the **americas**

SEX AS A POLITICAL CONDITION

7/23/19
For
Mimi Hittes

Thanks
for literary
a wonderful
experience)

Carla Nichole Flores

SEX AS A POLIT

COND

Carlos Nicolás Flores

ICAL
L

CAL

TION

**A BORDER
NOVEL**

Texas Tech University Press

This book is typeset in Minion Pro. The paper used in this book meets the minimum requirements of ANSI/NISO Z39.48-1992 (R1997). ∞

Designed by Kasey McBeath
Cover illustration by David Austin Gutierrez

Library of Congress Cataloging-in-Publication Data
Flores, Carlos Nicolas.
    Sex as a political condition : a border novel / Carlos Nicoas Flores.
        pages ; cm. — (The Americas series)
        Summary: "A satirical account of the cultural wars on the Mexican-American bor-der"—Provided by publisher.
        ISBN 978-0-89672-930-8 (softcover) — ISBN 978-0-89672-931-5 (ebook) 1. Culture conflict—Fiction. 2. Mexican-American Border Region—Fiction. 3. Political fiction. I. Title.
        PS3606.L587S49 2015
        813'.6—dc23   2014044590

15 16 17 18 19 20 21 22 23 / 9 8 7 6 5 4 3 2 1

Texas Tech University Press
Box 41037 | Lubbock, Texas 79409-1037 USA
800.832.4042 | ttup@ttu.edu | www.ttupress.org

Epigraph excerpt from "Towards a Greater Love" by Rogue Dalton (1997) reprinted with permission from Curbstone Press

For Roque Dalton
the Salvadoran revolutionary and poet
whose poem "Toward a Greater Love"
inspired this novel

From "Toward a Greater Love":

"Sex is a political condition."

—*epigraph, Kate Millett*

". . . the difference between the sexes
burns much better in the loving depth of night
when all those secrets that kept us
masked and alien are revealed."

—*Roque Dalton*

CONTENTS

Contents

ACKNOWLEDGMENTS

Since the people who contributed to the writing of this novel are substantial, I do not want to tax the reader with a long tedious series of curtseys and bows as, it seems, has become customary among some authors. However, the three key figures I must thank publicly are Antonio Cabral, the Chicano ex-Marine, union organizer, and journalist who got me involved in an adventure of a lifetime; Randy Koch, poet, journalist, professor, and take-no-prisoners editor who guided me through the writing itself; and Robert Mandel, former director at Texas Tech University Press who acknowledged the book's value from the moment he received it and stuck with it until it saw the light of day. Finally, I wish to thank everyone else who contributed to the book, especially my friends and, pardon the expression, political enemies. Some are dead, while others still stand on the ground level of history—that insatiable devourer of men, women, and their obsessions.

PART 1

A man on a horse galloped across a field. Suddenly, something squeaked in the bathroom. Honoré, sitting in his favorite chair next to a window, paused, ignored the noise and continued reading. The man raised a saber as he charged the Spanish troops aiming their rifles. Then gunshots. Ears ringing, Honoré stopped, as the riderless horse galloped across the field of his mind. But the gunshots were not gunshots. It was his wife Maruca banging a metal bucket across the bathroom tiles. The ringing became a tingling that spread from his ears to the tips of his fingers, from his belly to his neck, where it ran up the carotid to his eyes. He looked outside, among the limbs of a *cubreviento*, a salt cedar. On the sidewalk across the street, a boy with glasses, his hair thick and black as a wig, stood looking at the sky through binoculars. It was Tercero, Tequila's son.

As Honoré turned back to reading about the last day in the life of Cuba's most important hero, José Martí, the bathroom door swung open.

"When are you going to cut down that tree?" Maruca asked, her voice loud as the tin bucket she was then dragging into the bedroom.

Honoré slammed the book shut. "*¡Chingao! ¡Maruca, por favor!* Can't you see I'm working?"

With long black hair falling across her cheek, she clutched the end of the mop handle like an Adelita, one of the young women holding a 30.30 in photographs from the Mexican Revolution. She wore tight jeans and a partially unbuttoned parakeet-green blouse. "And what do you think I'm doing?"

His eyes wandered to her bed in the middle of the room, then to his, in the far corner next to a window, where he had been sleeping like a baby at night ever since returning from a dangerous and frenzied trip to Oaxaca. From the early days of their marriage, they had been able to do every-thing in the same bed, except sleep. She claimed he took up all the space; he claimed sexual harassment. Of course, it did not take much to arouse him—a flash of leg or a peek at her gorgeous *maracas*. Twin beds had been the only solution.

His eyes wandered back to Maruca, now mopping between the chest of drawers and the bathroom door. "Can't it wait?" he asked.

She stopped and fixed him with weary eyes. "I'm not asking for much. All I ask is that you cut down that tree. And not even the entire tree. Cut the branch scraping Bonita's window. Hurricane season is here. If a strong wind comes, it'll knock that branch down and God knows what will happen. I asked you to do this last year. I have not bothered you since."

Bonita was their fifteen-year-old daughter. "Mañana," he said.

"Mañana you might be gone again with that madman Trotsky!"

Trotsky was Juan Sánchez Trusky. "Please leave Trotsky out of this."

"He's using you."

Few understood Trotsky. "He's doing important work. And I wouldn't be alive if it weren't for him and his wife."

"Well, one day he's going to get you killed—that's for sure."

"I said leave Trotsky out of this."

She froze, eyes on the floor. She crouched, showing plenty of cleavage. "Wherever you sit starts to look like a trash can."

The thought of *maracas* made him shudder. *¡Ay, mamasota!*

She got up and carried a dirty white sock between her fingers into the bathroom. Upon returning, she gave him the evil eye. "What if I ask the neighbor to cut down the tree?"

Suddenly, he felt like a tortilla aflame on a grill as hot blood roared into his cheeks. The neighbor was Joshua T. Cuervo—otherwise known as Tequila Cuervo. The kid playing outside with binoculars was his eldest son.

"*¡Chingada madre!*" cursed Honoré. "Why do you have to drag that *cabrón* into this?"

"It's just an idea," she said as she kneeled on the floor and rinsed the mop in the bucket, its handle flying about under her arm. "You don't have to get upset."

He loved her dearly, but sometimes Honoré didn't know whether he wanted to slap her or kiss her. After taking a deep breath, he propped the book on the windowsill and rose to his feet. "Maruca," he said and walked across the room. "Maruca, honey."

"What?" she said, rising abruptly.

The mop handle flew through the air like a saber, clunking against his head, which sounded like a hollow watermelon.

He clutched the side of his head. "Ahhhhhh!"

She came up close. "Oh, my God! I'm so sorry! Are you okay?"

"Watch it with that damned mop!"

She touched his elbow. "*Perdóname, papacito.*"

"Okay, okay, okay!"

Honoré massaged the knot sprouting on his skull as she dragged the bucket out of the room, making more racket than before. She's always been like this, he thought, even before we bought this house, before we married—always mopping the floors, dusting the furniture. The woman belongs in Housekeepers Anonymous.

When the pain subsided, he returned to his chair, picked up the book from the windowsill, and opened it. Today, his first day off in weeks, he wanted to let his mind wander among the ghosts of the past, read about José Martí, the Cuban poet, journalist, and revolutionary who lived in New York, the belly of the beast, and in the last glorious days of his life returned to Cuba to lead a revolution against the Spanish imperialists. But Honoré couldn't get Maruca out of his mind—the nagging about the tree, the mop handle, the *maracas*. So he tried thinking about Martí, who had done so much, been everywhere—Cuba, Spain, Florida, New York. He even lived and taught school in that bloody country Guatemala.

Honoré owed more than his life to Trotsky. If it hadn't been for Trotsky, he never would have discovered the magic and wonder of books—and history. He would not have learned about Martí and Cuba's fight for independence from Spain. Though a bullet killed the Cuban patriot on his first charge, his death inspired a generation of revolutionaries that terrorized an entire hemisphere and changed the course of American history. Still. Still. Honoré couldn't stop thinking about, couldn't stop seeing *maracas*.

"*¡Qué hombre!*" he said and closed the book.

In the stairwell he found his face served up in a silver-framed Mexican mirror hanging on the wall. Long sideburns, large dark gloomy eyes, skin neither dark nor white, even mouth, broad shoulders and well-cut arms—he was a handsome man. But this had only brought him problems. Honoré came from a long line of vain and violent men, always in trouble with women or the law or both. His father died in a gunfight over a married woman in Sabinas Hidalgo, a town midway between Escandón and Monterrey, Mexico. Coyotes, *narcotraficantes*, drunks, womanizers—that was his legacy. So he knew the danger women posed. With just a look or smile, they could undo the toughest of men, turn them into pigs or howling dogs. Once they got you in bed, they could, as Tequila loved to say, "*desaguacatarte*," meaning they could "de-avocado you."

In the hall downstairs, he opened a closet jammed with clothes and boxes and found the Father's Day gift from Maruca still in its box—a chainsaw. He also found a can of oil and safety goggles in a corner.

In the kitchen at the other end of the hallway, pipes groaned as water filled the sink, and a pot clattered against dishes.

"Where's Bonita?" he called over the racket.

Maruca's voice rose from the kitchen. "She's out with Misty. Why?"

Though Honoré liked his niece, Misty, mostly because Bonita looked up to her as an older sister, he didn't trust her. Not only was she the daughter of Maruca's older brother—a nasty and corrupt cop who had never forgiven him for marrying his beautiful sister and had been trying to bust Honoré ever since—but she had a big mouth. "I need Bonita at the store. Otherwise, my mother will call me all day."

"What about your cousins?"

"You know I can't trust those faggots."

"Honoré, please!" she yelled. "Don't talk like that! I don't want Bonita to hear you talking trash!"

When he opened the front door, a flood of white light poured into the living room and the hot breath of South Texas struck his face. "¡*Chingao!*" he cursed.

Then he saw it again, up close. Huge, black, gnarled, the *cubreviento* should never have been planted—not in the middle of this desert, not in this barrio, and not in front of this house. Not only did it suck the earth dry, but it had grown too big for the yard. No grass grew now, just Maruca's yellow daisies along the edge of the porch and clumps of purple sage around the ever-dripping water spigot.

As beads of sweat sprouted on his arms, he crouched, opened the oil can, and poured some oil in the chainsaw, realizing that with several six-packs of nirvana waiting in the refrigerator, he could survive the heat.

Suddenly, a gray pickup roared around the corner and screeched to a halt across the street. Out jumped a short brown man wearing oil-stained overalls and black boots. With a smirk full of trouble and bullshit, Tequila slammed the door and waved. Honoré waved back but not too friendly. They had played football in high school and after graduation smuggled tons of dope across the river. Then Tequila married his high school sweetheart. A tribe of kids and a hundred pounds later, she died. Some said from cancer, others from *brujería*. Unable to manage the brats, Tequila married the first woman he could get his claws into, a somber, light-skinned ex-nun from Guadalajara, thin and ugly as a scarecrow but tough as a piston rod. Then he inherited a mechanic's shop from his uncle and bought the house across the street.

Puro cabrón, Honoré thought as Tequila walked into the sprawling house with a red-tile roof, green lawn, and fat shrubs surrounded by a white wrought iron fence.

Why had Honoré not been born like this *pendejo*—happy, untroubled, no brains? Or like his other neighbors, who had lawns which they cut and watered regularly? They went to work and came home; they watched television. Nothing was wrong with the world. Six-pack Josés. Yet this town had all kinds of problems. The schools were a mess. The churches helped no one. Legions of souls were lost every day. Across the river in Mexico, people were starving to death. Every day someone was shot and killed. Did his neighbors care?

He checked the slack in the chain of steel teeth.

Once, he didn't give a shit—about anything or anybody. Pot, coke, pussy, and moolah—that's all that mattered. Then he met Trotsky. To this day Honoré didn't understand the hold this forty-four-year-old stranger from California had had over him for the last four years. All he knew was that he had never felt better since Trotsky helped him get off the drugs, or since Honoré began avoiding old friends like Tequila and the Governor. In fact, he liked to think he was becoming a man of ideals, a man with a social conscience, as Trotsky would say.

On his recent trip to Oaxaca, Honoré delivered medical supplies to organizations working with indigenous groups fighting for their rights. Another time he made arrangements to deliver radio transmitters to guerrillas working to establish a communications network in the state of Guerrero. But why couldn't Maruca, who hated the local men, including her dope-trafficking cousins in federal prison or her brother Comino, the local yokel, the cop from hell—why couldn't she understand that Honoré was no longer like the men of Escandón? In fact, he was trying to live up to the legacy of the man his father had named him after—the French novelist, Honoré de Balzac. God knows where he discovered the name since he never read. Maybe among his sister's books. According to Honoré's mother, his father had prophesied that his newborn son would one day save the family. Destined to be "a man of honor," he would be a better man than the rest of the men in their family. His father was drunk at the time.

The phone rang. Maruca yelled something.

He put down the saw. "What?"

"Trotsky. On the phone!"

"I'll be right there," Honoré said and stood up.

Sometimes Trotsky called in the middle of the night. Sometimes to request something simple like giving a priest a ride to the bus station or airport across the river in Nuevo Escandón, Mexico. At other times he called for help in crossing a refugee from Mexico or Central America, like last year when under a hail of gunfire between the Border Patrol and a gang of smugglers, Honoré crossed a Sandinista *comandante* in a boat—a woman.

In the kitchen he picked up the phone. "Hello."

The voice was young and lucid. "Can you talk?"

Honoré looked around for Maruca. "Yeah, why?"

"La Usada may be listening."

La Usada was a joke, a pun on USA. In Spanish it meant the "used one," implying "the whore." It was also a code for U.S. intelligence or the CIA. "Everything's cool," said Honoré with a grin. "What's up?"

"The dolls will arrive today."

Trotsky had told him about the shipment two months ago. So this shouldn't have come as a surprise, but it did. "How many?"

"They didn't tell me. But you have plenty of room at the store, no?"

"No. The warehouse is full."

"Sorry. There's not much I can do. I fly out of Nuevo Escandón in an hour. I'm already late."

Honoré looked around. The room in back. There was plenty of storage space there. Maruca would object. But this is the life of a revolutionary, he told himself. Sacrifices must be made. "I'll figure something out."

"I'll be back in a week."

"Where you going?"

"Nicaragua."

"What's up?"

"I'm meeting some Vietnam veterans in Managua about a major new project. I'll tell you about it when I get back."

After hanging up, Honoré walked outside and lugged a small stepladder from the backyard, spread its legs, and set it up next to the tree. Working for Trotsky could be a pain in the ass, but Honoré knew he wouldn't be alive today if it weren't for him. Besides, what little he did for Trotsky wasn't much compared to the risks he had taken as a *narcotraficante*. Also, while in his old line of work he dealt with a bunch of scumbags, he admired Trotsky and his colleagues.

The branch looked like the back of an alligator crawling into an arbor of leaves and raising its snout high above the window. It was too high to saw in parts from the ladder. If he cut the limb at the trunk, it would fall on the porch roof and break Bonita's bedroom window, so he decided to start with the lower branches. He picked up the saw, put on the goggles, and climbed the ladder. Steadying himself, he gripped the handle and squeezed the trigger. The chainsaw roared like an AK-47, and a branch fell. Soon he got lost in the racket of steel teeth gnashing through the white flesh of Mother Nature and filling the air with a green smell. The chainsaw whined, and another limb fell and slipped through the other branches to the ground.

When Maruca nudged the screen door open with her hip, her face slick as a lollipop, he killed the saw, pushed back the goggles, and wiped his forehead. How was he going to explain the dolls?

She pulled the bucket to the edge of the porch and dumped the water on the dirt with the vigor of a construction worker, arms brown and strong, legs muscular and shapely in tight jeans. She knelt by the bucket, leaned forward, and as she reached across the plants in her garden, the blouse opened and reminded him of the first time she took off her clothes, *maracas* rolling out of her unlatched brassiere.

She looked up, shading her face with her hand. "What's wrong with your eyes?"

"Why?"

Her white teeth flashed. "I feel them all over my body."

"Just making sure a branch doesn't fall on you."

"Which branch?"

"The big one."

"I'll bet," she said and went back inside.

He wiped his brow, adjusted the goggles, and balanced on the limb. The chainsaw roared again. Easy, he thought as a branch dropped from the steel teeth. Any *pendejo* could cut down a tree. The real challenge was cutting down an entire society rotten to the core. That required real men. Men like Trotsky and Martí. Women, too. Like the Adelitas. So he climbed and stood on a branch, resting his butt against the trunk. Careful, he thought, as he raised the chainsaw into position. Who knows what you might cut off? Maybe you could live without a finger or a hand, might even put up with losing an entire arm—but if something else got cut off, you might as well blow your brains out.

Once Maruca asked him, "Why did you marry me?"

He wanted to tell her the truth, but his father said you could never tell a woman the truth. So Honoré told her she was an intelligent, kind, morally upright woman who would make an excellent mother; he loved her warmth; and she not only reminded him of his mother but in many ways was better than his mother. He never told her he married her because of her *maracas*. Oh, he might tell her that after making love, his mind lost in eyefuls of flesh, in the midst of nipples brown as chocolate waiting to see if they were going to be sucked. Still it was no joke. *Maracas* mattered.

The phone rang. She came outside. "Phone!"

"Now who?"

"Doña Pánfila," she yelled.

"Tell her I'll call her when I'm done here."

She went inside, then came back. "She wants to talk to you."

"What does she want?"

"I don't know. She won't tell me."

His mother always did this to him, called him about the stupidest things, things she could take care of herself. But he understood her. She was a lonely old woman. "Coming!"

His head boiling like a cabbage in soup, he climbed down slowly and walked inside the house, relieved to be in the cool kitchen. He picked up the phone. "Hello."

"*Hijo.*"

"*Diga, señora.*"

Sometimes she sounded like a little girl, sweet and helpless. "Your cousin wants to talk to you. "

"No, señora," he pleaded. "*¡Por favor, no!*"

He heard her put the phone down and talk to his cousin. Then she returned, breathing so loudly Honoré thought he could see her purple gums and yellow teeth. "*Hijo*, how much do you owe your cousin?" she said. "Let me pay him. If not, he says he'll quit."

"That idiot never does any work. And if you pay him, he won't show up until tomorrow. Don't give him a cent. Buy him a pizza."

She hung up.

"Idiots!" he muttered and slammed the phone down.

Pots and pans rang loud as steel in a sword fight as Maruca prepared to cook lunch. In this household, cooking was a serious matter, like going off to war. Maruca came from a long line of traditional Mexican women. Then, the smell of female flesh, pungent and sweet, reminded him that he hadn't had *any* in weeks. He forgot the store, his mother, and his cousins. He forgot the tree and Trotsky and the struggle for peace and justice. He crossed the room, slipped his arms around her waist, and nuzzled the back of her neck.

She pushed him away. "Can't you see I'm cooking?"

He slipped his hand under her blouse. "Just a little, give me just a little bit."

She pushed him away, a strand of hair falling across her brow. "That's what you told me the first time. Just the tip! Just the tip! I said, okay, just the tip, and since then I've not been able to get you out of me!"

Memories of their honeymoon made him shudder. "*Por favor*, Maruca! You're driving me crazy!"

She let him kiss her on the mouth, then bit his ear. "Later."

The monster awakened, yawning, snarling. He held her in both arms and pressed himself against her. "Oh baby, serve me a bowl of *menudo, un menudazo*. A lot of chile, a lot of *panza*, a lot of pig. A lot of meat."

"Sexist remarks," she said with a grin while pushing him away, "never bother me. Men are such silly pigs."

He pinned her against the kitchen counter. "When?"

"When what?"

"When are we going to have some *menudo*?"

"First cut down the tree."

The phone rang. "Oh, fuck!" said Honoré and let go. He picked up the phone. "Hello."

"Some gringos called," said his mother.

"Gringos call every day. Which ones?"

"The ones that speak that funny English."

"They all speak funny English."

"They sounded like they were drunk."

"Oh, okay," he said. "The gringos from Mississippi. Well, if they call again, tell them I'll be there tomorrow."

After hanging up, he turned to Maruca, who looked really good in those tight jeans as she crouched and pulled a skillet from the cabinet under the kitchen counter. Then thoughts of the tree and Trotsky and the dolls came flooding back. He needed to get back to work. In a drawer at one end of the kitchen counter, he found a nylon rope.

"You don't have to hang yourself," Maruca said, rising to her feet.

He looked up. "What'd you say?"

"You don't have to hang yourself. You'll get some *menudo*. Eventually."

He grinned. "Tonight?"

"Depends."

Outside, the rope glistened like a long yellow garden snake in the sunlight. After moving the ladder, he climbed up and lassoed the branch. Once he cut down this damned tree, he thought as he secured the rope, Maruca would smile and kiss him not because he had cut down the tree but because he had done something for her, and tonight they would find each other in their bedroom, where she would feed him his favorite candy, nipples, and together they would roll across the bed, lock and load, and then chop away—whack! whack! whack!—until suddenly the timber between them, heady and unstable as a *borracho*, would come crashing down in an explosion of leaves, vines, and limbs.

Then he climbed down and repositioned the ladder. After wiping his brow with the back of his arm, he got the chainsaw from the porch. The ladder wobbled as he climbed back up.

Steel teeth spit yellow sawdust like oatmeal where the limb met the trunk. No big deal, but the roar was deafening. Look at that, he marveled as the tree-eater chomped through the wood. A chainsaw was like an animal. You had to feed it, awaken it, then feed it some more. But like a wild animal, unless he kept his eyes on its teeth and his finger on its throat, it could very easily turn on him.

Yet no machine was going to scare him. The men in his family—at least, the men on his father's side of the family, the men from Sabinas Hidalgo— might be crazy, but if there was one thing Honoré admired about them it was their code of manliness. Any form of cowardice was unthinkable.

That's what Maruca did not understand. The night after he dropped off the Sandinista commander at Trotsky's, he made the mistake of telling her about the gunfight on the river between a gang and the Border Patrol.

"Aren't you afraid?" she asked.

They were lying in bed. "My greatest fear is dying in front of a television."

She glanced sideways at him. "What's wrong with that?"

"Trotsky says most men die like that. Stupid, inconsequential deaths. Me—I want to die on some beach in Central America, before a firing squad."

"¡Estás loco!"

He rose on an elbow. "Can't you take a joke?"

She was such a lovely woman, but she could drive him crazy with her right-wing politics. "No," she said.

"Do you know what it feels like to wake up in the morning and discover you're in bed with a Republican?"

"Do you know what it feels like to wake up in the morning and discover you are in bed with a communist?" she said. She was not joking.

"I am not a communist."

"I am not a Republican."

He lay back and gazed at the ceiling. "The feminists are right. Sex is a political condition. Sometimes you can't tell if you're sleeping with your wife or your political enemy."

After a while, she said, "You live in a world of dreams. First, you said you were going to make a lot of money with Tequila and the Governor. Nothing came of it. Instead you almost got killed. Then you got involved with Trotsky and said you were going to change the world. When are you going to grow up and be a man?"

And before he realized it, he was on top of her, holding her down as she kicked hard, *maracas* flattened like eggs sunny-side-up. He closed his hands around her neck, having no choice but to strangle her. Blood poured into his skull and stuffed his eyes, like Easter eggs brimming with red confetti. His hands trembled. Saliva dripped. Then he saw himself in a federal prison with a bunch of lonely, horny men, and Maruca a ghost, *maracas* and all, haunting him the rest of his life. So he let go and climbed off. With a flying kick she took a swipe at his balls but missed. After she stormed out of the room and went to sleep in Bonita's bedroom, he lay down in his bed and stared out the window like an idiot.

"You look like an idiot!" a male voice scoffed.

Honoré turned off the saw and removed his goggles. "What the hell?"

Tequila, beads of sweat on his cheeks, stood a few feet below. "I see Doña Maruca finally got you to do some work around here. Why didn't you just hire a gardener? The barrio is full of them."

"Get lost," Honoré said, then put his goggles back on.

The roar of the saw drowned out Tequila as it cut deep into the bark. Honoré didn't want to cut too deep. Otherwise he ran the risk of the limb falling on the porch and hitting Bonita's window. He needed to cut just enough so he could pull the rope and direct the fall away from the house. There, that was enough. Good, he was almost done. He killed the saw.

Then he removed the goggles and climbed down. "You're still here? What do you want?"

"Wanna make some quick money?"

Honoré put the saw on the porch. "*No mames.* I told you I was through with all that shit."

Tequila smelled of booze and oil. "Listen, *cabrón,*" he muttered. "You need to stop wasting time. There's a lot of money to be made."

"Get out of the way."

Honoré grabbed the rope hanging from the limb. A good pull was all it needed now. He pulled. The branch fought back, refused to move, even though it was attached to the trunk by less than an inch of its original base. So he pulled in earnest, and the branch resisted in earnest. The rope felt like a coarse braid of hair. Again, he gave it all he could, the way he might pull the reins on a spooked horse.

"Let me help you with that," said Tequila.

"Get out of the way."

Tequila shook his head as he moved to the curb. "Trees are dangerous."

Honoré wrapped the rope around his hand and made a fist. For a moment he imagined he had lassoed a steer as he dug his heels in the dirt and threw his weight against the rope. The wood moaned. It wouldn't give, so he pulled again. Nothing. He pulled again. Then the wood cracked and screamed.

"*¡Águila!*" yelled Tequila.

Like an alligator gone mad, the branch lunged at the house. Honoré yanked the rope. The branch swung toward him. Suddenly, stiff long-fingered hands wrapped his face in a storm of leaves as a monstrous arm hit him hard where God had made him a two-legged animal and sent him flying through a galaxy of stars, his butt landing on an asteroid. When he rolled over, he realized he had slammed against the dirt in front of his house. Only one thing hurt more than being kicked in the butt: being kicked in the balls. He hurt so much he must have been kicked in both places. Then Tequila took him by the elbow and helped him up.

Honoré staggered to his feet and yanked his arm loose. "*Ya*, let go!" he yelled.

The screen door flew open. "What happened?" asked Maruca.

Even though his butt hurt like hell, Honoré, a little dizzy, stood dusting off his jeans. "Nothing."

Then, he collapsed, face first.

Hot dirt mauled his cheeks. His fingers sizzled. Daggers of heat tore through his jeans. As the world grew dark, he found himself at the bottom of a well. Then like pigeons warbling among the trees, voices gathered about his head. In the distance a car honked, and a dog barked.

"Is he dead?" asked a boy.

"No," sneered Tequila. "*Cosa mala nunca muere.*"

"What happened?" asked Tequila's wife.

Tequila laughed. "*¡Pobre compadre! ¡Por poco lo desaguacatan!*"

"Let's take him inside!" said Maruca.

Like rats or snakes or *tlacuaches*, hands crawled all over his body. Some-one grabbed his head. Someone grabbed his feet. Someone grabbed his butt. Honoré opened an eye. Up, he went.

Tequila peered at him. "*¡Pendejo!*"

As they carried him upstairs, he glimpsed his handsome mustachioed Mexican face upside down in the mirror. The bubble-gum-chewing mug of Tequila's four-eyed son, Tercero, poked in and out of the reflection. Then Tequila, smirking. Finally, a worried but lovely Maruca. Slowly, they carried him to the bedroom, where they tossed him in that old battlefield, Maruca's bed. While Señora Cuervo kneeled at the end of the bed and prayed to St. Francis on Honoré's behalf, Tequila grinned at Honoré, who lay stretched out on the bed, his head in Maruca's lap.

Tercero, after wandering around the room and poking his nose into Honoré's bookshelf, stood before the window and looked outside. "¡Apá!"

"What?"

"There's that bird I told you about."

"A buzzard."

"No, Apá. It's big, bigger than a buzzard. Come see for yourself!"

"Forget it. Let's go, let's go!" said Tequila, heading toward the door.

"Wait, one last look."

Tequila crossed the room and grabbed the boy by his shirt and yanked. "I said let's go."

"Don't treat him like that!" yelled Señora Cuervo, on her feet. "Children are not animals! They're gifts from God."

"Wait, Apá! Please!"

Tequila halted halfway to the door. "What?"

"That was the bird I was telling you about. The bird I saw with my binoculars."

Then Tequila glanced at Honoré and shrugged. "This is what happens when you have intelligent kids. You can't shut them up." He fixed Maruca in a gaze. "Señora, next time you want a tree cut down, give me a ring."

Outraged, Honoré threw a leg over the side of the bed as he got up until a sharp pain cut through his butt and he fell back on Maruca's lap, muttering, "Ahhh!"

Tequila laughed.

Then he pushed his son ahead of him, and the two walked down the stairs and out the front door, Tequila's dumbass laughter booming even after they left the house.

"What an idiot!" Honoré said.

Maruca massaged his temples. "Who?" asked Maruca.

"Tequila!"

Downstairs, the front door opened again. Someone stomped up the stairs. Suddenly, the bedroom door swung open, and in flew his daughter, Bonita, with black braided pigtails and a few frizzy strands of loose hair glowing about a round angelic face with pink cheeks and lips. Such an innocent, obedient girl, thought Honoré, even though he was sure she would grow up to be a stunning beauty like her mother and drive some man crazy. But she had been a disappointment from the start. He had wanted a boy.

"What's the matter, Dad?" she asked, breathlessly.

"Nothing."

"You don't look so good."

"I said, 'Nothing.' How many times do I have to say it?"

She bit her lip. "Oh, okay. Two men outside are asking for you. They have a U-Haul."

"What do they look like?" he asked.

"Mexicans."

"The *oaxaqueños*," muttered Honoré, sitting up and throwing his legs over the side of the bed. Slowly, he pushed himself up, rose to his feet, and staggered to the window. At first, his vision was blurred. Then he made out the *oaxaqueños'* cowboy hats as they lounged against an orange and white U-Haul truck. But no bird. God knows what Tercero was talking about.

"Tell them to park in the driveway. I'll be down in a minute."

Bonita turned to Maruca. "Misty and her mom gave me a ride home. Can I spend the night at their house?"

"Not tonight," said Maruca. "You have to help your grandmother at the store today. She's been very sick lately."

"Can Misty help, too?"

"Yes."

"We'll be at the store." She ran out of the room, then came back. "Dad, are you going to be okay?"

"Go on. Do as your mother says."

She kissed him on the cheek. "Thanks, Dad!"

As soon as she left, Honoré limped back to the bed and sat down next to Maruca. "That tree almost killed me," he muttered. "It fought back. It tried to kill me. Amazing!"

Maruca raised an eyebrow. "What's amazing? You were just careless. You should have asked Tequila to help you."

He stood up, steadying himself with a hand on her shoulder. "You don't understand. When you try to change something, you expose yourself to danger—"

"You've done that plenty of times here," she sneered.

Honoré shook his head. "You'll never understand. That's the great paradox of men like me. In trying to destroy something, you always risk being destroyed. That's what happened to José Martí."

"Who?"

"Never mind."

"You never mind. Take care of your family. You're not going to change the world."

He moved, felt weird, queasy, as if the tree had cut him in half. "I have to go downstairs."

"You can barely stand up."

He steadied himself on her shoulder. "Wait!" He touched himself. "Am I okay?"

Maruca reached between his legs. "Why?"

"I can't feel a thing!"

She probed, squeezed, pulled. "Everything is there."

"I don't feel a thing!"

"Good," she said. "Maybe I can get some rest tonight."

With Maruca holding his arm as if he were an old man, he crept out of the room and climbed slowly down the stairs. Hanging onto the railing, he stopped, wincing as pain cut through his ass like a chainsaw. Then Maruca helped him through the kitchen to the den in back, where he eased into a chair beneath the glass-enclosed case on the wall where he kept his rifles under lock and key. A few feet away stood a cage containing a pair of canaries his mother had given Bonita as a birthday gift.

"Tell them to come in," he said.

Maruca opened the back door. "*Adelante. Pasen, por favor.*"

The sing-song voices of the short, brown men with bright eyes and dusty hair floated inside as Maruca left the room.

The first man removed his hat and bowed. "Don Honoré?"

"Yes," Honoré said.

"My name is Pedro, and this is Juan."

"*Bienvenidos.* Welcome."

"Sorry about this being done at the last minute," said Pedro. "Either we moved them today or lost everything." He lowered his voice. "There have been a lot of raids up north. The government has spies everywhere. Señor Trotsky told us he would call you."

Honoré winced.

"Are you all right?" the man asked.

The pain could have been worse. "Yes, I'm fine," said Honoré. "I had a little accident."

"Cutting down that tree?"

Honoré nodded, shifting to one side.

"Please don't get up. We'll take care of everything."

Honoré relaxed.

Pedro looked up and down the long, narrow room. "Where would you like them?"

"How many are there?"

"Twenty crates."

"*Chingao*, that's a lot!" Honoré said as Maruca walked back into the room.

"And dolls?"

"Sixty. Three per crate."

"Okay, put them there," Honoré said and pointed at the corner between the wall and the back door. "If that's not enough space, you can put the rest on this side of the door."

As the men walked out, Maruca frowned. "Dolls?"

"I'll explain later."

"No, tell me now!"

The door swung open as the two men carried in a four-foot-long pine crate with cord handles on each end. The wood looked old but sturdy. The lid was hinged and had a latch on the front. They set the crate by the wall and went back outside.

Maruca stared at the crate. "This smells of Trotsky. Is this his idea?"

"I told you. Leave Trotsky out of this."

"Not until you tell me what this is about. What's in the crates?"

"Lower your voice."

Maruca put a hand on her hip. "I can't allow this."

The door opened again. Maruca got out of the way, biting her lip as the men brought in another crate and slid it like a coffin on top of the first one.

As soon as they were gone, she asked, "Why didn't you take them to the store?"

"There's no room. Besides, I don't want my mother snooping around."

"Why? What's in the crates?"

"Look," he said, wincing again, "don't mention this to anyone, especially your brother."

The men brought in more crates, stacked them on top of one another, and left again.

"I knew it," she said. "I just knew it. The minute Trotsky calls, there you go like a puppy. I can't allow this."

Honoré faced her. "Tell me. What do you want?"

She halted a few feet from him. "What do you mean, 'What do you want?' I want these boxes out of the house—that's what I want!"

"Look. Just help me this one time. I'll cut down all the trees you want. I'll do anything. Just tell me what you want."

"How long are they going to be here?"

"Not long," said Honoré.

"You always break your promises. I asked you to cut down that tree over a year ago. I asked you to cool it with Trotsky and mind the store for the sake of your mother and for your daughter and me. So far, nothing."

"What do you want?"

She gave him a dirty look. "Money."

"How much?"

"Not much."

"What do you want money for?"

"Things for the house." Her eyes wandered thoughtfully, then lit up. "Maybe a TV."

"Forget it. We don't need a TV. We already have one."

"A black and white TV?"

"What's wrong with that?"

"The poorest people in this barrio have color TVs! All of Bonita's friends have wide-screen color TVs!"

"We'll get one next Christmas."

"You said that last Christmas."

"Take it or leave it. You can buy whatever you want except a TV."

"All right, all right, maybe a dining table."

The smell of old pine grew strong when the men returned with more crates, as if some strange spirit from a cemetery in the north had entered the room. Soon they had a stack of five crates, about six feet high against the wall. Maruca went upstairs to clean Bonita's room while Honoré watched the men carry the remaining fifteen crates inside.

After they put the last crate on the floor next to the bird cage, a few feet from Honoré, Pedro stood before Honoré, wiping his brow with a red handkerchief. "We're done," he said to Honoré. "Can we bother you for a little water?"

"Yes. There's some ice in the refrigerator. If you need to use the restroom, it's down the hall from the kitchen."

"Gracias, *maestro*."

The men did not take long in the restroom or drinking a glass of water from the faucet in the kitchen or thanking Honoré before walking out the back door and leaving him alone with the smell of pine.

As soon as the men were gone, Maruca returned. "Can I look?"

"No."

She stood before the crate next to the bird cage. "Are they really dolls?"

"That's what the Nicas call them."

Brown knots in the pinewood looked like eyes, eyes watching as she crouched and unlatched the crate's lid. After opening it, she slowly stood up, hand to her mouth, eyes wide as she stared at the shiny orange wooden stocks and the steel-blue barrels snuggling side by side in burlap. "*¡Dios mío!*"

A week later, Honoré still had not recovered from his encounter with the tree. In fact, he was having trouble sleeping at night. Then he began hearing strange noises outside his bedroom window. One night, even though the window was shut, Honoré heard it—soft and hollow, loud as an unearthly voice and lonely like a muted oboe. "Boooo!"

He opened one eye, then the other. After peeking at Maruca, who slept with her face in the pillow and a white sheet drawn up to her waist, he raised an arm and looked at his watch's phosphorescent digits: 1:30 a.m. Quietly, he rolled to the edge of the bed, then cringed as a bolt of pain shot from his ass to his legs; he waited until it passed. Then he crept to the window. Outside, stood the tree that had done him in, its arms filled with light from the street lamp on the corner.

He froze. Among the limbs and shaped like a Hollywood Oscar was something black and ominous, like a bird, a big bird.

"What's the matter?" muttered Maruca.

He pressed his face against the window. "I think there's an owl outside."

The springs in her mattress jangled. "Did you hear a whistle?"

He looked at her. "No. Why?"

She stretched a fabulous leg across the mattress. "Because if it's a *lechuza* you're in trouble."

He shook his head at his wife's idiocy. "So what?"

"A *lechuza* is a witch. If it whistles, that means it's coming after your soul. But if you say four Our Fathers, the evil sent to you will be returned to whoever sent it, only double."

"My mother says a *lechuza* is a *puta*."

"Then you don't have anything to worry about. You've had plenty of experience with those."

A car, loud with music like a jukebox on wheels, stopped at the corner and then took off. After a while, he slumped into bed, dreading another long night, fitful, wide-eyed, haunted. Anytime he woke up in the middle of the night, he couldn't go back to sleep. So he closed his eyes and counted sheep. It didn't work. Then he counted naked women. That made matters worse.

"Boooooo!"

His eyelids popped open.

"You're right, it's an owl," said Maruca with a yawn. "That means only one thing. Someone's going to die."

"Bullshit!" he said, climbing out of bed, stopping as pain sizzled throughout his butt, then throwing on his bathrobe, and stepping into some slippers. "People die every day at the hospital. Why aren't the trees around the hospital filled with owls? I'm sick of all this Catholic mumbo jumbo. If anyone is going to die, it's going to be that owl."

More pain halted him at the door. Then he eased down the stairs and crept through the kitchen to the room in back, where he tried to ignore the long, silent wooden crates of death-dealing technology. He quietly unlocked the gun case on the wall; he didn't want to disturb the canaries. A shotgun or 30.06 or an AK-47 would be too much, so he took out his lever-action .22 and loaded it with hollow-point shells. He froze as pain, piranha-like, nibbled his tailbone. Then as he walked back through the kitchen, he spotted the bottle of mezcal his father-in-law had left on the counter.

He grabbed it and, in accordance with his father-in-law's advice, "*Para todo mal, mezcal*," took a swig.

He shuddered. Feeling better, he went back upstairs with the bottle.

In the bedroom, he put the bottle on the nightstand and sat on the edge of his bed. He cocked the rifle and clicked off the safety.

After propping it against the wall, he took another swig. The Mexican liquor sent the hot, bitter roots of a cactus through his body until they reached his toes. He felt better. He took another swig. Like hot Mexican soup, the heat scalded his lips, warmed his guts, and soothed his tomahawk, which had been aching to go on the warpath.

"Honoré."

He lay down. "What?"

"What about the AK-47s?"

"What about them?"

"When are you getting rid of them?"

"Soon."

He took another swig. Then he lay down and stretched out his legs, his head resting on a pillow. The warmth of the liquor reached his tongue and tied it in knots, soaked into his ears and washed away the sound of Maruca's voice. He had turned into a tamale, white on the outside with plenty of red-hot chile inside. Suddenly, he was sweating and opened the window next to his bed. Ah, that felt good, he thought as a stream of fresh air swept into the room.

"If I hear one peep out of that owl," he muttered, glancing at the rifle to make sure it was within easy reach, "I'm sending it back where it came from—hell."

Maruca's mattress jangled. "I wish you wouldn't talk like that. One day God will hear you and send *you* to hell."

The next morning, Honoré, sitting in his office at the store, contemplated the piles of paperwork on his desk. Not only had he just received more new merchandise from Mexico such as heavy wooden doors, mirrors, and porcelain dishware, but a truck load of tin men had arrived. Now the warehouse was so packed he had even less room to store the dolls. Plus, thanks to his mother's mismanagement of the business, they had fallen behind on their payments at the bank and needed to make some money quick. He thought of Trotsky, who should be back any day, wondering how things had gone in Nicaragua, what the new project was about.

On the walls around his desk hung paintings of La Virgen de Guadalupe and dozens of crucifixes. They had been there as long as he could remember, and like everything about this job, he hated them. In the years before his mother got too old to manage the store and he was still smuggling dope, Honoré had plenty of money, which kept everyone happy, including Maruca, and allowed him to come and go as he pleased, but now that he had taken over the store, he had to lead a double life. Every day he had to pretend he was something he was not, putting on a stupid, sweet smile for his mother, his cousins, and the customers while helping Trotsky on the side. But this was the nature of the underground life, Trotsky had cautioned, and all revolutionaries led an underground life.

"Honoré!"

A buzzard flew past the window. It was his mother, who stomped up the porch steps, opening the door and slamming it behind her. For such a small woman, she had a loud mouth. Probably because she was going deaf.

"Honoré," she screamed, "your friend Trotsky is here!"

"I can hear you!" he yelled, rising from the desk. "You don't have to shout!"

In the hallway, the wooden floor creaked as he walked toward the front of the store, where his tiny shriveled mother stood inside the front door, Mexican newspapers under her arm. He could not believe that at one time she had been one of the most beautiful women in Escandón. Now look at what she had become, a *chicharrón* or a *chicharra*, a creature not long for this world, half-blind, half-deaf, shriveled. Everyone in the family hoped she would die soon. After kissing her lightly on the top of her head, he went outside.

A band of tin mariachis with bellies the size of barrels, sombreros wide as trash can lids, and violins and guitars in their wire-fingered hands, stood across the dirt yard, a few feet from the main gate. He climbed down the porch steps. Doors and windows and benches were stacked against the side of the house-turned-store, as if all of Mexico were on sale. A six-foot-long bull made from cast iron guarded the path to the warehouse. Standing in the sun's glare, Honoré waited for his friend to park his jeep in the street.

Dressed in a guayabera, jeans, and cowboy boots, Trotsky climbed out of the vehicle. His black hair fell in curls about his neck, and he wore a black eye patch held in place by a strap on a brown face. During an attack in Vietnam, one of his buddies got shot a few feet away. His head exploded like a ripe melon and spewed teeth in Trotsky's face, blinding him in one eye. Upon returning to California, Trotsky ended up in a mental ward, where he tried to do what a black master sergeant had done earlier in the week—hang himself with a shoelace stolen from a combat boot. While the sergeant died, Trotsky was cut down by an orderly.

"Welcome home," said Honoré.

Trotsky crossed the yard. "Thanks. It's great to be home. Sorry about the dolls."

"No problem."

"Everything cool with the wife?"

"Let's talk in my office," said Honoré.

They went inside, and Trotsky sat in the chair next to the desk. Slowly, he looked at the crucifixes on the wall as if either he had never seen them before or they reminded him of something he didn't want to think about.

Honoré handed him a fresh cup of coffee and then poured his own. "So how did it go in Nicaragua?"

"You've got to hand it to those Nicas," said Trotsky, cup in hand. "They took on the colossus of the north. But there's a price to pay for that, and they're paying it."

Honoré put his cup on the desk and sat in his chair. "I read about the contras' attack in the north."

"Can you imagine? Attacking civilians. Destroying schools and hospitals. The people of Central America are strong, but they need all the help they can get. The Vietnam vets I met with in Managua want to organize a convoy carrying humanitarian aid to Nicaragua this summer. But I have my doubts."

Honoré's chair squeaked as he accommodated himself. "Why? Can't be any tougher than any of the smuggling that goes on around here every day."

"Well, first there are the politics of organizing a convoy through Mexico and Guatemala to Nicaragua. But the thing that worries me the most is the guy heading the project, Jack Halligan. Very idealistic. A good man. Vietnam vet. Tough and courageous. But he's been sick a lot lately."

"Get your friend in San Antonio to help. What's his name?"

"El Capitán?"

"Yes."

"We'll see what happens. Also we need to talk to Don Sixto. He'll be out of jail today. We have a reception planned for him soon at La Clínica del Barrio."

A few months before, sixty-year-old Don Sixto and his supporters protested election fraud in Nuevo Escandón by unloading a herd of goats on the international bridge. While protestors with banners and placards packed the sidewalks, the goats ran loose among the long line of cars waiting to cross, bleating loudly amid the honking and shouts of passersby, shitting everywhere. One goat reached the American side of the bridge and rammed an unsuspecting American customs inspector in the butt. They shut down the bridge for hours.

Two days later, the protestors set fire to the house of a prominent political boss, but the fire got out of control and burned down a nearby church. After Don Sixto was arrested, people rallied daily for his release. While Trotsky's wife, Altagracia, had helped provide food, water, and medicine to the protestors camped outside El Calabozo, Trotsky had pulled strings on both sides of the border so Sixto would not be killed in jail.

"And the dolls?" asked Honoré.

"Sixto's son could help us, but I'd rather talk to Sixto."

Suddenly, the office door opened. "Buenos días, Señor Trotsky," said Honoré's mother.

Trotsky stood. "Buenos días, Doña Pánfila."

"Are you here to get my son in more trouble?"

Trotsky grinned. "No, señora. Quite the contrary."

"Look at him. He's never looked healthier. He has a job. A real job. He has a beautiful wife and a beautiful daughter."

"I'm keeping him out of real trouble."

She opened a desk drawer and took out some keys. "As long as my son puts his life in the hands of Our Lord Jesus Christ, he won't have any problems. I pray for him—and you—every night because I know that deep in your hearts you're trying to do something good for people."

A grin wavered on Trotsky's lips. "*Muchas gracias, señora,*" he said and sat down.

Doña Pánfila turned to Honoré. "Something's wrong with the restroom door in the warehouse."

"I'll take care of it." He took the key.

"And I told you not to feed stray dogs. We can't get rid of them. They've been coming in here and pooping all over the place."

"I don't feed stray dogs. Your nephews do."

Her eyes flashed with impatience. "Clean up the warehouse before the gringos show up."

"Gringos?"

"The ones who talk funny English."

"Oh, the drunks. The Savages. I thought they'd be here next week. Did they say when they'd arrive?"

"In a couple of days," she said and left.

Trotsky smiled. "A real matriarch, no?"

"After my father's death, she ruled with an iron hand. Had no choice. We would have lost everything if it hadn't been for her. Now she's too old to work, but she refuses to stay home. She has to have her hand in everything. The books are chaos. Money is missing. My wife and daughter help when they can. Of course, my cousins are more trouble than they're worth." He stood. "Let's go check that door."

Outside, Honoré led Trotsky past the horns of the cast iron bull and the thick wooden hacienda doors leaning against the side of the store. As they headed down a narrow dirt path between a stack of ovens, urn-like pieces of baked clay with a mouth for a fire and a small chimney on top, and wrought iron deer and birds stacked like tumbleweeds, Honoré noticed the smell. Probably a dead *tlacuache.* Or maybe the sewer backed up.

A tin roof slanted across the steel rafters. An army of knights made from tin in Mexico and shipped north, some four feet tall, others six feet, and the rest over eight feet, stood at attention. All wore helmets with visors and a metal feather on top. Black soot covered half of them, and many were twisted, hunched over, crumpled like old soldiers.

"What's this?" asked Trotsky, studying the tin men as if he were a general reviewing his troops. "The survivors of the last crusade?"

"No, a fire. A friend of mine owns a warehouse by the railroad tracks. It burned down. He wanted to get rid of them fast so he sold them to me cheap. As long as I took the damaged ones, too."

With his one eye, Trotsky looked at a sword, the tip of its blade on the ground, the hilt held by a gloved knight. "At one time a knight stood for something." He gazed down a row of men. "The Knights Templar. Soldiers of Christ. Real warriors, the backbone of the crusades. A red-cross knight was a hero." He tapped one of the tin men, which rang hollow. "Kitsch, an imitation of an imitation. Like men today. Hollow men."

Honoré got another whiff. He looked around. Where was it coming from? The rest room at the back of the warehouse? No. Too far away. Nonetheless, he walked back there. First, he checked the door. Sure enough, the lock needed to be replaced, but the smell wasn't coming from the restroom. Then he joined Trotsky.

"A soldier," said Trotsky as he turned to Honoré, "can endure a lot as long as he believes that what he and his buddies are willing to die for is worthwhile."

Honoré sniffed. The smell was worse here.

"But after seeing men, women, and children massacred," Trotsky continued, "or seeing your friends killed on behalf of a country that not only lies but doesn't give a shit, you risk losing everything."

Honoré glanced at the ground, then at Trotsky's boots. Apparently, this Vietnam veteran's sense of smell wasn't very good, probably a result of the wound to his face. He stood in what looked like a pile of shiny prunes swarming with green flies. Dog shit.

The next morning, Honoré served himself a cup of coffee in the kitchen and then walked into the dining room. A stack of unread newspapers lay on the long dark wooden table, where he sat. The *Escandón Morning Times* was crap, but he loved *El Nuevo Amanecer* from Nuevo Escandón. The *San Antonio Express-News* and *Dallas Morning Times* were almost as good as the Mexican newspapers, but *The New York Times* was the mouthpiece of the enemy. According to Trotsky, a revolutionary had to be better read than an English professor.

Upon opening the *Escandón Morning Times,* he froze.

The ugly face of a killer, welts above the brow from a blow or birth defect, glared at him from the front page—Maruca's cousin, Carlos. Also nicknamed Chale or La Chancla because he resembled an old shoe. There were photographs of three other men. Honoré put down his coffee, picked up the paper, and read closely. The report stated that Maruca's *primo* drove to a *colonia* south of Escandón, apparently to pick up some money owed him, and a fistfight broke out with the debtor and his sons. As he returned to his truck, they ran inside the house, got their rifles, ran back outside, and opened fire. He was sitting behind the steering wheel of his pickup when the smell of gunpowder turned him into an Italian meal—spaghetti and meatballs in red sauce.

Maruca came downstairs. In the kitchen she opened the refrigerator and then walked into the dining room with a glass of orange juice and sat at the other end of the table.

"Not a bad way to go," Honoré said.

"What are you talking about?"

"Your cousin. He was shot and killed yesterday."

"Oh," she said, picking up a Sears catalogue from among the stacks of newspapers.

"You don't even feel it when the bullets hit you. But dying over drugs is the pits. No dignity. No self-respect."

"Like you and Tequila when you were smuggling pot?" she said off-handedly.

"I've changed."

"You always go from one extreme to another," she said without looking up from the catalogue. "Yesterday a coyote, today a revolutionary."

Honoré and Maruca never had much to do with the dead man though he had lived in the plain yellow brick house down the street—where he sold heroin, cocaine, and marijuana—and despite the fact that he was Maruca's *primo*.

"Well?" asked Honoré.

"Well what?"

"How do you feel about your cousin's death?"

She flipped a page. "I already told you. My mother says that when you hear an owl at night, it means someone is going to die. How do you oppose prophecy? Besides, if you live by the sword, you die by the sword. Everyone in my family is surprised my cousin lived as long as he did."

Maybe if Honoré had shot that owl, none of this would have happened. Was Maruca right? Who was next? His mother? Tequila? Now *that* wasn't such a bad idea.

"By the way," said Maruca as she leafed through the catalogue, "what about the money you promised me?"

"I'm working on it."

"What does that mean? Another broken promise?"

"No, it means I'm meeting some customers today."

Sunglasses aslant on his red face, golden hair all over his red legs as if a swarm of bees had gathered on them, and wearing Bermuda shorts and a loud baggy shirt as he entered the yard, Hank Savage looked like an asshole. His eighteen-wheeler stood parked on the street.

"Well, hello, Ornery," he said and held out a hand. "Long time, no see."

Honoré shook the bony fingers of this hillbilly from Mississippi. "The name is Honoré."

Hank, red as a lobster boiled in tequila the night before and teeth dipped in yellow glue, rubbed his jaw. "Well okay, Ornery. Sorry. At least it ain't Horny," he said, and laughed. "Remember last time?"

"Last time?"

"Last time we went to Boys' Town."

"That was over a year ago."

"I've been itching to go back. You still hang with some of your old friends, like that short little guy."

"Tequila."

"Yeah."

"No."

Another man climbed out of the cab of the eighteen-wheeler. He wore blue denim overalls, steel-toed black boots, and a straw hat over a square face, craggy and sunburned as a chunk of granite. But it wasn't a man.

Arms thick as salmons, with a notebook tucked in an armpit, Mrs. Savage marched toward them.

Honoré knew she could beat up any man in a fair fight. "Good day, Mrs. Savage."

"Good day, yourself," she growled like a truck driver after a cross-country haul. Her gray eyes took in everything in the yard.

"How can I help you?" Honoré asked.

"Your mother here?"

"Inside."

Buttocks wobbling, she crossed the yard but stopped a few feet from the cast iron bull. "One day, someone is gonna get gored on this *toro*," she said before walking inside.

While old man Savage wandered off toward the warehouse, another truck pulling a flat-bed trailer parked behind the first one. Two gringos got out. Hank Savage's nephews.

"Long time no see, amigo," said Johnny Paint Savage to Honoré as he walked into the yard. He was lanky with bamboo-thin limbs. They called him "Johnny Paint" because back in Mississippi he painted houses for a living.

Tennessee Savage, sturdy and full-bodied, joined them. "Boy, you've got a lot of new stuff."

Johnny looked around to see if anyone was within earshot and leaned toward Honoré. "Can we talk?"

"About what?"

"Moolah."

Honoré suspected something. "I'm doing okay with what little I got."

"We're talking about some *real* moolah," sneered Johnny Paint. "Like that motherfucker down the street, moving coke in religious statues. Making millions. You can't be making much selling this crap. Ain't you interested in a little extra cash?"

"Nope."

"We'd like to meet some of your old buddies," said Johnny. "Pa told us about them. We're looking for a connection deep in Mexico. Maybe *Ass*-capulco."

"It's Acapulco."

"Same thing."

Tennessee moved close. "We've been having trouble getting past the checkpoint. One of our men got busted about a month ago. Lost a lot of money."

Honoré had not forgotten that some of these gringos were always looking for the easiest way to get illegal stuff past the checkpoint north of Escandón. Nor had he forgotten that sometimes they were undercover agents snooping around for leads. "I don't know what you're talking about."

Tennessee grinned. "No shit?"

"No shit."

Tennessee fixed Honoré in a gaze. "You got that I-don't-trust-you look. I understand, bro. In this town there's spooks everywhere you turn. Don't worry. We're cool. But I tell you—there's a shit load of money to be made on this border. Man, if we lived here, we'd already be retired, living off the fat of the land, maybe down in Acapulco with all that Meskin pussy."

Note pad in hand, Mrs. Savage stormed out of the store. Honoré joined her and Pa Savage in the warehouse among the vases, ovens, pots, and Mexican doors. Johnny Paint and Tennessee trailed close behind.

"Your prices are a lot higher than the last time we were here," Mrs. Savage growled.

Honoré stood next to her and her husband as they looked down a row of medieval soldiers covered in black soot. "I'm giving you Chicano prices," he said. "Anywhere else you get Mexican, Mexican-American, or gringo prices."

"How about a twenty percent discount?"

"No way, José."

She stood next to Pa Savage. "There's a place down the street that's slashed its prices. Let's go check it out, hon."

"Where?" asked Pa Savage.

"That place where they sell religious statues."

Honoré grinned at Johnny Paint and Tennessee and then said to Ma Savage. "Go ahead. But you'll get nothing but crap."

The next morning, it rained cats and dogs. Honoré didn't bother to open the store and spent the next two gloomy, overcast days listening to rain pound the roof of his house like bricks of Acapulco Gold. While Bonita stayed in her room talking to Misty on the phone, Maruca filled the house with the smell of enchiladas and did not utter one word about the dolls or the money. For the first time, Honoré wondered whether there might be some truth to what Maruca had told him about the owl. Maybe a curse had descended upon the barrio. However, if the men in the family—at least, the men from Sabinas Hidalgo—were not afraid of man or machine, should *he* be alarmed by black magic?

When the rain ceased on the third day, it was time to get back to work. Tequila crossed the street and accosted him as he climbed into his pickup. "Did you hear about El Sapo?" asked Tequila.

Honoré sat in his pickup. "No."

A man with the belly and face of a frog, El Sapo lived at the end of the street near the arroyo. A month ago, explained Tequila, he got into trouble with his wife, a fair-skinned hag from Monterrey with sharp, bony elbows. Anyway, because he didn't hand over his paycheck, she cut him off at the pass and sent him to the doghouse.

"*Panocha*less," smirked Tequila. "*¡Qué horror!*"

El Sapo, a maintenance man at one of the local high schools, was driven crazy at work by the sight of so many teenage girls running around in shorts or mini-skirts and tank tops. Fearful of losing his mind and doing something illegal at school, the poor man did the right thing, the humane thing, and headed for the red light district in Nuevo Escandón. Amid a rainforest of mangoes and man-eating plants, he let his anaconda loose among three women. Outside rain fell as if the world would be destroyed by water again.

"Anyway," Tequila continued, "the poor bastard got drunk, roaring drunk."

Though the lovely women begged him to spend the night as they stroked his exhausted limb, he refused, explaining he needed to get back to his wife and children. After emptying his wallet of his monthly salary, he stumbled into the rain, climbed into his pickup, and followed the same route home he had taken hundreds of times since he discovered Mexican whores when he was twelve. He took the road that ran along the river and beneath the black bridge, over which trains carried a thousand color televisions to the American market every day. He never came up on the other end.

"Yesterday," Tequila said, "the Mexican newspaper reported that the underpass had been flooded."

When Honoré arrived at the store, the first thing that caught his attention was the eighteen-wheeler with Mississippi license plates sporting a tiny Confederate flag. After parking behind the massive truck and climbing out, he waited for the Savages on the sidewalk.

"That was quite a storm," said Pa Savage to Honoré as he exited the cab, smelling of booze and piss. "We were stuck in that dingy hotel down the street. I thought about calling you."

Just then Ma Savage descended. "You were right," she said. "Those folks down the street may have cheap prices, but they're selling nothing but crap."

Honoré nodded and then headed toward the office.

But they didn't follow him. They started squabbling about something the old man said or did last night at the hotel. While Honoré unlocked the store's front door, the other two Savages showed up in their truck with the flat-bed trailer and parked in front of the eighteen-wheeler. When the phone rang, Honoré ran inside. His mother and cousins called in sick. What a relief!

Sturdy wooden doors from haciendas and churches in southern Mexico brought in the most money, so the gringos loaded them first in the eighteen-wheeler, where they would be protected from the elements, including theft. Next they stacked pot-bellied vases, clay ovens, and boxes of porcelain dishware between the doors. The band of tin mariachis with violins and guitars in their wire-fingered hands were loaded on the flat bed trailer. Pa Savage considered taking the six-foot-long bull made from cast iron, but changed his mind when he and Johnny Paint tried to move it and found out how heavy it was.

Tennessee walked across the yard. "You guys about ready to vamoose?"

Ma Savage snapped, "Hold your horses."

"Take your time," Tennessee said. "I ain't anxious to get back. Fact is I wouldn't mind spending another week here. Best Meskin food north of the Rio Grande. Next time we come, we'll come with plenty of time and plenty of dough so we can party."

"Not a bad idea," said Pa Savage.

Ma Savage glared at him. "You've been drunk the entire week. Isn't that enough?" Then she said to Honoré through gray teeth, "What about the tin soldiers? How much?"

Honoré led them back inside the warehouse. "We haven't priced them yet."

"What do you think, hon?" she asked Pa Savage as she maneuvered between rows of tin men.

Pa Savage slouched close behind her. "Ain't worth it. Got all the scrap metal we need in Mississippi."

"You can have all the damaged tin men for free—about twenty-three—if you buy the fifty good ones."

Mrs. Savage knocked on a soldier's breastplate with her knuckles. "How much?" she asked.

"Depending on the size, between thirty to fifty dollars each. Let's say $2,500."

"Naw," said Pa Savage. "No need for knights in Mississippi."

"Pa," she said, "that's not a bad deal. Some elbow grease—that's all we need. And a little straightening out. The good ones we can sell to the developers building those Tudor houses in that new subdivision in Vicksburg. Yard-art, they call it."

"Or just plain crap," said Johnny Paint, his mouth shiny with scorn. "That's what I call it."

Tennessee said, "I say we take 'em, all of 'em."

Johnny Paint frowned. "You plan to sell this shit back home?"

Pa and Ma Savage were looking at the mirrors and dishware in the metal storage shed at the back of the warehouse when Tennessee whispered in Johnny Paint's ear. "They're hollow, you dumbass. Plenty of room for stuff inside."

Johnny Paint rubbed his chin with a long-fingered hand. "You're a fucking genius."

Honoré didn't know how the hell the tin men would help them get past the checkpoint. There were all kinds of tricks, he knew, having pulled off some himself, but thank God getting dope past the checkpoint was no longer his problem. He was just glad to sell them.

Mrs. Savage wandered back. "You have a deal."

"Let's go to my office," Honoré said with a smile.

They paid in cash, bundles of it. Honoré was delighted. Now he could face Maruca, and there would be peace at home.

After everything was loaded, he walked the Savages to their vehicles and stood on the curb. "Good luck," he said to Johnny Paint and Tennessee as they leered at him from inside their pickup.

"Think about what we told you," Johnny Paint said.

Honoré grinned. "Sure will."

Then the gringos took off, waving out the side of their windows as they headed north on Tamaulipas Avenue. The tin men, standing guard in back of the flat bed, stared at him as they were hauled away. Trotsky was right. They looked pitiful, as if the shadow of death had reached them as well. Arms mangled by fire, swords melted, and helmets black with soot, they looked like an army of crusaders who never had a chance.

If the idiots had paid Honoré with a check instead of green-eyed Washingtonians stuffed in duffel bags, his hands wouldn't have gotten dirty—and he'd be home by now. Though he didn't know what that dirtiness consisted of, he knew, after counting hundreds of dollars in small bills, it was there—a fine dust that clung to his fingers and reminded him of the old days when he and Tequila sat in a swanky Dallas hotel suite, counting millions while snorting cocaine and drinking whiskey before the long-limbed lovely white hookers showed up, huge breasts pouring out of brassieres like vanilla malts topped with pink cherries. If he had only saved that money. If he had invested it in something, like a ranch or a forwarding agency or a hotel, he wouldn't be stuck in this dead-end job.

After stuffing the bills back in three duffel bags, he got his revolver from the desk drawer and took the bags out to his pickup, where he hid them under a tarpaulin on the bed. When sheriffs up north, anxious to empty their poorly funded jails, began giving prisoners one-way tickets to Escandón, where they had a better chance of surviving in the warm weather, the main drag out front filled with homeless people and prostitutes, and so he could not leave money in the store, not even in the safe. He locked the back door and switched off the lights.

What scared him most, however, as he headed south on Tamaulipas, an eye on the rearview mirror, were the old debts, unfinished business, wounds that never healed from his drug-dealing days. He still remembered the late afternoon he was cruising in a lowrider with a friend who had just gotten out of Leavenworth and had returned to Escandón to visit his family. They stopped at a railroad crossing, red lights flashing as the guard rails came down. Then, a truck rumbled to a stop next to them, and a *vato loco* with a black pin-stripe mustache rolled down a window and sprayed the lowrider with an AK-47.

Honoré turned left on Kennedy Street and drove under the interstate overpass. Several traffic lights later, he cruised past the cemetery across the street from Burger King and Wendy's. At the intersection near the H-E-B supermarket and the post office, he turned south and headed toward his wife's old barrio, Sal Si Puedes, passing car washes, small corner meat markets, hole-in-the-wall restaurants, a *washatería*, and a Buttercrust bakery.

A block past the second traffic light, he turned left and saw the Sears Roebuck truck parked outside his house. "Oh, brother!"

His head began to boil like a cabbage in a pot of soup. As he parked behind the other truck, he remembered what his father had cautioned many
times, that in dealing with women it was often best not to say anything.
After tucking the pistol inside his belt, he climbed out and pulled the duffel
bags from the bed of the truck, hefting one over his shoulder with his right
hand and carrying the other two in his left.

Then, he heard a strange whistle. He halted, looked around. Nobody.
The sound of cars on a distant boulevard carried in the air. A bird flew high
above.

Giggles floated like bubbles. "It's me, *pendejo!*" yelled Tequila from
across the street. Looking like an American tourist in shorts, a Hawaiian
shirt, and flip flops, Tequila approached on hairy legs. "Have you heard?"

Honoré put down the duffel bags. "No."

"Some *güey* died last night."

Honoré couldn't pry his eyes from the Sears truck. "Mexicans die every
day."

"*No mames, pendejo.*"

Honoré fixed Tequila in a gaze. "Are you talking about Maruca's cousin?"

"No, *güey*. That was two days ago. I'm talking about Gustavo Ulibarri.
He fell over dead in front of his television."

A salesman at K-mart, Gustavo was Honoré's age. A nice guy and a
great salesman, he always got Honoré good deals. He lived down the street,
and occasionally Honoré saw him come out of a bar downtown, drunk on
his ass, his face dark and hard like a well-done steak. "Too bad."

"Well, have you thought about it?"

"About what?"

"Why do you act like a *pendejo*?" demanded Tequila, hands on his
hips. "Did that tree limb crack your brains and fuck up your memory? I'm
talking about making some money."

Honoré picked up the duffel bags and turned toward the door. "No
thanks."

"Ah, you're right," Tequila sighed. "Why leave this paradise in Escandón
and go to some dump in Acapulco?"

Honoré stopped and turned. "What do we have to do?"

"An honest day's work. Some guys in Acapulco asked me to work on
their yacht. Made me an offer I couldn't refuse. It would be just like the old
days, only better."

"How many times do I have to tell you I'm through with all that shit?"

Tequila blinked. Then he shaded his eyes with a hand and looked up at the sky. "*Mira.*"

Above, a bird flew in a wide circle.

"A *lechuza*," said Tequila. "You know what that means."

"*No chingues*," said Honoré, turning away. "It's a buzzard."

"Wait, wait!"

Honoré halted. "What?"

"What do I tell my friends in Acapulco?"

"Tell them to go fuck themselves."

With one duffel bag slung across his back, Honoré carried the other two past the tree. On the porch he set down the two and pulled open the door. Then he picked them up and walked inside.

Bonita sat on the edge of the sofa with the remote in her hand as two delivery men in blue uniforms unpacked a large-screen television. "Ooooh! Aaaah!" Then she saw Honoré. "Look, Daddy, it's just like Christmas."

Maruca stood in a daze, eyes on the TV, smiling. She didn't even bother to greet him. Suddenly, a terrible thought came to Honoré's mind. *The dolls.*

The short man smiled. "Buenas tardes."

"Buenas tardes," Honoré said curtly.

The tall man addressed Maruca. "Señora, where do you want us to put the TV?"

Annoyed, Honoré pivoted and stalked into the kitchen, where he was relieved to see that Maruca had had enough sense to close the door to the back room. He opened it, walked inside, and dumped the duffel bags on the floor. When he turned on the light, eyes stared at him from the pine crates and followed him to the gun case on the wall. Not a peep from the bird cage. After securing the pistol under lock and key, he returned to the living room.

"There's an outlet here," Maruca said, pulling a chair away from the wall. "Yes, this is where I want it. Against this wall."

Honoré asked the tall man, "May I see the invoice?"

"*Desde luego*," said the man, unclasping a piece of paper from the clipboard.

A blizzard of chills swept Honoré when he saw how much Maruca had paid for the TV, his tongue curling like a piece of *chicharrón* on dry ice. "*¡Chingada madre!*" he muttered.

"Something wrong?" Maruca asked without looking at him. "*Perfecto,*" she said to the men as they set the TV against the wall.

The tall man handed Honoré the clipboard with the work order. He signed it and handed it back. Suddenly, his knees felt weak. His bones froze like bamboo in a cold front, and nuggets of sweat popped out on his arms. The men opened the front door and trudged to the truck as evening settled on the barrio. After they rumbled down the street, a dizzy Honoré staggered into the kitchen. The phone rang.

"What?" Honoré growled into it.

"Are you okay?" asked Trotsky.

Honoré got control of a jumpy tongue. "Yeah, sure."

"Are we going to Nuevo Escandón?"

"Yeah, give me about an hour."

"Okay."

Still dizzy, Honoré returned to the living room and sat on the couch just as Bonita turned on the television with the remote. He stared at the dazzlingly bright sixty-inch screen.

"All we need now," she said, sitting on the floor with eyes glued to the screen, "is some popcorn."

Maruca sat down next to her.

There was a time Honoré could not watch American television without plenty of saltpeter in his coffee. Scantily dressed white cheerleaders were interesting until he sensed something unreal about them. Then there was all the shooting and cars flipping in mid-air—this was worse than the pornography Tequila watched at home. Like Trotsky, Honoré hated that TV reduced men to homebodies, fags, *pendejos*.

"I don't know," he said, "what this world is coming to."

"Shhhh," said Maruca, leaning forward and changing channels.

Bonita turned her head. "Daddy, please."

"Please don't call me Daddy," said Honoré. "Do I look like a gringo?"

Bonita said softly, "Apá."

Maruca turned to him. "What do the gringos have to do with this?"

"Everything. They tell us was what to eat, how to dress, how to think."

She sat next to Bonita. "That's Trotsky talking."

"Gustavo Ulibarri just died in front of his television."

"He was a drunk. Everyone knew he was going to die sooner or later. And his wife must be very happy to get rid of that *pendejo*."

The back of Honoré's tongue tickled like he was getting a sore throat, like he was coming down with a bad cold, maybe pneumonia. Slowly, he got up and stood behind Maruca, who was flipping through the channels.

"What's the matter?" she asked matter of factly over her shoulder.

He really didn't want to get mad. No, he was already mad. He didn't want to explode. He wanted to do what his father had always told him to do when dealing with women: keep his mouth shut.

Suddenly, against his will, his mouth opened. "What do you think I am, *un pendejo*?" he yelled.

She jumped to her feet. "Did I say that?"

"No, but I know how your mind works."

"*¡Honoré, por favor!*"

"You're ruining my daughter! You're spoiling her! I don't give a shit what the feminists say! I am the head of this household, and no one buys televisions without consulting me!"

"What the hell is the wrong with you?"

"You said you were going to buy a dining table. Instead you went and bought this TV. That's what's wrong!"

She stood directly in front of him. "Well, I just got sick and tired of you breaking your promises. Besides, I paid for it with my own money."

His mouth quivered with rage. "You paid too much! Where did you get so much money?"

She looked at one side of his face, then the other. "You look like you're about to have a stroke."

He opened his mouth, but nothing came out. When he closed it, everything wanted to spew out, like when he had drunk too much tequila and couldn't keep anything down. "I hate all this gringo bullshit. And I refuse to die in front of a television!" he yelled. "That's what's wrong with me!"

Maruca pointed the remote and turned off the television. "Why are you angry at the gringos? Because of Trotsky? Or is it because you're not in Hollywood? No, no, I know," she said and laughed. "What you really want is to die in a movie! On television!"

He stormed out the front door.

At Herrera's Stop-n-Go grocery, Honoré eased up on the gas pedal and let the pickup coast along the street's downward slope toward the Mexican flag unfurling like a giant *zarape* above the squat buildings downtown. He couldn't see the river, but it was there between Escandón and Nuevo Escandón. In the old days, he drove this same route with Tequila when they headed out to the red light district in Nuevo Escandón. In fact, if he needed anything right now, it was a boys' night out on the town. Getting soused, strung out, fucked up, plastered.

A train whistle ripped through the blue evening. Amid the clanking and groaning of the railroad cars against each other, Honoré stopped at a crossing, where the graffiti on boxcars, the blinking red lights, and rumble of metal lulled him until a monster truck, snorting and farting, pulled up next to him, on the driver's side.

"Fuck!" he muttered.

This is exactly how his friend's lowrider, an old convertible, had been positioned when they stopped at a railroad crossing, his friend sitting in the driver's seat smiling, talking about how glad he was to be home, a tattoo of the Virgen de Guadalupe on his right arm as he gripped the steering wheel and waited for the train to clear the tracks. Then after the train disappeared around the bend, the red lights stopped blinking and the gates lifted. Suddenly, blinding flashes of lightning from the barrel of an AK-47 sprinkled rose petals across the dashboard. A geyser of blood struck the windshield as the man-eater roared.

Honoré slid to the floor. Three bullets hit his leg. The burning spread slowly and then quickly and fiercely. He flung his door open and lunged out, where his face slammed against the gritty pavement. Then he rolled away from the idling lowrider and crawled toward its back wheel, away from the gunfire. His leg felt as if someone had poured sizzling grease on it. He kept crawling. Then the shooting stopped, and the monster truck screeched and burned rubber as it sped away. Another vehicle pulled up.

A boot descended from the black sedan and stood on the asphalt inches from his face. A long-haired stranger with a black eye patch pulled him to his feet and pushed him in the backseat of the car. "Get in!"

They sped off.

"When I heard the AK-47," Trotsky said later, "I thought I was back in Nam. It was all so familiar. Like a dream or a movie. A flashback. I opened the door, and there you were on the pavement. You looked like one of my friends. So I grabbed you and threw you in the car."

Trotsky took him to his wife's ranch south of Escandón, where a Mexican doctor from across the river tended to him. Since members of the rival gang were looking for him, Honoré couldn't go back into town, so he called Maruca and told her to go stay with her family until things cooled down. Meanwhile, Trotsky spent day and night with him at a small clapboard house at the ranch as he went through withdrawals from pot and coke while the doctor from Mexico checked on him once a week. At night a fireplace kept them warm.

When his mind cleared, Honoré found out that the stranger who had saved his life was the son of an American of Bohemian descent named Trusky, once stationed at the naval base in San Diego, California, where he grew up in a family of women—his mother and several aunts. Soon after graduating from high school with honors, Trotsky left his mother after a fight with one of her boyfriends and enlisted in the Marines. They didn't waste any time shipping him to Vietnam.

What Honoré or his friends had experienced as narcotraficantes on the border was child's play compared to what Trotsky endured in Vietnam. He should be dead. And from the looks of it, his ordeal wasn't over. The thought of suicide was never far.

"Latinos kill each other in LA every day," Trotsky intoned the night before Honoré left the ranch. "Stupid deaths over territory. Over women. Money. They die like *pendejos*." Brown face gleaming in light from the fireplace, he looked directly at Honoré. "And that's how you're going to die."

Had any other man spoken to him like this, Honoré would have beat the shit out of him. "I can change," he said.

Trotsky gazed at him coolly. "I doubt it."

A twinge of pain in his thigh reminded Honoré of the railroad crossing. Then it subsided. "Is there any way I can pay you back?"

"Maybe."

Nothing happened. As soon as the train disappeared beyond a warehouse and the lights and clanging stopped, the monster truck sped off. Relieved, Honoré started his motor and crossed the tracks.

The historic district lay a few blocks east of downtown. Grand old Victorian homes of clapboard and brick sat amid spacious lawns filled with old trees whose gnarled leafy limbs shaded the neighborhood. Some of the city's prominent families still lived here, but since most had died off or left town, a few of the houses had been converted into law offices. The old railroad station wasn't far off. The district was so close to the river that there was a constant flow of undocumented workers. Years ago, Honoré and Tequila had smuggled a lot of stuff through here.

After parking behind Trotsky's jeep, Honoré climbed out of his pickup and stood on the narrow sidewalk along a wrought iron fence, gazing at the two-storey house Trotsky's wife had inherited from her family. Then he opened the gate and walked up the porch steps.

He rang the doorbell.

After recovering from his wounds in Vietnam, Trotsky returned to his mother's home in San Diego. As he wandered the streets looking for direction in his life, he found he hated California's endless highways, suburban sprawl, groovy lifestyles, Hollywood royalty, and trendy cliché-ridden

minds. So he joined a group of hippies, hooked up with a gorgeous California girl, and months later ended up on the sands of Isla de Mujeres, just off
the coast of Mexico in the Caribbean, running on the white beaches half
naked, long black hair down to his shoulders, his one good eye red from
pot-and-tequila visions, knees sore from screwing on sand at night. After
the hippies left for Guatemala, Trotsky moved in with an aunt in Mexico
City and enrolled at the University of the Americas. Then he won a fellowship to a university in South Dakota, where he began work on a doctorate
in political science.

Tortured by flashbacks of the carnage in Vietnam, he spent nights walking in freezing weather, pursued by phantoms of his dead buddies. In class
one morning, he assaulted a professor who called Vietnam veterans baby
killers. The police arrested Trotsky, but the professor dropped the charges.
After the university kicked him out, he moved to Arizona, where he lived
on an Indian reservation. Peyote ceremonies and sweat lodges kept him
from killing himself. Then, during a visit to the Audie Murphy Memorial
Veterans Hospital in San Antonio, he hooked up with an old army buddy,
El Capitán, then a veteran turned anti-war activist, who convinced him to
live there and join the anti-war movement.

Honoré rang the bell again.

No answer. Grackles clicked and whistled in the trees next door. Cou-
pling railroad cars boomed on the tracks a few blocks away. He rang the
bell again.

Amid the screaming and bottle throwing and the smell of pot and the
anti-war posters and slogans bellowed through megaphones and hippies
pissing in front of the Alamo, Trotsky saw a lovely young woman holding
a sign, with the classic looks of a flamenco dancer—the black hair, the light
skin, a trim mouth, and even nose. Poised and unperturbed as if she were
in line for communion at church, she caught him staring at her. He smiled,
she smiled, and they spoke. Three months later they married. Repulsed by
the military bases in San Antonio, Trotsky found the desolate Texas-Mexico
border appealing. He especially loved this part of town—and this old house,
in particular—where Altagracia's family had lived for generations.

The door opened. "We're under surveillance," Trotsky said quickly and
stepped outside.

Honoré waited for Trotsky to lock the door. "When haven't we been?"

Trotsky wore suspenders over a loose white shirt with its sleeves rolled
up. "This is different. There's no telling how they might try to set you up. It
could be through one of your customers at the store or a neighbor." Trotsky

headed down the porch steps. "And remember that in the Cold War the real intercontinental ballistic missiles have been women."

"When haven't women been dangerous?"

Trotsky paused on the sidewalk. "All I'm telling you is that we have to be especially cautious."

They climbed in the jeep. Trotsky turned on the engine, and they headed toward downtown. After cruising past the federal courthouse on their left, and the plaza with memorials for the veterans of WWI, WWII, Korea, and Vietnam on the right, they turned south on Washington Avenue and sped toward Mexico. They paid at the toll booth, the guard rail lifted, and then they rolled across the Bridge of the Americas. After getting through Mexican customs, a two-storey bunker-like building with brown-faced officers lolling about in blue uniforms, they cruised west along the river. Streams of evening sunlight fell across dirty gray houses.

A train moved slowly over a bridge toward the river as they shot into the underpass echoing with the metallic grinding of wheels above. It was the same underpass where El Sapo drowned. They came out on the other end and drove around a palm-lined plaza to an avenue running parallel to the river.

"What's the matter?" asked Trotsky.

"Just thinking."

"Maruca?"

"No, about a neighbor. He died in this underpass."

"I read about him."

Honoré glanced at Trotksy. "Strange things have been happening around my house."

"I told you we're under surveillance."

Honoré turned his attention to the road ahead. "It's more than that. Men in my neighborhood have been dying. Maruca says it's because of an owl in the tree outside my bedroom window. My neighbor claims someone hexed the men in our barrio."

The evening sank in a haze of blue. Cars reminded Honoré of fish with yellow eyes glowing in the inky darkness of a fish bowl, red lights on their tail fins, like strange deep sea creatures. Night fell as they drove toward the city's outskirts.

"I want to show you something," said Trotsky.

At the top of a low hill, an eerie scene unfolded before them: the huge well-lit ultra-modern Motorola complex with tractor trailers lining its docks and security lights amid dark rows of shacks made from wooden pallets abandoned by maquiladoras and trucking companies. Honoré had been impressed that so many American companies had factories in Nuevo Escandón until Trotsky explained that workers assembled TVs for peanuts and shipped them to the American market, where they sold for hundreds of dollars. Here an employee worked a full week, eight hours a day, and made about thirty dollars.

"Each day," he said, "a woman makes enough to buy a hamburger in the United States. We don't need an owl to tell us that people are dying in droves every day."

As they hit a dirt road, a volley of rocks clattered against the under-carriage of the jeep. Soon they approached the neon lights of nightclubs, bright as flames rising from a lake in hell. Honoré grew up thinking pros-titutes were a necessary evil—and he had clearly loved the carnival atmo-sphere of Boys' Town, where he could have anything he wanted as long he had money. Then, one day he heard Trotsky's wife explain how some women from barrios and villages throughout Mexico and Latin America came looking for the American dream and ended up working in the red light district, where they made more in one night than a week at Motorola or Sony.

"Americans want to keep out undocumented workers," said Trotsky, hands on the steering wheel, eyes shifting to the mirror and back to the road. "But they don't mind exploiting the workers in Mexico. They say it's the responsibility of the Mexican government to provide jobs for their peo-ple, yet every time Mexicans try to establish a government that responds to the people's needs, Americans oppose it. Meanwhile, these poor women's hard work at meager-paying jobs subsidizes the American dream. "

Bouncing over potholes made deeper by the recent rain, they turned and went down another dirt street and then another, long roads with few lights, until they stopped in front of a plain two-storey white house with a stairway to the second floor. A wooden sign said La Clínica del Barrio. Laughter and music drifted from the roof as they got out of the jeep.

At the top of the wooden stairs, Honoré opened a door with a bloated screen and followed Trotsky into a small crowded kitchen, hot and smell-ing of tamales in large kettles on the stove. Beyond a second screen door at the far end of the room, music played and people laughed.

Dr. Heriberto Longoria, a short, dark man with frizzy hair and a thick-lipped smile, embraced Trotsky. "Trotsky, the Russian revolutionary!" he cried. "Welcome to Mexico, *cabrón*!"

Dr. Longoria had tended to Honoré at Altagracia's ranch, removing two bullets from his right leg and another from his left buttock. A few more inches to the right, the doctor told Honoré, and the bullet would have unmanned him.

The doctor's wife, a slender woman with a plain, warm face, stood at his side, wiping her hands on an apron. "Señor Trotsky, *bienvenido*."

"Gracias, gracias," said Trotsky, shaking her hand. "Altagracia couldn't come. Family. She sends her regards."

"We understand," she said. "Tell her we miss her."

"You've met Honoré, haven't you?" asked Dr. Longoria.

She turned to Honoré. "Yes, of course. Welcome."

"Gracias," said Honoré.

"Don Sixto is here," Dr. Longoria said. "He's been asking for both of you."

"How is he?" asked Trotsky.

"He can barely walk. But he's alive."

When water boiled out of the kettle of tamales and sizzled on the stove, the doctor's wife excused herself. Honoré stepped aside, his back to the door leading to the rooftop patio, as she lowered the flame and lifted the lid.

"Go ahead," Dr. Longoria said to Trotsky. "We'll join you as soon as we're done here."

Voices, laughter, and music filled the night as Trotsky opened the screen door and Honoré followed him outside. About forty people sat scattered among tables arranged in rows on the roof-turned-patio girded by a waist-high parapet. At one table several journalists stood and greeted Trotsky and Honoré. At another table Alejandro Mireles, the new president of the opposition party, introduced the two men to his wife, a shapely light-skinned woman with a regal bearing.

After chatting briefly with them, Trotsky led Honoré to a table in back, where Sixto sat with a slender woman young enough to be his daughter. Face dark as coffee and black hair in braids, she wore sandals, a turquoise blouse embroidered with flowers, and a long black skirt. Must be his latest conquest, thought Honoré. On the table, empty bottles of beer surrounded a bottle of tequila. Then he saw an AK-47 slung from the back of her chair and wondered whether she might be his body guard as well. According to Trotsky, the two had been living together since Sixto left his menopausal middle-aged wife.

Assisted by the young woman, Sixto rose to his feet on crutches, bruises on his face and a turban of bandages on his head. "*¡Adelante! ¡Adelante!*"

Trotsky embraced Don Sixto. "You're alive, *cabrón*! When they jailed you on Black Tuesday, none of us thought we'd see you again."

"Mexicans are difficult to kill," said Don Sixto, his hand on the young woman's shoulder. He grinned at Honoré, teeth sturdy beneath a thick black mustache. "*¿Y tú, cabrón?* How are my *camaradas* in Oaxaca?"

Honoré shook an iron hand vigorously. "They send you *saludos*."

Sixto put his arm around the young woman. "This is La Morenita. She's from Oaxaca."

Honoré said, "Buenas noches, señorita."

"Buenas noches," she replied with a shy smile.

Trotsky exchanged greetings with her as well.

Then Sixto lay his crutches aside and with her help resumed his chair. "Sit down," he said to the men, "sit down. We have much to talk about." After Trotsky and Honoré pulled chairs from the end of the table and sat, he patted the girl on the butt. "*Hija*, can you bring us some cold ones?"

With a bounce in her step, La Morenita left. A few minutes later, she returned with beer bottles in each hand. Then, knowing when to get lost, she left.

Don Sixto raised his bottle high. "*¡Salud, dinero, y amor!*"

"*¡Salud!*" everyone cheered and then drank.

Sixto lowered his bottle. "How are things in Nicaragua?"

"Tough," Trotsky said, "especially in the north, where the contras are operating. I met with some Vietnam vets in Managua. They want to organize a convoy to Nicaragua. They're looking at several routes, one of which comes through here."

"When?"

"This summer."

"What do you think?"

"Well, first I'll be surprised if they get it off the ground. And second, we have our hands full with Lucero."

Lucero was a small town about fifty miles southwest of Nuevo Escandón. Reputed to be the capital of *brujas* in the region, people from throughout South Texas and northern Mexico went there seeking cures for everything from cancer to alcoholism. It also had some excellent bakeries. Honoré's father loved to eat empanadas from there, and so Honoré had been there several times as a child when they visited his father's family in nearby Sabinas Hidalgo. Now it was a beacon of light in the struggle for democracy as its inhabitants fought to get the PRI government out of power.

"I'm headed down there as soon as I can walk," Don Sixto said. "Doña

Catarina and her supporters need all the help and encouragement they can get."

Trotsky leaned close to him and softened his voice. "One more thing. The dolls need to go home."

Sixto nodded. "Come by the shop."

"When?"

"Soon. We're thinking of organizing a press conference for Doña Catarina."

Trotsky glanced at Honoré.

Honoré nodded, his mind still on Maruca and how much he hated fighting with her. "I'll be there."

While Sixto and Trotsky talked about Lucero, Honoré's attention wandered beyond the rooftop to the lights of Escandón and Nuevo Escandón converging in the distance. He couldn't see his old friend, the Rio Grande, but he knew somewhere in the dark between the two cities it flowed toward the Gulf of Mexico. In high school he smuggled drugs across the river because he was bored and because Tequila convinced him it was a quick way to make cash. Besides, everyone was doing it, so why not take advantage? Then his father got killed, and his mother had to fend for herself and the family. When they were on the verge of losing the store, Honoré started smuggling in earnest. Soon he got hooked on pot and coke, and Maruca threatened to leave him. He didn't quit until after the shooting at the railroad crossing.

Slowly and unsteadily, a huge man wandered across the patio toward them. "Ah, my dear friend Trotsky, there you are! I heard you were in Cuba."

Trotsky stood and gave up his chair to El Profe. "No, Nicaragua."

Legend had it that El Profe had returned to the borderlands in the early seventies, after being hunted down for his involvement in a communist plot to overthrow the Mexican government. Now he taught economics at a small private college in Nuevo Escandón and wrote a popular left-wing weekly column for a local newspaper. Trotsky had long claimed El Profe was an infiltrator who used his drunkenness as a cover-up.

A car honked in the street below. "Your wife is here," said La Morenita, who had wandered back. She peered over the parapet.

The car honked again. "*¡Pinche vieja!*" El Profe muttered, wavering to his feet, then flopping back in his chair.

Sixto leaned toward him. "I think it's time for you to go home, Profe. Let Trotsky help you downstairs."

The drunk sat upright like a good student anxious to respond to a teacher's question. "Caballeros, there is no need. There has never been a need. Freedom is freedom. And bondage is bondage. We prefer bondage."

The car honked again.

El Profe stumbled to his feet. Then as he lurched toward the parapet, Honoré shot to his feet and helped La Morenita pull the drunk from the edge of the roof. Below, the Profe's wife, a speck of a woman, stood outside her car.

"Gentlemen, please," said El Profe, jerking loose from Honoré. "Let us be gentle. Let us be men. Let us be gentlemen."

"*Tranquilo, Profe*," purred Honoré, taking hold of the drunk's elbow. "*Tranquilo.*"

"Okay, okay," El Profe said. "But please let me say something. Let me address my good friend, Trotsky."

Honoré tried nudging the drunk away from the parapet. "Profe, please."

"My dear Trotsky, listen to this. As you know, in the second temptation of Christ, Satanás told Christ to cast himself from the top of the temple—" El Profe leaned over the edge of the roof as if he would cast himself from the parapet. He backed away. "But Christ told him to fuck off. Well, not in so many words."

More honking.

"Let's go downstairs," said Honoré, pulling the drunk's arm.

The honking stopped. From below, the wife shouted, "Get down, *hijo de tu rechingada madre*! Fool!"

"Caballeros, if you were married to my wife, you would drink as much as I do."

"We better go, Profe," Honoré said.

Suddenly, a hand solid as a chunk of granite nicked Honoré's nose as the drunk stumbled and fell. Now the big man lay grumbling on the floor. Honoré and Trotsky helped him to his feet. La Morenita waited near the parapet.

"*Tranquilo*, Profe," purred Honoré. "*Tranquilo.*"

The drunk wobbled. When he stepped forward, he tripped and sagged against Trotsky, who held him up. The giant stood, wobbled again. Suddenly, he lurched forward and crashed into Trotsky, who reeled backwards, arms pinwheeling over the edge of the roof.

Honoré jumped, clutching him by a trouser leg. When it ripped, Honoré clasped an ankle and hung on for dear life until La Morenita grabbed Trotsky's belt. Honoré felt his grip slipping. An otherwise ever-somber Trotsky looked ridiculous hanging over the side of the building, shock of black hair waving. Beads of sweat sprouted on Honoré's forehead. The muscles in his arms ached. La Morenita huffed and puffed. Then slowly, they hauled him back on the roof.

Trembling and breathing hard, Trotsky stood and straightened out his clothes. "Fucking Stalinist!"

"Are you okay?" asked Sixto from where he sat.

After some other men came and dragged the drunk away, Trotsky sat down. "I need a shot of tequila."

Sixto handed him the bottle. "El Profe is a good man," he said. "A dedicated father. A good husband. A great activist."

Trotsky took a slug and swallowed hard. "When he's sober," he said, then adjusted the black patch over his eye. "That wasn't an accident."

"Yes, it was."

"He's a spy."

"No. An alcoholic. The best kind of spy. Why do you think I keep him around? Who do you think got me out of jail today?"

Honoré sat down.

At the other end of the rooftop, the kitchen screen door swung open, and out walked Dr. Longoria and his wife carrying a steaming bucket. "The tamales are ready!" he shouted. "The best tamales in Mexico! Tamales from my wife's country, the proud state of Veracruz! ¡Adelante!"

La Morenita took off across the patio.

The pile of thick green leaves wrapped in flat bundles steamed through the crowd, drawing eyes and tongues after them as the canister arrived at a table in the middle of the patio. La Morenita carried several tamales to Sixto's table along with a fresh round of beer bottles. She kissed his head.

Sixto unwrapped the banana leaf from around the glossy body of dough filled with pork and chile. "I love tamales from Veracruz. But these are so delicious they're dangerous. Eating too many will get you in trouble. So watch it." He turned enthusiastically to Honoré. "¡Éntrale! ¡Éntrale!"

Honoré looked at the tamales doubtfully until hunger got the best of him. "I'll take a bite."

"No, no! Eat all you want!"

Meanwhile, Dr. Longoria set up a microphone at the other end of the roof, a few yards from the kitchen door. After welcoming a number of guests, including Trotsky and Honoré, everyone applauded. Then he introduced Don Sixto, who rose to his feet grinning broadly, like he was finally getting a chance to do what he did best. Everyone stood and applauded as Trotsky helped him across the patio.

"Gracias, gracias," Sixto said in a low, firm voice as he held himself erect on the crutches. "I wish to thank Dr. Longoria for his generosity and you for this welcome." The crowd cheered. "Thank you for all of your support while I was in jail."

The crowd roared and whistled.

Then Sixto handed a crutch to Trotsky and stood straight, shoulders square, head high, much like his old self, strong and powerful, handling the microphone with the aplomb of a nightclub entertainer, snapping the cord like a whip. "*¡Estos hijos de su rechingada madre no valen madre!*" he said.

Cheers and applause swept the patio.

"These government bureaucrats," he continued, "have never been able to do anything for themselves, so they have lived off the *chichi* of their mother, the PRI. These men stand for nothing! These are not even men! Eunuchs—that's what they are! *¡Ya basta con este gobierno!*"

More cheers and applause.

"Our work is not over," he added. "Even if the PRI-government steals this election, we must fight with everything we have. Why? Because our calling as revolutionaries is a noble one. It requires real men and women. Men and women like Don Esquivel and Doña Catarina in Lucero. They have been fighting for better government ever since I've known them. They could have had wonderful political careers and made a lot of money, but they chose to fight for *el pueblo*. So, as soon as I am able to walk, you will find me there fighting alongside the people of Lucero!"

People pounded on tables and yelled encouragement. Meanwhile, La Morenita picked up the AK-47 from her chair, slung it from her shoulder, and like an Adelita from the Mexican Revolution walked across the patio to where Don Sixto stood.

As soon as the applause died down, Sixto added passionately, "May the men and women throughout our great republic triumph in their struggle to create a true democracy! May we triumph in our struggle in Nuevo Escandón! And may all our comrades-in-arms throughout Latin America—in Cuba, in Guatemala, in El Salvador, in Nicaragua—triumph in their struggle for peace and justice!"

Holding the AK-47 upright, La Morenita came up behind Don Sixto, raised the assault rifle, and shouted in the microphone, "*¡Viva Mexico, hijos de la chingada!*"

At home, in the wee hours of the morning, Honoré heard it again. Knowing exactly what he had to do to get rid of it once and for all, he shot up and grabbed the .22. Then as chills ripped through his body, he realized it wasn't coming from the window after all. It sounded like a huge wet balloon being deflated.

A ghastly smell filled the room. "¡Ay, Dios mío!"

He threw the rifle on the bed and ran to the bathroom. Dizzy, nauseated and weak, he sat on the toilet, shivering like a wet dog. He didn't even have time to turn on the light. A torrent of diarrhea threatened to take intestines and everything else along with it. His cheeks sizzled as chills sliced up his ribs, drying out his mouth. His tongue swelled until it felt big as a cow's.

"Maruca!" he pleaded.

"Go to sleep!" she said from her bed. "It's late!"

"Maruca, this is no joke!"

Her voice lost its patience. "What's the matter?"

"I'm sick as a dog!"

Head swirling, he wobbled on the stool and then keeled over. With knees up to his chin, hands on his stomach, he rolled on the floor, feeling as if someone had reached inside his gut and wrung out his intestines. Briefly, the pain subsided, but then the cruel fists came again, twisting, pulling, wringing out his insides.

"Where are you?" she asked from the darkness above him.

The words stuck in his throat. "Down here, on the floor, goddamn it!"

She flipped the light switch. "What's wrong?"

"I'm dying!" he cried. He groaned, gasped, clutched his bowels, and then passed out.

Next, he found himself in the middle of Alaska, slumped on a pack of ice, probably a glacier, amid a blizzard, shivering. It was so cold that not even the thick Mexican blankets Maruca piled on top of him warmed him. But it wasn't Alaska. It was his bed at home, with the two thermometers Maruca had stuck in him, one up front and one in back, God knows for what. His body seemed to have shut down, and now the only joy in his life was the stream of fresh oxygen coming in from the window Maruca opened next to his bed.

"Is this how people die?" he muttered.

Her voice regained its matter-of-factness. "You're not going to die."

He spoke out of the corner of his mouth. "This is how people die. You get sick. You go to bed. You can't move. You don't want to move. People bring you things. You look out the window. You don't know when it will end. Then they turn off the lights."

She walked around the bed, stood there in her white bathrobe, and looked closely at him. "This is what you get for eating tamales from Vera-cruz and boozing it up." Then she sat on the edge of the bed.

He clenched his teeth as the spasms in his gut came and went. He thought about going back to the bathroom.

Then, as he began to feel relief, Maruca said, "Honoré, we can't go on living like this."

He closed his eyes, thinking, I'm dead.

"Honoré?" she said.

He saw his spirit leave his body and cross a river of shit. Maruca and the Catholic Church had been right all along: because of his politics, he was on his way to hell. After trudging several miles, he came upon a bunch of Mexicans, illegals looking to cross the Rio Grande. Though he could not stop to speak to them, he recognized them—the dead men from the barrio. La Chancla, El Sapo, Gustavo Ulibarri. They had stopped to rest and drink water from plastic milk jugs under a tree in the middle of a vast plain. Flames shot up on a distant horizon, and above flew an owl whose dark wings stretched like clouds across the sky.

Next he saw himself dressed in a suit of armor, wearing a white smock with a red cross on it and carrying a heavy sword. Maybe he hadn't gone to hell after all. When he turned, he saw a thousand knights in shining armor riding on beautiful steeds and carrying white banners with red crosses. He saw himself on a battlefield strewn with dead knights. At one point he thought he had been slain as he looked up from a pool of blood at a young woman in white kneeling next to him and praying the rosary. When her gown opened and revealed her *maracas*, he did not know whether he was lying on a lance or something else. But how could that *something else* ever find its way into heaven or hell? For the first time he thought he might not be dead. He woke up in the red light district in Nuevo Escandón drinking with the enemy, a gringo.

"What do you do for a living?" asked Hank Savage.

What a stupid question, thought Honoré. "I work in the kitschen."

"Oh, you're a cook, is that it?"

"No, I'm a salesman."

Hank's face was red. "Oh, really? I guess we're all salesmen. I'm a sales-man. What do you sell?"

"I sell kitsch."

Hank scowled. "Shit?"

"Kitsch, Mexican kitsch."

"What's that?"

Honoré rested his arm on the table. "Something you buy and then don't have any use for. An imitation of something that was once valuable, like knights or knighthood. Now you just reproduce it for mass consumption."

Hank put down his glass of tequila. "Too complicated for a redneck."

"Look at it this way, Hank. I sell souvenirs. Memories or pieces of memories, pieces of a dead past."

Then, Honoré heard Maruca's voice. "What are you talking about?" she asked.

Doubts about whether he was still in hell were so strong that he dared not look. Eventually, he opened an eye. With fat cheeks and a brown pug nose, a lovely *maraca* smiled at him from beneath Maruca's robe. Electricity tingled in his veins. Something else tingled.

He rose on an elbow. He looked across the room. He was lying in his bed. "Where's the owl?"

"There's no owl."

"Didn't it come back?"

"No. It never came back. You were hallucinating."

He sat up. "I must be going crazy."

"Honoré."

"What?"

She stood and kissed the top of his head. "You need help."

Then, he thought about his outburst over the TV and wanted to say something but didn't.

"Let's go to bed, honey," she said.

After she turned off the light, he lay down and closed his eyes. He tried to stop thinking. Instead he imagined the slaughter of the tin men, turning black in the flames. Then, he remembered the blue-eyed devils that carted them off in their U-Hauls to be sold as scrap metal in Mississippi. He remembered the night in Nuevo Escandón. Trotsky, Don Sixto, La Morenita, the drunken Profe. "The tin men have died," he muttered. "They're not even good for souvenirs."

CHAPTER 4

Black Hole—Or the Horrors of Good Sex

Usually, Honoré heard the sound of a hammer driving a nail home on the weekends, late Saturday or all day Sunday, when the men were home from work and the sky was bright and sunny. It reminded him of his childhood, when his father built their house, when his mother didn't work, when he and his cousins played cowboys and Indians in the arroyo that emptied into the Rio Grande, when questions about peace and justice didn't matter. But one morning he noticed a change—the hammering that for weeks had come from Tequila's house stopped.

That night, as he got ready for bed, Honoré looked out the window. Flashes of an intense eerie light from an acetylene torch spouted from the roof across the street. Fortunately, Honoré was not especially concerned about God or the Devil. Nonetheless, this glimpse of hell was troubling.

He closed the venetian blinds and climbed in bed. "Have you talked to Señora Cuervo?"

"No," said Maruca. "Why?"

He lay his head on a pillow. "Tequila's up to something."

"Why don't you just ask him?"

"Because Tequila Cuervo has done nothing but get me in trouble ever since I've known him."

Maruca rolled over and yawned. "Then mind your own business."

"In this barrio, in this town, that's impossible."

"Then pray."

"P-r-a-y or p-r-e-y?"

A week later, something appeared on the roof of Tequila's house. At first, Honoré thought it was a deer blind or a clubhouse for Tequila's kids until he saw what resembled a metal-and-glass turret like the one on top of a B-52 bomber he had seen at the air show in the Valley. After a few days, a tarpaulin covered the turret, and all activity stopped. One morning he dared look again. He could not believe what he saw: a small observatory stood on the red-tile roof of Tequila's home, and a telescope pointed at the sky.

Is this what Trotsky was talking about? A CIA plot? Or just business as usual in South Texas? With neighbors like Tequila, who needed the CIA? He didn't think. He rushed into things. He had never read a book. In school he had done nothing but torment the teachers and everyone else, either jabbering away or cutting deadly farts. He knew nothing about the world beyond the barrio and didn't care.

Was he interested in astronomy?

No, gastronomy was all that idiot knew, Honoré concluded and headed downstairs, where he found Maruca in the kitchen washing dishes. "Have you seen Tequila's new addition on the roof of his house?"

"Yes. So?"

"Has his wife told you anything?"

"No," she said, shutting off the water in the kitchen sink. "By the way, someone may be watching us."

"What do you mean?" he asked.

She dried her hands on a towel. "Before those guns arrived, Bonita's friends dropped by all the time. Now she makes up excuses explaining why they can't come over. Meanwhile, Misty has been asking all kinds of questions. So I think my brother suspects something."

He glanced at the crates in the back room. "When hasn't Misty asked all kinds of questions?"

"She's my brother's spy."

"Oh, really. Is the Pope Catholic?"

"Look, I've seen some of his men drive by."

He faced her. "They're cops. That's what cops do."

She came up close, put her hand on his arm. "He'd love to have any excuse to put you in prison. You better get rid of the guns soon. You have plenty of space at the store now."

"*Tranquila*," he said. "*Tranquila, por favor*. I've already talked to Trotsky. Tomorrow the dolls will be gone."

That night under cover of darkness, Honoré and Maruca loaded the dolls in an old Buttercrust truck Honoré borrowed from the forwarding agent who had sold him the tin men. It was a long night, and Honoré got splinters in his hands from the wooden boxes. Meanwhile, Bonita lay asleep in her room.

The next morning the truck shuddered and farted as he drove under the interstate and turned north on Tamaulipas Avenue. He puttered past Tamaulipas Wholesale Imports, Los Reyes Auto Sales, and Art by God, a new pottery shop owned by a gringo couple from southern California. He cruised past another used car lot, a rustic furniture store with the figure of Don Quixote sitting in the front yard, his head resting on his hand as he

contemplated, according to Trotsky, his dilemma as an idealist. Some gringos milled around rows of ovens lined up to be loaded into two U-Hauls.
A block later, two homeless men, their hair thick as dusty oil-stained rags,
sat on a bench on a street corner. Several blocks down stood The Lazy Mex
Cantina. Across the street, some blacks, faces dark and shiny as eggplant
and strange in a town full of Mexicans, descended from two buses parked
in front of La Quinta Motel.

At one time Honoré's family owned entire blocks of real estate along this
strip. Today they would have been wealthy if his grandfather had not been
a drunk, a gambler, and a womanizer. His son, Honoré's father, established
their store on a lot he inherited from his mother, but the family would have
lost that too if it hadn't been for Honoré's mother. In fact, Honoré and his
family would have been migrant workers like so many of his friends in
school.

Across the street from Pizza Hut, he slowed down. Then, he stopped
in front of the store and climbed down. One of his cousins, Big Rig or
just plain Rig, arms swinging high and clear of his belly, waddled out of
the warehouse. Then, with his help, Honoré turned the truck around and
backed into the dirt yard and up to the warehouse.

Honoré climbed out and walked to the truck's back doors. "Where's my
mother?"

"Inside, asleep," said Rig. "What's going on?"

Honoré swung open the doors.

Rig peeked inside. "What's in these crates?"

"Medical supplies."

"Who's sick?"

Honoré pulled out a crate by its cord handle, and the two men carried it
past the iron bull and then under the warehouse's corrugated tin roof and
across the dirt floor abandoned by the tin men. They put it in an empty
storage shed in back.

As they returned to the truck, another belly the size of a barrel came out
of the store—his other cousin, Cachetes—and hovered blimp-like on the
porch. "What's in the truck, *primo*?" Cachetes asked.

"Medical supplies."

"Who's sick?"

Honoré approached the back of the truck. "An entire nation."

"Boss," said Rig.

Honoré slid a crate to the edge of the truck. "What?"

"We're starving."

Annoyed, Honoré let go of the cord handle and faced the two pink-cheeked squinty-eyed hippos confronting him. He took a ten-dollar bill from his pocket and flashed it in their faces. "Unload this truck, then I'll feed you."

The hogs took their time. Meanwhile, customers came and went, and nobody asked what the cousins were doing or what was in the crates, not even Honoré's mother. Wanting nothing more than to get Maruca off his back, he was relieved to get the dolls out of the house.

When the hogs finished, they came inside and reminded him about the pizzas, so he gave them the money. Two hours later, after stuffing themselves at Pizza Hut, they came back and complained they had eaten too much and wanted the rest of the day off. His mother, in turn, started complaining about her arthritis, so he gave all of them the day off. As soon as they were gone, he plunged into the paperwork on his desk. It was amazing how much he could do without them around.

In the late afternoon, Honoré finished and was getting ready to close the store when the phone rang. The sunset deposited a mix of blue and orange in the window as he sat down in his chair.

It was Trotsky. "Hey, good to hear from you," Honoré said. "I just got the dolls moved. What's up?"

"The meeting with Sixto has been cancelled," Trotsky said.

Honoré tensed. "What happened?"

"Sixto is very sick. He's in hospital right now. La Morenita is with him."

Honoré got a sinking feeling in his stomach. The owl came to mind. The CIA. Everywhere he turned danger lurked. Everything and everyone was suspect. "Is it serious?"

"I don't know. I'm going to see him now. I'll get back to you as soon as I find out what's going on."

After locking the store, Honoré headed south on Tamaulipas. Downtown, he turned right toward the railroad tracks. At his friend's warehouse, he dropped off the Buttercrust truck and picked up his truck. Then, he headed home through the evening's fading light.

When he pulled up in front of his house, he couldn't tell, in the yellow glow of the streetlight, if the kids running back and forth and throwing a ball on the next block were playing soccer or dancing to the cumbia blasting from someone's backyard. Suddenly, their mother came out and yelled, and the kids ran inside. Across the street, some of Tequila's friends stood around a grill in the driveway, drinking beer and cooking *carne asada*. Honoré climbed down and headed across the asphalt.

Salvador, a tall man with a dark face under a cowboy hat, tossed him a beer. "We heard you were dead."

Honoré snapped the can open, a huge white golden beard of foam splattering on his shirt. "What *pendejo* told you that?"

Behind the grill, Chango looked like an overgrown kid in tennis shoes, shorts, and a Dallas Cowboys jersey. "Tequila said they tried to poison you in Nuevo Escandón."

Honoré took a sip of beer. "*Puro pedo.* Since when has Tequila told the truth about anybody?"

"Never."

"Did you hear the latest?" asked Chango, a meat fork in his hand. "Tequila's going to Acapulco."

"Who knows what that *cabrón* is up to," said Honoré, checking out the hamburger patties sizzling on the grill. "One time he told me he got hired to work on a yacht in Mazatlán. Turned out he was shacked up with some *puta* in *la zona.*"

The men were still laughing when the front door swung open and a tribe of little mechanics, all dark brown, pesky as Tequila, swarmed out. The one with the thick glasses, Tercero, stopped and stared at Honoré. Like his father, he was nosy. Worse than his father, he thought he was an intellectual.

"My father is building an observatory," he said.

"Oh, really."

White teeth beamed in Tercero's face. "Yes, sir. Would you like to see it?"

A door slammed. Dressed in a blue mechanic's shirt, blue trousers, and steel-toed boots while carrying a six-pack tucked under an arm, Tequila stood on the porch. "*¡Ya llegó el mero mero!*" he shouted, reminding everyone he was the boss.

"Have you been telling everybody I was dead?" asked Honoré.

Tequila walked past him. "Of course not! Why would I do that? Is the salsa ready?"

Chango took the six-pack from Tequila and deposited it in the ice chest. Then he took the patties off the grill and stacked them on a tray. "The meat is ready, *jefe!*"

"*Dale gas,*" said Tequila, without looking up. "Tercero, take the meat inside." Tercero picked up the tray heaped with steaming burgers and carried it slowly back to the house, crowded by his three brothers, sniffing all the way inside.

"Where are the jalapeños?" asked Tequila, looking around.

Chango went down on one knee, opened his knapsack, and took out some peppers that looked like fat green fingers. "Here."

"And the onions?"

Chango reached inside the knapsack again. "Here."

"Hmmmm," said Tequila, holding a huge onion in each hand. "Where'd you get these?"

Chango got up and brushed off his bare knees. "We grow them in our backyard."

"These are big. They look like *chichis*."

Everyone laughed.

Honoré's eyes burned as Tequila took *la mano*, a basalt pestle, and crushed a jalapeño in the *molcajete*, a basalt mortar for crushing chile, on-ions, and tomatoes into salsa. "You got here just in time, Coyote," Tequila said. "How about a taco?"

Then, in a deep voice, Salvador asked, "How about *un taco de ojo*? Look at what's coming down the street."

A young woman with wild long black hair sashayed toward them. What the hell, wondered Honoré, was she doing in a mini-skirt, a tight-fitting blouse, and high heels in this barrio? Looking for trouble—or selling something? A car throbbing with the sound of a cumbia cruised past them slowly, headlights lighting up the Aztec goddess with *maracas* bigger than onions or tomatoes.

Tequila's lips were bright with grease. "*¡Ay mamacita, come to papacito!*"

Honoré punched Tequila on the shoulder. "*¡Cállate!* Show some respect, *cabrón*! If not for her, then for your family!"

But no question about it, thought Honoré. On a dark, hot night like tonight, the *molcajete* between the young woman's two legs could undo a hundred men's pestles.

"Buenas noches, señorita," said Tequila.

"Buenas noches," she said to no one in particular, glancing at them, lift-ing her head, heels digging into the asphalt. She lived in one of the houses down the street.

One damned good-looking woman. However, unlike Tequila, Honoré refused to give in to the snarling below his belt.

Tequila's trousers bulged but not because of a wrench stuffed in his pocket. "Did you see what I saw?" he drooled.

Salvador's eyes were glazed like fresh donuts. "I saw *panocha*."

"I saw *chichis*, big ones," sighed Chango.

Salvador said in a sweet voice. "I saw a flower."

"I saw God," swore Chango solemnly.

Honoré scraped the ground with toe of his boot. "I saw a *lechuza*." He turned to the men. "*Águila, compadres.* Or you'll lose your balls—and your money—to that woman."

"That woman," Tequila snarled, and like a dog in heat, he fell on all fours, "can do anything she wants with my balls—and my money." He howled at the moon.

Honoré grabbed him by the collar and pulled him to his feet. "Swine! That *puta* won't look at you twice. Her boyfriend is a *narcotraficante* in the Valley. He was busted and put in prison in Mexico. She's hiding out."

Tequila rubbed his neck. "How do you know?"

Honoré threw his empty can in the trash. "You know men from South Texas don't fuck around when it comes to their women. They don't have balls for much else, but they have balls for that."

"How do you know she's from Matamoros?"

"The same way I know everything about this town. My brother-in-law, the cop from hell."

"So Comino told you?"

"Of course not. He doesn't have to. All he has to do is open that big mouth of his, and before you know it, everyone is talking about it."

"Apá?" Tercero called, poking his face out the front door.

"¿*Qué*?"

"Can we show Señor Castillo my telescope?"

Tequila straightened his collar. "Can't you see Señor Castillo and I are talking? Don't be bothering people. Go help your mother."

As soon as the kid closed the door, Honoré asked, "*Qué chingados* have you been building?"

Tequila wiped his mouth. "Tercero wants to be an astronomer."

"No way."

"*Sí, güey.* Come, I'll show you."

On the floor in the living room, the tribe of little Tequilas sat eating hamburgers, drinking Cokes, and watching Batman on TV. In the kitchen, Señora Cuervo stood at the counter, her face plain and white as a communion wafer. Tequila opened a cabinet door next to her and took out some keys.

"Buenas tardes, señora," said Honoré.

Señora Cuervo, who had grown up in a large family in Zopilote County before studying in a convent in Guadalajara for several years, spoke Spanish like a Mexican. "Buenas tardes, Honoré."

The keys jingled. "I'm showing him the *observatorio*," said Tequila.

Tercero ran into the kitchen. "Apá, can I go too? *¡Por favor!*"

"No!"

Señora Cuervo dried her hands on a towel. "Why do you buy these things if you're not going to share them with your children? Do you want them to turn out like your brother's children, a bunch of dunces? Traumatized? *Acomplejados?*"

"*Ya, por favor,* woman." Then Tequila pointed at Tercero. "You can come along—but only if you behave. Understand?"

Tercero nodded enthusiastically. "¡Sí, Apá!"

Outside, Tequila climbed the stairs to a wooden landing. After unlocking a door, he entered a room about the size of an ordinary bedroom. At one end stood a television, and at the other, a desk. A window looked out on the backyard. Bookshelves rose along one wall while maps of the stars covered the other. In the middle of the room, under a small dome in the ceiling, stood a black and white plastic telescope on a tripod with legs extended across a wooden platform. The dome or cupola was made from metal and glass, and evidently it could move on small wheels like those on a lawn mower. Next to the telescope stood the control panel, a small podium-like wooden structure with a light switch and some metal knobs.

"This must have cost *chingos*," said Honoré.

"The dome is made from car parts, and the telescope is a cheap one. I'd like to get a really powerful one. Look." He hit a switch on the control panel and turned off the lights in the room. Then he moved a knob, and the dome squeaked open. Millions of glittering stars and fresh air spilled into the room. "Just like a real *observatorio*."

Tercero climbed on the platform and put an eye to the telescope. After a while, he exclaimed, "There's Venus, Apá."

"Let Señor Honoré take a look."

The kid looked up, his thick glasses catching glints of light from a lamp in the corner, "Can I tell him about black holes?"

"I said let Señor Honoré take a look."

The kid went on, boiling over with excitement. "Black holes are holes in the sky. They're black because you can't see them. They eat up light. Black holes eat up everything. Right, Apá, they eat up everything?"

Tequila grabbed Tercero by the back of his shirt and raised him in mid-air. Like most uneducated people in Escandón, Tequila was proud to have a son with some brains but could only take so much of his gibberish. "Did you hear what I said, *mijito*?"

Tercero, glasses lopsided on his nose, whimpered, "Sí, Apá."

Tequila dropped him. "Go watch TV."

Tercero, rubbing his neck, got up from the floor. Eyes dull as a lizard's behind thick lenses, he stared at Honoré, turned around, and walked toward the door, casting one last loving glance at the telescope before pulling the door shut behind him.

The wheels squealed as Tequila moved the dome again. Then he adjusted the telescope so it faced south. "Check it out."

The blue lights of Escandón and the weak yellow ones of Nuevo Escandón appeared in the circle of glass an inch from Honoré's eye. There were the lights of Hotel Washington, the Escandón National Bank, and the Hilton Inn. The interstate ended at the river, where construction for the new international bridge had begun. There was the old bridge—bridge Number One or the Bridge of the Americas. There were some of the old two-storey houses in the historic district. He couldn't see the river.

"Let me show you something else," said Tequila. "Stand back." Tequila made the dome turn again. "Lower the telescope."

Now the telescope faced east. An inch from Honoré's eye, a dog walked through a pool of light. A man sat in a sleeveless T-shirt in a chair watching television and drinking beer in his living room. An old woman stood on a porch, and at least a dozen black cats sprawled on an old couch.

Tequila spoke, "Check out the house with the wall around it."

On a corner about three blocks away rose a six-foot cement wall. Soft yellow lights burned in a lush yard of grass, prickly pears, and palm trees. On the side of the house were a swimming pool, a barbecue pit, and a picnic table. The wall reminded him of those he had seen in wealthy neighborhoods in Mexico, but there was no broken glass along the top of this one.

"So?" asked Honoré.

"*La mamacita* goes skinny-dipping in her pool."

"Are you talking about the Aztec goddess who just walked by?"

Tequila smirked. "Who else, *güey*?"

Honoré straightened. "I knew this wasn't about astronomy." He shook his head. "It's about *ass*tronomy."

A few days later, the telephone in Honoré's office rang, and his mother answered in the next room. Then the old woman, brittle as a sun-baked branch of mesquite, peeked in the door. "Your wife."

He reached for the phone. "What's up?"

"Tequila disappeared."

He sat back in his chair. "What do you mean?"

"His wife came over after you left this morning. She was crying."

He turned on the television. "She's a hysterical woman. What can you expect from an ex-nun who married a *pendejo*?"

"She'll be back in a few minutes. What do I tell her?"

Zigzags flashed across the black-and-white television screen on his desk. "Tell her he's probably in Acapulco. He was supposed to go there and fix an engine on a yacht. Was supposed to make a lot of money. Dying to get out there because he could drink all he wanted and go to the beach every day."

"She told me he's been involved in some illegal business. Some men were after him."

On TV, a shapely blonde in a mini-skirt handed a microphone to a man in a three-piece suit. "Good. And I hope they get their hands on him. That bastard owes me money."

Maruca's voice spilled out of the receiver. "Honoré! This is serious. His wife thinks he's been kidnapped or worse. What do I tell her?"

"Tell her to do what everybody else does—call the police."

In the afternoon Honoré saw the missing person's report broadcast on television, mug shot of Tequila and all. Smirking stupidly, he looked more like a mafioso than a victim. He always had such a high opinion of himself. Many short people were like that, as if a rebellious attitude could undo the work of God or Nature.

Throughout the week, Honoré heard rumors that Tequila had been spotted in Houston or was seen crossing the border with a gringa or that his bullet-riddled body had been found on a ranch in northern Mexico. Tequila looked like so many Mexicans that he could be confused with anybody, but Honoré knew that the longer the police couldn't find Tequila, the more likely it was they would come after Honoré. After all, everyone thought they were good friends because they grew up in the barrio and played high school football together.

As Honoré gazed at the icons of Jesus Christ and La Virgen de Guadalupe on the wall, he wondered if they could help him. "Please, Almighty God and Mother of the Mexicans," he muttered, "save me from Tequila Cuervo and the Mexicans."

After that, no more phone calls, and he went back to work. His mother, overdosing on painkillers for her arthritis, slept in the back room while Honoré ran the store.

Then Trotsky dropped by. "Sixto is feeling a lot better. We'll meet with him as soon I get back from Boston."

They stood outside on the curb, where Trotsky had left his jeep idling. "Boston?" asked Honoré.

"I'm meeting with the Vietnam vets. It seems there might be a convoy after all. I'm not all that excited about it, but I'll attend out of solidarity."

Trotsky seemed in a rush, so Honoré didn't explain about his troubles with Tequila. "How long will you be gone?"

"A week, maybe two. Depends. But I already met with Sixto about the dolls. He said he talked to his son about them. We should be getting them across the river soon."

Three days later, the phone rang. "Hello," said Honoré.

It was Maruca. "They found him."

"Where?"

"In the river. Dead."

"Good," he said. "God answered my prayers."

But he had his doubts. God did not give people like Tequila looks or brains, but he gave them the stubbornness of a mule and the strength of an ox. They might not have beautiful wives or attractive children, but they could do all kinds of crazy things and survive like weeds.

The next day he was attending to some customers in the warehouse when the phone rang in the office.

His mother answered and then yelled through the screen door. "Your wife!"

He walked inside and picked up the phone. "What's up?"

Maruca was breathless. "Señora Cuervo is going crazy. She can't sleep. She screams at her children. She hasn't eaten in days."

Honoré sat in his chair. "Isn't she praying?"

"She's cursing God and the saints!"

He gazed outside. "So what do you want me to do? She's an ex-nun. Why doesn't she ask God for help? I did."

"Talk to her. Just talk to her. She respects you."

In the street outside the store, a squad car cruised by. "I can't get involved. I'm trying to help people who are fighting for a cause, willing to sacrifice everything for a better world. They're not some fat ugly capitalist pig who goes nuts once a month and gets lost because he doesn't have anything better to do."

"Fine. I'll tell her."

The squad car returned, slowly. "What are you going to tell her?"

"That you won't talk to her."

"Fine."

But he regretted his words the moment he hung up.

The next morning the consequences showed up: a tall gringo in a gray suit, white collar and dark tie. Honoré didn't get up from his desk when he saw the white car with a long antenna park in front of the store or when the gringo strode through the front gate looking around as if for some escapee from Leavenworth, entering the store, going straight to Honoré's office. His boot heels thumped through the open door, and he settled in a chair next to Honoré's desk. He didn't flash his badge. He didn't have to. The butt of a pistol stuck out of a shoulder holster like a bull's horn.

"I suppose you know why I'm here, Honoré," said Rex, his eyes gray and his hair red. His voice had the twang of an out-of-tune electric guitar.

Honoré opened a ledger on his desk. "Yup."

"You know where he is?"

Honoré flipped the page. "Nope."

"Do you know what happened to him?"

Honoré checked off some figures with a red pen. "Nope."

"What can you tell us about him?"

The pen began to bleed on the paper. "Nothing."

"Nothing?" asked the shit-kicker. "He's your neighbor. You grew up together. You went to school together. You've been involved in shady business dealings."

Honoré glared at the freckles, wondering how anybody could live with thousands of them on their face. He threw the pen on the desk. "Are you accusing me of conspiracy?"

"Look, Honoré," Rex said, leaning forward in his chair. "I don't care what happens to your neighbor. I have more important things to do. His wife claims dope smugglers kidnapped him, and that brings the case under my jurisdiction. I don't believe a word she says. All I want is to keep my telephone from ringing off the wall. And I sure as hell don't want the telephone ringing off the wall in Washington." He sat back. "Now what can you tell us about him?"

Honoré leaned back and thumped his cowboy boots on the desk. "What can be said about a *pendejo*?"

Rex shifted to the edge of his chair and peered around the bottoms of Honoré's boots. "Did you notice anything unusual before he disappeared?"

"Once a *pendejo* always a *pendejo*."

"Any idea what might have happened to him?"

Honoré glanced out the window. "Probably. He's been *embrujado.*"

"What's that?"

"Bewitched."

Rex pressed on. "Look, Honoré, stop dicking around. You know who you are and what you do, and you know I know. So if you don't cooperate with me, not the FBI *but me*, I'll have to turn up the heat, put you under surveillance twenty-four hours a day. And in this town you know what that means."

Honoré saw red, but it was not the FBI agent's hair or the ink oozing from the pen on the ledger. It was his own blood exploding in his head as he pulled his boots off the desk, sat forward, and slammed the ledger shut.

"Ready to play ball, big boy?" the gringo said.

"Fuck you."

Rex got up and stomped out of the store, laughing.

This is precisely why Honoré had not wanted to get involved in some dumb-ass murder mystery—he had too many political enemies in this town. Twenty-four-hour surveillance meant that the dogs—the local cops, led by his brother-in-law Comino—would be let loose on him.

That evening Tercero opened the door, and Honoré walked into the Cuervos' living room. Then, while waiting for the boy to get Señora Cuervo, he looked at the wood paneling on the walls and sofas strewn with popcorn and plastic straws, hoping the kid would get lost but knew there was no way to get rid of him. Honoré would have to exercise caution.

Pale and thin, Señora Cuervo, a rosary wrapped around a hand, walked into the living room. "Buenas noches."

"Buenas noches."

She stood next to Tercero, who watched from behind thick glasses. "Any news of my husband?" she asked.

"Maybe," said Honoré. "Can we go to the observatory?"

She made a face, wringing her hands. "I locked the room, and I don't want to open it. There is something evil in that room, a demon."

"I know. That's why I need to go up there."

She raised her eyes to the ceiling as if pleading for God's intercession. "Can we do this some other time? I don't feel well. The thought of going up there sickens me."

"There's no time to lose, señora."

She bit her lip. "I don't understand why my husband spends so much time up there. And now that he bought that stupid telescope, my son wants to be there all the time. Tercero is already too much like his father. I'm afraid he's going to get worse unless I oppose all this nonsense."

"Then give me the key," said Honoré, "and I'll go up there."

Tercero grabbed Señora Cuervo's arm. "I want to go! Can I go?"

She pulled her arm away. "No!"

"Please, Mamá!" he said, jumping up and down. "Pretty please!"

"I said no!"

He got down on one knee, hands in prayer. "Please, Mamá! I'll be a good boy. I'll wash the dishes. I'll take out the trash. I'll go to the store when you ask me to. I won't hit my brothers."

She looked at him with surprise. "You promise?"

"I promise."

She drew near. "And you'll stop spitting on the floor?"

"Yes."

"All right then," she said and left the room.

After returning with the keys, she led Tercero and Honoré outside, up a flight of metal stairs to the observatory.

She unlocked the door.

Nothing had changed since the last time Honoré was here. The desk next to the window, the telescope under the dome, the books on the shelves. Suddenly, he saw something he hadn't noticed before—a photograph of Tequila in a football uniform taped to a map of the heavens on the wall. Honoré could not believe that one time he and Tequila had been like brothers, that they had played football in high school, had even walked home together after school—but they had. The moment Señora Cuervo, who was still cowering in the doorway, saw the photo she sat on the couch and wept, the rosary dangling from one hand. Meanwhile, Tercero opened the observatory dome and pointed the telescope at the heavens.

Good, thought Honoré. Now I won't have to deal with him. Like a detective in a murder mystery, he began the investigation. Papers, maps, photo albums, notes, and books revealed nothing.

"Look at Venus!" shouted the kid, standing with one eye to the end of the telescope.

"In a minute," said Honoré as he rifled a drawer and found a stash of X-rated videos. He closed the drawer.

"Look at Venus!"

Clueless and annoyed as he took a chair, Honoré considered whether he should abandon the search until Tequila's photograph on the wall caught his attention again, and he wondered why anyone would put it there. May-be a joke. An arrow drawn with a crayon pointed to a section of the map marked and delineated as "a black hole." Tercero must have done it.

Honoré didn't know how long he had been sitting there when a hunch hit him. "Tercero."

Like a good straight-A student, Tercero responded, "Yes, sir!"

Honoré rose to his feet. "See that box in the corner?"

"Yes, sir."

Honoré crossed the room. "Can you get all the information you can on black holes—books, magazines, photographs—and put it in that box? Tonight I want to read everything I can on black holes. Tomorrow I want you to tell me everything you know about black holes."

The kid let go of the telescope. "Yes, sir!"

Honoré climbed on the platform and lowered the telescope. He aimed it at the barrio, at the house down the street, adjusting the lens until he found what he was looking for and broke into a cold sweat. "Oh, my God!" he muttered.

"Are you looking at Venus?" asked Tercero from across the room, where he was flipping through a magazine.

Honoré wanted to tell the kid the truth—so he did. "Yes."

Tercero stood up and smiled. "It's beautiful, isn't it?"

Honoré raised the end of the telescope. "Did you get all the material on black holes?"

"No. Some of it is in my room."

"Could you get it while I talk to your mother?"

"Yes, sir." The boy flew out the door and down the spiral staircase, which twanged until he reached the bottom and went inside the house.

Honoré sat next to Señora Cuervo. "I need your help."

Señora Cuervo clutched the rosary. "I'll do whatever you ask."

"Good," he said. "First, don't let anyone in this observatory. No one, understand?"

"Why? Is there really a demon in here?"

Honoré nodded solemnly. "Yes, ma'am."

"*Le doy mi palabra*. No one will come in here."

"Second, I need a thousand dollars."

"Okay."

"Third, tell no one—especially the police."

She nodded.

"Fourth, you must be patient—this might take a while."

A tear came into her eye.

"And fifth," he said and pointed at the beads, "you must pray for your children, for me, and for yourself." He looked at the telescope. "But mostly for Tequila," he said under his breath. "You must pray for Tequila."

"Okay."

"And one more thing. Don't call the FBI."

At the store the next day, Honoré headed to the back of the warehouse and unlocked the door to the storage shed. Metal bars and cobwebs on a small window filtered gray light from the east as he led the hogs inside. After flicking the light switch, he walked across the dusty room and removed the tarpaulin from a stack of boxes. Then he knelt by a crate on the floor, the eyes in the pinewood staring at him, and he unlatched the lid.

"Why are we here?" asked Rig.

He pulled on the lid. "We're going on a mission."

"Like *Mission Impossible*?" mocked Rig.

Honoré took a screwdriver from his back pocket and pried the lid loose. "*No mames*. This is serious."

"Okay, okay, boss, gotcha."

When the lid finally came unstuck, Rig gasped. "I thought you said these were medical supplies. These are guns!"

Honoré handed an assault rifle to Cachetes, who sounded like a little girl—no, a big fat girl. "Guns scare me."

"Listen, *pendejo*," Honoré said. "You work for me. If you don't like it, let's see if some other asshole will put up with your bullshit. Besides, the plan is simple. All you have to do is drive me to the house and wait outside. I walk through the front gate. I take the prisoner. I bring the prisoner back. I put him in the truck. And we drive off. "

He gave another AK-47 to Rig, who asked, "What are the guns for?"

"How do people act when they see a *cuerno de chivo*?"

"Scared shitless," said Rig, raising the rifle to his shoulder and aiming it at the window.

"Okay," said Honoré as he threw the tarpaulin over the boxes again, "then that's what they're for, to scare people."

"What if someone else shows up with a *cuerno de chivo*?" asked Cachetes.

Honoré stood before his cousins. "That won't happen. No one expects us. The real danger is something else. But you won't have to worry about that because I'll face the *real* danger myself."

Beads of sweat sprouted on Cachetes' brow. "What's the *real* danger?" he asked.

Honoré turned to the door and shook his head. "You wouldn't understand, even if I told you. It's worse than cancer."

Rig piped up. "Cancer? That's serious business."

"I know," said Honoré as he watched the fatso lower the assault rifle. "But this is worse. First it infects the mind, then the body." He hated dealing with idiots. "But just to make sure nothing happens to you or me, we're going to take some antibiotics before we go in."

"Some what?" asked Rig.

"Some medicine."

"What kind of medicine?" said Rig.

"Saltpeter."

"Salt cedar?"

"No, *pendejo*," Honoré said. "That's a tree. A *cubreviento*. I said 'saltpeter.'"

"Never heard of it. What's that?"

Honoré rolled his eyes. "A tranquilizer."

"Oh, okay."

Honoré took his cousins out to his mother's ranch on the River Road, two acres several miles northwest of Escandón, where he fed them pepperoni-and-saltpeter pizza and showed them how to use the AK-47s, just in case. But the damned things were so loud they couldn't hear each other for hours afterward.

Saturday night Honoré borrowed the Buttercrust truck again. Rig drove; Honoré rode shotgun while Cachetes sat between them, crunching his second bag of *chicharrones*. "This is how the DEA does it," Honoré explained as they drove across town. "They park a Buttercrust truck full of surveillance equipment down the street from a dope dealer's house and monitor every movement until they're ready to make the bust."

After circling the block where *la puta* lived, they parked amid frothy breakers of music surging from beyond a six-foot wall hemmed in by trees and cactus. The smell of *carne asada* mingled with the aroma of fresh flowers.

"I'm going over the wall," whispered Honoré. "If I'm not back in an hour, you break down the front gate and come get me."

Dressed in a black jumpsuit, black boots, and a black ski mask, Honoré disappeared among the foliage. He crept along the wall until he found a tree, which he tried to climb, but the lower limbs got in the way. Sweat rolled into his eyes, and branches twisted the mask so his ear stuck out of an eyehole. He pulled it off. Then, as he pushed the leaves out of the way, a long-fingered branch broke loose and slapped him in the face.

"*¡Chingao!*" he cursed under his breath, one eye shut.

He waited for the burning to stop. Then he climbed to the top of the wall, where he sat and put the ski mask back on before jumping and landing in the grass on his hands and knees. He waited, trying to control his panting. All he needed to do now was crawl like a hunting dog to the other end of the yard.

Dozens of needles bristled on the green tongue-like cacti. Along the fence, palm trees rose against the night sky. Tulips big as breasts guarded a lush carpet of grass. It was like the Garden of Eden. Next, he smelled perfume. He stopped, looked around, saw nothing, kept going. It didn't smell like flowers or a fruit tree. It smelled too good to be true, like an expensive woman or the whores in *la zona*.

Then, he heard a giggle. He froze on the ground behind a bougainvillea. Maybe it wasn't a giggle. Maybe it was a bird in a tree. Then he heard a whistle, like the one outside his window at home when that owl showed up, the one Maruca said might steal his soul. The noise was close, perhaps a foot away, but he couldn't tell if it was a giggle or a whistle. The muscles in his legs and arms were ready to spring. Someone giggled above his head. He looked up at none other than La Virgen de Guadalupe! In a bikini! She raised a lovely hand, giggling. All at once, his cranium exploded like a bongo drum as she blessed him with a basalt pestle and turned his brain into a bowl of *menudo*.

Next he found himself at the bottom of a dark well when he caught a glimpse of a woman grinning at him. "*¡Pendejo!*" she said.

Then a man showed up, and both looked a him, as if he were a piece of shit at the bottom of a toilet.

Honoré must be dreaming. Reluctantly, he opened one eye, then another, his head throbbing. He sat in a chair, hands tied behind his back.

A demon with a pitchfork in his hand smiled stupidly in front of him. "*¿No, que no, chiquito? Ya te chingamos.*"

"Who the fuck are you?" asked Honoré, a buzz in his ears.

"I'm Adán," said Tequila, who stood about two feet away, in a speedo, a two-pronged meat fork in one hand.

"You're Nada," sneered Honoré.

Tequila's smile was laced with barbecue sauce, which he wiped with the back of his hand. "Welcome to paradise," he said and returned to the grill.

Honoré wiggled his wrists. "This is a black hole, *pendejo.*"

Tequila flipped the meat on the grill. "Tercero says nothing ever gets out of a black hole."

"Well, I've come to take you home."

"No way, *güey.*"

The rope burned Honoré's wrists. "Your family needs you."

"*Ya cállate.*"

"We need to talk."

"*¡No mames!*" Tequila took a long red handkerchief hanging from his speedo, forced it between Honoré's teeth, and tied it tightly behind his head. He stepped back and admired his handiwork. At length, he took the fork from under his armpit and waved it in Honoré's face. "Now you listen to me, *cabrón.* You come in here trying to act like 007, and look where you are. You think you can take me back just like that? Have you asked me if I want to go back?" He got so close Honoré could smell the booze. "No, don't close your eyes, *cabrón.* Let me tell you why I'm not going back. I'm not going back because I'm happy. In high school you were the star quarterback. Most popular. Most handsome. All the chicks were after you. And then you married the head cheerleader, the most beautiful woman in Escandón, and got all the pussy you wanted. You and Maruca were the envy of everyone in the barrio. You smelled of pussy everywhere you went. And what happened to me? I married a scarecrow who died from TB. Then I go and marry a nun."

Honoré lowered his head and fought back the smile wiggling across his lips like a worm.

Tequila brought the fork close to Honoré's eye. "You think that's funny?"

Feet in the pool kicked the surface of water hard, and a shark-like form glided beneath the waves of aqua-green reflections until they broke with a slurp. Long black hair strung out across the water as a young woman grabbed the side of the pool with one hand and wiped her face with the other.

"*Papacito,* I'm hungry," she said like a spoiled child, in Spanish.

With a dumb-ass grin, Tequila blew her a kiss, and she dove back under the water and swam to the other end. "And you came to save me from that?" he said to Honoré. "*¡Estás loco!*"

Suddenly, the young Mexican woman, *maracas* ripe as mangoes, climbed out of the pool in a bikini, long silver ribbons of water running down her shapely legs. After pulling her bikini bottom up, she picked up a towel, wrapped herself in it, and sat in a lawn chair.

Tequila whispered in Honoré's ear. "Now I understand what you meant when you used to talk about the horrors. I thought you were crazy. You were drunk on your ass. 'The first horror of good sex,' you said, 'is finding out that you're not getting any.' Remember that?"

Honoré tried spitting out the handkerchief.

Tequila yanked it from Honoré's mouth. "Well, you were right. When I first stuck my dick in this Aztec goddess's pussy, I was horrified by how much I'd been missing."

Honoré was finally able to breathe right. "Would you shut up?" he said, wriggling in the chair as he tried loosening the rope around his wrists.

Tequila pushed him back in the chair. "Settle down." He untied the handkerchief and removed it. "Then you said the second horror is finding out just how good it is. Now that one really doesn't count because it's like the first horror. But let me tell you about the third horror: not getting enough. That's where I'm at. I can't get enough of this woman. The smell of sweat on her buns drives me crazy. Or the taste of her pussy when dripping wet. Cream pie, the gringos call it. Do you know what else the gringos call a pussy? Camel toe. I checked it in Tercero's *Encyclopedia Britannica*, and sure enough it looks like the bottom of a camel's foot."

"Shut the fuck up!"

Tequila stuffed the handkerchief back in Honoré's mouth and tied it again. "No, you shut up. You're the one who put all these ideas in my head. I was a good little boy until I started hanging out with you. Anyway, listen. The fourth horror of good sex is getting too much. I'm not there yet, and from the look of things, I have a long ways to go. 'The fifth horror,' you said, 'is the fear of losing it. And the sixth horror is losing it.' Remember all that shit?"

Honoré glanced at the young woman in the lawn chair staring at him. She whined, "*Papacito*, I'm hungry. I want a taco."

Drops of sweat sprouted on Tequila's upper lip as he straightened. "She wants a taco."

"*Un taco de chorizo.*"

Tequila's eyes flip-flopped. "She wants a *taco de chorizo.*"

"A lot of red chile."

"One *taco de chorizo* coming right up!" Tequila replied. "Just give me a minute, baby!"

Smiling from ear to ear, Tequila turned and walked along the edge of the pool. He stepped behind the grill and one by one turned over the sizzling steaks and sausages while singing a refrain from his favorite Mexican ballad, ". . . *pero sigo siendo el rey.*"

Chunks of gray smoke stung Honoré's eyes, and the delicious smell of *carne asada* reminded him that he had made a grave miscalculation—he forgot to eat. Hunger made men vulnerable. That's what got him in trouble at the party in Nuevo Escandón.

"What an idiot!" he muttered into the handkerchief.

Chile dripped from the tacos Tequila carried to the young woman rubbing lotion on a leg. "*Papacito* wants to go hippity hop," he said. "How about a real *taco de chorizo, mamacita*?"

She took the taco. "You said we were going to torture your friend first."

Tequila glanced at Honoré. "We can torture him later."

"How about some coca?"

"Right away, Mamacita," he said, and then ran inside the house.

Moments later, he came back with a plastic bag of white powder, a small mirror with a gold frame around it, straws, a razor and a spoon. He put everything on the picnic table. The young woman watched him pile several spoonfuls of the white stuff on the mirror and separate it into thick white lines with the razor. First, he walked over and put the mirror beneath Honoré's nose.

Honoré puffed, and the white powder skittered across the glass.

Tequila pulled the mirror away. "No, no, Coyote," he said. "Let's not waste a good thing. You're not going to piss me off like that."

Then Tequila went over to the young woman, who took a few hits. He snorted the rest through the straw as if he were drinking a milk shake with his nose.

"Mamalicious," he said, wobbly on his feet.

"What, *papacito*?"

Tequila ran his fingers through her hair. "*Papacito* wants to go hippity hop."

She tucked a *maraca* back in her halter. "Let's torture the prisoner first. That'll be more fun."

Tequila's face glistened with sweat. "*Ya, mamacita*, I can't stand it any-more. Look. First we'll show him what he's missing out on, and then you can do whatever you want to him."

She smiled. "Promise?"

Her skin shone like the wood of a fine violin as she stood up, her hair black as a grackle's feathers. Walking past Honoré, she brushed a strand of hair from her face and smiled.

Tequila sprang after her and fell on his knees on the cement. Snarling like a dog, he crawled on all fours into the house.

What Honoré heard next was not the sound of love or even sex but the sound of a woman undoing a man. The idiot forgot to close the bedroom window. Or maybe this was how they planned to torture him—by letting him hear everything.

One minute Tequila wept and wailed like a kid denied a piece of candy, and the next he howled as if he had gotten his dick caught in a vise. They went on and on, breathing hot and heavy, grinding, squishing, slurping. Trotsky called these "the sounds of the universe"—the sounds of breathing, eating, shitting, and fucking. According to his unified theory of the universe, these were the sounds of creation.

Suddenly, Tequila groaned as if someone had kicked him where God had made him a two-legged animal, and there was a thump on the floor. The lights came on in the house. A door swung open. Wrapped in a towel, the young woman ran out, trembling from head to toe. Then, she calmed down enough to untie the bandanna around Honoré's mouth.

"What happened?" he asked.

Her eyes were feverish. "Too much coca." Her towel came undone.

And just as he got a good look at her *maracas*, the gate flew open, and two men the size of beach balls carrying AK-47's rolled into the yard. But when they saw the naked woman, they halted, lowering their barrels and removing their black ski masks.

Obviously, Honoré thought, he had not given them enough saltpeter. They sniffed and drooled. She ran inside. But it wasn't female flesh that halted his cousins.

"Boss," said Rig as he untied Honoré's hands, "that *carne asada* sure smells good. Can we have some?"

Honoré stood up, rubbing his wrists. "I thought you ate before we came out here."

The beach balls rolled toward the grill. "We did."

Honoré ran to the house. A thin carpet led to the living room, furnished with a television, a couch, and coffee table. Pictures hung on the beige wall, pictures of a boy, two girls with white teeth and pink smiles. Evidently, she had children. Maybe she was married, but then why live this kind of life? Unlike the Cubans, he seriously doubted that revolution could eradicate prostitution.

He came to an open door, and there she was, sitting at her vanity and gazing at her large, dark eyes in the mirror as she put on lipstick, cool as a cucumber, as if she had spent her entire life confronting men armed with AK-47's. Honoré sensed he was in grave danger when he saw the white sheet covering Tequila, whose brown feet stuck out at one end. If you lived like a *pendejo*, thought Honoré, you died like a *pendejo*.

She eyed Honoré in the mirror. "Now that we got rid of Tonto," she said in Spanish, "it's just you and me." She dipped her finger in the plastic bag and wiped the white stuff on her lips. "How about some mustard on that foot-long hot dog, *papacito*?"

She stood, the towel wrapped around her. She stepped on Tequila's *pan-*

za and jumped into bed where her towel came undone. She stretched out her long, mahogany legs, and her *maracas* spread like swirls of chocolate. When she rubbed some coke between her legs, Honoré shuddered. He now stood face to face with one of God's deadliest creations. His hot dog felt as if it had been left too long in the microwave, bloated, threatening to rip apart, sizzling in mustard. The saltpeter failed.

Suddenly, a car horn, distant and urgent, sounded like a bugle. He listened, heard it again, calling men to arms. His ideals as a revolutionary rose through his veins like flags strung up a flagpole.

Tequila rolled over, pushing back the white sheet, and raised himself on his elbow. "*Mamacita,* let me lick your pussy."

If the Spanish conquest of the Americas failed, it was because of bastards like Tequila. Nothing could kill them. Now, Honoré would have to take him to the emergency room instead of the morgue, which meant he'd have to talk to the police, Comino's men. Comino, always on the lookout for an opportunity to bust his political enemies, might have Honoré arrested for assault and battery. They might even plant some weed on him. So he picked up Tequila's steel-toed workman's boot and clobbered him on the head. Arms flopping like loose rubber oars, Tequila rolled on his side and fell unconscious.

Then, from his pocket, Honoré took Señora Cuervo's thousand dollars and handed it to the woman. "Here. Take this and get out of town."

She grabbed the money and threw it his face. "*¡Cabrón!*" she screamed, mouth ripped by anger, her white teeth lovely.

Next, a butterfly appeared. Silver, it glinted, suspended in mid-air. Honoré didn't know where it came from, beneath the mattress or under the pillow. It was a razor, long and sharp enough to serve him up like spaghetti and meatballs. He was quick, though, catching her wrist, and throwing her back on the bed, falling with her. But she rebounded and crawled on top of him, pummeling his face with her *maracas,* which left him breathless.

After teetering on the edge of the bed as if about to be sucked into a black hole, he lost his balance, and the two rolled onto the floor. This time he landed on top of her, holding her wrist in an iron grip.

"Drop it!" he yelled.

Her mouth was wet. "*¡Chinga tu madre!*"

"I know who you are," he said, "and why you're here. You're from the Valley. You used to live in Matamoros. If you're not gone in twenty-four hours, I'll turn you over to the FBI. You hear me?"

She spit.

"Drop the razor!" he gasped, spit running down his cheek, "or I'll break your wrist."

"*¡Me la mamas, cabrón!*"

He twisted her wrist. She cried out, and the razor fell. He let go and picked it up, climbed off. Holding her wrist, she rolled on her side, lifted a knee, and rose to her feet, *maracas* flying as she ran out of the room and down the hall, crying like a little girl, though her buttocks were not those of a little girl. A door slammed. Honoré rose on one knee and then another, and sat on the bed. Exhausted, he gazed at Tequila, who lay there with his ass looking like two piles of brown sugar at the mercado in downtown Nuevo Escandón.

At last, he stood up and saw himself in the vanity mirror, a tall man with a handsome light-skinned face and thick black hair and a mustache. He would have been a great actor, but he was not an actor, and this was not a movie. This was life on the border, in South Texas, his life, more dangerous than anything the bastards in Hollywood could imagine.

CHAPTER 5
Deconstructing Olive Oyl

Clouds sparkled in the morning sky. While long lines of cars crowded the bridge's northbound lanes, the side taking Honoré and Trotsky across the Rio Grande to Nuevo Escandón was empty. Not only had Honoré survived the mission to rescue Tequila but Trotsky had returned earlier than expected. Now they were headed to a press conference organized by Don Sixto at his shop in support of opposition leaders traveling from Lucero to protest the army's civil rights abuses.

After getting through customs, Trotsky directed the jeep into the crowded, boisterous streets of Nuevo Escandón and then took the main street past the first plaza. At the second plaza, they turned left and passed a movie theater, then some unfinished cinder block fences and corrugated tin roofs slanting above swollen wooden walls and dirt yards stuffed with mesquite trees. Dozens of cars squatting on both sides of the street forced them to park a block from Don Sixto's garage. Still sore from the fiasco with Tequila and the Aztec princess, Honoré followed Trotsky slowly, picking his way among the potholes in the sidewalk, until they spotted some men inside a car across the street from Sixto's garage.

"*Águila*," Trotsky said.

Honoré halted and gazed at the two men wearing sunglasses, which he had seen before, not these men but men like them, at rallies or meetings throughout Mexico—*gobernación*. The so-called Mexican FBI.

"The *cabrones*," Trotsky muttered, "can't cope with the real criminals, so they prey on people trying to do something good for this godforsaken country."

Then Honoré followed him through a squealing metal gate. The latest butt-swinging cumbia blared from a radio and carried across the oil-stained dirt. Dozens of cars, hoods opened like mouths ready for a dental examination, sat side by side amid the ringing of hammers and wrenches in the hands of young men whose arms glistened in the morning sunlight.

"Don Sixto!" yelled the boy standing guard on the roof of the shop's two-storey whitewashed building that towered above the metal gate. "Someone's looking for you."

"*¡Ya voy!*"

Wearing a newsboy's cap pulled low over a sunburned face and pulling a red cloth from his back pocket, Sixto walked from behind a Volkswagen van.

"You look like Pablo Neruda in that cap," said Trotsky.

Sixto wiped his hands. "Well, today I feel like Pablo Neruda. I'm alive. I slept eight hours last night. Of course, La Morenita warms my bed and sweetens my sleep. What more can I ask for?"

Honoré stood next to Trotsky. "Sorry we're late. I couldn't leave the store unattended."

Don Sixto's oil-stained hands were big as wrenches. "*No'mbre*, don't worry about it. Waiting is our favorite pastime. We live in a different century from the gringos. Those *cabrones* can't wait for anyone. But my *compadres* from *gobernación* are never late, are they?"

"Yeah, we just saw them," said Trotsky. "How's security?"

"No problem here," said Don Sixto, nodding toward the boy on the roof and then at two young men removing a tire from a school bus. "All these men are armed. And they shoot very well. I trained them myself. No one dares bother me here. Sometimes a helicopter flies over, but like everything else in Mexico, that's just for show." Sixto stuffed the red cloth in his back pocket. "Where's the American reporter?"

"I gave him directions to your shop," said Trotsky, glancing at his watch. "He knows Nuevo Escandón well, so he should have no problems getting here."

If there was anything the Mexican government hated, it was publicity in the American press. So Trotsky called a reporter at the *Escandón Morning Times* and asked him to interview Doña Catarina. Meanwhile, Sixto arranged for his friends at *El Nuevo Amanecer* and *El Machete* to be at the press conference, but Honoré doubted they'd show up.

However, that wasn't why he had tagged along. Sixto had promised to cross the dolls soon, and Honoré wanted to see where things were. Besides, he needed a break from his mother and cousins who had been at each other's throats all week.

"Where's your son?" Honoré asked.

"Monterrey," said Sixto. "Getting everything ready for us to move the dolls."

"When?"

"Soon."

Honoré hated to nag. "A week? Two weeks?"

Sixto patted Honoré's shoulder. "We're doing the best we can. Speaking of which, can you get a plane?"

"A plane? I don't know."

"Check it out." Then Sixto addressed Trotsky. "I've told everyone about the convoy to Nicaragua. Some support the idea. Others say we should stay out of international politics. We have enough to do here and in Lucero."

"Well, I wouldn't worry about it. The veterans probably won't get it off the ground. Let's worry about Lucero."

Next, Don Sixto led them around the back of the Volkswagen bus to the two-storey building. Inside, they entered an office lined with metal shelves sagging with car parts, tools, and cans of oil.

Doña Catarina, a matronly woman with a pale face and blond hair, rose from a chair and smiled. "Señor Trotsky," she said, "I'm so glad you came." She looked at Honoré.

He shook her hand. "It's an honor, señora. I've heard wonderful things about you."

Sixto laid an iron hand on Honoré's shoulder. "This is the man," he said to Doña Catarina, "who helped us with the Sandinista commander last year. Several weeks ago he took some medical supplies to the villages in Oaxaca."

The woman's eyes glistened. "Oh, yes. I've heard about you." She brushed Honoré's arm with her hand. "Maybe you and Don Sixto can help us in Lucero when he's ready to travel."

"Sí, señora."

Then she turned to an old man sitting in the chair next to her, a cane between his knees, shoes polished as if they had been dipped in black ink. "This is Don Esquivel, the party's secretary and advisor. We didn't have a car or money for this trip. Don Esquivel paid for the gas, and Xavier brought us in his Volkswagen."

A tall slender young man with a girlish face behind gold-rimmed glasses, Xavier, Don Esquivel's son, stood up, shook hands with Trotsky and Honoré, and then sat down. Next to him sat a young woman named Rosa, who wore faded jeans and tennis shoes. She barely nodded.

Sixto walked behind his gray metal desk and plopped in a swivel chair. While Trotsky sat in a creaky chair next to a shelf of mechanic's manuals, Honoré settled on a wooden stool and stared at a poster on the wall advertising Cerveza Superior. A blond woman with an ivory smile looked at him; his eyes were drawn by the gravitational pull of tits big as *calabazas*. As soon as he could pry his eyes loose, his curiosity traveled the length of her gorgeous white legs to her toes. At her heels, in the corner, stood an AK-47.

Meanwhile, Catarina recounted what happened in Lucero. "Party officials in Monterrey sent ruffians to organize a counter-demonstration, but a big turnout of el pueblo helped us drive the intruders out of town. Then the governor sent in the army, and they set up a blockade. About a week ago, a soldier raped Rosa."

Rosa bowed her head and sobbed quietly as Catarina put her arm around her shoulders. "*Ya, ya, hija,*" Catarina said. "You'll be okay."

Rosa wiped her nose. "I'm sorry."

Catarina's eyes swept across Sixto's desk. "We've complained to the authorities, but nothing has been done. I don't know how much longer we can hold out without some kind of support from the outside."

The wheels on Sixto's swivel chair squeaked. "If men in this country," he said, "had half your courage and moral integrity, Mexico wouldn't be in the mess it's in. Just remember, you're not alone. We're going to do everything we can to help you."

"Gracias," Doña Catarina said. "You're very kind."

The noon sun poked Honoré's eyes. Beneath the two lanes of vehicles waiting to cross the border, the bridge swung slowly, almost imperceptibly. Honoré and Trotsky had been in the sweltering heat for over an hour, moving in fits and starts. Below the muddy waters of the Rio Grande flowed. Above clouds the shape of Spanish galleons sailed across a blue sky. Up ahead rose the white walls of the US Border Inspection station, and the officers in blue uniforms with badges bright as gold doubloons took their time as they leaned toward the driver's window of each vehicle.

Black patch across one eye, Trotsky turned to Honoré. "His editors probably told him to interview some jackass at the Chamber of Commerce. I don't understand it. In Lucero we have a genuine struggle for democracy, and nobody up and down this border is interested. It all turns my stomach."

Honoré watched the cars ahead. "Catarina is a brave woman."

"You've got to hand it to the Mexicans. In Mexico being a member of the opposition can be fatal."

Honoré shifted in his seat. "How are we going to help them?"

"We should ask the Chicana activists in Escandón for support."

Honoré glanced at Trotsky, probably the wisest man he had ever known though at times like this he had his doubts. "Forget it."

"I've always wanted to join forces with Olivia."

Suddenly, the mirage-like figure of Dr. Olivia de la O appeared among the cars, walking between the bumpers into Honoré's mind, long skinny legs and arms, big teeth in an uneven mouth, thick black hair, and the posture of an arthritic. Her large but poor family lived in El Rincón del Diablo, a barrio near the river. After graduating from the local college, she won a fellowship to a university in California and was gone several years. Next he heard that she was back, a flaming Chicana radical who had landed a position as director of Casa Jovita Idahr, a small women's center funded by a wealthy South Texas rancher named María de Lourdes Smith. One day in a plaza downtown, he ran into Dr. de la O, skinny and lopsided as ever, toes big as turnips, in huaraches. She hadn't shaved her legs or armpits in months. She walked right past him without a glimmer of recognition, her head back, nose high, elbows swinging back and forth like Olive Oyl in a Popeye cartoon.

Trotsky rested a hand on the steering wheel. "They could be very—"

"No way."

"Why?"

"*Tortilleras* frighten me," said Honoré. "My cousin got into a fight with one at the Soul Español. She beat the hell out of him. You never know what you're dealing with—a man, a woman, or a nut."

"But Olivia has done some good work in Escandón," said Trotsky.

"What? Getting a bunch of women to come out of the closet? Everywhere she goes marriages fall apart."

"Homophobia is a serious problem here," said Trotsky.

The bridge moved under the long lines of cars glowing like great beetles of glass and metal blasted by heat and light in an industrial furnace. "Yeah," Honoré said, "but what pisses me off is that at the national level she's a flaming feminist lesbian leader, but here she puts on a show for everyone suggesting she's a traditional Mexican woman."

"She just doesn't want to embarrass her family in Escandón, especially her eighty-year-old father."

"She's a fucking hypocrite." Honoré knew Trotsky and Olivia had never gotten along. "So why are you political enemies?"

Trotsky wiped his forehead. "Several years ago," he said, "when I first arrived in Escandón, I went to a party given by a drinking buddy, a young lawyer, and I took Altagracia. We were going out for a night on the town. Altagracia looked stunning in a mini-skirt. At the party, Dr. de la O was dressed like a hippie, looking cool. Pot is interesting, but I hate the pot scene. Too much paranoia. We didn't stay long. But just before we left, I overheard Olivia talking to some women. She sneered, 'Oh, he just married a pair of legs.'"

"You're pissed because of that?"

"No, not really, but it shows you where she's at. She thinks I'm hopelessly sexist, old-fashioned. All I ever wanted was to be part of el pueblo, to lead a normal life, have a family and kids because I've had plenty of the other—no roots, no family, no one giving a shit whether I live or die. The fact that she's never been married, never had children—all theory, no practice—blinds her. Yet she presumes to speak on behalf of womankind. I suspect one day we're going to have a major knock-down drag-out."

Honoré gazed at an inspector walking a black dog on a leash around the car ahead. "Then why would you want to work with her?"

"Why let a grudge stand in the way of social progress? Why execute potential allies when there are so few of us working for peace and justice? We need all the help we can get, and this project in Lucero is ideal for Olivia and her feminists. Plus, it'll take some pressure off of us."

Upriver, an engine buzzed. A helicopter, like a huge mosquito with a big plastic bubble for a head and skis for feet, flew low along the water, the wind from the main rotor blade smoothing the surface like a fresh tortilla. Then, the chopper rose and leaped over them, filling the jeep with the thumping racket of its engine, and circled over the bridge. A Border Patrol agent peered through binoculars from inside before the chopper flew down river.

"They're flying awfully low," said Trotsky, squinting at the sky. "Must be some illegals or drug runners crossing."

On the sidewalk some Anglo women wore shorts, leather sandals, and huge Mexican straw sombreros; their legs glowed like cabrito on a spit. The large round gourds in their hands, painted in the colors of the Mexican flag, paled by comparison to the *maracas* in their halter tops. Every Mexican male worth his salt on that bridge locked his gaze on the white goddesses. The long pink tongues of the dogs on US government leashes were not the only ones salivating though the young Anglo men, new on the job, seemed oblivious.

"Tits and ass," Honoré said. "That's what those bastards in the helicopter were looking at."

Trotsky moved the jeep a few yards forward, braked. "Someone needs to approach Olivia."

Like a bucket of ice-cold water, a realization hit Honoré. Terrified, he straightened. "Me?"

Trotsky didn't smile. "I can't think of anyone else. You don't have a history with her."

"Well, I wouldn't say that."

"You've not seen her in years. You're in a better position to talk to her."
Honoré slammed his knee. "But I'm a man—"
"So?"
"Olivia hates men."
"Go see her lover, Ty Cobb Ramírez."
Honoré frowned. "*¡Chingao!* She's a first-class bitch. And a drunk."
"How do you know?"
"She's Tequila's cousin."

Trotsky took out a handkerchief and wiped his forehead. "They live down by the river. Pretend she's Olivia's husband or boyfriend. Get her drunk. Treat Ty like one of the boys. The important thing is to get the women in their group interested in Lucero. Some of Olivia's supporters are some of the wealthiest women in Escandón."

The customs inspector with the leashed black dog walked past the jeep. Like most new recruits from up north, he was tall, young, and serious, with a pink face that had just begun to turn into a sausage in the hot skillet of South Texas.

A dog with a spiked collar growled. Honoré knocked again, and the porch exploded with at least five small bulldogs jumping and barking like demons, their broad, wrinkled snouts hammering the screen. He could still feel the cold tremors in his bones when one morning, down by the river, a dog sank its teeth in his ankle and wouldn't let go. He pulled out a .45 semi-automatic and shot the motherfucker. He ended up in the hospital, unable to walk for days. Fortunately, the dog wasn't rabid. Otherwise, he'd have had nurses sticking needles in him for weeks.

And if it was true that dogs were like their owners, it looked like he was in for a lot of trouble. Sure enough, when the door opened, a short, round young woman in an apron and a spiked collar around her neck came out. She got down on one knee and chained the dogs to the porch's wooden posts. When the ugliest and most vicious snapped at her, Ty Cobb Ramírez stood up and with a hard kick in the butt sent it flying across the porch.

Honoré thought the yelping dog should be grateful. At least, she didn't shoot it.

After unlatching the screen door, Ty said gruffly. "C'mon in." She wore a faded denim shirt with brass buttons, jeans, and cowboy boots. "Don't worry about the dogs. They don't bite."

The pack of demons strained at the end of their chains, pulling hard against their collars, their ivory meat-cleavers flashing with drool, their eyes fierce as a jaguar's or a shark's or an enraged wife's. When she closed the door, the dogs' racket softened. Many years younger than Dr. de la O, Ty looked like a boy—plump, with a soft, girlish face and close-cropped dark brown hair.

In the living room, Ty put her hands on her hips. "So you're Trotsky's friend?"

"Yes, ma'am."

She frowned. "You don't have to say 'ma'am' to me. I'm not an old woman."

Honoré swallowed. "Yes, ma'am."

"If you don't watch your tongue, you can leave right now. We don't tolerate sexist language in this house."

Then, Honoré remembered how Trotsky had handled the same situation in Austin one time. "Sorry, comrade."

Ty nodded. "That's better. What do you want?"

"Trotsky and I are helping a group of women in Lucero, a small town about fifty miles from here, near the mountains, in Nuevo León. We hoped El Grupo Femenil would support them. That's why I want to talk to Dr. de la O."

Ty shook her head. "If I don't get to see enough of Olivia, I don't see how you can. She's always on the go. She has time for no one. You have to catch her by surprise."

"Well, who runs El Grupo Femenil?"

"Olivia. And if she doesn't like you or you're politically suspect, which you are, no dice."

"Me—politically suspect?"

She nodded solemnly.

"Why?"

"Well, first you're a man. Men cannot be trusted. Second, you're a friend of Trotsky. He cannot be trusted."

"Do you know Trotsky?"

"All I know is what Olivia told me. *Es un cabrón, hecho y derecho.* First, he seduced that beautiful girl, Altagracia, with all kinds of lies. I hear he's Jewish. A Mexican Jew, worst kind. Too much of a loose cannon to be a real Marxist. He thinks he's a great man of history, but he's just a wannabe living in historic times. A tourist, a dabbler, a dilettante, a fop."

Honoré didn't enjoy hearing trash about a man he admired and respected. "He and his wife have helped a lot of people in Mexico."

"Well, Olivia still doesn't like him."

Honoré felt a tickling at the back of this throat. "I know, but I'm here to help some women in Mexico."

"There's something else."

He cleared his throat. "What?"

"Olivia doesn't like you either."

"Oh?"

"Can't say I blame her. I've heard about you. Tequila loves to brag about all the shit you and he did together—drugs, booze, hookers. So any friend of that asshole must be an asshole."

Honoré felt light-headed, as if an explosion were coming on, like he was getting ready to beat the shit out of this *tortillera*. But he couldn't. He had come on a mission. He considered his next move. "Well, I'm not going to tell you what Tequila said about you."

Ty was taken aback. "Has that bastard been talking about me?"

He pivoted on a boot. "Look, I gotta go."

She ran between him and the front door. "What did he say?"

He paused. "Ask Tequila."

She grabbed him, fat fingers on an arm of steel. "Tell me!"

"Not if you're going to treat me like shit."

The phone rang. Ty froze, eyes wide open. It rang again. "Wait here." She ran to the kitchen. Two minutes later, she was chirping and cooing on the telephone like a lovebird. Suddenly, there was silence, the silence of bad news and broken hearts. "Oh, no!" she cried. "You promised, baby!"

Honoré hated when adults sounded like this. No dignity, no self-respect.

Upon returning, eyes downcast, dragging her boots, she stopped next to him. "She does this to me all the time," she said. "I prepared dinner for her."

"Was she *really* going to be here tonight?"

"She was, but for Olivia going to a conference out of town is like getting laid for the rest of us."

"I better go."

She hooked her fingers in his belt. "Wait. *Ya estuvo.*"

"Why?"

"Have you had dinner?"

In the kitchen, he took a stool next to a window. Outside, smoke unwound from a grill built from a metal barrel on four legs. Beyond the mesquite trees at the back of the yard, the sun sank in an orange haze. This part of the Rio Grande he knew well, having crossed it with Tequila and tons of *mota* many times, just upriver.

"Here you go," said Ty, putting a plate stacked with grilled beef and tortillas wrapped in a dish towel on the table. After placing a bowl of guacamole next to the tortillas, she opened the pantry and took out some bright yellow plates she claimed Olivia bought in Oaxaca and gave one to Honoré.

"Smells great," he said as he served himself a plate full of meat, sausages, tortillas, and guacamole. "If not for the drug trafficking and mosquitoes," he added, "I wouldn't mind living by the river. Must be cheap, too. How much do you pay?"

First, she got two cold ones from the refrigerator and plunked them on the table. Then she sat down with her plate of food. "Not much. It belongs to Olivia's family. As long as we do the upkeep and pay the yearly taxes, we live rent-and-mortgage free. Olivia wants to buy a house in north Escandón with the money she saves here. But I don't want to move. I love it here."

He took a bite. "Mmmm. You're a damned good cook."

"I do everything here," she said, flashing the fork with the same flair and gusto as Tequila. "I get free room and board, and I don't have to work while I go to school."

"Oh, yeah. What are you studying?"

"Poetry."

"How you plan to make a living?

"Teaching."

"Teaching what?"

"Poetry."

"So is Ty Cobb Ramírez your pen name?"

She grinned. "*No mames, cabrón.* That's my real name. My father wanted a son. Ty Cobb was his favorite baseball player, so he named me Ty. *¿Qué loco, no?*"

"I wanted a son, too," he said. "Then my wife got sick."

"Well, my father didn't know whether I was a boy or a girl," she said. "He was drunk most of the time."

"Sorry to hear that."

A mosquito buzzed a few feet away. "But when I discovered that I liked girls and that girls liked me and that I was a poet, I saw that my father, bless his soul, did the right thing. Don't you think Ty Cobb Ramirez is a great name for a dyke poet?"

"Sure," Honoré said doubtfully.

Buzzing loudly, the mosquito shot between Ty and Honoré. "That's the only thing I hate about living by the river," she said, slapping it away. "Mosquitoes. And the Border Patrol."

"Why BP?"

"Because they're Big Brother—or Big Prick—keeping an eye on us Mexicans."

She downed a bottle in a few gulps and then got another one from the refrigerator, snapping it open as she sat down. He, on the other hand, took it easy. You could get away with all kinds of shit with drunken women, but not if you were drunk.

"Thanks for staying," she said. "Sometimes it gets lonely around here."

He cut off a piece of sausage. "Why is Olivia gone so much?"

On the porch outside, the meat cleavers barked. "She attends every conference in her field. It can be frustrating, especially at night. I can put up with not talking, but I can't put up with not getting enough."

"Not getting enough is serious business."

The dogs stopped barking and whined like babies. "I bought Olivia some red panties. She looked great. We had a romp in bed one night, really turned me on. But then she never put them on again. It's like sex really doesn't interest her."

He swallowed and then said, "I know what you mean."

Her eyes narrowed. "Liar. Men aren't interested in what women feel."

If she's butch, he wondered, why is she interested? "Everyone says men want only one thing from women," he said, "but no one seems to know what women want."

She arched an eyebrow. "We want freedom."

"From what?"

She slapped the mosquito on her neck. "Men."

Bewildered, he said, "I could never live without a woman."

"That's because you're a man. And men in this town expect women to be at their beck and call."

Annoyed, he wiped his mouth with a napkin. There was really no point in talking to this dyke. "Where's the bathroom?"

"Down the hall, to your right."

He threw down the napkin and stood up.

"Wait." She glared at him.

He halted a few feet from the table. "What?"

"You still haven't told me what Tequila said about me."

"He didn't say anything."

She slammed the bottle on the table. "See what I mean? There you go, lying again. Olivia was right. Who knows what you and Trotsky are up to? It might even be a trap. Forget it. Get lost. Tell Trotsky to go fuck himself."

His hand became an iron fist as he thought about beating the shit out of this dyke. A slap across the face would send her flying across the kitchen like a mosquito. A fat mosquito. Then he remembered why he had come here. To help some women in Mexico. "I'll be right back."

The wooden floor in the hall wobbled beneath his cowboy boots as he walked toward a door that squealed when he opened it. Inside, the room smelled of fresh paint, soap, and mint. A douche bag and a new tampon lay on the sink. When he finished, he washed his hands with perfumed soap and rinsed them in hot water before stepping back into the hall. As he closed the bathroom door behind him, he felt someone staring at him. He turned around. Inside the room across the hall, Frida Kahlo, with a tiny sketch of Diego Rivera above her cockroach eyebrows, stared at him from a poster on the wall. Even here, this *feminista* fortress, he observed, women could not get men out of their minds. On another poster the brown rugged face of César Chávez squinted in sunlight. This room, with all four walls heavy with hundreds of books, must be Olivia's library.

Down the hall, Honoré peeked in another room.

Pictures of Ty and Olivia, like Bluto and Olive Oyl, stood on the dresser. What must the sexual politics be like here? he wondered as he skimmed the surface of the waterbed, blue as the sea and piled with pillows, round and big as mounds of dough. *Tortilleras*, Trotsky claimed, lived in a parallel universe. Some denied the male–female duality yet couldn't help but imitate it in their relations with each other. Some took the role of men while others took the role of women. Here Honoré couldn't tell who was what. Ty was very butch, but Olivia was the breadwinner. Ty did the household chores, but Olivia was the intellectual giant. On the walls were pennants from Berkeley. On another wall was a poster of La Virgen de Guadalupe. A drawer stood open. Inside were red panties.

Sex is a political condition, he reflected. Or was it the other way around? Politics is a sexual condition?

Then, something occurred to him, and he returned to the kitchen. "All right," he said as he sat down, "I'll tell you what Tequila told me about you."

She perked up. "Okay, what?"

"He said you liked *pechuga*."

Her eyes danced. "I love chicken, especially chicken breast." She paused, frowned. "So what?"

"He said you were a lot like him. He says he's a *cabrón*. So that makes you a *cabrona*. He said you love *pierna* and *pechuga*, but you weren't getting enough."

She stared at him in a daze. "What are you talking about? *¿Pierna y pechuga?* Like tits and ass?"

"More or less."

She arched an eyebrow. "How does he know? That cokehead never knows what's going on in the world. Last I heard he had his head up some bitch's ass."

"I'm just reporting what I heard. Oh, he also said that if anybody needed to go to *la zona* it was you, where there's plenty of *pecho* and *pierna*."

Ty took off her apron, rolled back her sleeves, and moved her stool directly in front of him. "Can we have a man-to-man talk?"

He tried not to grin. "Okay."

"Do you have a problem with *tortilleras*?"

Mexican humor was cruel. They called dykes *tortilleras* because when they made love, pussy to pussy, it was like the hands of a *tortillera* coming together as they patted and molded the dough into tortillas. The action was between the palms.

"I don't think so," he said. "As long as they don't give me any shit."

She stood and took two more beers from the refrigerator and set one in front of Honoré. "I'm not like Olivia. I'm a *tortillera*, and I love it. I don't have to hide it or make excuses." She sat on the stool. "Is it true the *pechugonas* run around topless at *la zona*?"

Mexicans loved to play with words. *Pechugonas* were women with big *pechos* or boobs. *Pierna* meant leg. "Nothing but *pierna* and *pechuga*," he said.

She sat on the edge of her chair. "Are they really nice?"

He sighed. "Some are very beautiful."

She leaned so close he smelled the sausage on her breath. "Are they young?"

What a silly question. "Of course."

"The *pechos*—are they really big?"

He was beginning to like her. "Like *calabazas*."

"Do they let you touch them?"

"Sometimes."

"How much do they charge?"

He took a slug. "Thirty bucks for thirty minutes."

An eye sharpened. "What else do they do for you?"

"It depends on how much they like you. Sometimes everything except kiss."

She sat back, eyes wild as a lovesick javelina's, a smile wavering on her moist lips as she looked into the future. Then she burped. "I'll make a deal with you, *cabrón*."

"*Dale gas.*"

"In two weeks there's a women's conference at Casa Jovita Idahr. Olivia is organizing it. A major Chicana writer is speaking, Danielle Mujica. And some Chicana heavyweights are coming from California. Scholars, literary critics. Dr. Genoveva Malecón from Berkeley. Dr. Cherry Bustos from Stanford." She drank from her bottle of beer, swallowing hard, and then said, "Cherry is something else. A real *pechugona*." She wiped a streak of foam from her lips. "I wouldn't mind getting in her pants." Then she stood up and punched him hard on the shoulder.

The pain spread quickly. He thought about slapping her. Grin and bear it, he told himself.

She leaned so close he smelled the beer on her breath. "Here's the deal," she said. "I get Olivia to talk to you at the conference and maybe get her women's organization to support you—if, and only if, you do me a big favor, *cabrón*."

Perched like giant fighting cocks in the night sky, the neon signs of the bordellos cast their plumage of light on the dirt along the cement wall enclosing the red light district. Honoré had told Maruca he was going to Nuevo Escandón to visit Don Sixto and would get back late. In light of what happened at the Clinica del Barrio the last time, she warned him to be careful about what he ate and drank.

Slowing his truck down, he glanced at Ty. "So are you ready for *noche de carnaval*?"

"Yep. I brought the masks."

"Great!"

As the headlights of cars leaving the compound bore through sheets of dust, he rumbled over a cattle guard and bounced past an inspection booth, where a uniformed guard sat dozing with a submachine gun on his lap. Across the dirt road, a young man in a white apron prepared tacos at the stand in front of the wall surrounding the Heaven of the Dead Man. A guard at the gate directed Honoré to a paved parking lot inside, where he eased the pickup among the trucks and cars smoldering in the neon light.

After he turned off the engine, she pulled a bag from the floor board. "Where'd you get them?" he asked.

"Our last Halloween party." The blond hair and red lips of Cinderella hung lopsided from her hand. "This is Olivia's. She's the princess. Too girly for me." She dropped Cinderella and pulled out the face of a man with a ghastly mouth, a thick brow, and a sunken forehead—Frankenstein. "I don't want to be a monster." After groping deep in the bag again, she took out a third mask—Batman. "Look, this one is for me."

He picked up Frankenstein. "I'll wear this one."

"But it's not fair."

"What?"

"You're too manly to be Cinderella and too handsome to be Franken-stein. Trotsky should be Frankenstein."

Honoré laughed. "Trotsky doesn't need a mask. Besides, it doesn't matter. We're going to a party." The rubbery smell of the mask made him feel like a dick—or, a dickhead—slipping on a condom. "Even in bed that doesn't matter because you usually turn off the light, crawl under the covers, or shut your eyes."

He slowly climbed out of the pickup because he was having a tough time seeing through the slits. Just outside the entrance to the nightclub, a woman checked him out. Maybe the mask of Frankenstein scared her. Then a man wearing a cowboy hat joined her, and the two disappeared along the walk toward the rooms in back.

Honoré gave the guard a big tip, just to make sure the truck was still there when he and Ty got back. "Ready?" he asked her.

The spiked collar around Batman's neck sparkled. "*Sale.*"

Ostriches, vampires, can-can dancers, and witches packed the night-club. Even the waiters wore masks. The only ones who did not and didn't need them were the gringos, who were not from here, so no one would recognize them anyway.

"There," Ty said and pointed to an empty table across the large room.

They sat down, and a waiter brought them a dish of black olives. Then he left and came back with two cans of Tecate. Meanwhile, a herd of masked gazelles, their legs long and curvaceous, escorted three smiling red-faced gringos in Panama hats, Hawaiian shirts, and white tennis shoes toward another door at the back of the club and disappeared outside.

Ty lifted her mask and fixed her gaze on a tall young woman. "Oh, mama," she sighed.

The woman, wearing a richly embroidered headdress of sequins and standing on shapely white legs, stuck her ass in Ty's face as she leaned over Honoré. "Are you a monster?" she whispered in his ear.

He spoke as best he could through his mask. "Why?"

She sat down in a chair. "Because you look like Frankenstein." Her fingers crawled, tarantula-like, slowly and frighteningly, along his leg. "And because you're built like one."

He removed his mask and grabbed her hand. "Would you do me a big favor?"

"What, baby?"

He pointed at Ty. "Put this young woman out of her misery."

She pushed him away. "Do I look like a *tortillera*? The twins over there," she said to Ty. "They'll do anything as long as you pay them, even a donkey." Then she stood, taking his hand and pulling hard, her ass wagging in Ty's face. "Come on, *papacito*, just you and me."

She seemed unusually strong for a woman. "Cool it," he said, still planted in his chair. When she stumbled against the table, giggling, leaning forward, pursing her lips, a bottle fell, rolled, and crashed on the floor. Then, she shot straight up, swallowed hard, and blinked. "*¡Auxilio! ¡Auxilio! ¡Policía!*" she screamed.

Meanwhile, Ty sat behind her, gazing at her middle finger.

What the hell, thought Honoré. Suddenly, he found himself staring at the barrel of a machine gun. He raised his hands slowly.

"*Qué chingados* is going on here?" yelled the cop.

"Someone raped me!" yelled the woman.

Ty grabbed Honoré's arm. "Let's get the fuck out of here!"

His hands aloft, Honoré said, "Sit down! Calm down!"

The cop, still pointing the gun at Honoré's face, said to the woman, "How can anyone be raped in this place?"

"I was standing there talking to this caballero when suddenly something went up my backside."

The cop looked around for evidence. "Where?"

"*¡Las partes nobles, pendejo!* Where else?"

Another cop showed up, a submachine in his hands, an eye zeroing in on the woman. "It's you again, *cabrón*! What's going on?"

Cabrón? wondered Honoré. Why call a woman *cabrón* unless she was a man? A transvestite?

"I asked you what's going on?" repeated the cop.

"A finger," whined the woman.

"A finger?"

"The public has the right to look at my *partes nobles*," the woman whimpered, "but no one has a right to finger me!"

"*No mames*," said the cop, pushing the first cop's machine gun out of Honoré's face and clutching the woman.

She yanked her elbow free. "Stop it! That boy did it!"

"What boy?"

She pointed at Ty. "That one!"

"That's a girl?"

"She's a *tortillera!*" the woman yelled.

"Who? Me?" Ty cooed and draped one leg over the other.

The cop pointed the machine gun at Honoré. "And who are you—her father?"

"No, just a friend."

"They're gringos," the other cop said.

"Good. We'll arrest all three."

"No, let them go. I don't want trouble with gringos. Besides, this isn't the first time this *cabrón* gives us trouble." The cop turned to the transvestite. "You're drunk. We already told you that if you caused any more problems we'd arrest you. Now get the hell out of here, *pinche puto culero.*"

The *puto* left, escorted by the cops.

Honoré rested his arm on the table. "What did you do?"

Ty put her mask back on. "Nothing," she mumbled through the slit in the rubber.

"Listen, Ty," said Honoré, leaning forward. "I agreed to bring you here in exchange for a favor. But if you're going to take advantage of me, there will be consequences."

"Like what?"

"Like how would you like to get arrested and come out in the Mexican newspapers tomorrow morning? Or how would you like to just disappear and end up bubbling in a drum of acid?"

A set of twins—two women wearing white capes that flowed to their ankles, their fair-skinned faces covered by silver masks—walked over from the bar where they had been lounging on stools, throwing their capes over their shoulders and displaying *pechos* whose nipples glittered.

"Buenas noches, *jovenes*," said one of them. "Want to see what you've been missing?"

Drawn by the *pechos* wiggling inches from her face, Batman rose to her feet. "You're right. They're big, just like *calabazas*." She caressed one, squeezed a nipple. "I knew I was missing out on something."

When someone raised the volume on the jukebox, a cumbia exploded like a public harangue. "¡A mover el bote!" yelled one of the twins, taking Batman by the hand.

The other twin took Honoré's hand. "Come on!"

"I hate to dance," protested Honoré.

She led him to the dance floor. "Just shake it."

He stood there like an idiot.

"Just move *el bote*," she said and swung her beautiful ass to the crashing, rumbling, uplifting beat of the cumbia. *Pechos* bobbing, she spun around, smiling, and showed him the two big lovely scoops of vanilla that were her buttocks glistening with beads of sweat. Everyone, including the gringos who had the biggest *botes*, rose to their feet and began moving it, back and forth, up and down.

"Let's go to the room," whispered the lovely creature in Honoré's ear.

"I didn't come for that."

She thrust her pelvis against his. "Then why are you here, *papacito*? Don't you want to feed your monster, even for free?"

Ty and her new friend came over. "This is great!" beamed Ty.

The twin slipped her arm under Honoré's. "Let's go warm up some tortillas. Three of us, one of you."

Honoré grinned, raising his hands. "No, no, no."

The other twin put her chin on Ty's head and wrapped her arms around her shoulders. "Okay," said the twin, "then *we'll* go warm up the tortillas. We make the best tortillas in Nuevo Escandón," she said. "Plenty of *masa*." She raised a lovely *pecho* with one hand.

The other one took out from her purse a flesh-colored dong with French ribbons. "And plenty of metate."

He blinked, amazed that Mexican whores had become this savvy. "I'll wait here for you. But remember. No *macho gacho* bullshit. Treat these women like señoritas, even if they're not. Behave like a caballero from South Texas."

"Okay, okay," muttered Ty under her breath.

As the two blond bombshells escorted the would-be boy toward the exit, Honoré sat down at the table, remembering when his father brought him here and waited for him while a naked woman unzipped his trousers in a back room. In his family, fathers and uncles traditionally took the boys out for a night on the town to make men of them.

Then another *pechugona* arrived at the table. "Buenas noches, *papasote*." She sat down. "So what's your name, *cosotas*?"

"What's yours?"

"Vuelve a la Vida," she said, a smile lounging amid the glow of her lipstick.

"Vuelve a la Vida? You mean like the shrimp cocktail with oysters, octopus, onions, and cilantro?"

"And a lot of salsa picante."

Casa Jovita Idahr was a renovated Victorian house in downtown Escandón, a few blocks from Trotsky's. Since Ty told Honoré to wait in the hall for Olivia on her way to the lecture hall, he stood next to the entrance. If that did not work, he would try catching her during one of the breaks. Otherwise, he would have to wait until after the conference, but then it might be too late because she always rushed off with her friends from out of town. Honoré would have preferred going with Trotsky and Don Sixto to Lucero today, but Trotsky insisted that the sooner Honoré got Olivia's support, the better served their cause would be.

Maruca hadn't been enthusiastic about letting Bonita accompany him, but she didn't oppose it, especially after Misty found out that Danielle Mujica, the Chicana poet from San Antonio whose work was being taught at some schools in Escandón, might be there. Honoré agreed to bring the girls, who now stood chattering about an upcoming volleyball game with a rival school; they would ensure his safe passage through what he suspected was enemy territory.

An office door opened at the other end of the building, and a woman carrying a pile of books stacked across her chest entered the hallway— none other than Dr. Olivia de la O, wearing her legendary huaraches and a long black skirt over skinny legs. Flowers embroidered on a white blouse reminded Honoré that no matter how much she tried to imitate the Indian women of southern Mexico, she couldn't get rid of the look of a spinster left to dress saints in the Catholic world.

Honoré stepped forward with the manners of a caballero from South Texas and, as she approached, held open one of the two doors leading to the lecture hall.

"Dr. de la O?" he said. "Honoré del Castillo."

Without removing her chin from the stack of books, she peered—like a cat, or maybe a dog, sniffing trouble. "Can't you see I'm busy?"

"Did Ty tell you I called on behalf of Trotsky?"

"Later, later."

Then, she spun about face, books firmly beneath her bony chin as she backed through the other, unopened door.

Pinche vieja, thought Honoré, wanting to let the door slam in her face. Some of the worst scumbags he knew in Escandón had more manners than this—drug dealers, whores, thieves. Even the *jotos* were polite. He thought about leaving.

Then it occurred to him that this humiliation was nothing compared to what the women in Lucero had been suffering at the hands of the Mexican army. So he signaled Bonita and Misty to follow him. After greeting and shaking the hands of a few locally prominent women, mostly college professors and a few students, a newly appointed federal judge and two probation officers, all Hispanic women, he sat in the third row from the podium. Bonita and Misty sat next to him.

He relaxed until a noise distracted him.

Voices gathered outside before some strange-looking women stormed inside. With close-cropped hair, they would have looked best in Nazi uniforms, swaggering around in construction boots, slouching hangdog style. He couldn't tell if they were from Escandón or from out-of-town. Maybe Austin. Halting in mid-step, they shot nasty glances at Honoré.

"Dad?" whispered Bonita.

He kept his voice low. "What?"

"Why are those women looking at you that way?"

"I don't know. Maybe because they've never seen a man before."

"Are you sure we came to the right place?"

"*Ya*, be quiet, *por favor.*"

As soon as everyone had settled into their seats, Dr. de la O walked to the podium. "The last two days of this conference have been wonderful," she oozed. "Every time I get together with my *comadres* I am so energized. But all good things must come to an end. We thought it would be best to end with poetry. But since some of our presenters are running late, we've had to change the schedule. So first the poèts—" She looked up the middle aisle to the back of the theater. "Everyone ready? Yes?" She nodded and smiled. "And now our own Chicana poet from Escandón, Texas."

Applause swept the room as a short, fat boy with a round face with dimples beneath a black ten-gallon hat, swaggered down the middle aisle to the podium—Ty Cobb Ramírez. In blue jeans and lizard boots, a belt with a silver buckle and a red bandanna around her neck, Ty had everything she needed except a pair of six-guns to look like a tough hombre walking into a bad death saloon at the turn of the century.

She laid out the sheets of poetry on the podium. "*¿Qué pasó, raza?*" she boomed in the microphone.

The women giggled. Some broke into applause and whistled. "*¡Échale! ¡Dale gas!*" shouted someone in back.

"*¡Qué viva la raza!*" someone else shouted.

Ty grinned. "*¡Simón que sí!*" She raised a fist in a Chicana power salute.

"*¡Arriba las mujeres!*"

"*¡Y abajo los hombres!*"

Some women stomped their boots. Others clapped with glee. The federal judge and a probation officer grinned politely. Some cast mean glances at Honoré, who ignored them, wondering whether he should wait in the restaurant down the street for everything to finish, then sneak back and catch Olivia in the hall afterward.

"Now, *raza*," said Ty, a little too close to the mike and breathing heavily, "I want to read to you a poem about *ideals*, Chicana ideals. Because what we Chicanas feel is very important. Very important, *raza*. Very important. If we can't say what we feel, then we're not very important. So this poem is also about feelings. Chicana feelings."

Whales and the sea and the desert and the names of Hernán Cortés and La Malinche and a few *chingazos* delighted the crowd as if they had never heard a woman curse before. What the poem entitled "The Sadness of Cortés" had to do with Chicana ideals or feelings, however, was beyond Honoré. Though her delivery was warm and loud, Honoré would have preferred to listen to the real poetry of the border such as the *narcocorridos*.

"Dad," said Bonita.

"Lower your voice," whispered Honoré. "What?"

"Misty wants to know why are all these women acting like men?"

"I don't know, *mijita*."

"When is Danielle Mujica reading?"

"I think she's next."

When Ty finished, he applauded enthusiastically.

"Thank you, *raza*," said Ty as she waved to the audience. "Thank you, thank you."

Olivia appeared at the podium again, smiling for the first time as she waited for the applause to die. "Our next guest almost didn't make it today. She's been caught up in a flurry of book signings and public appearances across the country. Yet she was willing to sacrifice her precious time and come in support of the women's center, pro bono." Olivia waited for the thought to sink in, and then she put her mouth close to the mike and said with passion. "One of the fastest rising stars in the Chicana literary firmament—Danielle Mujica."

Applause exploded.

Down the middle aisle walked a young woman in her early thirties, wearing a stiff tutu-like skirt above shapely legs in black stockings and cowboy boots. Her hair was cut like a flapper's, and her mouth was the shape of a small valentine. A sigh arose among some of the women. As she sashayed past Honoré, he couldn't help but notice the flirtatious glance she cast him.

Behind the podium, she looked across the audience. "Thank you, thank you, thank you, *comadres y carnalas*, gracias, beloved *público*."

She was one hot mama. However, the only thing Honoré found irritating was her voice, which squeaked like that of a little girl. "I'm so happy to be here with my people."

"*Échela*, girl! *¡Aviéntate!*"

"*Me fascina la Mujica*," whispered a woman behind Honoré. "It's so refreshing to hear a woman say what's on her mind, does what she wants, dresses the way she wants, no man to tell her what to do. *Es una chingona*."

"Yes, but sometimes she goes over the top," said the other woman. "She has a filthy mouth."

Danielle took her time opening her book, long fingernails flashing in the light from the ceiling. After casting flirtatious glances at some women in the first row, she sighed and rolled her eyes when she couldn't find the page she wanted to read. Then, she stopped.

She sighed again and read a poem:

Something happened to Blanca Nieves
In a gray northern city
Something terrible.
She lost something precious.
She left,
Lived in the desert among the nopales
Y los indios
Learned to love her *raza*,
Awoke,
Learned to love herself.
Her bronze-colored self,
Her true self,
Her Malinche self.
Became famous.
Came back.
Then there were *chingazos*!

Honoré's face grew hot with embarrassment as she described her years as a rebellious bitch, using words such as *cabrón* and *chingar* and *caca* and *pendejo*. Had he known better, he never would have brought Bonita or Misty, who might tell her father.

Then Mujica read a poem about Pancho Villa, not giving a shit what she said or whom she offended as she described herself hunkering on her cunt on a hard leather saddle as the Pancho Villa in her came out, as if saying, "Oh, look at us. We Mexican Americans are so cute. I'm Chicano pussy."

Bonita grabbed Honoré's arm. "Dad, do you mind if Misty and I wait outside?"

Relieved, Honoré said, "No, no, go ahead."

"We'll be in the park down the street."

Fifteen minutes later, Honoré couldn't understand what all the excitement was about as applause flooded the room and Mujica finished amid a standing ovation. Honoré stood up, too. She curtseyed and smiled and blew kisses in every direction before walking to the table where Olivia had arranged a stack of books to be signed.

Olivia took the microphone again. "And now we'll have a short intermission while we wait for our other presenters to arrive. In the meantime you can all get your books signed by Danielle."

Honoré moved to the back of the lecture hall, where he could see what was going on and plan his next move.

Someone tugged at his elbow. "What did you think?" said Ty, holding the ten-gallon hat at her side.

"You were great."

Her eyes widened. She glanced at Danielle Mujica. "What do you think of Mujica?"

He lowered his voice. "I prefer your stuff."

"Really, *cabrón*?" she asked, raising a doubtful eyebrow. "You'll say anything to get what you want. Tell me the truth."

He laughed. "I am telling you the truth."

She grabbed his arm. "Listen. We need to have another man-to-man."

His mind wandered to Olivia standing behind the table of refreshments. "Well, let's see how things turn out here."

"Promise?"

"Promise."

Then she led him across the room. "Olivia," she said, "I've someone who'd like to talk to you. He's the gentleman I told you came to the house the other night. Honoré del Castillo."

Olivia straightened, glass of punch in hand, and gazed at him as if seeing him for the first time. "Yes, I remember you." Her voice was thin as a reed. "Escandón High. Star quarterback. Most handsome. You married

Maruca Santiesteban, the homecoming queen. Your family sells Mexican curios."

"Yes, ma'am."

She put down the glass and shook his hand. "I was surprised to see you here. I couldn't imagine why a man from Escandón would be at a women's conference."

"I've come on behalf of Juan Sanchez Trusky."

Her eyes wandered off. "Oh, really? Trusky." Her eyes returned. "Why didn't he come?"

He lied. "He's sick."

She smiled. "Do you think he'll *ever* get well?"

"I don't know, ma'am," he said, his hand opening and closing slowly, as if that would ease the tension in his throat. "I only know he wasn't feeling good and asked me to come. He felt you could help us."

She glanced at her wristwatch. "Ty," she said, "can you wait for Dr. Malecón in the parking lot? She should be here any minute. I don't want her getting lost."

Ty whispered, "What if she's bombed?"

Dr. de la O snapped, "Just go!"

"Okay, okay," said Ty, glancing at Honoré.

Dr. de la O became all business. "Okay, Mr. Castillo," she said. "What do you want?"

Honoré cleared his throat. "The leaders of the opposition party in Nuevo Escandón have been supporting a struggle in Lucero. The people have been protesting the corrupt government and election fraud. The government sent in the army. El pueblo have been at the mercy of the soldiers. One of them raped a girl. The organizers have been at this for months, but they won't be able to hold out much longer unless they get help."

"What kind of help?"

"Well, just about anything you can offer," said Honoré. "Money. Donations of food and medicine. Public support. We organized a press conference in Nuevo Escandón for them, but no one showed up. Perhaps if you organized one here, at Casa Jovita Idahr, the media would pay attention. Coverage by American newspapers would ease some of the pressure."

"Why me?"

He opened and closed his hand. "Because the struggle in Lucero is being led by women. We thought it might interest you."

"Are these women members of the opposition party?"

He felt the tension growing. "Yes."

"We're non-partisan."

"These women are involved in a struggle for democracy and respect for human rights."

She frowned. "We're an apolitical organization."

Honoré did a double take. "*Apolitical?*"

She rested an arm thin as a stick of bamboo on her waist and shook her head slowly, eyes half-closed as if imparting great wisdom to a child. "We don't take sides along party lines. We advocate on behalf of all women."

"Even if women are part of the problem?"

"I said," she emphasized, her voice brimming with school-marmish contempt, "we're non-partisan."

The desperation in his throat grew. He couldn't argue with her. Only Trotsky could do that. "Maybe you should talk to Trotsky."

"That coward."

He felt as if she had shoved him without lifting a finger. "Pardon me?"

"Why didn't that coward come directly to me? He knows where to find me." She cocked her head. "Besides, I don't trust Trusky. He's sexist. Anti-feminist. Claims to be a Marxist but knows nothing about Marxism." She looked around and then said slowly, very quietly. "I've heard rumors he's been smuggling guns into Mexico. Do you know anything about that?"

A Siberian wind sent his bones into a deep freeze. "No, ma'am."

She looked at him long and hard. A noise in the hall made her eyes flicker. "As I said, we're an apolitical organization. I don't see how we can help you."

A door swung open. Like barrels of booze rolling across a wooden floor, voices poured into the room. A heavyset fair-skinned woman with close-cropped hair and arms as thick and powerful as a weightlifter's— not because of the iron they pumped but because of what they put in her mouth—swaggered down the aisle. Wearing black-framed glasses on an unhappy face and decked out in a black skirt and gray satin short-sleeve blouse, she looked like a fat academic nun.

Behind her strode a beautiful young woman with a striking resemblance to Elvis Presley, wearing sunglasses on a fine, even nose, a denim jacket with a sequined Virgen de Guadalupe in back, and tight jeans filled by curvaceous hips. Her lava-black hair sprang thick and wavy across small elegant white ears and ended in a ducktail. She wore a dark blue T-shirt with a yellow bear with big eyes and a big smile above the yellow lettering of the University of Berkeley. Ty was right. Dr. Cherry Bustos was a *pechugona.*

Ty guided the women directly to Olivia and Honoré. "Dr. Genoveva Malecón and Dr. Cherry Bustos," she said. "Honoré del Castillo, a local Chicano activist."

When the smell of tequila hit Honoré, all he could see was Dr. Malecón's mouth, shiny with uneven gray teeth and a big tongue.

"A Chicano activist?" she asked. "I thought Olivia was the only chicanery in Escandón." She burst out laughing. Then suddenly, she weaved on her feet, burped, stumbling against Dr. Bustos. "Well, glad to meet you, señor." She offered him a pale dough-like hand.

Her grip was surprisingly powerful; he thought she was going to turn his fingers into mush. "*El gusto es mío*," he said, wincing.

Dr. Bustos, shoulders bouncing slightly as she chewed gum like a teenager, pushed her sunglasses back on her nose. "When will this *jale* be over, girls?"

"We've been waiting for you, Cherry," Olivia said, her tone so sweet she could have been a doting mother.

Then the women conferred. Cherry wanted to cancel the rest of the conference and head across the river to the cantinas in Nuevo Escandón while Dr. Malecón claimed she had lost her notes on the empowerment of women and didn't feel she could give the lecture. Olivia, surprisingly kind and sweet with the two drunks, kept talking.

The smell of perfume reached Honoré before the fingers touched his arm.

"Who are you, caballero?" asked the ballerina in cowboy boots.

She smelled too good to be true. "Honoré del Castillo, *a sus órdenes*."

"Honor of the Castle?" said Danielle with a smile. "And whose honor are you protecting today?"

"Mostly my own," he said with a chuckle. She wasn't cold or bitchy like Dr. de la O. He liked her.

He liked her even more when she flashed a fabulous leg as she raised her skirt and checked a seam in her black stocking. "I'll bet."

But she was dangerous. Not only did Dr. Malecón glower like a truck driver who had just climbed out of a tractor-trailer, sleeves rolled up on biceps ready to smash faces, but Dr. Bustos, her shoulders high and head held back in a defiant *'chuco* stance, was ready to rumble. Honoré felt he was back in middle school facing off a rival gang because he had flirted with one of their *rucas*.

Danielle squeezed Honoré's bicep. "So what do you do? You look like a bouncer." She giggled.

He told her.

"*Es un vato de atole*," said Ty.

Danielle ignored her. "Say again."

"I sell kitsch," he said.

"What?"

"Kitsch."

Dr. Malecón turned around like a Sherman tank rolling into position. "What did you say?"

Clearly and precisely, he repeated, "I said I sell *kitsch*."

Eyes spun behind the bifocals. "That's not what I heard. I heard *bitch*."

"Well, you may have heard that, but that's not what I said."

Cherry elbowed her way into the conversation. "What's the matter?"

"This shit-kicker said *bitch*," said Dr. Malecón.

Ty stood at his side. "No, he didn't. He said *kitsch*."

"I heard *witch*," said Cherry.

"He did not say *witch* or *bitch*," insisted Ty.

Olivia turned on her. "Stay out of this! You're always getting into things you don't understand!"

Cherry eyed Honoré over her sunglasses. "Those are fighting words where I come from."

"Not here!" said Olivia. "Ty, why did you bring him? Get him out of here!"

As Cherry swaggered into Honoré's face, he found himself admiring her mouth. "Do you think," she said, "you're man enough to back up those words?"

Cherry was a hot mama. Good-looking people had more in common with each other politically than anyone else. Honoré could not understand what she was doing with these dogs. "Señorita," he said in the respectful tone of a caballero from South Texas, "if you were a man, I'd gladly step outside with you. But you're a woman. My father taught me not to lay a hand on a woman. Especially if she deserves it."

She poked his shoulder with an exquisitely manicured finger. "Yeah? What else did your old man teach you?"

He stood tall in his boots, hands on his waist. "That it's better to get killed over a woman than to kill one."

Cherry turned to Olivia. "Man, where did you find this relic?"

Dr. Genoveva Malecón broke into a fit of laughter. "This is Texas, Cherry, for crying out loud! South Texas! The nineteenth century!"

"Girls, please!" cried Olivia. "Girls! Girls!"

Suddenly, Dr. Malecón, teetering at first, slammed into him. He went
flying into Cherry, who pushed him away, hard. As he toppled backwards,
arms flying, he accidentally slapped Olivia in the face. She screamed
and fell. After landing on the floor on his back, he rolled on his side and
considered scrambling to his feet like a high school quarterback about to
be pummeled as he looked for an opening to throw the ball. Instead, he
crossed his legs just before a Sherman tank in a black skirt and gray blouse
rolled over him.

"Girls! Girls! Girls!" squealed Olivia, struggling to get up.

Honoré's face was flattened on the polished floor, where he couldn't
avoid gazing at Olivia's red panties as she sat with her skirt up to her waist.
Was her underwear communist-inspired? Was this a *real* red scare?

"Girls! Girls! *¡Ya!* Stop it!"

More legs flew through the air, fat and white as cheese but with varicose
veins, and once again he found himself contemplating some red panties,
big ones this time, belonging to Dr. Malecón, who sat up and glared at
him as he tried to crawl away like an alligator but soon discovered that the
women's construction boots had steel toes. His ribs didn't collapse when a
woman kicked him, but he stopped breathing.

Worse, when Dr. Malecón put him in a headlock, he found himself staring at what looked like a mustache, pubic hair, or a tarantula crawling out
of an armpit. God, it smelled! As he tried to pull away, she cinched her grip
tighter. Suddenly, the women wearing construction boots sat on his back,
and he felt like the international bridge at five on a Friday afternoon.

He yelled, "Get off! My back is not a bridge!"

"Did you hear what this motherfucker said?" yelled Dr. Malecón. "He's
making fun of us!"

"*¡Dale en la madre al güey!*"

"*¡Todos los hombres son iguales!*"

"Animal!"

"Monster!"

On Monday morning, Honoré found himself in a bed at The Sisters of
Divine Providence Hospital. His mother called and told him she wanted
to visit him but couldn't because she was too tired and so sent the hogs,
who showed up with boxes of pizzas and sat there eating for an hour
without saying much. After Big Rig farted, Honoré summoned the nurse,
who kicked the two out and then came back and sprayed the room with
air freshener. As soon as she left, Rex, the FBI agent, phoned to report the

chisme throughout the law enforcement agencies downtown, laughing so loudly he sounded like a wild goose honking. Supposedly, Misty's father, Comino, spread the rumor that he had finally found out what was wrong with Honoré all these years—he was gay.

His neck still hurt, but the doctor said he would go home soon. From where he lay on his back in a neck brace, all he could see was an empty bed, a window, the television on a metal fixture hanging from the ceiling, and a crucifix above the entrance to the room. His biggest regret was not going to Lucero with Trotsky.

The door swung open slowly, and a young woman in green scrubs entered. "This way," she said. "In here."

A wheelchair hauling a man with a white turban on his head rolled into the bedroom. He looked like a terrorist. All he needed was a camel. But, no, it wasn't a turban. They were bandages, and a neck brace kept his chin in the air, but Honoré couldn't get a good look because his own brace kept him facing the ceiling. The nurse and a male orderly helped the new patient into the adjacent bed, holding his arm and pushing his butt until he was under the covers.

The nurse said, "The doctor will be here in an hour. If you need anything, just push the call button."

"Gracias," said the Arab in a familiar voice.

The nurse and orderly left. And now as the two men lay side by side in neck braces, Honoré felt slightly ridiculous. "Trotsky," he said, "is that you?"

"What the hell are you doing here?" asked a surprised Trotsky.

"I got beat up by some women. You?"

"All hell broke loose in Lucero."

Honoré spoke without moving his head. "I've been here since Friday night."

"What happened?"

Honoré wanted to sit up. Instead, he kept his eyes on the television, which hung there silent and asleep like a huge eye blinded by lack of interest.

He described Ty Cobb's poetry reading. "You should have seen her. Ten-gallon hat, cowboy boots, a huge belt buckle, jeans, a red bandana." Then Honoré described Mujica's poetry reading.

"Like newborns," said Trotsky, "we've started by naming our body parts. This is a Chicano cunt. This is a Chicano dick. This is Chicano shit."

"Taking my daughter was a big mistake," said Honoré.

Trotsky propped himself up with a pillow.

"Dr. Cherry Bustos and Dr. Genoveva Malecón showed up," added Honoré. "You know them?"

"By reputation only. Beauty and the beast."

"Are they lovers?"

"I hope not."

Honoré described the rumble. Trotsky laughed until his neck hurt so badly that he had to buzz the nurse. Fifteen minutes later she came into the room with a handful of painkillers, which she washed down his throat with a glass of water. Then she left.

Soon Trotsky sounded woozy. "Didn't Olivia do anything?"

Honoré rolled his eyes. "She screamed."

"And Mujica?"

He remembered the shapely legs in stockings under the ballerina skirt. "She screamed some more."

"And the rest of the women?"

"Ty helped, though not much."

Trotsky stretched out his legs. "Sickening. But what sickens me is Olivia saying that El Grupo Femenil isn't a political organization. She just refuses to help because she hates me."

People passed by in the hall. A door opened and closed. A young woman laughed. Rubber soles squeaked as they rushed down the polished floor. Wheels spun, and a young man laughed. Then the air conditioning came on, and fresh cool air flowed across Honoré's face.

"By the way," said Trotsky, "I must warn you. Next time you're at my house watch your tongue. My wife and I agree on most things, but there is one thing she's very sensitive about—Dr. Olivia de la O. She really doesn't like her, but she supports the feminist cause."

Honoré lay there thinking about what had happened at the women's conference. "Trotsky."

"What?"

Honoré hated asking stupid questions. "Don't you feel like a *pendejo* lying in that bed?"

"No. Why?"

"I do."

"So? What's a man without a contradiction?"

Honoré couldn't help but ask a stupid question. "Are *tortilleras* part of the revolution? Because if they are, the revolution is beginning to feel like a free-for-all among freaks."

"I'm afraid so," Trotsky said. "Sometimes things make sense, and some-times they don't. Sometimes your closest allies turn out to be your worst enemies. Do you know what all of this is called?

"No."

"History."

Outside, an engine droned in the sky. The chopping came close, a helicopter flying over the roof of the hospital, probably the helicopter that flew patients to San Antonio, coming so close he thought it would fly in the window at any moment. Then, like a pesky mosquito, it flew away.

Honoré looked at the constellation of tiny holes in the ceiling. "So what happened in Lucero?"

"Oh, man," said Trotsky, his voice picking up strength as it painted a picture of a Mexican village in the mountains of Nuevo León and soldiers with Indian faces arriving in trucks. "Imagine an entire company of Mex-ican soldiers marching over you as they beat everyone in the way with the butts of their rifles. There were *chingazos* for everyone. They were brutal with Don Sixto. He cursed them until they beat him unconscious."

Suddenly, the dull gray eye of the TV on the wall blinked. Wide awake, the screen livened up with a vivid blue until puffs of black smoke marred it and an airplane roared into the room. Piloted by a gringo with blue eyes and a yellow mustache, the B-25 bucked amid the explosions of flak. A WWII movie.

Trotsky turned off the TV. "Sorry," he said. "Hit the remote by accident."

The pilot reminded Honoré of his old buddy, the Governor, who had ac-cess to a private plane. "I think I know where I might find that plane Sixto asked for."

"Where?"

"First finish your story."

Trotsky cleared his throat. "Anyway, the army had *chingazos* for every-one. And the women hadn't counterattacked yet. I don't know what hap-pened. It was the most incredible thing I've ever seen. As you know, Lucero is known as the capital of witches in the region. Supposedly the witches cast some kind of spell on the town and removed the women's fears. Witches, ex-Priistas, and lesbians. Ex-Spaniards, mestizas, and Indians. No Chicanas or Mexican Americans. I was the only Chicano there. They went crazy and drove the Mexican army out of Lucero with everything they could get their hands on—machetes, kitchen knives, brooms. The rolling pins and skillets were deadly. The Mexican army didn't know what to do. They were ordered to shoot; they retreated instead. The last thing I remem-ber is watching a woman beating a soldier with a brassiere full of stones."

CHAPTER 6
The Governor and the Hog

A hog roared. Loud and frightening as a fighter jet strafing an anti-aircraft installation on a ship, the motorcycle belched and howled and throbbed down the strip. The Governor.

Honoré, getting up from his desk, smiled. Reluctantly. First because his neck was still sore. Second because asking his old sidekick for help wasn't a good idea. At one time the Governor, Tequila, and he had smuggled tons of pot across the river until they got busted on a dirt road east of Cotulla. Though they managed to escape into the *monte*, their little gang broke up, and the Governor left for California, where he got busted again and sent to the slammer. Then he came back and got in trouble with the sheriff.

Honoré headed toward the front of the store. While a porcelain owl tried staring him down in the hall, a flock of green and red parrots accosted him in the showroom. After the Savages had bought and carted off just about everything in the store, Honoré's mother got it into her head to order birds made of porcelain from Oaxaca, which she then hung from wires in the ceiling. At the front door, he paused, thinking twice about what he was going to do. Finally, he walked outside.

With silver spokes spinning and chrome handlebars flying high, the hog, rumbling and snorting, rolled into the dirt yard. The Governor, platinum-blond hair tied down with a red bandanna around his head and mirror sunglasses on his red face, brought the animal between his legs to a halt. On the seat behind him, a Mexican bombshell wore a cowboy hat tied with a leather thong under her chin. Tight, skimpy shorts showed shapely brown legs. Red cowboy boots clung to the side of the hog. Shades, black and eerie as eyes on a bumblebee, hid a gorgeous face, which looked vaguely familiar. But then all good-looking women looked vaguely familiar.

Honoré clambered down the steps. "Well, look who's here," he sneered. "Thought you were dead."

The Governor turned off the hog, which grunted and died. Then he cracked a smile while the bombshell put on a sweet but deadly grin. Honoré had seen that grin before. Probably couldn't speak a word of English, thought Honoré, but with the Governor she didn't have to, of course, since he didn't speak much English either.

"I heard *you* were dead," said the Governor.

Honoré felt the sunlight on his face. "Oh, really?"

"You know how this fucking town is. You can't fart in peace because everyone will hear it."

The sun was warm. "What did you hear?"

"I was down at the county courthouse when some tall, redheaded guy laughed and told some fat cop that a bunch of feminazis beat the shit out of you."

"That's pretty much what happened."

"So, Comandante," said the Governor, sounding congested as if he had stuck his nose in some trough brimming with female body fluids that morning. "What's up?"

The Governor had been in a nuthouse in Minnesota trying to get off horse. Maybe that's why his nose was running wild. "You finally dry out?"

The Governor took a cigarette from his sweat-stained khaki shirt and lit it. "Well, they didn't dry everything out." He inhaled and released the smoke in Honoré's face. "Honey, this here's the Comandante. Comandante, this here's Honey."

Honoré extended a hand. "*Mucho gusto.*"

"*El placer es mío,*" said Honey and shook his hand.

Her fingers were hot and clammy.

"The Governor and I are old friends," he said in Spanish.

"So I've heard," she said, her voice hollow as if her words contained nothing. That too was unusually familiar.

While the Governor had a knack for getting into trouble, his real talent was surviving it—the county jail, federal penitentiary, drug dealing and shootouts in California, migrant work in the San Joaquín Valley, and the boycotts with César Chávez. He was descended from bank robbers who had holed up in Escandón around the turn of the century and then made a bundle through crooked land deals and intermarriage with the local señoritas. Now he and his family were one of the wealthiest clans in South Texas. However, the local white aristocracy considered them scumbags—and the Governor, the worst of the lot.

One morning years ago, the Governor, an eye swollen, half-closed and black, limped into Honoré's store and asked if Honoré would get him some dynamite. The sheriff and his deputies had just beaten the shit out of him at the county jail. Honoré said he didn't sell dynamite but could get some for a good price across the river. Days later, they drove out to a ranch east of Escandón, where the Governor packed the sheriff's house with explosives. As the two stood a hundred yards from the house with the detonation box between them, the Governor offered Honoré the chance to do the honors.

Honoré shook his head. So the Governor plunged the handle, and the beautiful pink two-storey house with French doors exploded like a birthday cake crushed by a fist.

The Governor blew a ring of smoke. "So what's up, big daddy?"

Honoré stepped up close. "I got a problem." He measured his words. "I need to export some dolls to Mexico."

The Governor showed gray smoke-stained teeth. "Dolls? Like in guys and dolls?"

"Nope. Like toys."

Blue eyes glimmered. "Like in games? What kind of games? Cops and robbers?"

"More like cowboys and Indians."

"Cowboys and Indians?" The Governor grinned. "I'll bet. More like gringos and Meskins."

"Same thing."

The Governor glanced over his shoulder and said, "Honey, the Comandante and *yo hablar*." He nodded toward the store. "Go inside, *adentro*, where it's cool. You might want to buy *un regalo*."

The bombshell climbed off, pulling her shorts loose between her curvaceous buttocks as she pranced across the yard. Honoré had seen those chops before. All at once, it occurred to him who she might be. But the coincidence was too great—well, maybe not in a small border town like Escandón. In the meantime, he better keep his mouth shut.

The Governor stood. With his boot heel, he swung out the kickstand and leaned the machine against it. Then he dismounted and followed Honoré around the side of the store, past the cast iron bull, into the warehouse.

"Who's the broad?" asked Honoré.

"My maid."

Honoré halted. "*Chingao,* that's quite a maid."

Smoke unraveled past the face of the blond desperado. "Not only is she well made, but she's on the make. I may have to send her back to Mexico. All the women I've known are interested in only two things—my money and my dick, usually in that order. Says she loves me, but what she really wants is her papers."

"Does she have a twin?"

"Not that I know of. Why?"

"Just wondering."

At the back of the warehouse, Honoré opened the storage room and switched on a light. After pulling a tarpaulin off a stack of narrow wooden boxes the size of baby coffins, he said, "Any day now my brother-in-law Comino and his goons will raid this place. The only reason they haven't is because our daughters are good friends. That won't last forever. I've got to get these across the river *pronto*."

The Governor walked around the boxes. "Where you moving them to?"

"North of Monterrey."

The Governor rested his boot on a box. "Mind if I ask what's in the boxes."

Honoré frowned. "Does it matter?"

"No," said the Governor, a twinkle in his eye. "But I know it has to do with the revolution. Or should I say 'revolutions'? You've been involved in so many I can't keep count any longer."

"AK-47s."

Cigarette dangling from the side of his mouth, the Governor pulled off his black leather gloves and scratched his head. "It'll have to wait until after the honeymoon."

"What honeymoon?"

"The one that just got off the hog."

Honoré shook his head. "What? You have to be married to have a honeymoon."

The Governor took the cigarette out of his mouth. "A honeymoon is a month of honey—that's all."

Something tickled at the back of Honoré's throat. "Does that mean we can't move these guns for another month because you're too busy fucking?"

The Governor took his foot from the box. "She loves to ride the hog. Says she loves the way the hog makes her pussy feel. Better than a vibrator. How about two weeks?"

Frustration gripped Honoré's throat. "How about one week?"

"All right," said the Governor as his eyes roamed the warehouse. "I'll see what I can do, but it all depends on Honey." His gaze returned to Honoré. "She can take a lot of wear and tear, if you know what I mean, but a month of lovemaking in a week might be too much. Course a lot depends on how soon Cuz gets back from Montana."

"Hear he's been sick," said Honoré.

Cuz was not really the Governor's cousin. Honoré had nicknamed him "Cuz" so the politicos at the Washington Hotel wouldn't know who they were talking about whenever Honoré and the Governor ate lunch there. That was before the Governor was sent to the penitentiary. A pilot in Vietnam and member of a wealthy land-owning family in South Texas, half-Anglo and half-Hispanic, Cuz represented everything Honoré and his comrades-in-arms were fighting to overthrow—American imperialism. Cuz gave the Governor his nickname, and the Governor hated Cuz, but now they needed him.

"Cuz has a bunch of old planes," said the Governor as they walked out of the warehouse. "Maybe we can use one. That way, if we crash in Mexico, it won't be any big loss to anybody."

"Not a bad idea."

The Governor climbed back on the hog, pulled on his gloves, and threw his weight into the kick starter, the engine coughing and sputtering and farting. Honey came out of the store, carrying a beautiful owl made from enamel painted bright red, with splashes of yellow in the wings, with blue eyes under a black brow. Honoré had asked his mother not to order owls from Oaxaca, but she ordered them anyway as soon as she discovered they sold better than the parrots. This was the only one left, and Honoré was only too happy to get rid of it.

In long strides Honey crossed the yard. The Governor gazed at the owl indifferently and took out a wad of cash from his jeans as she climbed on the hog behind him.

Honoré declined the money. "Consider it a wedding gift."

The Governor, golden hair gleaming in the sunlight, put the money back in his pocket. After gunning the engine and filling the yard with the smell of an iron hog, he looked at Honoré from behind his mirror sunglasses. "Anyway, that's my story," he said, "and I'm sticking to it."

Money bought all kinds of trouble. So the worst thing that could have happened to the Governor after he got out of prison was that his father croaked and left him a fortune, which included a ranch northwest of Escandón on River Road, some commercial property downtown, and a big house in north Escandón. With plenty of money to squander, he was having a hard time staying off dope. So there was no telling what condition he might be in today as Honoré walked past a steel pole with the flag of Texas flopping from it and pushed a button on the iron-grill gate, which swung open electronically. He stepped inside the Governor's spacious veranda and stood before a thick dark wooden door.

Soon it opened, and there stood the Governor buck naked, his platinum blond hair a mess, face red and dazed from many hours between the sheets, legs covered with golden hair, and his dick raw, round, and uncooked as a big Vienna sausage from a just-snapped-open can.

"Comandante," said the Governor with a smoke-stained grin, "come right in."

Yellow walls rose high around a spiral staircase as they headed toward the living room and walked past the kitchen with its stainless steel stove. In the den at the side of the house, a large window opened on a huge back-yard, a swimming pool, and palm trees. Honoré tried to keep his eyes on the saltillo tile or the paintings on the wall, but the Governor's red buttocks kept getting in the way.

"How about a dead one?" asked the nudist.

"Sure."

"Honey," the Governor yelled in the direction of the kitchen, "two dead ones."

The Governor opened the back door and led Honoré outside. In a moment of déjà vu, Honoré thought he had stepped into the Garden of Eden again: the backyard was lush with thick grass, ears of cactus big as flour tortillas bristling with spines, mounds of red and yellow and blue flowers, and the slender, gray-ringed trunks of palm trees lolling against a blue sky. He sensed danger.

A wrought iron table with two chairs stood under a small palapa at the back of the house, where Honoré sat down. The view of the pool was nice.

The Governor dumped a pack of cigarettes on the table. "I forgot my matches," he said. "I'll be right back."

Dong swinging, he turned and walked away. Just then the back door opened again, and out pranced Honey, carrying a tray with two bottles of beer. After exchanging a few words with her, the Governor went inside.

Chills went down Honoré's back, his eyes ricocheting between the sparking bottle and the palm trees, as he wondered, how the hell do you keep your eyes off a woman's bare *maracas*?

As she bent over the table, one *maraca* hung in mid-air with a nipple ready to be deposited in his mouth like a drop of chocolate. He shuddered as he remembered that a pair of powerful tits just like these had knocked the shit out of him one night. Who the hell was this woman? It had to be the Aztec goddess.

He did not stand up as Mexican custom demanded; he couldn't. "Gracias."

Nonchalant as a fully dressed waitress in a restaurant on Tamaulipas Avenue, she glanced at him with a white-toothed smile that hit him like a surge of warm salt water on a beach in Acapulco. "It's good to see you again, hot dog," she murmured in Spanish.

Honoré sat up, a sudden snarling in his groin. "I thought I told you to leave town."

"I did."

"So what are you doing here?"

She peeked across her shoulder. "Shh. If I lose this job, I'll be out in the street. The Mexican mafia is looking for me."

He kept his voice low, "And if I tell the Governor?"

"Then I'll tell him you fucked me."

He gripped an armrest as she walked away. "*Pinche vieja cabrona*," he muttered.

But as soon as she went inside, he sighed with relief that he could sit there and not have to stare at her buttocks, brown and firm as clay from the river bottom, or those *maracas*, heavy and slow-moving and gripping as glue. The snarling waned.

The door opened again. Out walked the Governor, wearing a blue terry-cloth robe, hairy legs pale above the dark leather of his old, beat up cowboy boots. "Want to hear the latest on Cuz?" he asked and sat down.

Honoré picked up his beer. "Shoot."

The Governor lit a match and held it to a cigarette dangling from his lips as he cupped a hand around it. He flung the smoking match on the lawn. "Cuz doesn't trust a fucking doctor in this town, right? Can't say I blame him. So he flies all the way to Dallas. Walks in there, and they check him out. First thing they tell him is that he's a goner. If he doesn't go in for a quadruple bypass right there and then, he'll never see his wife or Escandón again. So they take him straight from the doctor's office to the operating table. They slice him down the middle, pull his ribcage open, and pin him back on the operating table just like a *cabrito* on a stick. Of course, we all know he's always had a bad heart, even before he began eating like a hog. So they cut up his legs, take out some veins, and do a plumbing job on his ticker. They put him back together like Humpty Dumpty. Tell him he's good for another five to ten years. You think a close brush with death would humble him. But no. Even after all that, the motherfucker thinks he's so superior he can't give me the time of day when we cross paths at the bank."

Honoré had never thought much of the aristocrats in Escandón, and he didn't especially like Cuz, who could be a stuck-up asshole. But he also knew that money is thicker than blood, and so he didn't want to speak badly about him. "You've got to feel sorry for the man," said Honoré. "No one wants to die before his time."

The Governor picked up his beer and looked thoughtfully at the swimming pool. "I've always felt sorry for that sonuvabitch." Then he cracked a smile. "Care to go for a swim?"

"No."

"Just peel off your clothes and plunge in."

Honoré smiled, too. "Maybe next time."

The Governor put down his beer and picked up his cigarette. "What Escandón needs is a nudist resort."

"Why?"

Smoke climbed past the Governor's red face. "Well, you know how narrow-minded people in this town are. They need to open up. We can start by taking off their clothes. First, we'll free their bodies; then, we'll free their minds. Nudity cleans you of all kinds of bad thinking. Gets you close to nature."

"Bullshit."

The Governor flicked some ashes on the grass. "No, listen. One time I was sunbathing at the ranch. Down by the river. Suddenly, I hear a helicopter. Sure enough, it's our pals, the BP. So I pull a towel over my face and chest, and I cross my legs so that you can't see the sausage. They fly over. Seconds later, they turn around, come back, stop, and hover. They do this at least two times. Bastards think they're looking at a naked woman. Then I open my legs." He chuckled. "They took off in a jiffy."

Honoré shook his head. The Governor was one of the craziest motherfuckers he had known. That's what a crazy father—and horse—had done to him.

The Governor flicked some more ashes. "They're supposed to be guarding the border, and all they need is a naked body to distract them. In the meantime, a terrorist might sneak across. Nudists don't ogle each other. Too busy enjoying their God-given birthright, which is freedom."

"You're just asking for trouble."

The Governor sucked on his cigarette and then blew rings of smoke that spun lazily across the table. "The only obstacle right now is Cuz. My aunt died and left me some property on River Road, which I want to develop. It has a nice lake, an A-frame bungalow with running water and restrooms. My aunt loved to take her family and friends out there. But she died without a will. So there's a dispute. Cuz claims she left my portion to him. Plus the road to the property runs right through his ranch. Until that's settled, I can't build the resort."

Honoré was not listening. The *maracas* were still on his mind. "What do you know about your maid?"

"Why?"

"Has it ever occurred to you that she might slice your throat in the middle of the night and rob you?"

The Governor closed his eyes in dismay. "Who do you think you're talking to? They don't call me the Governor for nothing. Look, she's from Matamoros. She used to be Dagoberto González's squeeze. Dagoberto is rotting away in a jail in Mexico. But his men are looking for her. Can't say I blame them. She's so hot she sizzles. Isn't she a doll?"

Then, remembering why he had come here, Honoré sat up straight. "What about the dolls?"

"Which dolls?"

"The AK-47's at my store. You promised you'd help me move them into Mexico."

The Governor flicked his cigarette again. "We've got a plane."

"From Cuz?"

"Yep."

"How?"

"Just like the old days. I pulled him aside one day at the bank and whispered some sweet nothings in his ear, told him I'd send someone to cut off his balls if he didn't cooperate."

Honoré nodded and smiled. "I miss the good old days."

"Well, they ain't over yet," the Governor said. "The problem is getting a pilot. After that last bust, some aren't flying until things cool down in Mexico. You know about the latest crash, right? Well, the pilot is pushing up daisies somewhere in Mexico. And two others are in prison right across the river. Waiting for a prisoner exchange to get back to the States. There's only one guy who might do it, a good pilot too, one of the best pilots for American Airlines and the CIA—Killeen."

A lizard of fear ran down Honoré's back. "That fucker is a drunk."

The Governor took a swig, swallowing hard as his face turned red. "I know. Can't fly 'less he's drunk. The drunker, the better."

The idea of flying into Mexico with a drunk and a heroin addict gave Honoré goose bumps. "One more thing."

The Governor wiped his mouth on the back of his sleeve. "Shoot."

"Have you given up *horse*back riding?"

Like the flowers in the garden, the Governor's blue eyes smiled. "What do you think, motherfucker?"

"The last time we worked together you were so strung out on that shit you almost got us killed. If Tequila and I hadn't been there to drag you out of the line of fire, you'd be dead today."

"And I ain't forgot, amigo. If I had, I wouldn't be risking getting blown out of the sky by a bunch of Meskins."

With red wings wide and sharp in the eerie fluorescent light that washed the small airport at night, the DC 3's two propellers flung sheets of hot air across the asphalt. Honey, in hip-hugging jeans and cowboy boots, ran ahead of Honoré, their boots clanging on metal steps as they climbed into the red belly through a side door. Bringing up the rear came the Governor. As soon as he stood in the cargo bay, he turned around and pulled a rope that transformed the steps into a passenger door, which he then slammed and fastened with a latch.

Cardboard boxes full of electronic parts didn't leave much space to maneuver in the cargo bay. The crates with the AK-47s lay hidden underneath. Suddenly, Honoré bumped into Honey, who glared and then smiled at him from under a perfectly plucked eyebrow. Then, she turned and climbed over a box into a tunnel-like crawl space lit by recess lights in the ceiling that led down the length of the plane to the cockpit. The Governor brought her on the trip at the last minute because she swore she had seen some of her former boyfriend's men in their neighborhood and refused to stay at the house alone. Behind her, Honoré crawled into the wake of an expensive coconut-scented perfume left by the valentine-shaped butt in tight jeans wobbling inches from his face. On all fours, he felt like a dog.

An old olive-green army field jacket hung from the bulkhead that separated a chair, bolted to the floor, from the cockpit where Killeen sat in the pilot's seat. Honey plopped herself in the chair while Honoré waited for the Governor to edge past and climb in the co-pilot's seat, where he sank behind the control yoke and put on headphones. Like rattlesnakes, wires coiled among two-way radios on an oil-stained table standing against the fuselage behind the Governor's seat. On the floor underneath the table, a long plastic funnel lay on its side. The windshield, which consisted of sharp narrow triangles of sturdy glass through which the darkness of the night poured into the cockpit, was smaller than he had expected. Outside, the engines idled, and the plane shuddered.

Headphones on, Killeen sat in the pilot's seat. With the control yoke at his lap and his fingers on the engine knobs, he turned to the Governor and yelled, "These fucking motors make so much noise, you can lose your hearing!" He glanced at Honoré. "Put your headsets on!"

Honoré took two headsets from among the radios on the table and handed one to Honey. After putting his on, Honoré dragged a small tool box from beneath the table, placed it at the foot of the doorframe, and sat down.

Killeen, the gold stripes on his captain's jacket glowing in the blue light of the control panel, growled, "Ready for takeoff."

"We haven't got any seatbelts back here," said Honoré.

Killeen spoke over his shoulder. "No problem. Just hold on tight."

Then he slowly pulled up the throttle as he peered out the windshield at the man in a red jumper walking backwards and eased the bird onto the runway. Weighed down with cargo, the plane taxied evenly across the asphalt, then gathered speed, which intensified as Killeen gunned the engine. The runway was long and smooth. Honoré wondered whether they would be able to take off with so much weight until Killeen pulled the yoke and the plane rose like magic over a small lake and swung over the lights of Escandón. Five minutes later, they crossed the border into Mexico.

The Governor turned to Killeen. "How about a drink?"

Killeen's eyes swam in a pool of blue light, his face deeply lined as if tattooed. His profile and the cut of his brown hair under his captain's hat must have had a dignified look when he worked for American Airlines. "Roger."

The Governor turned around in his seat. "Honey, how about some honey?"

"¿Qué?"

"Some tequila."

She reached for the box under her chair and opened it. She took a bottle from among the six the Governor had brought and handed it to Honoré, who passed it to the Governor. "Killeen used to work for the Company," the Governor said, as he poured tequila in a jigger. "This fucker can land on a dime in the middle of the night as long as he has plenty of booze."

Killeen wore his dark blue American Airlines suit, with neatly pressed lapels and gold around the sleeves. After the Governor got him out of jail in Nuevo Escandón smelling like a pig, they could find no other clothes for him to wear at the rundown motel where he was staying on Tamaulipas Avenue. Some homeless people had broken into his room and stolen his belongings. Like so many other American pilots Honoré had seen on the flights between Escandón and San Antonio, Killeen looked relaxed, experienced, and reliable.

But his hand trembled as it took the jigger of tequila. After downing it, he growled, "Ah, that hit the spot."

The Governor offered Honoré a glass. "Comandante?"

Nauseated by the rocking of the plane and the smell of tequila, Honoré shook his head. "No. Not yet."

The Governor's red face shuddered as the spirit of maguey went down. "Booze helps, but it ain't nothing like smack. Smack smacks. That's why they call it smack."

"Why does it smack?" asked Honoré, who had never understood or liked *tecatos.*

"Because when it hits you, you hardly feel it and it feels so good you don't have to get smashed."

"Well," said Honoré, an eye on the stars outside, "I just hope we don't smack into something."

"Or get smacked by someone," growled Killeen.

In the glow of the instrument panel lights, the Governor looked pink as roasted ham. "When you're smack in the middle of Aztec territory, anything can go wrong. But Killeen here has a knack for getting out of cracks."

"Cracks or crackups?" asked Honoré.

"What's the difference?"

Killeen turned toward them with a smile. "Depends. On whether you're talking to a crackhead or a crackpot."

The Governor's word games bored Honoré. "Can we cut the crap?"

"Not until I get a last crack at that bottle," said Killeen,

"Now that," grinned the Governor, "smacks of the truth."

Darkness covered the desert below as they droned south. According to the flight plan, they would fly toward Sabinas Hidalgo, then over the mountains to a ranch just north of Monterrey. Trotsky had already made arrangements, through Don Sixto, with a revolutionary committee that, with the help of some electronics smugglers, would receive the shipment. However, in order to make the run worthwhile for everyone at both ends, Killeen especially, most of the boxes contained electronic parts.

And there were risks. Much depended on how things worked out on the ground with the Mexican authorities, whether the right people were paid in time, whether word of the shipment got out. Sometimes things didn't go well. Earlier that year one bird was forced to land by the Mexican air force, and another was stopped at the end of a runway by submachine gun fire. Two pilots from Escandón were now serving time in federal prisons in Monterrey and Saltillo, and both had been left to rot by the investors who had underwritten the transport company.

"Just this month," said the Governor, "thirty-six pilots have been killed, all flying out of Escandón. Engines catching fire, slamming into the side of a mountain, or shot down by the Mexican army."

"It's risky business all right," said Honoré.

"Killeen here is a veteran. He'll never get out, will you?" said the Governor.

Killeen glanced at them with the smug look of someone who loved to talk about this. "First, there's the excitement of flying," he said, his voice full of stones. "But like everything else, that wears off. Then there's the money. That never wears off. Eight trips a day. Eight thousand dollars. Cash. No questions asked."

The Governor's voice was sour and groggy like he had been suffering all week from cedar fever, a terrible allergy to juniper pollen. "A lot of people in Escandón have made fortunes off that little airport. Some investors have slush funds for downed pilots. If a pilot lands in a Mexican prison, he gets a private cell, someone to cook for him, good food, and always plenty of pussy."

Suddenly, the plane shuddered, tossing as it hit turbulence, throwing the bottles in the box against each other. "Whoa," muttered Killeen.

The smell of tequila wafted through the dark. "You thinking what I'm thinking?" asked the Governor.

Killeen nodded. "Afraid so."

"We're in deep shit."

Killeen raised the bottle of tequila. "Is this all the fuel we got left?"

The Governor gave a flashlight to Honoré. "Check out the box."

Brandishing the flashlight like a lance, Honoré lit up Honey's legs. She smiled, then moved them aside. Hesitant as he crouched on the vibrating floor, he wondered briefly which of the two boxes he was supposed to check out, hers or the one underneath it, which he opened. The strong aroma of tequila rose from bottles that sparkled like the teeth of a shark under a beam of light. "Not one bottle left as far as I can tell."

Governor said, "We'll have to ration the booze.

Honoré returned to his seat.

Killeen put off taking the next drink until his face grew so pale he looked as if a noose had been tied around his neck and he was ready to be lynched. "I ain't feeling too good."

"Here," said the Governor.

Killeen's hand flew like a white dove in the light from the control panel, fingers opening like wings. "Just give me the fucking bottle."

"Now, now, Killeen, take it easy."

Killeen swallowed hard. "Ahhhh, that's better!"

The Governor wrested the bottle from the pilot's hand, slowly but firmly. "We need to save some for the flight back."

"Roger."

Ten minutes later, Honoré stood up to stretch his legs and got a glimpse outside as the plane skirted a pond of lights on the ground. "Sabinas Hidalgo," he said.

The Governor peeked outside. "That's a wild town. Honoré's family is from there."

"I've heard about it," growled Killeen.

"Honoré and I got into firefight with a rival gang. They tried to highjack us one night, but we got away. Your friend was with us. Tequila. One crazy motherfucker. What ever happened to him? Didn't he retire from the business?"

"He's thinking about getting back into it."

Honey leaned forward. "You know a guy named Tequila?" she asked.

The Governor glanced at her. "Yeah. Why? Do *you* know a guy named Tequila?"

She sat back. "No."

"You sure?"

"I'm sure, baby. 'Tequila' is a funny name for a man. I was just curious."

"Well, just remember one thing. Curiosity killed the cat."

She glanced at Honoré and then said to the Governor. "Baby, *por favor*. No jealousy, please."

Leaving Sabinas Hidalgo behind, they flew over the mountains and dropped into a valley. At length, they saw the lake of lights in the distance.

"Monterrey."

"We're not far off," said Killeen, his voice crisp over the intercom. "Better get ready."

"We won't be on the ground long," said the Governor. "Fifteen minutes at the most."

The plane veered east, flying along the city's periphery until they reached a dark, desolate area. The descent began. In the distance two tiny lights burrowed like fireflies through the middle of the night-covered desert. The plane banked steeply, plunged, and then flew low along a dirt road until the lights on the ground turned into the headlights of a pickup. Moments later, some flickering orange lights marked a makeshift landing strip, over which they zoomed. Killeen turned in a wide circle, came back, and aligned the plane with flames leaping from cans of kerosene. Honoré's stomach clenched. He wondered if a drunk could land on a dirt road in the middle of the night.

The wings glided evenly until the landing gear hit the ground and the plane bounced. Swaying from side to side like a huge cardboard box about to fall apart, it slowed, settled on its tail, and eased to a stop. The DC-3's headlights lit up the arms of joshua trees standing like giants in the middle of the desert.

Killeen remained in his seat while the Governor, Honey, and then Honoré crept through the tunnel to the back of the plane.

As soon as the Governor unlatched the door and pushed it open, the hot desert air leaped inside like an iguana scampering for cover. "You talk to them," he said to Honoré.

A pickup backed within inches of the door, and two men with flashlights jumped from the cab.

"Buenas noches, *jefe*," shouted a man. "*Somos del Comité Rojo de la Sultana. Y ustedes?*"

Honoré stood at the door. "*Somos amigos de Don Sixto de Nuevo Escandón.*"

The man climbed on the back of the pickup and peeked inside the plane. "*Malas noticias*. The *federales* are on their way."

"What happened?"

"Someone didn't get paid off."

"How far away?" asked Honoré.

"We don't know. Ten minutes, thirty minutes."

"Okay."

"*¡Rápido, muchachos!*" the man yelled at the rest of the men standing beside the truck. "*¡Si no, nos mandan a la chingada!*"

The Governor and Honey pushed a heavy cardboard box the size of a small air conditioning unit toward Honoré, who pushed it toward the Mexicans. They worked rapidly, shoving box after box across the metal floor. The wooden crates containing the dolls were the easiest to pull by the cord handles, but they were the heaviest and most unwieldy to lower from the plane. As soon as the pickup was filled, it took off, and another took its place. Boxes tumbled into the night until the metal floor and aluminum walls shone like the inside of a large, empty cigar canister.

"*¡Ya!*" shouted the man and the last of the pickups drove off.

Honoré slammed the door and locked it. Next, he followed the Governor and Honey to the cockpit, where they found Killeen passed out and the bottle of tequila in his hand.

"Oh, shit!" The Governor shook the pilot by the lapels and slapped him. "Killeen, wake up! We've gotta get this bird in the sky!"

Killeen raised his head, his eyelids pale as white grape skin in the beams of the flashlight. "I'll drink to that."

The Governor dragged him out of his seat and laid him on the floor. "We've gotta wake this guy up. Honey, got any coca?"

She sat on the chair and opened her bag. "No powder. Just tampons."

"With coca?"

"Yes," she said and handed him the stringed tampons in slender cardboard applicators. "*Aquí están.*"

"Perfect. Coked up, this guy can drink all three of us under the table," said the Governor to Honoré. "Pull down his pants."

Honoré untied the pilot's belt and rolled him on his side. Two masses of white flesh with pink pimples glowed like a cratered moon under the Governor's flashlight.

"I hate to do this greaseless," said the Governor.

Honey unscrewed a small bottle of Vaseline. "Here."

Like a skilled urologist, the Governor spread Killeen's cheeks with one hand and slipped the plastic applicator between them with the other, leaving a white string hanging from between the chunks of white cheese. "Turn him around."

Honoré sat the pilot up against the fuselage.

"Guess what?" said Honey. "I found some English Leather in your jacket."

"Perfect!" said the Governor, taking the funnel from the floor and kneeling next to Killeen. "Now open his mouth."

Honoré held the pilot's head back as the Governor put the funnel in his mouth and poured. Suddenly, the poor man's legs twitched. Then, his entire body shuddered as if an electric current ran through him; he sat, choking on the English Leather. He pushed the funnel away.

A beam of red light penetrated the cockpit like a blood-soaked javelin. "*¡Chingao!*" said Honey. "Look!"

Then a siren screamed, and a loudspeaker squawked. "*¡Alto! ¡Alto!*"

"The *federales!*"

Someone banged on the door. "*¡Policía! ¡Policía!*"

"Let me talk to them," said Honey. "I've dealt with these assholes before."

The pounding on the door intensified. The Governor put an arm around her shoulders and whispered in her ear. She nodded. "*Sí, sí.*"

The Governor turned to Killeen. "Got any weapons?"

"Some wrenches in the tool box is all," Killeen muttered.

The Governor walked past Honoré and squatted by the tool box. He pulled out two wrenches, one of which he slipped in his boot before standing up. "Killeen," he said, pausing for a moment as the pounding continued, "be ready to take off."

Killeen stood, wobbled, and pulled up his pants. Then he staggered back to the cockpit. "Roger."

The Governor handed Honoré the other wrench. "Put this in your boot."

"What's the plan?" Honoré asked,

The Governor turned to Honey. "Now listen, Honey, we need a first-rate show. Otherwise our ass is grass. *¿Comprendes?*"

"*¡Seguro que sí!*"

The Governor went first. Beams of flashlights exploded in their faces as they descended into a thicket of machine gun barrels. "We'll need a goddamn miracle to get us out of this," the Governor muttered over his shoulder to Honoré.

A male voice leaped from the darkness. "What did the gringo say?"

Another male voice joined in. "Hey, gringo, what you say?"

The Governor shouted, "Hello, amigos!"

"*¡Manos arriba!*"

Once a Mexican, always a Mexican, and all *real* Mexicans look alike. Short, brown, and fat, these greasers could have been Tequila's brothers or cousins. The only difference was that they wore brown uniforms and spoke Spanish so fast even Honoré couldn't understand them. A descendant of the Spanish conquistadors, he had never considered himself a *real* Mexican since his dear mother had done a good job reminding him of his European roots when he reached the age of reason. *Real* Mexicans were *indios patas rajadas*.

Now the Governor and Honoré, hands in the air, stood on the desert floor surrounded by five *federales*, when a strange whistle came from inside the airplane, so loud everyone heard it above the din of the engines.

"Look at what God has sent us!" yelled an officer, who shone his flashlight on the woman standing in the plane's entrance.

"*¡La Virgen de Guadalupe!*" yelled someone else and laughed.

"*¡Una bruja!*"

A short brown man with a swollen belly under his brown uniform aimed his flashlight from the foot of the ladder. "*¡Qué bruja ni qué bruja, pendejos! ¡Es una vieja bien buenota!*"

Amid the racket of the idling engines, Honoré could have sworn they were all barking and howling like dogs as perfume wafted through the night air and their tongues hung like pink ribbons on an Easter basket full of hard-boiled eggs.

Suddenly, she yelled, "Are *cuernos de chivo* the only things you can get up, *pendejos*?"

Everyone fell silent as she descended to the ladder's last rung. "Then show me some real *cuernos!*" she yelled.

Honoré was ready to howl like a dog when she pulled off the T-shirt and stood there in a thong and cowboy boots amid a frenzied bubble bath of flashlights licking every curve and shadow of her body. At first he thought he saw cup cakes, big ones. Then mangoes. Then boxing gloves. Yes, boxing gloves, which didn't waste much time in hitting him below the belt.

"*¡Pendejo!*" shouted the commanding officer as he stuck his flashlight in the face of the man at the foot of the ladder. "Arrest this woman!" He screamed at another, "Pull up your fucking pants!" He hit another man over the head with the flashlight. "And you, you imbecile, put that tiny thing back where it belongs! That's an embarrassment to a nation that takes pride in its manhood."

Suddenly, Honoré looked up and thought he saw a flying serpent, like the one on the Mexican flag. Impossible. Maybe a bird. At this hour of the night? Maybe a bat. No, it was thinner. Deadlier. It was a thong floating through the flashlight-pierced air before landing on top of the commander's head.

Blinded, he yelled, "*¡A la chingada!*"

The .45 semi-automatic exploded, shooting a yard-long white flame into the night sky. The Governor toppled over.

Ears ringing, Honoré ducked down on one knee. Then, after pulling the wrench from his boot and like a man possessed, he jumped to his feet and hit the officer over the head, who collapsed on top of the Governor. Since the other *federales* were still under Honey's spell, Honoré methodically knocked them out one at a time, turning hot dogs into a pile of tamales wrapped in brown uniforms on the desert floor, some with their pants halfway down their legs, tongues hanging out, still wagging.

Suddenly, the Governor crawled from under the officer and sat rubbing his ear. "What the fuck?"

Honoré grabbed his hand and pulled him to his feet. "You okay?"

"Yeah."

"Let's get the hell out of here!"

Honoré helped the Governor up the steps. After slamming the door behind them, Honoré followed him to the front of the plane, where Honey sat naked on her chair as she put on the field jacket. Her knockers wiggled.

Suddenly, a bullet ripped a hole in the windshield and whizzed past Honoré's head. "Holy shit!"

A spotlight lit up the end of the dirt road as jeeps and trucks aimed their beams at the plane. "There's more at the end of the runway," Killeen slurred.

"Motherfuckers!" cursed the Governor, climbing in the co-pilot's seat. "You sure you can fly this damned contraption?"

Killeen's hand trembled on the joystick. "Hell, yes!" he yelled and then burped as if he were farting. "On cocaine I can do anything. Hang on, cowboy! Keep your heads down!"

Honoré crouched behind the Governor as they taxied toward the *federales*. Most of the lights on the instrument panel went out as bullets hit the fuselage, and the wind roared through the bullet holes.

"No instruments," said Killeen.

With the cargo bay empty, the plane felt light and hollow as an enormous kite suddenly lifted by the wind, its string unwinding powerfully as the fragile piece of paper on a wooden cross rose into the heavens and just kept lifting until all they could hear was the hum of the engines and the wind.

"Man, that was close," said the Governor.

"Let's hope," said Killeen, "that the instruments are the only thing they hit."

Honey held up a brand new bottle of tequila. "Look what I found!"

"Here," said the Governor. "Let's party."

She gave him the bottle. "Let me put on my clothes. I'm cold."

The Governor opened the bottle and handed it to Killeen. Then he glanced at Honey. "I have a joy stick here that'll keep your bottom warm."

Killen drank from the bottle as if he were drinking a Coke. "Great stuff," he growled and wiped his mouth on the back of his hand.

The Governor took the bottle and offered it to Honoré. "How about a drink, señor?"

Honoré downed a shot, feeling the roots of the cactus spread through him almost immediately, the warmth soothing his stomach and then his throat and tongue. "Gracias," he said and returned the bottle.

Honey, wearing nothing but the Governor's army jacket, climbed into the cockpit and sat on the Governor's lap, wrapping an arm around his neck as she took a swig of tequila with the other.

"Nice and warm and cozy," said the Governor.

The plane hit some turbulence, dipping suddenly. "Whoa!" snarled Killeen. The engines droned steadily along until it bucked again, creaking and moaning in the wind. "This was not in the weather forecast."

All at once, it bucked hard, up and down, so hard that Honoré took flight. "Ahhhhh!" he yelled as he was thrown against the roof and hit his head, landing on his butt on the metal floor, where he lay, rubbing his head where a hot chile jalapeño sprouted.

Creaking and moaning, the plane went up and down. "Ahhh!" yelled Honey, her voice full of terror.

The Governor held her tightly on his lap. "Whoa! Hang in there."

The plane bucked again, and everyone yelled as if they were on a roller-coaster at the carnival in Escandón.

"Oh, my God!"

"We're gonna crash!"

"Ahhhhhhh!"

Then it was over, and the plane flew steadily, as if cruising along a flat surface.

"Ah!"

"Oh!"

"Ooh! Ah!"

What the hell? wondered Honoré as he sat up on the floor and saw Honey going up and down.

The plane bucked again, slightly.

"Oooooh!"

"Aaaaaaah!"

"Ooooooh!"

What the hell was he doing with these assholes? wondered Honoré. No matter how much he tried to get away from this shit, it was impossible. Then, he remembered that men like Trotsky and José Martí and all the heroes before them had dealt with this kind of shit way before him. If they were heroes, it was because they weren't assholes.

"Whoopee! Ride 'em, cowgirl!" yelled the Governor.

She cooed in his ear as they finished. "¡Qué rico chorizo!"

The Governor, his head lolling from side to side, muttered, "Man, oh man, what a ride! My kind of rodeo!"

Holding the army jacket shut around her waist, she climbed out of the cockpit, legs glistening with sweat. She smelled of cod liver oil.

"Sorry about that, Honoré," said the Governor with a wicked smile. "A man's got to do what a man's got to do."

Rubbing his head, Honoré reminded himself that beggars can't be choosers. "No problem. We delivered the guns."

Flying north over the mountains, they droned along for some time before they spotted a highway and flew a parallel course. When a streak of gold on the eastern horizon broke the grip of night, they came within sight of a city's lights.

"Sabinas Hidalgo," muttered Killeen.

Then he banked right, the plane humming steadily. In less than thirty minutes, they would get to the border.

Suddenly, two glints of blinking lights sped toward them.

"What's that?" asked Honoré.

"Moving too fast to be smugglers," said Killeen. "Must be jets."

"Jets?" Honoré peered over the Governor's shoulder. "I knew the Mexicans might send propeller planes but not jets."

Killeen wiped sweat from his cheek with the back of his hand. "The U.S. sells trainer jets to the Mexican government. They convert them into attack jets and use them for interdiction."

The Governor stared out the window. "Mexican air force ain't nothing to worry about. We've got anti-aircraft guns."

"You gotta be kidding," said Honoré.

After removing his headset, the Governor climbed out of the cockpit and swung the flashlight through the cargo bay. "Where's the funnel?"

Now dressed in jeans and boots, Honey found it under the table. "*Aquí*," she said.

The Governor took the funnel. "Follow me."

In the back of the plane, the Governor handed Honey the flashlight. "Hold this," he said.

Honoré stood next to Honey.

After removing the tarpaulin, the Governor knelt on the floor and stuck the funnel in the round mouth of a pipe rising from the floor like a fat cobra. "Here," he said to Honey.

Kneeling, she held the funnel in place.

"What's in the bags?" asked Honoré.

Crouching, the Governor untied a bag. "Balls."

"Balls?"

The Governor opened the bag and scooped out a handful of silver marbles that sparkled under Honoré's flashlight.

"Ball bearings," said Honoré.

"Like dogs in heat, those jets will nose right up behind us to check us out. Killeen will wag the plane's tail and change altitude. They'll follow us.

Then we give them a good *balling*, right up the nose. You'll see. Now go to the window and holler when they're behind us."

At the window Honoré peered outside. "They're still a ways off." Two or three minutes later, they swung up behind the DC-3. "Okay!"

"Roger!" Killeen shouted.

The plane climbed and banked. "Bombs away!" the Governor shouted.

The balls clicked and clacked against each other as they rolled out of the bag and into the funnel. Honoré couldn't see the hundreds of ball bearings pouring out the back of the plane, but he could hear them rattling as they went down the pipe. He looked out a window again. Banking in a wide circle, the cargo plane left a spiral of balls behind as if it were decorating a Christmas tree in the morning light.

Suddenly, the first jet let out a trail of smoke and swung to the right. The second pilot followed close behind.

Seconds later, the tiny figure of a man dangled at the end of a parachute bloating like a Portuguese man-of-war against the sky.

"How did you do that?" asked Honoré.

"All you need is one ball bearing to get sucked into a jet engine," said the Governor matter-of-factly. "We created a storm of balls."

The engines hummed steadily. "Where'd you learn that?" asked Honoré.

"From a pilot serving time in California. That's what he did when flying loads out of Colombia. It always worked."

A golden eastern horizon poured light across the desert. Ahead, a copper snake sparkled—the Rio Grande. Soon the snake slithered between the lights of Nuevo Escandón and Escandón, and a few minutes later they descended over the twin cities and banked toward the American side, toward the tiny airport, where long lines of landing lights burned steadily along the runway and a control tower stood watch.

"Goddammit!" shouted Killeen over the roar of the engine. "The landing gear ain't working!"

"What!" shouted the Governor.

"Get it down."

Killeen worked the controls frantically. "I'm trying."

"We got time," said the Governor.

Killeen yelled, "Oh, shit! We're losing power fast!"

"What's wrong?"

"They nicked one of the oil lines on the left engine! And the other engine is so old it won't hold up! We're going down—fast!"

"Can we make it to the lake?"

"Only God Almighty will get our asses out of this crack!" Killeen shouted over his shoulder.

The Governor turned to Honey. "Pray."

She frowned. "Why me?"

"Because you're a Meskin and Meskins are closer to God than gringos."

"*¡No mames, güey!*"

The Governor looked outside. "The lake! The lake! Head for the fucking lake!"

Killeen's face was red. "This fucker is not responding."

"Shut up, and head for the lake!"

"You know how to swim?" asked Killeen.

"Hell, no!" said the Governor.

"Me neither!"

"Well," said the Governor without taking his gaze from the window. "Looks like we'll have to learn pretty quick!"

The wings roared as they dropped over the water surrounded by barbecue pits, cement picnic tables, and palm trees, the plane's flaps opening and braking, skimming the surface of the water. Waves of shiny copper rose and fell in the morning sunlight, and the water smelled of dead fish.

The Governor, his face close to the windshield, shouted, "Ditch it!"

The water blinded Honoré. Then, he heard the noise out front and straightened up, pulling a towel from a rack on the wall. A motorcycle rumbled and coughed like a lion let loose in the yard. As soon as he finished drying his face, he stepped out of the restroom. Since his mother was dusting off the parrots in the front of the store, he opened the back door and walked around the side.

The Governor, his face sweating like he had just taken a hot shower or had come down with a bad cold, sat on the hog which he held upright with a boot on the dirt. "Howdy."

Honoré stopped at arm's length and peered. "You okay?"

"Sure. Why?"

"You look sick"

"Looks are deceiving."

The Governor's hand was cold as ice, pretty much as Honoré suspected. "You feel like death warmed over."

The Governor took a cigarette from a sweat-stained khaki shirt. "The dolls get through?"

"Yes. As a matter of fact, my friends asked me if we'd try it again, if you'd be interested in flying to Nicaragua."

The Governor lit the cigarette. "I wouldn't mind getting back into the business. But I'm really not interested in smuggling revolutionaries or guns."

That drop of sweat gathering on the tip of his pink nose meant only one thing. "You look like you've been *horse*back riding."

With blue eyes dilated, the Governor blinked slowly, lizard-like. "And you're beginning to sound like Cuz."

"Speaking of Cuz, what did he say about the crash?"

After sucking on the cigarette, the Governor released a stream of smoke. "When it got out on TV and newspapers that he was the owner of the plane that crashed in the lake, he went through the roof. He hates bad publicity."

A police car cruised past, a fat cop behind the steering wheel. "My wife," Honoré said, "wasn't too happy to see me on TV either. It's been two weeks now, and she's still pissed."

The Governor flicked some ash on the dirt. "Cuz wants to build a WWII museum on my aunt's property. He's even thinking of buying a Russian Mig. Wants to build an outdoor museum that'll teach Meskins in this town the price of freedom. He doesn't think they're very patriotic. Well, he's fucked up if he thinks he's getting my aunt's property. Over my dead body."

"I heard Killeen left town."

The Governor rested a hand on the handlebars. "Yep, died and gone to heaven."

"Killeen's dead?"

Sunlight split the Governor's blond hair. "Well, not quite. Should be, though. Went down. Carrying dope this time. Army showed up. Someone didn't get paid off again. Shot the plane out from under him. So he's doing time in a Mexican prison. But his investors are making sure he's taken care of. He'll probably get out in a year if the booze and the pussy don't kill him."

With the sun warming his back, Honoré stood tall, glad to be alive, glad to be home. "Can he still get it up?"

"Well, I don't know about that," said the Governor with a sly grin. "Killeen always said that as long as he has use of his eyes and tongue he'll be okay. Thank God I don't have to worry about that. I got plenty of pancakes at home, Meskin pancakes."

Honoré shifted his weight. "Oh, really? What's the difference between Meskin pancakes and gringo pancakes?"

"Meskin pancakes are spotted," the Governor said, "toasted nice and brown in places. Gringo pancakes are plain, blond."

"Which tastes better?"

The Governor gazed thoughtfully at Honoré through another stream of smoke. "I guess it all depends on the kind of syrup you pour on them."

Troubled by the drop of sweat dangling on the tip of the Governor's nose, Honoré said, "Can I ask you a personal question?"

"Shoot."

"Why don't you get off the smack?"

The sound of cars in the streets poured into the silence. "Because nothing gives a man like me more peace than smack. Better than poontang, to be honest."

Honoré stepped up close. "It's going to kill you."

"And the revolution is going to kill you."

Honoré kept his voice low and gentle. "You could help me. At least you won't die for some dumbass reason. You won't die like a *tecato* or a *pendejo*."

The Governor tossed the cigarette away. "Listen, Comandante. I gotta go."

Honoré put his hand on the Governor's shoulder. "Wait."

The Governor straightened the hog. "Look, right now I got to get back to the battle of the Alamo."

Honoré recalled the Texas flag in front of his Spanish colonial house. "Your house does look like the Alamo. Who's winning?"

Holding the handlebars firmly with both hands, the Governor aimed the front wheel toward the street. "Tough to tell."

"Well, thanks for everything."

Eyes half closed, the Governor gave Honoré a quick military salute. "Comandante," he said, "glad to be of service. Adiós."

"Adiós."

Then, gunning the engine, the Governor rolled out of the yard and stopped at the curb, where he looked up and down the street before skidding across the asphalt in a burst of gasoline fumes and rubber, straightening out and picking up speed. Farting like a hog and making as much racket as an AK-47, the Harley set off car alarms up and down the strip as the blond desperado sped home.

CHAPTER 7

Sex

Standing at home in the room once occupied by the death-dealing Third World technology of the Cold War, Honoré gazed at the two birds in the cage. Moving their beaks this way and that, caressing each other's necks, kissing, stroking each other's feathers, they made sweet noises, tweeting. At one time, his marriage had been like this. Everything seemed full of promise, not a dark cloud in the sky. Life was good. Now he lived in a world of idiots, and he suspected he was becoming one himself.

"These are the sounds of the universe," he muttered, "and this is the way things should be."

"Oh, really," said Maruca matter-of-factly, behind him.

Suddenly, dust shot up his nostrils as if he were caught up in a desert storm. "What's the matter?" he said.

Maruca swept past him with the broom. "Why?"

"Looks like you're mad."

She went on sweeping to the end of the room. "Nothing's the matter."

"Doesn't look like it, not the way you're handling that broom."

"Can't you see I'm busy?"

It had been like this for more than two weeks. He had tried to talk to her, buying her flowers, leaving them on her bed, cleaning up after himself, watching his tone of voice. He had even cut an opening on the side of a log-shaped piece of mesquite so the canaries could build a nest where the ladybird could lay her eggs. But nothing did the trick, and the nights had been lonely.

However, the birds' sweet noises reminded him that anything was possible. "Look at these birds. That's the way things ought to be between men and women."

Maruca swept past again, flinging dust in his face. "That's what my mother—may she rest in peace—said."

His mother-in-law was an idiot. "Your mother said a lot of things."

Maruca stopped, broom upright in one hand. "She said men and women should live in harmony, just like those birds. But she said it's impossible."

With her long black hair falling past her dark razor-sharp eyes, Maruca looked lovely but deadly. "Why?" he asked.

She swept past him. "Because men are swine. Beasts. Men may have beautiful, faithful wives, but because they're swine, they go after the first *puta* that walks past them."

"She was talking about your father." The broomstick missed his head by less than an inch. "Maruca! Goddamnit, stop it!"

Someone ran down the stairs. The tiles in the kitchen squeaked. Pigtails flying, Bonita skipped into the room. She stood before the bird cage and screamed. "Oh, Dad, look at the tweety birds!" She put her nose to the wires. "How cute! Dad, come here! Look! They're building a nest. They're getting ready to have a baby. See? They're building a nest in the log. They look so happy."

Maruca stood with the dustpan in one hand and the broom in the other. "Have you cleaned your room?"

"Can I feed the lovebirds first?"

"No."

Bonita's face collapsed. "Mom, please!"

Suddenly, Maruca stiffened as her eyes settled on the floor by the cage. She crossed the room and got down on one knee. Slowly, she rose, and with a pink sock dangling between two fingers, she turned to her daughter. "What's this?"

Bonita gaped at the sock. "Mom, please."

"Bonita, I don't see how you and your father can stand living in a mess. Look at this! Didn't I tell you to pick up after yourself?"

"Mother!"

Maruca moved in close, dangling the sock in Bonita's face. "I already told you I don't want to raise a daughter who can't do anything, can't cook, can't clean, can't look after herself or her children."

Bonita looked at Honoré, then Maruca. "Mom, what's wrong?"

She thrust the sock in Bonita's hand. "Look at those canaries. No one has to be after them to do what they're supposed to do."

Bonita turned to Honoré. "Dad, what's wrong with Mom?"

Maruca grabbed her by the arm. "Pay attention when I speak to you!"

"Sorry, Mom."

Maruca let go. "Today, young women can't do anything for themselves. All because of these so-called revolutionary ideas about men and women. The first thing a woman needs to understand is that she is not a man. And because a woman is not a man, she lives in a dangerous world."

Bonita rolled her eyes. "Mom, I'm only thirteen."

"Well, that's exactly why I'm telling you this. When my mother first told me all of this, I thought she was so old fashioned. Over the years I've seen what's happened to many of my friends from high school, all because their mothers never taught them how to be women. Today in Escandón we have an army of single mothers on welfare. Children by different fathers. No dignity. No shame."

"Mom!"

"What?"

"Please!"

Maruca thrust the dustpan in Bonita's hands. "I don't want you coming back and having me raise my grandchildren. So first clean your room and then feed the lovebirds."

Bonita made an ugly face. Maruca pointed at the door. "Don't make that face or you'll be grounded the rest of the day."

Bonita left.

Honoré, who dreaded fights between women, peered out the window. "The day looks yellow."

"It's the hurricane."

"Is that why it's been so humid?"

The phone rang. "Would you get that?" she said. "If it's for me, tell them I'm busy."

He walked to the kitchen and picked it up. "*Bueno.*"

Rig's breathing was heavy. "Doña Pánfila is sick."

"Well, give her some medicine."

His speech was slurred. "She wants to go home."

"Well, then take her home."

Like a spoiled woman, his cousin let out a long sigh. "The truck won't start. We forgot to get gas last night."

Rage sent chills down his arms and legs, into his gut, his tongue. Honoré hung up, then tried calming down before returning to the den, where Maruca sliced him from head to foot with a nasty look. "What's bothering you?" he asked.

She swept toward him. "I already told you!"

He grabbed the broom. "No, you didn't!"

She pulled back. "Stop it! Let go!"

He refused. "Trotsky? The dolls? Is that it?"

"What about that whore?"

"What whore?"

"The Governor's *movida.* My brother told me all about her. She's the same bitch that got involved with that idiot across the street."

"I didn't want her on the trip, but the Governor wouldn't listen."

"Next thing I hear is that you're back in the business."

"I had nothing to do with that woman."

"What about all the other things?"

He let go. "What things?"

"Sixto, Lucero, Dr. de la O, and those lesbians who almost killed you. Why did you expose Bonita to all that crap? Why do I have to worry all the time whether you're coming home or not? This is worse than when you were smuggling dope."

"And what about your family?"

"Leave my family out of this!"

His voice thickened. "Look at your cousin, shot and killed over a bad drug deal just a few months ago. Look at Comino and all of his illegal bull-shit. Look at the people of Escandón. This is the way people live here. This place is a war zone. This is *la frontera*. The Wild West, in Technicolor. What do you expect? At least I'm trying to do something good."

Her voice rang throughout the house. "I don't care how our neighbors live! I don't care how the people of Escandón live! All I want is peace!"

He stormed into the yellow gloom. He tripped on a root big as an arm sticking from the dirt and nearly slammed into the *cubreviento*. Halting inches from the thick, gray trunk, he looked around. A weird stillness reek-ing of electricity and danger had descended over the barrio while a flotilla of dark iron-bottom clouds waited on the horizon. Suddenly, a strange whistle came from the tree. What could that be? Must be his ears, still ring-ing from the screaming match.

He climbed in the truck. As he drove around the block and headed west toward the highway, he turned on the radio. A somber voice announced that they would soon feel the effects of the hurricane in the Gulf of Mexico. A tornado watch was in effect.

At the store everything was doom and gloom. The venetian blinds were shut, nobody inside, no radio blaring butt-swinging cumbias, no dogs wandering around, no customers, no traffic. After parking, he walked to the back of the store, where snores rumbled from inside.

He stopped. Worse, the shit-like smell of pot turned his stomach.

He opened the door. In the back room the hogs were stretched out like huge pork chops, their heads thrown back on the couch, eyes closed, stoned on their asses, while his mother sat in her rocking chair in front of the television, smoking a thick cigar. Empty boxes of pizza lay in stacks.

"Mom," he said as he took the cigar from her, "what are you doing?"

"Why didn't you tell me about *los churros*?"

He doused the *churro* with water in the sink and then dumped it in the trashcan. "Mom, are you okay?"

Bloodshot eyes tried to focus on him. "What'd you say?"

"Are you okay?"

"I've never felt better."

He slipped an arm under her and picked her up. "I'm taking you home."

"Don't worry about me. Put me down!"

She was stiff and dry as mesquite. "I'm taking you home."

While the hogs snored, he backed out of the room with her. Next, he carried her around the side of the store and eased her into the pickup's cab, where she fell asleep with her gray head against the window. After making a U-turn on Tamaulipas Avenue, he headed south, about six blocks, made a left turn, sped under the highway, and barreled toward Las Lomas, a neighborhood of two-storey clapboard houses that had once provided housing for the Air Force base before it was closed in the seventies.

He drove around the back of a hill overlooking the neighborhood, now infested with drug dealers, and stopped in front of an old wooden one-storey house with a tin roof. A barbed wire fence held up by wooden posts enclosed a yard full of prickly pears and mesquite and palm trees. Two dust-covered cars on rims lay in back. The house had not been painted or repaired in years because his mother wanted everything to stay the same as the day his father died. Honoré honked.

Lupita, a short skinny but sturdy black-haired woman with a grave arrowhead-sharp face, came outside. She held the door open as he carried his mother up the front stairs.

"What happened?" she asked as she followed him to a bedroom at the end of the hall. "Is she sick?"

"She's just tired," he said, gingerly laying her on the bed.

Lupita took off the old woman's boots. After putting a pillow under her head and throwing a thin blanket over her, Lupita asked, "Why are her eyes red?"

"An eye infection," he said and then stomped out of the house.

A bull with sharp horns and a muscle-bound body ready to undo any bullfighter glared at Honoré as he marched past. Huge dark brown doors, recently imported from a monastery in Puebla, stood against the side of the store. The warehouse was jam-packed again with new merchandise. Outside the store's back entrance, he paused, listened, sniffed the air. Nothing.

Then he opened the door and stormed inside. "Okay, motherfuckers!" he yelled as he pulled Rig from the couch by the scruff of his neck and dumped him on the floor like a sack of flour.

Rig yelled, "Boss, I can explain everything!"

"Don't give me that 'boss' shit!" Honoré shouted, then kicked him in the ass, so big his boot almost got caught in it.

"Ouch!" whined the hog. "That hurt!"

"On your feet!" Honoré yelled and grabbed him by the shirt. "I'm sick of dealing with you motherfuckers!"

"Doña Pánfila!"

"Doña Pánfila is gone!"

"I want to talk to her!"

"You're not talking to anyone!"

Finally, Cachetes sat up, rubbing his eyes. "Are you sure you know what you're doing, boss?" he whined like a spoiled woman, a bitch, or a faggot. "I don't think you want us talking to your FBI friend about all the shit you're into."

With a clenched fist ready to fly, Honoré froze. "What?"

"You heard what I said," Cachetes whined.

In one stride Honoré crossed the room and grabbed him by the collar. "Listen, asshole, imbecile, pork chop. If you breathe a word to my political enemies, you're headed to the slaughterhouse in Nuevo Escandón, where my friends will turn you into pork sausage for the dogs."

Eyes filling with tears, Cachetes squeaked, "Okay, boss, okay!"

Honoré thrust him away. "Now get the fuck out of here! And don't come back! You're fired!"

Most women had more dignity than these idiots. In fact, Honoré could no longer tell if they were men or women. Pizza and hamburgers and malt shakes and Coke and pot and TV and shitty wishy-washy teachers and slobs for parents and the American nightmare had turned them into hogs crawling on all fours out the back of the store.

The phone rang. He slammed the door shut and ran to his office. "Castillo's Mexican Curios."

"What's the matter?"

"Why?"

Maruca's voice was as unkind as ever. "You sound like you're ready to have a heart attack."

He paused, caught his breath, and glanced out the window. "I just fired the hogs."

"What about your mother?"

In the front yard, the hogs waddled toward the street, taking forever to leave. "I took her home. Bonita should stay with her tonight. I don't want those assholes spending the night over there anymore."

"When are you coming home?"

The hogs crossed the street, headed straight for Pizza Hut. "I don't know," he said. "Probably late."

"Can you get some bird seed?"

"Bird seed?"

"Yes, for Bonita's birds."

Suddenly, brakes squealed as a U-Haul rumbled to a stop in the street, tailed by a beat-up van. "Look, I gotta go. Some customers just arrived." He stood up.

"When will you be home?"

"As soon as I finish with the gringos."

The Savages had done such a good job of promoting their store in Mississippi that a bunch of their friends and their children climbed out of the vehicles. Their mothers, wearing cuffed biker shorts and pink tank tops overflowing with big tits, stood on chunky white legs and flip flops as they lit cigarettes and watched their children run wild in the yard, while the men, with long blond hair down to their shoulders and sporting muscle-bound sun-toasted arms, marched toward the store. Honoré met them on the porch.

"Señor Savage sends his regards," said a lanky man with a hillbilly twang and shifty blue eyes. A gray work shirt over gray work pants and black army boots and black leather belt with a brass buckle reminded Honoré of a Confederate soldier. The man smelled like a mechanic. And of booze.

"How's the old man doing?" asked Honoré.

"Fine."

"Ma Savage?"

"Mean as ever."

By noon, Honoré sat in his office, astonished by bundles of green cash big as heads of lettuce rolling across his desk, more than they had made in weeks. "Gracias," said Honoré, writing out a receipt. "Any word on Johnny Paint and Tennessee?"

"They're in jail."

Honoré looked at the man. "What happened?"

"DEA busted their asses smuggling dope inside tin men."

Honoré closed early that afternoon and headed out to the ChiChiB, which was what Escandonians called the new H-E-B supermarket across the highway from his store. Two pointed canopies on metal poles tied down with rope in front of the store's entrance looked like the cups on Madonna's cone-shaped brassiere. He parked and walked inside.

Red balloons rolled down the cement floor of an aisle as kids chased them and the mother chased the kids. More balloons, big balloons—no, beach balls—rolled toward him. But these were not balloons or beach balls. They were people, fat people, dressed like overgrown kids in cutoff shorts and sandals and floppy T-shirts. You would have thought they were gringos, who dressed any which old way, but most of these were Escandonians. The rest were *real* Mexicans—that is, Mexicans from Mexico.

He turned down the third aisle and walked into the smell of soap, which reminded him of Maruca's obsession with housecleaning chores and the small pleasures of domesticity. No danger here. It was a place for housewives and old men.

He walked to the next aisle.

A dog glared at him. Not a real dog. The picture of a dog on a package of dog food.

He turned. Now yellow eyeballs gazed at him amid white whiskers—a cute little monster, a cat. Dogs and cats live better in America than most people in Latin America, he thought as he headed down the aisle.

Where was the bird seed?

He hunted for a bird among the cans of dog and cat food, leashes, and spiked collars, which reminded him of Ty Cobb and her friends from California. The American identity was so fucked up that Americans often had no choice but to identify with their pets. In fact, some women were turning to dog trainers to help them domesticate their husbands.

"Wild birds!" he read on a bag.

But where's the seed for love birds?

He paused, wondering, what was a love bird? Was it a cockatiel? A cockatoo? What's the difference?

A bird peeked at him from a bag plump with sunflower seeds. Another bag swelled with khaki-colored pellets that resembled bird shit. Parakeets? Maybe, he thought and picked up a plastic bag full of the seeds, tiny and white and black, mixed like cereal.

He headed to the front of the store with the bag. A ten-year-old girl blocking the aisle glanced at him with blue eyes and then said something to her mother in perfect Spanish.

Mexicans, thought Honoré. *Real* Mexicans.

The mother, light-skinned, with blue eyes like the daughter's, ignored her as she raised a lovely foot with toenails polished red and put on a slipper that was on sale, her skirt opening the length of her long white legs all the way to her panties, red with blue lace. Slowly, she raised her head. Unsmiling, she arched an eyebrow at Honoré, as if saying, "How dare you look at my pussy?"

And he felt like telling her, "Why the hell are you flashing your pussy in public?"

Moments later, he stood in line at the cash register trying to recover from the kick in the balls. She didn't kick him, of course, but that's how the *taco de ojo*, an eyeful of skin, left him. Aroused, he walked out of the supermarket like a cripple, slowly and deliberately. Fresh air didn't help. You need some saltpeter, he told himself.

In the parking lot, a drop of water blinded him. He stopped, wiped an eye. In the sky, an armada of dark gray battleships had gathered for an attack. Suddenly, a fine drizzle broke. People ran. Sun-pierced drops of water struck the asphalt like gold needles.

"*¡Chingao!*" he cursed as he climbed in the truck and slammed the door.

Lightning flashed as the battleships released their barrage. Rain fell in torrents, flooding the windshield, the parking lot. He didn't know whether to sit tight or head home. Eventually, someone turned on their headlights and took off. Honoré followed, slowly. While the car turned right on the avenue and headed west, Honoré turned left, windshield wipers flapping back and forth. Like a gold-filled eye, the sun winked at him from beneath a black eyebrow of a cloud as thunder rolled across the earth and the wind grabbed his pickup and shook it hard.

After a long tedious ride through congested streets, he parked in front of his house, where the wind pulled the *cubreviento* back and forth. With the bird seed under his arm, he jumped from the pickup and splashed through puddles. Soaking wet, he unlocked the door.

"Maruca!" he yelled in the living room.

No answer.

After closing the front door, he went to the kitchen. "Maruca!"

Honoré heard the front door fly open and someone yell. "*¡Pinche huracán! ¡Me ha mandado todo a la chingada!*"

Honoré walked into the living room, where Tequila stood in a puddle, his hair wet, eyes blinking, shirt and pants soaked. "What's wrong?"

"The *pinche huracán* knocked down the observatory. Now there's a big hole in the roof of the house and everything is getting wet. The electricity is off. The phone is dead."

Honoré led him to the phone in the kitchen.

Tequila dialed. "Pancho? *Oyes, cabrón. El huracán me ha mandado todo a la chingada.* Get your ass over here. Close down the shop. Yes. Good. And bring the tarpaulin. Yes—oh, and a ladder. *Lógico*—oh, and some wood. *¡Ándale! ¡Pronto!*"

He hung up the phone and turned to Honoré. "I need your help."

"Apá! Apá!" The door opened, and there stood four-eyed Tercero. "Amá is going crazy! Come. Hurry!"

"*¡Vámonos!*" said Tequila.

Honoré took off with them, running out the front door and into the cold downpour, splashing through the stream hurtling down the street, wading through the lake on Tequila's lawn, and dashing inside.

Señora Cuervo, rosary dangling from one hand, stood in the kitchen yelling, hands held out in supplication to the heavens. "The world is coming to an end! It's the apocalypse! *¡Es el diluvio!* Save us, Almighty God!"

Tequila grabbed Tercero's shoulder. "Take her to her bedroom. Give her a shot of tequila. Keep her there until I get back."

"Dad."

"What?"

Behind his glasses, Tercero's eyes looked like raw oysters. "Mom doesn't drink tequila."

"Then give her some valium. She eats that stuff like candy."

"No, she doesn't."

"Shut up and do as I say."

Then Honoré followed Tequila out the back and up the stairs to the observatory. The wind had blown the telescope to one end of the room and the papers were sticking to the walls, and books lay open and wet. *Playboys* lay scattered all over the place, tits and ass everywhere.

Honoré shook his head. "The wages of sin."

"*No mames.*"

Outside, a car honked. "Pancho," muttered Tequila.

Honoré followed him downstairs. After helping him and Pancho carry the tarpaulin, a ladder, and some planks to the observatory, Honoré climbed through the hole in the roof, where the wind was blowing so hard that the tarpaulin filled like a sail on a ship and threatened to carry him off. As soon as the two men joined him, he fell and slid to the edge of the roof but clung on all fours until Pancho pulled him back up.

When lightning struck not far away like an arrow hitting a bull's eye and a thunderclap shook the world, Tequila yelled, "Hurry! *¡Si no, nos mandan a la chingada!*"

As soon they finished nailing the tarpaulin on the roof, holding it down with boards, they climbed down a tree on the side of the house, their faces streaming with water.

In the washroom Tequila gave them towels, and they dried themselves. Afterward, he went to check on his wife, dripping water on the tile floor all way into the living room.

Honoré and Pancho followed him and waited next to the front door.

As soon as Tequila returned, Pancho said, "I gotta go, *jefe*. Call me if you need more help."

"No, wait," said Tequila.

Pancho opened the front door. "For what?"

Honoré stepped outside. Suddenly, the sky lit up as if a huge acetylene torch had been ignited, and again Honoré had that sinking feeling he was glimpsing into the bowels of hell.

Suddenly, a blinding white light shaped like a pitchfork struck the *cubreviento* in front of his house.

"*¡Mira, cabrón!*" yelled Tequila and pointed.

Amid a rolling thunder of railroad cars hooking up across the sky, the *cubreviento* wavered, looking like it was about to fall on the house, then toppled toward the street, bringing down the power lines with it in explosions of electricity that turned the wires into snakes sizzling and snapping in the water.

"*¡A la chingada!*" said Tequila.

As they crossed the street, Pancho warned, "*¡Águila! ¡Águila!* Watch out for those wires!"

"*¡Mira!*" said Tequila and stopped.

A huge black bird crawled from among the limbs, opening its wings as it hopped around in the street. Then it spread its wings, hopped once more, and took flight.

"*¡Una lechuza!*" said Pancho.

Standing shoulder to shoulder with Honoré, Tequila said, "That means only thing."

"Bullshit!" said Honoré.

Out of the house stepped Maruca, long legs in tight-fitting jeans and sandals on bare feet. For a moment Honoré forgot where he was and what happened to the tree and remembered why he had married this beautiful woman. All at once, it hit him that she was too beautiful to live in such an ugly house. She was right. They needed a nice house in north Escandón.

"Oh my God!" said Maruca as she stared at the fallen tree. "I knew this was going to happen!"

More thunder rolled across the heavens as another armada of gray battleships appeared and a drop of water hit Honoré in the eye. "We better go inside before we get killed."

Yellow and gloomy, Honoré stopped before the mirror in the stairwell and wondered where he got the notion that he was handsome. From women, of course, especially his mother, who always reminded him that he came from good stock—Spaniards, not Indians like Tequila or Maruca.

Good looks meant good genes. Social standing, even if you didn't deserve it. But did they mean sanity? Though good-looking, his uncles and cousins were insane—smugglers, coyotes, drunks, whoremongers, liars, thieves. The women were worse—great beauties, saints, and ballcutters. His mother was the exception. Well, maybe not. She had spoiled him rotten, raising him so he couldn't live without a woman.

He climbed the stairs. After walking past Bonita's empty room, he opened the door at the end of the narrow hall and entered the master bedroom. He thought Maruca was still downstairs until he saw the light under the bathroom door and heard the water in the shower.

He sat down in his chair by the window and stared outside. Rumbling, the battleships were moving on, leaving the *cubreviento* lying in the yard like the leg of a fallen elephant. It was late afternoon. He thought about the past.

Since he had always wanted to court Maruca the way Mexicans court women in the Mexican movies his mother loved to watch, he arrived at her house in the barrio one night with a band of mariachis smuggled from across the river. Her father and mother loved it, but her brother Comino hated him from the moment Honoré stood in the light cast by a streetlamp and waited for her to come to her window on the second floor. If he could, he would have sung. Instead, his bosom buddy, Tequila, sang a solo like Pedro Infante. He was terrific. A scene straight out of a Mexican movie. After that evening, Honoré and Maruca went everywhere together—the prom, football, and rallies, *quinceañeras* and weddings, and then the nightclubs in Nuevo Escandón. Everyone envied them.

One Sunday about fourteen years ago, she came to the store to do her homework. They were still in high school. He had just quit the football team because he had to help his mother at the store on the weekends. Both eighteen, they would graduate that year. So while he worked on the books in the office, Maruca studied in the room in back. When it was time to take a break, he walked back there—and that's when he saw her black hair shiny as a crow's feathers in afternoon light, her eyes curious and tender, and her lovely ankle dangling from the side of the couch. Pink nail polish glimmered on her toes. He kneeled and kissed them. Then, he kissed her hand. Then, he kissed her mouth. Then, they lay together on the couch and kissed for an hour. He spent another hour taking off her clothes, her shoes, then her socks, her blouse, her bra, her jeans, and then her panties. For weeks, he refused to wash his right hand.

Pipes shrieked throughout the house when Maruca turned off the water. The bathroom door opened. Black hair damp and shiny, barefoot on the tiles, she walked into the room wrapped in a white terrycloth robe. "Bonita called and said your mother is okay," she said as she sat on her bed.

"Good."

"How are you going to run the store without your cousins?"

He crossed his legs, propping an ankle on a knee. "I'll find some help. The men here in the barrio are always looking for work."

She rubbed her hair with a towel. "What if your mother takes your cousins back?"

He pulled off a boot. "Look, my mother is dying. If she takes back those idiots, not only are they going to kill her soon but they're going to bankrupt the store." He pulled off his other boot. "I won't hire them no matter what she says."

"Well, someone has to take over that store and run it the way it's supposed to be run. Otherwise we'll end up in the street."

He sat back, sighed. The writing was on the wall, had been for a long time. He just refused to see it. If he didn't start laying plans to transfer the property to his name, it would be lost like everything else his family once had. But that meant giving up his work with Trotsky.

His mother compared him to a street lamp once. "*Luz de la calle, oscuridad de su casa,*" she said, meaning that while he might "light up" the street he kept his home in "darkness."

He was doomed.

Eventually, Maruca said, "Guess what? I saw the cutest, most beautiful house I've ever seen, brick-veneer, red-tile roof, a nice lawn, a big yard, lots of nice shade trees, and a carport. And nice neighbors. Very cheap, too. We could sell this one or rent it and pay for that one. What do you think?"

"Sure," he muttered.

"Would you like to look at it?"

"Yeah."

"Really?"

He glanced at her. "Really."

With a smile she got up from her bed, closing the robe, tightening the rope around her waist, and walked around the end of her bed. She sat down on his lap and slipped an arm around his neck. "How are you doing, baby?"

"Tired."

She ran her fingers through his hair. "Honoré, I wish we could be happy for once. There's been a lot of craziness."

"We come from crazy people."

"I'm tired of craziness."

He lay his head against her chest. "I know, I am too."

"What is it about those men that draws you?"

"I don't know. They're fighters. They lead interesting lives. Trotsky's been everywhere, read everything, done everything. Me—I'm a nobody. A Hispanic statistic."

She took his face in both hands and looked deeply in his eyes. "But you're not a nobody."

"You don't understand."

"Yes, I do. You have your family. You have a wonderful daughter, who adores you. If it weren't for you, your poor mother would have nothing. We would have nothing. You're the only thing that stands between us and the street. Oh yes, I could live without a man. This town is full of women living like that. But I don't want to live like that."

Then, she kissed him on the mouth.

Something sprang loose, uncoiled, snarling. Swiftly, desire turned his mind into an aquarium swimming with all kinds of fish, a shark long and muscular and menacing as a woman's inner thigh, a blow-fish round as a woman's *maracas* or plump as a buttock.

"Take a shower," she whispered in his ear.

He took a shower.

Shivering, he returned to the bedroom wrapped in a towel and climbed in that old battlefield, Maruca's bed, and pulled the covers up to his chin and turned toward her, knees touching hers. Goose bumps sprung on her flesh as his fingertips glided along her thigh. He rose on an elbow and scooted toward her, slipping a hand under her ribs, while his other hand advanced along her waist. She opened her legs, and he opened his. They intertwined, his thing flopping about as it sought to get out of the way and came to rest against her belly, where it wept. Her *maracas* flattened against his chest as he embraced her with tenderness and desire and they kissed the way they used to, tongue to tongue, gulping each other down as if they were drinking fresh water from a fountain.

After a while, the heat under the sheet was too much, and he untangled his legs from hers and kicked it off. Streaks of gold ran along the contours of her legs, and her thigh glistened like a python ready to uncoil. No sunset, no ocean, no landscape, nothing was more inspiring than her naked body in the golden light from the lamp.

He held her again, burying his face in her neck, kissing the sweet-smelling flesh. He closed his eyes, and his lips roamed. Then, twin puppies stuck their warm, round snouts in his face. Opening his eyes, Honoré took a thimble-shaped brown nose in his mouth.

"*Ay, papácito*," she yelped.

The other puppy wanted some attention, too.

Maruca yelped again.

When she sat up next to him, he ran his hand along the *cordillera* of her backbone until his fingers found their way between her buttocks, warm and moist as buttered pancakes.

Suddenly, her fingers alighted on his sack of grapes, ripe and heavy with desire. "Oh, God!" he shuddered.

With both hands she took him as if she were getting ready to play a flute. "Oh, God!" he said, digging his heels deep in the bed.

After a while, it was too much, too sweet, too painful, and he pushed her away. She lay back. He lay back gazing at the ceiling, thinking.

"Everywhere you turn," Trotsky had told him, "you see fucking. Pollination. The birds and the bees. Dogs in the streets. Cats. Roots penetrate the soil. Spengler once wrote that technology is the extended use of your fingers. *Technology* comes from *tech*, which means *finger*, and *ology*, which means *knowledge of*. A penis is a kind of finger, like God's finger in Michelangelo's painting of God touching Adam. What is an arrowhead, a needle, a knife, a spear, a bullet, blackjack, or a rocket if not an extension of the penis? Look at the Milky Way. Why, when you look at it, does it seem like God had an orgasm last night? But a penis without a vagina is something else by the same name. It's a pestle without a mortar, a *mano* without a *molcajete*."

At long last, it was time to become a beast, Honoré thought. How embarrassing! Romance was supposed to be beautiful and poetic like the world of the angels. Romance was supposed to be gallantry and serenades.

Getting on his knees like a dog reminded him that he belonged to the animal kingdom, a resentment, Trotsky observed once, that put him in the same category as white Southerners who refused to believe they descended from the apes, though, if anyone qualified to be their descendants, it was white Southerners. On the other hand, getting on his knees was the same thing you did when you prayed—hence, the kinship between praying and preying. Sex was humbling. Sex was more powerful than wine. Tell me whom you fuck, and I'll tell you who you are.

"Sex," said Trotsky, "is prayer and confession."

So like a dog, he got on his knees and put God's finger where God made Maruca a two-legged creature. Moist, exquisite, thrilling, it was like kissing. It was like swallowing or being swallowed as his ass went up and down. How awkward! How embarrassing!

At length, he forgot he was a beast and became a rolling pin pushing through a mound of dough and flattening it, flipping it over and rolling back and forth, in and out, roundabout, squish.

"God—oh, God!" cried Maruca.

Honoré closed his eyes. "Oh, my God!"

The beast grew. He became a green frog swelling between Maruca's legs and continued to swell as the connection between them got sweeter, a delicious in-and-out, until in his mind he became a giant inflatable frog that floated over the bed. The sweetness reached such intensity that the connection between him and Maruca came unplugged and the liquid boiling inside him poured into her, and in his mind he shot from the bed like a deflated balloon and his face struck the ceiling and flapped against it until all the hot air swooshed out of him.

Then, he fell back, face down, on Maruca. He rolled off her chest and lay exhausted, breathing heavily, as she jumped out of the bed and ran to the bathroom, leaving a trail of bird seed on the tiles. The creature between his legs, tiny as a bat, now slept with its head down, and he listened to the water running in the bathroom.

PART 2

Blue kept the demons away. Not only did the Toltecs paint the interior of their homes blue for that reason, but that was the color Frida Kahlo had painted the exterior of her house in Mexico City, a few blocks from where Trotsky had lived with his aunt in Coyoacán while an undergraduate at the University of the Americas. More importantly, years later, when he awoke screaming in the middle of the night, he would stagger to the living room and sit in the chair across from where Honoré now waited on a couch, sip warm milk laced with vodka, and bask in the soft light cast by the lamps until the waves of blue washed away the faces and voices of comrades killed in Vietnam. Only then could he go back to sleep.

Honoré's eyes wandered. In the dining room, high-backed wooden chairs with woven seats stood around a long, thick rough-hewn wooden table, and Mexican silverware sparkled in a china cabinet from Oaxaca. The photographs of Trotsky and his wife during travels in Mexico, Cuba, and Europe stood on a nearby shelf. A door led to the kitchen, where Altagracia was preparing coffee and warming *empanadas*, taco-sized Mexican pies stuffed with pineapple and cinnamon apple, whose scent filled the house. From the pages of a book on the coffee table, a man wearing a floppy wide-brimmed cowboy hat and a holster with a six-shooter stared at Honoré. It was Augusto César Sandino, the great Nicaraguan revolutionary who led a rebellion against Yankee military occupation of Nicaragua.

Upstairs, a door closed.

Trotsky, his hair aflame and a black patch over his right eye, hurried down the stairs and strode into the living room. He wore jeans with a white shirt and black suspenders. "Sorry to keep you waiting," he said as he sat in a leather chair. "I just got off the phone with a newspaper in Houston. They're looking for contacts in Oaxaca. I recommended the priest at the Iglesia de los Descalzos."

"I heard good things about him while I was there."

"Did you meet him?"

"No. He was out of town."

"Too bad."

"Where's El Capitán?"

Trotsky pulled a pen from his shirt pocket and wrote in a small notebook on his lap. "He called earlier. Got lost, but he should be here any minute," he said.

Honoré picked up the book from the coffee table. "So how does it look?"

"We'll find out soon. Last time I spoke to the organizers in Boston they were having trouble raising money. And there was some question about the leadership of the convoy."

Honoré flipped through the pictures of Nicaragua and Somoza and a volcano in the middle of a lake. There was a picture of Daniel Ortega and tanks in the streets of Managua and crowds in a public square. Another page featured a picture of Sandino and a description of how Somoza had him executed shortly after hosting a party for him. Suddenly, someone knocked on the front door, so loudly and violently that Honoré thought it might be the police.

Trotsky got up and opened the door.

Bald and short, bifocals on an unsmiling no-nonsense face, El Capitán held a briefcase, looking more like an insurance salesman than a revolutionary. "*Buenas tardes*," he said in a voice surprisingly macho for a small man.

"*¡Adelante!*" said Trotsky.

After shaking Trotsky's hand, then Honoré's, El Capitán sat on the couch next to Honoré. "Somebody's out there in a car, looking at the house through binoculars."

Honoré asked, "Is he fat?"

"Yes."

Honoré kept a straight face. "Is he brown?"

"Yes."

"Is he ugly?"

"Well, I don't know—"

Honoré peeked outside. "Just as I thought," he said, resuming his seat. "My brother-in-law, Comino. Runs the county jail. He and his friends like to harass me, keeping an eye on everything I do, sometimes reporting back to my wife. If I had a *movida*, they'd keep their mouths shut because they know every man in Escandón deserves a mistress. But since I've been hanging out with Trotsky, they've been dogging me, looking for the first opportunity to bust me." He stretched his legs and relaxed. "Comino's never forgiven me for marrying his sister."

The men laughed.

Trotsky sat down as Altagracia carried a silver tray with coffee and *empanadas* into the room. She wore a fuchsia blouse and a flowered black skirt that reached her Mexican sandals. "Hola," she said.

El Capitán stood. "*Buenas tardes, señora*."

She set the tray on the coffee table and shook his hand. "*Buenas tardes,*
Capitán. Please, have a seat."

He sat.

After handing out napkins, she said, "Enjoy." Then she moved a chair
from the dining room table and sat next to Trotsky.

While taking a bite from an *empanada* and sipping some coffee, El
Capitán passed out fliers. "In June," he explained, "a convoy of trucks, buses, and cars will be leaving all parts of the United States, from as far away as
Vermont and Oregon, carrying medical supplies, food, and bicycles to Nicaragua. The vehicles will converge in San Antonio, then drive in a convoy
to Escandón, and cross the border here. The vehicles themselves are part of
the cargo. They will remain in Nicaragua, and the drivers and everyone else
will fly back. The convoy's humanitarian purpose is to take much-needed
food and supplies to the Nicaraguan people, but its political purpose is to
challenge the U.S. embargo against Nicaragua."

Trotsky folded the announcement and slipped it in his notebook. "I was
in Nicaragua when the veterans first talked about this. I had my doubts, but
it looks like they finally got their act together."

"By the way, is Olivia pissed off?" asked El Capitán.

Trotsky exchanged glances with Honoré. Word had gotten out about the
incident at Casa Jovita Idahr, but there was no telling how much El Capitán
knew.

"Why?" asked Trotsky.

"We've had a hard time getting a hold of her."

"She's very busy," Trotsky said coolly.

"The steering committee wants her women's group to sponsor this, but I
need a commitment now."

Trotsky brought the tips of his fingers together an inch from his nose,
almost prayerfully. "And?"

"Well, I don't think her group will commit—at least, not any time soon.
They won't do anything without Olivia's approval. So I'm asking for your
help."

"How?"

El Capitán's words floated across the coffee table as effortlessly as specks
of dust in the shaft of light from the window. "We need lodging for one
night, dinner, and breakfast the next day."

"How many vehicles?"

"Forty. About sixty to eighty people. Also I need you to coordinate your
efforts with Don Sixto."

Altagracia straightened the long black skirt covering her knees. "Father

Bernardino's church has a big parking lot, and there's a dormitory across the street. It's empty most of the time."

Father Bernardino was Altagracia's cousin. "What about the bishop?" asked Trotsky.

"What about him?" she asked.

Trotsky restrained his voice. "Do you think he's going to allow one of his churches to be used as a campground for the convoy? He's a Republican. And an SOB."

With the conviction of someone who knew her family well, Altagracia said, "My cousin is stubborn. He'll convince the bishop to help us."

Trotsky shifted in his chair. "I'd prefer not to deal with the Catholic Church in this town."

All this sounded too easy, mulled Honoré. "What if the *federales* don't let the convoy cross?"

El Capitán's black eyes wiggled as if caught off guard. "This administration," he said, "will stop the convoy if they can get away with it, but it probably won't happen until we try to enter Guatemala. Or on the border between Guatemala and Honduras. That way the Republicans can wash their hands of it and hold the Mexican or Guatemalan government responsible. Trying to stop the convoy on this border is too close to home, too much media, too much publicity. It'll never happen. Don't worry. We're not asking for much from you, just a nopal and a glass of water."

"What happens," Honoré asked, "if they change their minds?"

"What do you mean?"

"What if they stop the convoy?"

El Capitán grinned. "Well, then you'll have a siege on your hands."

Palm trees lined the sidewalk while the black limbs of mesquite trees lunged over the wrought iron fences of the two-storey Victorian houses as Honoré looked up and down the street. Comino and his goons were gone. Still, an old sensation made his skin crawl, and his palms grew sweaty as he remembered that he and his friends had often driven through this old neighborhood with tons of dope.

He climbed in his truck and left.

After turning the corner, he headed north, several blocks later skirting an old warehouse, rumbling over the railroad tracks and cruising past clapboard houses with slanting metal roofs, dirt yards filled with mesquite and palm trees, and cars lined up on the street. Some of his friends from the old days had lived in this barrio, in a white house on the corner. There it was, on the left, where they had had a lot of parties in the backyard. They were all gunned down in an ambush by the river.

He checked the rearview mirror.

And there they were, dark-tinted windows several car lengths behind him, a Ford sedan. He couldn't tell if they were Comino's men or old enemies from his dope-dealing days. Often there wasn't much difference. He yanked the truck onto a dirt road and sped past a brick warehouse covered by a corrugated roof sparkling like nickel in the sunlight. They followed him. After roaring through an explosion of stones under his chassis, he made another right and shot across gray asphalt, smooth as velvet under the tires. After making a sharp turn at a mom-and-pop corner store, he headed toward the river. At another intersection he turned behind the warehouses along the railroad tracks, sure he had lost them. He slowed down, turned left, and headed east, toward the highway, crossing the railroad tracks again. Then he spun into an alley and parked next to a huge dumpster behind a cantina, The Lazy Mex.

A motorcycle zoomed past.

Sometimes his enemies tailed him just to annoy him or because they didn't have anything better to do. Sometimes they were so stupid they confused him with someone else, but what scared him most were the old debts, unfinished business, old resentments, wounds that never healed. In fact, he had always feared that one day he'd die in a crossfire. Payback was tough.

A kid rode by on a bicycle.

A knock on his window startled him, and he sat up straight. The barrel of a shotgun was pointed at his face. Wait—no, it was a cue stick. He rolled down the window.

A young boy with fat cheeks loomed close. "What's the matter, *cabrón*?" said Ty Cobb. "Did I scare you?"

He climbed out, walked to the end of the alley, and peeked around the corner of a building.

"Playing hide and seek?"

The coast was clear. "No. Cowboys and Indians."

"*No mames, güey.*"

He stood before her. "What are you doing here?"

"I heard a car pull up. Thought it was a friend we've been waiting for."

"Who's *we*?"

"How about a beer? Come inside. I'll introduce you to my new friend."

"Sure."

A yellow cone of light fell on the pool table nestled amid cool shadows reeking of beer and cigarette smoke. At the other end of the cantina, a bartender in a white shirt stood drying glasses behind the bar.

Honoré sat at a small table against a dank cement wall. Cue stick in hand, Ty sat across from him and whistled at the bartender.

"Where you been?" Honoré asked.

"Busy."

The bartender brought the beers. "*Provecho*," he said and then left.

The ice-cold beer in his throat calmed Honoré. "I heard you and Olivia broke up."

She stood, chalking the cue as she circled the pool table. "Stupid bitch. I cook. I keep the house clean. I take care of her dogs. Then Danielle and her friends from Berkeley show up. She gets pissed off at me while she's at their beck and call. It's worse than being married."

A door across the room opened. A tall blond woman came out of the bathroom, a shy smile on her long bony face, and approached the pool table. "Hi," she said to Honoré.

"This is a friend of mine," Ty said to her, "Honoré del Castillo."

Like a good old-fashioned caballero from South Texas, Honoré stood up and held out a hand. "*Mucho gusto*."

"Shirley English," the blonde said in a soft pleasant voice and shook his hand with long white fingers.

Ty circled the pool table. "She's from New England. A news reporter for KAOS."

"Welcome to South Texas."

"Thank you."

After shooting and missing, Ty handed her the cue. Then, Shirley walked around the table, eyeing the balls on the green felt. No doubt she was a lesbian, thought Honoré, but her dainty movements, sweet voice, and hair tied up in a ribbon made it difficult to tell. Then, she leaned over a side rail and aimed the cue at the six and slammed it so hard the balls exploded, careening and clicking hard before they were swallowed up by the corner pockets and rumbled into the table's belly.

"She plays like a man," said Honoré in Spanish.

"That's not all she does like a man," Ty replied in Spanish.

Honoré finished his beer, which soothed his gut. The girl played well, but Ty won the game.

Afterward, just as he was beginning to enjoy a buzz, the front door swung open and daggers of white light butchered the smoke as two figures, one right after the other, stepped into the room, dark shades on solemn faces. Too far away to recognize Honoré, the men sat on stools at the bar and ordered a drink. He wasn't sure they were the men who had chased him, but he couldn't take a chance.

He got up. "I gotta go," he muttered to Ty.

"Something the matter?" asked Shirley, twisting the chalk on the end of her cue.

Ty grabbed his arm. "Wait."

He paused, eyes on the men. "For what?"

"We haven't had a man-to-man."

He pried his arm loose. "What's there to talk about?" he said and then headed toward the back door.

She ran after him. "Wait!"

He walked into the blinding South Texas sun. "What?"

"I want to go to *la zona*," she said, squinting. "Please take me."

He wanted to slap her sun-toasted cheeks. "Fuck you. The last time you broke your promise. First, you fingered that poor transvestite. Then, you let those lesbos nearly kill me."

"Look, I'm sorry. I'll make it up to you. What do you want me to do? I'll do anything."

He looked at her long and hard. "You're sure?"

"I'm sure."

Suddenly, he remembered the *carne asada* the afternoon he went to visit her at Dr. de la O's house. "Well, how about cooking a *carne asada* for me and some friends?"

"Is that all?"

"That's all."

Honoré's enemies never tailed him when he drove into his mother's neighborhood, not since the time she pointed his father's 30.30 at them. Though barely able to hold the rifle, she managed to get off a few rounds and smash their windshield. As he parked in front of her house, he didn't bother to check if anyone had followed him. He opened the screen door and walked inside.

Lupita stopped him in the hall. "Don Honoré."

"What happened?"

"She's getting ready to meet her Maker."

"Again?"

Lupita nodded solemnly. "Again."

His mother lay in her bed with eyes shut and hands clasped on her chest.

"What happened?" he asked Lupita.

"She fainted."

"Anything else?"

"She hasn't eaten all day."

Suddenly, Doña Pánfila's eyes snapped open. "Am I in heaven?"

He held her hand, crisp as onion skin. "No, mother. You're still alive."

The phone next to the bed rang, and Lupita picked it up. "Yes, ma'am. He's here. Doña Maruca."

He took the phone. "Hello?"

"What's going on? Lupita called earlier, said your mother's sick."

His mother, head on a pillow, stared at him. "She looks okay," he said.

"Take her to the hospital."

"Why?"

"Just take her. You never know. She has high blood pressure. She could be having a stroke. Her doctor has been worried."

His eyes wandered aimlessly across the room. "That guy's an idiot. I preferred her old doctor."

"Some customers just walked in. Take Lupita with you. Get your mother admitted, and have Lupita stay with her. Tell her we'll pay her extra. Then, come here as soon as you're done. I haven't been grocery shopping, and there's no food at the house."

"Okay," he said and hung up, then turned to Lupita. "Get her ready to go."

Lupita walked out of the bedroom and returned with the old woman's robe and a small suitcase. As soon as his mother was dressed, Honoré picked her up tenderly and carried her outside to the truck, where he sat her in the cab. She dozed off, mumbling, while Lupita put the suitcase in the flatbed. At length, Lupita climbed in, and he closed the door. The hospital, a huge ugly orange-brick building ten blocks away, was perched on a hill that overlooked the city. After Honoré laid his mother on a gurney, two orderlies in blue scrubs rolled her inside to a waiting room overflowing with old men, young mothers, and children. Honoré and Lupita followed through the swinging doors into the emergency room.

An hour later, a doctor strolled into the room.

"Good afternoon," Honoré said, rising to his feet. Honoré hated doctors in Escandón. Lawsuits were rampant. Wrong diagnoses were common. Healthy people died all the time, fatally ill people seldom died, and the ones who needed to die lived the longest.

"Your mother is dying," said the doctor as he flipped through documents on a clipboard. He was fit and trim beneath a white coat, eyes dead serious behind steel-rimmed glasses.

"Are you sure?"

The doctor put the clipboard down and regarded him. "What do you think we do here? Play doctor?"

Every muscle in Honoré's body demanded that a fist annihilate this guy's arrogant face, an easy task since the doctor was a foot shorter than Honoré. "No, sir. It's just that we've been through this with her several times, and it's always been a false alarm."

The doctor scribbled on his clipboard. "Your mother is so old it's a miracle she's alive."

"Hogwash."

The doctor stopped scribbling. "Look at her. Death warmed over."

His mother had been dying for so long that everyone agreed she would be better off in heaven. But no matter how much she pissed him off, no one should talk about his mother like this.

When the doctor saw Honoré's clenched fist, he raised an eyebrow and walked away, swinging his hips a little too much like a woman.

"Idiot!" muttered Honoré.

Blue-eyed television sets broadcast Mexican *telenovelas* in the rooms he passed on his way down a hall, bringing back memories of when he and Trotsky had been laid up on the hospital's top floor. In the lobby he walked past an old couple sitting side by side in plastic chairs while toddlers flocked around their fat, dark mother. As he stepped outside, he came across a young man on a gurney being lowered from an ambulance, his dark face wearing an oxygen mask, a dagger tattooed on his forearm, an earring sparkling on his left ear. Probably a gangster who just got his ass blown off, mulled Honoré before heading across the parking lot to his pickup.

Gonzales Avenue took him north toward Kennedy, where he turned west and drove past the cemetery. In the rearview mirror, he spotted a car with tinted windows. Following too close for comfort. At the next traffic light, the car turned south, and Honoré breathed a sigh of relief. Leaving the cemetery behind, he reached the interstate's overpass without incident, drove underneath it, and turned north on Tamaulipas. At the store everything seemed okay as he parked in the dirt yard. Good, he reflected, because he had a lot of paperwork to get out of the way. And don't forget to call the bank, he reminded himself.

When he walked into his office, Maruca pushed herself away from the desk and got up. "I think the telephone is tapped," she said.

"Why?"

"When I'm on the phone, I hear a click or breathing like someone is listening. Are you up to no good, again?"

He looked at her, feeling as if at any moment he would fall off a cliff. "I'm helping Trotsky with a new project, but it's nothing."

"I thought you were going to stop all that."

Honoré opened a desk drawer, looking for the keys to the file cabinet. "It's a small project, nothing to worry about."

"Honoré!"

He faced her. "What?"

Her black hair shone in the light from the window. "What are you and Trotsky up to now? All of your projects with him have been like that, nothing to worry about."

He closed the drawer. "Some vets are hauling humanitarian aid to Nicaragua. They'll pass through here. Trotsky and I are providing food and lodging for one night. That's all."

She stared at him doubtfully. "How is your mother doing?"

He surveyed the office, wondering where his mother might have put the keys. "I don't know. It's always the same story. One day she's dying. The next she's back here at the store telling everyone what to do."

"What are you looking for?"

"The keys to the file cabinet."

"In the bottom drawer."

"Thanks."

After he found the keys, she said, "Is there anything you need from the store?"

He looked at her and smiled. "A six pack of nirvana."

She didn't smile. "Fine."

When she turned to go, Honoré said, "Maruca."

She stopped with her hand on the door.

He approached her. "I owe Trotsky a lot, but I can't spend the rest of my life paying him for saving my life. This is the last time I work with him. I promise."

She kissed him and left. He opened the file next to his desk, took out the general ledger, and checked to see if the store was overdrawn at the bank. Ten minutes later, he called the bank to confirm. No, they were okay.

All of a sudden, the back door opened and someone yelled in a sickeningly familiar womanish voice, "Honoré!"

He walked to the back of the store. "What do you want?" he asked the pink-cheeked six-foot-tall hog standing in the doorway. Another stood just behind him.

His cousin smiled. "We heard Doña Pánfila is dying."

"So?"

Today the hogs looked so much alike Honoré couldn't tell the difference between them until Cachetes smiled like a pumpkin and showed his uneven teeth. "So we came to see if we could help."

Honoré said, "Things have never been better. So get the fuck out of here."

Honoré slammed the door in their faces and returned to his office. He picked up the phone and dialed.

A woman answered, "*Buenas tardes.*"

"May I speak to the Governor?"

"Hi, hot dog."

"Who's this?"

The voice was melodious. "Who do you think?"

"Oh," he said, shaking his head doubtfully. "How have you been?"

Her tone changed. "*De la chingada. Tu amigo está loquísimo.* You've got to get me out of here. Why didn't you tell me he was *un pinche tecato*?"

"I thought you'd fuck anything with gold on it."

"*No mames, güey.* I may be a *puta*, but I'm not a *pendeja.*"

"Let me to talk to El Gobernador."

Another phone was picked up. "Halloooooo!" wailed the Governor, his voice sluggish from fucking too much or coking out. "Is anyone out there?"

Honoré shook his head, grinning. "Nobody."

"Is there any hope?"

"*Nada, cabrón.*"

"Does God exist?"

Honoré repeated something Trotsky had said many times. "No. He's dead. The Christians killed him."

Bed springs jangled. A door opened and closed. Suddenly, the sound of a stream of piss hitting water in the toilet bowl came across the line.

The Governor cleared his throat. "Ahhh!" The toilet flushed. As soon as the Governor was back in his room, bedsprings squealed under his weight. "Sorry, Comandante. I couldn't contain myself, as my old man used to say."

"You sound like you've been fucking and shooting dope all morning."

He laughed. "The battle of the Alamo is raging. Today I played David Crockett. She played Santa Anna."

"Who won?"

"If you seen the condition she left my musket in, you'd know."

"Cut the bullshit."

The Governor laughed again. "Okay, honey, you can take that out of your mouth now. I need to talk business with El Comandante." The bed-springs jangled again. A door closed. "Okay, Comandante, shoot! What are you up to now?"

"I need your help."

That night in the kitchen Honoré removed the bottle of tequila from the cabinet and took a swig. After opening the refrigerator and taking out a can of beer, he headed to the porch and sat in a lawn chair amid a rectangle of light spilling from the window behind him. The beer was cold as ice as he gazed at the stars and the Milky Way. It was all so immense. A shooting star fell. Dogs barked. Bonita and Maruca were already asleep upstairs. Lupita called earlier and reported that his mother was feeling better. Tomorrow would be a long day at the store. He needed to get some rest tonight.

Suddenly, an eerie scrambling in the driveway, about ten feet away, just beyond the reach of the light, startled him. The scrambling grew into something the size of a cat. A snout poked the air. Honoré caught a glimpse of its ugly cord-like tail as it spun around and scurried toward the street. A *tlacuache*! Ugly as huge rats, thousands of *tlacuaches* lived in Escandón, coming out and going into all sorts of weird places when you least expected and scaring the shit out of you.

I can't believe I live here, he thought. I can't believe I've not been able to get out of this black hole. El Barrio Sal Si Puedes. What kind of a name is that? El Barrio Get-Out-If-You-Can? Maruca is right. We need to buy a new house in north Escandón.

A car approached from the west as the possum waddled across the street. Suddenly, it froze in the headlights. Honoré was sure it would be smashed. But the car screeched to a stop and missed the ugly thing, which bumbled through the white haze of the car's lights. People in this barrio are like possums, he thought. When life or history confronts them, they play possum. They play dead. Then, life or history just runs over them.

Trotsky had taught him things could be different. There was a world beyond Escandón. But the biggest lesson the tortured Vietnam veteran taught him was that there was a world of ideas beyond as well. Most people in Escandón did not know this. They didn't even understand their own world.

A pickup sped around the corner. A cumbia blaring from its radio, it cruised along the street and stopped in front of Tequila's house. The lights went off, and the radio got quiet. Mumbling some gibberish, the driver pushed the door open, the hinges screeching loudly, and out slid Tequila, singing in Spanish. Probably back from a night in the red light district. He slammed the door, staggered, and then halted in mid-street as if he had dozed off, bottle in hand.

Another *tlacuache*, thought Honoré.

Tequila unzipped. The sound of a cumbia grew loud as another car bebopped around the corner. Piss sparkled in the headlights and spattered on the asphalt like broken china.

"Tequila!" shouted Honoré.

The car screeched. The beer bottle crashed as the car sent Tequila flying through the air. Then, the car backed up, spun around noisily, and screeched away. Honoré jumped to his feet and found Tequila moaning on his back in the middle of the street. Honoré knelt next to him when a fart broke like a bubble in Tequila's trousers and rose like steam through the night.

"*¡Chingada madre!*" cursed Honoré, holding his nose.

Tequila rolled on his back. "*¡Yo sigo siendo el rey!*"

It was a corny old Mexican ballad claiming that a man could be a king no matter what. "*¡Que rey ni que rey!*" said Honoré, trying to pick him up. "You're not a king. You're a *pendejo*!"

Tequila hiccuped. "*¡Yo sigo siendo el rey!*"

Tequila weaved as he stood up, trying to decide which way to go, and just as he was about to take a step toward his house, he flopped on his butt. The headlights of another car swung around the corner and cruised down the street, thumping and vibrating like an amplifier on wheels. Honoré grabbed Tequila's ankles and dragged him to the curb and up the sidewalk to his house, wondering whether he should wake Señora Cuervo.

"What the hell do I do with this idiot?" Honoré muttered.

He dragged him through the thick grass to the back of the house and stood him up at the foot of the stairs leading to the observatory. He went through Tequila's pockets and found his keys. He was heavy and smelled like a garbage can as Honoré hauled him up the stairs, slowly and quietly. His only worry was getting a hernia.

"This is the last time I get you out of trouble," swore Honoré, unlocking the door. "The next time you die in your shit."

He opened the door and turned on the light. Then, as Tequila slid to the floor, Honoré looked around the room. The first thing that struck him was that the roof had been fixed. A slab of plywood now covered the opening where the observatory once stood. Suddenly, his mouth fell open.

Bundles of fifty- and one-hundred dollar bills lay everywhere—on the desk, the chairs, the floor. The telescope stood at the end of the room under a sheet of plastic. In place of the poster of the heavens identifying a black hole amid the Milky Way hung a poster of a Dallas Cowboys cheerleader, a blonde with big tits and long legs. Come to think of it, the two posters featured the same ominous phenomenon. A new TV, the same size as the one Maruca bought, stood against the wall. Then, after his eyes jumped from one bundle of money to the next, Honoré estimated there must be at least a million dollars in cash. It looked oh-so-wonderful, but it smelled dirty.

"¡Yo sigo siendo el rey!"

Tequila rolled on his side and got up on his knees with his pants at half-mast, showing the crack in his butt as he crawled across the floor. Honoré shook his head, remembering the time he and Tequila were strung out on cocaine and booze and hung out with a gang of drug traffickers at a cantina across the river and closed down the place, locking the doors with customers and prostitutes inside, and spent three days and nights in there. How Honoré did not lose his mind was beyond him. On the third day, a friend of the cantina's owner showed up, and the minute he saw Tequila and Honoré, he took out a pistol and dragged both to an empty lot in back. When the *narcotraficante* put the gun to Tequila's head, Tequila confessed he had failed to pay for a shipment of pot. Tequila, of course, spent the money and forgot to tell Honoré, who took out a wad of cash and promised to pay the rest if Tequila's life were spared.

The *narcotraficante* sneered at Tequila, "You aren't worth the bullet, you piece of shit," and put the pistol back in his belt.

Tequila now sat in front of the coffee table and opened a bag of sugar. He sprinkled some on a mirror on the coffee table and separated it into lines with a credit card. Next, he picked up the remote and aimed it at the TV.

Palm trees rose from white sand against a blue sky, and a dark blue ocean crashed on the beach. It was amazing what these huge television screens did—put you right there, in another world, in another reality, just like that, in the blink of an eye. This could be paradise. His eyes opened wide as a woman walked toward him, a young woman with long golden hair, a long-legged Scandinavian toasted golden brown by the tropical sun, a blue-eyed European with plentiful golden breasts bouncing in upward swoops. A golden Brillo pad shimmered where God had made her a two-legged animal.

Stirrings rose from the bottom of Honoré's soul. Then, three young men walked from the opposite end of the beach. With black curly hair and a sharply handsome face, one looked like a Greek statue he had seen in Trotsky's illustrated books on Greek civilization. The second one, with a beehive of golden ringlets on his bronzed face, looked like a Viking, his arms as thickly braided with muscle as the rope used to dock boats in Oslo. And with thighs chiseled and powerful as the flanks of a stallion and dark brown as Colombian coffee, the third one looked like a pharaoh from Egypt. Each of the men swung a six-inch version of the snake that tempted Eve into eating the apple.

But this is not the Garden of Eden, Honoré reminded himself. This is Hollywood.

Next, the beautiful young woman crouched on her hands and knees on the sand, hair down around her face. Like the sea, her eyes were blue. At first Honoré had to stop thinking and look closely at what he was seeing because he couldn't believe it. This is too private, too intimate; this does not belong on television. The woman's buttocks were spread out like two loaves, hot and golden, and in between golden twigs covered a strip of raw sirloin. Her magnificent breasts swung across the Greek's face, which rolled from side to side as his humping intensified. The other two men got ready to do her, one in the mouth, the other up the ass.

Suddenly, a silver cross flashed on the TV screen and swallowed the beach in darkness. "Let's have a toke," said Tequila, tossing the remote on the coffee table. He sat on the floor with a straw in his hand. "The Indians in Peru know what they're doing," he said. "They take this shit so they can work in the mines and in the cold. They can go days without eating and feel good. They've been doing it for thousands of years. Tercero looked it all up in the encyclopedia I bought him. But the best thing about this shit is that it lets you drink and fuck all night. I come here, snort some coke, have a few shots of tequila, watch plenty of porno, and then head out to *la zona*. With plenty of money, coca, and pussy, who needs a wife?" Tequila separated six hits of white sugar. "These are yours, *cabrón*." He snorted. After wiping his nose on the back of his arm, he took out a bottle of tequila and set some glasses on the table.

"¡Satanás!" muttered Honoré, half in jest, half in truth, as he imagined two horns sprouting from his friend's head. After all, it was Tequila who had gotten him into drugs and then drug trafficking.

"*¡Que Satanás ni que Satanás!* Don't tell me you've become a hallelujah! First a high school quarterback, then a coyote, then a revolutionary, and now a Christian! *¡No mames, pendejo!*"

Honoré stood before the coffee table, thinking that if he snorted some of this sugar, there was no telling what might happen, whether he would end up in the *zona* or in the county jail. Worse, it meant he might go back to his old ways. "When are you going to stop all this shit?"

Tequila wiped his nose with his finger, sniffling as if he were coming down with a cold. "Stop what shit?"

Honoré eyed the bottle of tequila on the coffee table. "You know what I mean."

Tequila opened the bottle. "Coyote, you make me sick. We're old buddies. But then you meet *el cabezón*—that Russian with the black hair and black eye patch—and you go crazy." Tequila poured some tequila in a glass and then another for Honoré. "A toast to our friendship."

"I gotta go."

"Wait," said Tequila, pushing a glass of the fiery stuff at him.

Honoré took the glass. "Okay, one drink."

"Coyote, listen. I don't care how many Russians you meet or how many big words you learn. We're both from the Barrio Sal Si Puedes, and you'll always be from here."

"I'm not from here. My wife is from here. I'm from El Rincon del Diablo."

"Same thing."

The smell of tequila and Tequila disgusted Honoré. "I gotta go."

Tequila, his nose glowing like Rudolf the Rednosed Reindeer's, leered at Honoré. "Oh, you gotta go?" he slurred. "Maruca didn't give you permission? Is that it?" He paused, burped, looked up, eyes glassy. "There was a time . . . you went, you did whatever you wanted, when you wanted." He wiped his mouth with the back of his oil-stained hand. "Now look at you . . . pussywhipped. Can't do this, can't do that, gotta go home. Look at how your mother has you running that shop!" He burped again. He eyed the money on the coffee table. "Now look at all this lettuce." He flung a handful of hundred-dollar bills at Honoré. "Half of it could be yours! We could be making lots of money!" He made an ugly face. "You think you're a revolutionary—" He paused, then fixed Honoré in a demonic gaze. "You're just a Mexican curio, *pendejo!*"

"Shut up," said Honoré and put down the glass of tequila, untouched. "If I hadn't dragged you up here, you'd be splattered on the street like a *tlacuache* right now."

The night was hot. After climbing down the stairs, Honoré walked around the house to the front gate, where, just as he strode past Tequila's pickup, something down the street seemed out of place—a strange car. He froze.

Nothing else looked different. There was his house across the street and his pickup. And up and down the street were the dark shapes of houses and palm trees and garbage cans. Suddenly, a stick of light blossomed and expired—someone lighting a cigarette in the car, probably a bunch of guys getting stoned. Maybe *tecatos*. No, those losers hung out in the arroyo several blocks away. The engine started. Honoré crouched behind Tequila's pickup as the car pulled out, came up the street slowly, its engine running smoothly, the chassis squeaking.

A chill went down Honoré's back as it drove past, a plain black sedan with a floppy antenna, windows tinted and rolled up, two men in the front seat. A cigarette glowed in the dark.

CHAPTER 9
A Nudist Colony

A lazy sunset flung a Mexican *zarape*, woven from streaks of orange and red, across the warm evening as Honoré drove the truck in the northbound lane through Escandón. Trotsky rode shotgun, his black hair frolicking like a war bonnet in the breeze as he gazed at the hundreds of cars from Mexico in the mall's parking lots. Palm trees, like flamingos preening on long, slender legs, stood in a row along the highway. In the southbound lane, eighteen-wheelers sped toward the border, where soon traffic on the international bridge would be backed up for hours. Meanwhile, Honoré headed toward the outskirts of town, where they would greet the convoy to Nicaragua arriving from San Antonio.

Suddenly, Honoré saw something red in the rear view mirror. Then, it grew, like a bright cherry on an ice-cream sundae, only bigger, until the mirror flung zings of red light in his eyes.

"We've got trouble," he said as he eased up on the gas and checked the speedometer. He wasn't speeding.

A cop car pulled alongside Honoré on his left. Then, as the two vehicles moved north at the same speed, Honoré glanced inside the other one. Sunglasses poised on the steamy brown face with full lips and a double chin, a police officer glared at Honoré.

"My brother-in-law!" groaned Honoré.

Suddenly, the squad car took off, red lights flashing, siren screaming as it disappeared around a curve.

"Put a Mexican behind a desk or in a uniform," said Trotsky, "and you create a monster."

"Comino should be arrested," said Honoré.

"On what charges?"

"Impersonating a police officer."

On the outskirts of town, cars whizzed by in the northbound lane, vanishing beneath a railroad overpass supported by two massive cement pillars, while Honoré slowed down. As he rumbled to a stop on the shoulder, an ambulance—siren wailing, red lights flashing—sped toward Escandón in the southbound lane. He reached for the ignition and killed the engine. Afterward, he and Trotsky climbed out of the truck about twenty feet from the overpass. Honoré opened the tailgate and took out the banner made by Don Sixto and his sons, who had been involved in so many demonstrations in Nuevo Escandón and northern Mexico that they had banners for nearly every occasion. Carrying the roll of canvas on his shoulder, Honoré struggled up the brush-entangled embankment to the railroad tracks and walked between them to the middle of the overpass. Trotsky followed closely behind, and together they unfurled the banner, which read, WELCOME TO ESCANDÓN, CONVOY TO NICARAGUA, and hung it on the north side of the overpass.

Standing above the highway, they could see for miles. "Looks like an accident," said Trotsky.

Like a dead cockroach, a tractor-trailer lay on its side in the distance. "An eighteen-wheeler," said Honoré.

"It doesn't take much to flip them over, does it?"

Honoré leaned against the siding. "Sometimes those drivers are drunk on their asses."

"There'll be a lot of trucks on the bridge."

"There's always a lot of trucks."

Trotsky's hair was black as the pavement. "I mean when the convoy crosses into Mexico. According to El Capitán, everything should run smoothly, but if the government tries to stop us, the crossing will be hell—especially in this heat."

"He made it sound pretty simple. Let's hope he's right."

"By the way, Altagracia won't be able to make the trip to Nicaragua. Are you interested? I'll cover all your expenses."

"How long will we be gone?"

"About a week," Trotsky said. "If everything goes according to plan."

"My mother," Honoré said, "is sick. She might die any day."

"I'm sorry."

"Of course, she's been dying as long as I can remember."

The honking began as a white pickup, with the flags of the United States and Nicaragua snapping on metal rods attached to the bumper, flew beneath the bridge. Two vans—the Cross of Malta, VFW, painted on their doors—hauled boxes in their luggage racks. Still other vehicles sported VVPX, which, according to Trotsky, meant "Vietnam Veterans for Pax." "Pax" meant "peace." Not "pox," which meant VD. A van with a black POW/MIA flag snapping on its antenna carried a stack of suitcases and duffel bags on its roof. A crow's foot inside a circle—the international peace sign—appeared on pickups loaded down with bicycles and wheelchairs. A yellow bus with NICARAGUA OR BUST painted on its side crept caterpillar-like around a curve and chugged past. Just like the good ole days when Honoré and Tequila were the stars of the football games at Escandón High, five more buses followed in sequence as if transporting a marching band and its cheerleaders to a football game.

"Thirty-eight or thirty-nine vehicles in total," Honoré said.

"I counted thirty-eight," Trotsky said.

"They don't look like they're in good shape. Probably already lost some on the way down here. Do they know how to get to the church?"

"Yes. We provided directions."

Honoré slid down the dirt slope on the heels of his boots, and the two stood on the shoulder as more vehicles flew past, honking like geese headed south in the fall. Honoré and Trotsky waved and then climbed in the pickup. Honoré started the engine, bounced through the grassy median, and headed south, honking as they caught up with the convoy.

Soon, as they passed a yellow school bus, Honoré turned and looked directly at a sickeningly familiar white face in the driver's seat. "Oh, fuck!"

"What's the matter?"

He looked again. "It can't be."

"What?"

They left the convoy behind. "If I saw what I think I saw, we're headed for big trouble."

"What did you see?"

"*Un pendejo.*"

Trotsky turned in his seat and looked out the back window.

"The guy driving that bus is a redneck *narcotraficante* named Johnny Paint."

Trotsky sat back. "Are you sure?"

Honoré shook his head slowly. "Well, he sure looks a lot like him."

"Let's hope you're wrong."

They passed an eighteen-wheeler and then another one. Three miles from the border, several more eighteen-wheelers bound for the maquiladoras in Nuevo Escandón moved slowly in the southbound lanes as cops directed traffic. Honoré slowed down. If the convoy tried to cross into Mexico tomorrow morning, it was going to be hell. To avoid congestion, Honoré got off the highway at the next exit and took the access road past several traffic lights until he reached Kennedy, where he turned left and then headed across town. At the cemetery they turned left again and headed toward the church, driving past a soccer field. A red tile roof rose in sharp angles above yellow brick walls. Honoré drove to the parking lot behind the church and stopped amid billows of white smoke pouring from a black metal drum converted into a barbecue grill.

Honoré climbed out of the truck and opened the tailgate. Then, with Trotsky's help, he carried a heavy ice chest across the parking lot toward the short, fat boy with an apron around his *panza* standing behind the grill.

After setting down the cooler, Trotsky said, "Well, look who's here, Ty Cobb herself. I thought the women's movement wasn't going to help us. Where's Dr. de la O?"

Ty wiped her brow with the back of her sleeve. "In Washington, at a convention."

Honoré leaned toward Trotsky. "Olivia and Ty are no longer partners."

"Really?" Trotsky said, grinning widely. "I thought you two would live happily ever after."

Ty turned a burger on the grill. "We outgrew each other. No big deal."

"Divorce is always a big deal."

"Not really. We don't have the hang-ups you breeders have about marriage and divorce and all that BS. We're free spirits."

Honoré rubbed his dusty right boot against the back of his left leg. "Ty is a true comrade. Despite Olivia, she convinced the women in her organization to help us. They're volunteering their time in the chow line."

"So my wife told me." Trotsky patted her on the shoulder. "Good. Great, in fact."

She shrugged.

Trotsky grinned. "Well, it's too bad Olivia is missing out on this. We need her. It would be good for the poor dear to see what the women in this town can do without her."

Ty ignored him.

Then he turned to Honoré. "I'll be inside," he said and headed across the parking lot to the church.

Ty Cobb, beads of sweat sparkling on her forehead, glared at the church as Trotsky disappeared inside. "That pretentious prick! Thinks he knows it all."

"Hey, give him some credit. He's sharp as a whip."

"Well, I don't like him."

"Doesn't Olivia think she knows it all? Even though she thinks she's God's gift to women, he tried to reach out to her. He asked for her help."

"So what? He's still a prick." She wiped her forehead with the back of her arm. "Did you bring the beer?"

Honoré opened the ice chest and took out a cold Heineken.

Ty snatched it from his hand, twisted it open, and tipped it back just like a man, wiping her mouth on her sleeve afterward. "So when are we going back to *la zona, cabrón*?"

Honoré inspected the meat on the grill. "Well, first let's see how things turn out here."

"Next week?"

"We'll see."

Ty cut a piece of sausage and offered it to Honoré on the end of a two-pronged fork. "Try this, Coyote."

The hot juices penetrated every taste bud. "Mmmmm."

"Olivia is pissed."

Honoré chewed the delicious chunk of meat. "What else is new?"

"She found out I got the women to help. What if she shows up?"

"I doubt it."

"I've never seen her so angry," she said, glancing past his shoulder toward the sound of engines. "I'm warning you. When she gets mad, she can get violent."

"No kidding?" said Honoré, turning around to see who had arrived.

"No kidding."

Three black Volkswagens, with battered fenders and smoke pouring from mufflers, stopped at the back of the church. Doors cracked open, and a bunch of men, short, with sunburned faces and matted black hair, climbed out. They wore safari vests with pockets bulging with cameras, pens, and packs of cigarettes. The Mexican press.

Honoré swallowed the meat. "Keep that booze out of sight or the priest will jump all over our asses. And keep your mouth shut."

"Why? What's up?"

He lowered his voice. "Look, in a few minutes this place will be jumping with all of my political enemies. There'll be spies everywhere."

"Who do I watch out for?"

"The cops, the gringos." Honoré wiped his mouth on the back of his sleeve. "Anybody from out of town. Anyone who's too friendly, asks too many questions. A red-headed FBI agent."

Ty made a dumb face. "Why would there be spies at a barbecue for a convoy hauling humanitarian aid?"

"Never mind. If anything or anyone looks weird, let me know. And stay out of trouble."

She pointed at the Mexican reporters with the fork. "Are these guys your enemies?"

"No, of course, not."

"They sure look weird to me."

A floppy black cowboy hat appeared. Some days Sixto looked like Pablo Nerudo. Today he vaguely resembled Augusto César Sandino. His lanky, sinewy son, El Víbora, stood next to him. They had accompanied the Mexican press.

Honoré crossed the parking lot. "*¡Mi general!*" he yelled.

Don Sixto threw back his head and opened his arms, grinning. "Honoré!"

They embraced, slapping each other's back hard. "Good to see you, *cabrón*," said Honoré.

"*¿Y el convoy?*"

"They should be here any minute," said Honoré. "They may be stuck in traffic. A lot of trucks going south."

"Yeah, the bridge is jam-packed. We barely made it over in time."

El Víbora, his arms looking hard as mesquite wood, stepped through a curtain of sunlight and shook Honoré's hand. "Everything is ready for tomorrow's rally in Nuevo Escandón," he said. "All the TV and radio stations and newspapers have been notified."

A KMEX van arrived and parked behind the Volkswagens. A young man in a red tie, white shirt, and gray pants clambered out, a pen and notepad in hand, and stood waiting as another young man followed him out, walked to the back of the van, opened the doors, and took out a camera. Then the KAOS van arrived, parking behind KMEX. The anchor, a popular young woman named Conchita Terrazas, climbed down from the vehicle wearing a dark two-piece business suit and high heels. Afterward, a tall blond girl climbed down with a camera, which she set on the pavement. Golden hair sparkling in sunlight, she crouched next to it and fiddled with a knob. She was Shirley English, the girl he had met at The Lazy Mex.

Suddenly, it occurred to Honoré that she was probably the reason Olivia was pissed. "Hola," he said from where he stood about twenty feet away.

"Hi," the girl said as she rose to her feet, camera on her shoulder.

Suddenly, Honoré felt different, like he was on TV, like he had become a character in a Mexican *telenovela*, like a star. His body shuddered; his hands felt damp. He straightened his collar.

Soon, the hum of engines filled the air. "Here they come!" yelled El Víbora.

First, the pickup with the flags on the bumper arrived. The van with the POW/MIA flag parked behind. More vans and trucks pulled into the parking lot and lined up in three neat rows across the pavement. Some elderly folks—men and women in their sixties and seventies, hair white as cumulus clouds, faces red as fresh apples—climbed down from the vehicles with the Cross of Malta, undergirded by the letters *VFW*. Wild-eyed, shaggy, tough, the men in combat gear jumped out of the van with the POW/MIA flag as if they were on a search-and-destroy mission in Vietnam. A tall black man with gold-rimmed glasses and a preacher's white collar climbed out of his van as if looking around for pagans. Finally, the string of yellow school buses loaded with boxes rumbled across the asphalt and parked in a fourth row. More vehicles arrived until at least thirty-eight stood in the parking lot. Doors flew open, and voices resonated like a flock of pigeons. If Johnny Paint was driving a school bus, he was nowhere to be seen now.

"Looks like the gringos emptied the nursing homes and morgues," said El Víbora.

"Watch your tongue," said Don Sixto. "These people are here to help us."

Another bus arrived. It coughed, chugged, and backfired with a blast that sounded like gunfire. A cloud of exhaust poured out of its tailpipe. "*¡Chingao!*" said Honoré. "How are these wrecks gonna get across Mexico and Central America?"

The old folks, warbling under straw hats like tourists at the racetrack in Nuevo Escandón, walked past the cameras and the Mexican press. The vets looked like extras from the set of *Apocalypse Now* searching for the fastest way to the red light district. The women were tall white mothers wearing shorts and looking for their children at a supermarket, but there were no children.

"Praise the Lord!" said the black minister, stopping three feet from Honoré, eyes excited in a face shiny and black as a polished eggplant. "The promised land! We have arrived! Indeed, we have!"

Honoré held out his hand. "Welcome, pastor."

"Thank you, son. Just call me Paul." He shook his hand and leaned toward him. "Can you direct me to the men's room?"

"Inside, to your right."

"*Mira, mira,*" hissed El Víbora, who stood behind Honoré. "Gringas."

Tall and skinny with bony shoulders under their T-shirts, braless, the gringas paused a few feet from Honoré. "And who are you?" asked the one with a hammer and sickle tattooed on her left arm. "Our tour guide?"

"Yes, ma'am," Honoré said.

The women left, suddenly giggling as they glanced back at Honoré and looked him up and down one last time. He smiled. They had nice long legs.

"I'll take the one on the left," El Víbora said.

"I'll take both of them," Don Sixto said.

"That'll be the end of you."

"Is there a better way for an old man to die?"

Then, Honoré faced a tall gringo, lively blue eyes in a craggy unshaven face, broad shoulders in a khaki shirt, accompanied by a short gringa in cutoffs and tennis shoes, an old gray T-shirt over a flat braless chest, a frown beneath a safari hat.

The gringo held out a sun-scorched hand as a drop of sweat dangled from the tip of his nose. "Howdy."

"Howdy," said Honoré.

"Name's Jack Halligan. Commander of the convoy."

Honoré shook his hand. "Welcome, sir. Don Sixto here is chairman of the convoy support committee in Nuevo Escandón."

"*Bienvenidos a la frontera*," said Don Sixto, shaking the Commander's hand vigorously. "It's an honor to be a part of this wonderful gesture by the American people to those of us who have fought for peace and justice in Latin America for years."

With a sincere but weathered face, the Commander said, "Gracias, gracias, gracias. This is Molly," he added. "An old friend, second in command of this outfit, a true comrade."

The woman's lips were dry and chapped. "I knew it'd be hot on the border but nothing like this."

The Commander looked around. "Trotsky already here?"

"Inside," Honoré said.

"Last time I saw him was in Managua, where all this started. What about El Capitán?"

"Mexico."

Suddenly, the Commander, his face pale as soap, teetered and grasped the woman's shoulder.

She held him. "Are you okay?"

The Commander regained his balance. "Yeah. Just not used to this South Texas heat yet."

"This is nothing," said Honoré.

"Are you serious?" she gasped.

Another man came up from among the vehicles. Rimless glasses on a long sharp nose, he wore shorts and carried a briefcase. Dark brown curly hair grew on his sturdy white legs. He wore tennis shoes. "Good day," he said, a smart ring in his voice.

The Commander spoke. "One of the finest civil rights lawyers in the country. On the staff of the ACLU, in fact. Pinchas Zuckermann."

"Pinchas?" asked Honoré.

"Yes."

"Do you know what that means around here?"

Everything about the man sparkled—his glasses, his pink lips, his voice. "Just call me Zuckermann," he said with a smile. "Every Hispanic I've met told me never to use my first name around Spanish speakers and especially Mexicans. I don't. But I'm proud of my name. Pinchas was Aaron's grandson."

Chuckling, the Commander slapped Zuckermann on the back. "That why he's such a fine lawyer—because he's *pinche*."

"*Bienvenido*," Honoré said with a smile.

"Gracias," Zuckermann said and then took out a silk handkerchief with "PZ" embroidered in gold and wiped his face. "I heard it could get hot in Texas, but I had no idea. Will it cool off once we head south?"

"Yes," said Honoré. "The *altiplano* begins in Saltillo."

All at once, the cameras gathered around, snooping into everything, and members of the Mexican press shouted, "¡Una entrevista! ¡Entrevista!"

Molly wiped her brow. "We better go inside."

"I second that motion," said Zuckermann and then turned to the Mexican press and TV cameras. "Let's go inside, ladies and gentlemen! We'll take questions inside, please! Inside! ¡Las entrevistas en la iglesia!"

As Honoré watched the crowd shamble toward the church, a raspy voice turned his stomach. "Hi, hotshot."

He had heard that voice before, and though he didn't want to see who it was, he turned, slowly. There stood Johnny Paint and Tennessee. "You're part of this convoy?"

"Hell, yes," said Johnny. "Wouldn't miss it for the world."

"How did you get involved?" asked Honoré.

"Hooligan," drawled Tennessee, blue eyes sad as ever.

"Hooligan?"

"Halligan. The Commander. A distant cousin. When we heard he was headed for the border, we decided to tag along."

"I heard you guys were locked up."

After looking around, Johnny Paint edged closer. "Shit, ain't no jail in these here United States of America or anywhere else that can keep a Savage under lock and key. So here we is, bro."

Honoré lowered his voice. "Where's your uncle?"

"Back there." He pointed at one of the vehicles. "Ma Savage's trying to wake him up. We need to get him some Meskin pussy. How about you tagging along, amigo?"

Tennessee sniffed the air. "Smell that!"

"Barbecue!"

"Let's go inside," said Honoré.

"God, that smells too good to be true!" chirped Johnny Paint and started toward the grill.

Honoré grabbed him by the elbow. "Look, why don't you guys go inside? The food's almost ready."

Johnny Paint looked past Honoré's shoulder. "You see what I see?"

"What?" asked Tennessee.

"I see green."

"Damn right," said Tennessee. "Heineken green."

Honoré turned around—and sure enough, there was Ty Cobb in plain sight, sucking on a green bottle like a baby. The idiot.

"I could use some of that," added Johnny Paint.

Tennessee nudged Honoré out of the way. "Let's check it out."

As the two gringos crossed the parking lot, Honoré wondered whether the Commander knew what he was doing by bringing these troublemakers along. At length, he decided they would cause fewer problems out here than inside, where a reporter might ask them questions. So he walked toward the church, which consisted of two wings connected by a walkway. On the right stood the church itself while the parish hall, on the left, overflowed with people.

Inside the hall, the polished wooden floor soon became a campground with lawn chairs set up and sleeping bags unrolled in the large cafeteria-like room with plenty of light from the windows. In fact, some people were lying down already, shoes off and heads on pillows, and the whole place smelled of gringos, who sweated a lot. At one end of the parish hall, Trotsky's wife and the women from de la O's organization had already set up tables with trays of food, stacks of tortillas, and a large coffee urn. At the end of the table stood ice chests filled with cans of soda, and next to them were plastic barrels of water. Men and women in shorts and T-shirts waited in line, and others sat eating at the long tables.

Trotsky's wife, Altagracia, left the serving line and stopped Honoré in the middle of the parish hall. "We ran out of ice," she said. "Can you send someone to the store?"

"Yes, of course," he said and then headed across the hall, where the Commander and Trotsky sweated in the glare of TV lights while El Víbora watched.

"The women need some ice," Honoré said to El Víbora. "Can you get some?"

"Sure."

Honoré took out some money. "There's a store on Kennedy."

"The convoy to Nicaragua," declared Trotsky before a television camera, "is an important humanitarian gesture on the part of the American people. It shows that many Americans, conscientious law-abiding citizens, oppose this government's foreign policy in Latin America. So, on behalf of the Escandón Convoy Support Committee, I wish to welcome the convoy to Escandón. As we love to say in Spanish, '*mi casa es su casa.*'"

Cheers went up, and people pounded the tables.

The Commander stepped up to the camera, his face somber, shoulders stooped from fatigue. "We have been deeply moved by all the support people have given us. We come from as far as Oregon and New England. In communities throughout this country, ordinary people have raised money and collected medical and food supplies. This has been in contrast to the brutal, terrorist policies of this administration toward the real freedom fighters in Latin America."

Suddenly, El Víbora was back. "*Problemas*," he whispered to Honoré.

"What's up?" asked Honoré.

"The dogs have arrived."

Honoré rushed across the parish hall and out the entrance.

Sleek white unmarked sedans with long steel antennae flopping about like rigging on shrimp boats in the Gulf of Mexico cruised into the parking lot behind the church. After killing the engines, big men in shiny gray suits and white Stetsons and cowboy boots climbed out, standing tall as they hitched their trousers and eyed the scene.

Never did Honoré think that one day he would prefer dealing with the *federales* rather than the flat-footed local yokels if only because these *federales* tried to do things right—that is, legally. In fact, the feds were investigating the DA's office, the Telaraña County sheriff, the Telaraña County jail, and the cops for money laundering, influence peddling, dope dealing, and corruption.

Honoré's old political enemy, the redheaded FBI agent, Rex, led the parade.

"Well, I guess it ain't no surprise to see you see here, with these radicals," Rex said as another gringo joined him. "This is Honoré, our local rabble rouser. Thinks he's Che Guevara."

Honoré looked at the other gringo. "You FBI, too?"

"No, Treasury."

"Washington?"

"Yes, sir."

Honoré hated that he preferred talking to gringos simply because he could joke around with them without wanting to kill them afterward. "Why can't you send educated agents to the border? All Washington ever sends is poor white trash. Send us some intelligent blacks."

The Treasury agent laughed.

"Cut the bullshit," muttered Rex.

"Ten four," Honoré said.

Sirens screamed. Squad cars arrived. Fat men in blue uniforms, heavy black belts, and holsters with guns big as cannons climbed out, slammed doors, and gathered around Comino, who wore a white cap with a big silver badge on its crown. The gun quivered on his hip as he crossed his arms on his chest and cast a sidelong glance at Honoré, who stood twenty feet away.

Honoré turned to Rex. "I'll get the Commander. Wait here." Then he went inside. After stepping around and over people lying on the floor, Honoré stood behind Trotsky. "Cops."

"Who?"

"INS, FBI, Treasury, and my in-laws."

A woman shouted, "Look!"

Honoré's stomach sank. First, the FBI agent, then the Treasury agent, and the other tall gringos in gray suits and cowboy boots filled the door-way. A buzz spread through the room. While the newspeople carried their microphones and cameras toward the suits, the Commander, Trotsky, and Zuckermann retreated in the opposite direction and huddled near a wall. Honoré joined them.

The Commander kept his voice low. "Get those pigs out of here!"

"Take them into the conference room!" said Zuckermann.

"Yes," said the Commander, "the conference room. Just get 'em out of sight. I don't want those bastards talking to the press."

"I'll take care of them," Honoré said and then strode across the hall. "This way," he said to Rex.

A door at the back of the hall opened on a long narrow room with plenty of windows and a mural of Franciscan monks in brown robes on a wall. Chairs stood around a long wooden table. All the men except Rex and the Treasury agent filed inside. Meanwhile, cameras on the shoulders of the TV crewmen filmed everything.

Suddenly, boots clattered across the floor as a herd of javelinas charged through the entrance, eyes flashing, breathing jalapeño fumes. Comino glared at Honoré and then grinned as he welcomed the opportunity to kick Honoré's butt.

Honoré turned to Rex. "The apes have to stay outside."

"Fine," Rex said and waved at Comino and his men. "Officers outside. Everything's under control here."

Comino approached him. "Sir."

Rex wriggled his nose as if he caught a whiff of something ugly. "Sir, *what*?"

Beads of sweat on puffy brown jowls, Comino froze as a TV camera zoomed in on him. "Sir," he said, "the Escandón Police Department is here to . . . um . . . ah . . ."

A uniform behind Comino leaned toward him and whispered, "To serve and protect."

"To serve and protect!" Comino said loudly.

Rex glanced at the Treasury agent and then Honoré, despairingly. "Officer, I understand that. The Escandón Police Department is one of the best in this country."

The Treasury agent grinned, looked away, and then walked inside the conference room, closing the door behind him.

Comino smiled at the camera. "We want our visitors from the north to know that they're safe in our city. This is not Mexico. If anyone needs anything, just holler. We *spik Inglish*."

Everyone except Rex laughed. "Thank you," he said. "Now would you mind waiting outside?"

Comino glared at Honoré. Then he turned to Rex. "Yes, sir." He saluted, turned, and herded the blue javelinas out.

As soon as the best and the brightest exited, Rex disappeared inside the conference room. Honoré joined Trotsky and the Commander, now pressed by the news media people.

"What do the feds want?" asked Conchita Terrazas, pushing a KAOS microphone in the Commander's face. "Why aren't they part of the press conference?"

The Commander cleared his throat. "We are on a mission of peace and hope for Central America."

"We understand that, sir. But—"

"Let me finish."

"Yes, sir."

"The feds are here to harass us. They're here to discredit our mission. They invited themselves tonight. We knew something like this might happen. We didn't think it would happen here."

"Is it true you're challenging the United States' embargo against Nicaragua?" asked a Mexican reporter.

Zuckermann eased between the Commander and the media and raised a hand. "Gentlemen—and ladies—please. May I have your attention?"

The Mexican would not back down. "Will you cross the border tomorrow?"

"That's the plan," said Zuckermann.

"Is there any chance of a violent confrontation?" Conchita Terrazas asked hopefully.

Zuckermann rolled his eyes. "Of course not. We are on a humanitarian mission. Please, everyone. Please. Thank you very much for coming, but right now we're very tired and we need some rest. Tomorrow we'll update you on any developments."

As soon as the media marched out of the parish hall, everything returned to normal: the unpacking of gear, the chow lines, the women serving food, the old folks stretching out on lawn chairs, and clumps of people talking and laughing. Honoré and Trotsky joined the Commander, Molly, and Zuckermann, who had moved away from the crowd.

"We've got to tighten security," said Molly in a low voice. "We've got plenty of spooks on board already. But now with the feds breathing down our necks, there's no telling what stunt they might pull."

"Who?" said the Commander.

"The spooks. Government spies."

"You're exaggerating."

"Am I?"

"Okay, okay," said the Commander, "post as many guards as you want, and let these people get some rest."

Satisfied that he had listened to her, she left and joined some veterans at a distant table.

"One more thing," said Zuckermann to the Commander. "We've contacted the head of the Rural Legal Defense Fund. Armando Sánchez. We've got to ready our petition in case the feds try to stop us at the bridge tomorrow."

Trotsky nodded. "Good."

Zuckermann added, "After I make a few calls to New York, I'll get back to you."

"Trotsky and I will be in the conference room with the feds," the Commander said. "Don't take too long."

As soon as Zuckermann and Trotsky left, Honoré approached Jack. "Excuse me, sir."

"Yes," said the Commander.

"Can we speak privately?"

"Shoot."

"Are the Savages your relatives?"

The Commander's eyes widened. "You know them?"

"My family has done business with them over the years."

The Commander saw the look in Honoré's face. "Several of our vehicles broke down in Mississippi. Ole man Savage helped us. First-rate mechanic. Offered to join the convoy after we told him we needed a good mechanic, especially once we entered Mexico. Then, my cousins showed up. Ma and Pa Savage didn't see anything wrong in their tagging along. Plus, they donated some of those trucks. I didn't have much choice."

Honoré said, "They can be a lot of trouble. If word gets out that these characters are on board, it'll hurt your cause."

"I know, I know," moaned the Commander. "But Ma Savage is with them. She'll keep an eye on them."

Honoré decided to cut to the chase. "Are you aware they're escapees?"

The Commander looked around. "Look, I know why they're dying to get to Mexico. I was hoping to dump them here in Escandón. Can you help?"

"I don't know," said Honoré. "I'll do what I can."

Jack's blue eyes were sad under the weight of the world. "Just keep tabs on them. Tell me if they cause trouble, especially if they get drunk or stoned. Okay?"

"I'll go check on them." But the minute Honoré walked outside, it was obvious that there was already trouble. The iron grill stood abandoned, and Ty had gone AWOL. And the Savages were nowhere around.

At the same time, Comino yelled, "Honoré!"

Honoré looked at his brother-in-law and the other cops milling around the squad cars.

Comino waved. "Come here! Don't worry. We won't do anything to you, *primo*!" The cops laughed.

That was it. That was all he needed to hear, the cackling of *pendejos*. He couldn't kick their asses now, but he couldn't turn his back on them either. Cowardice had never been in the repertoire of the men in his family. He headed across the asphalt.

"We're ready for whatever you have to dish out," said Comino. "From the looks of this junkyard and these hippies, it won't be much."

Honoré decided to follow his mother's advice for once and turn the other cheek. "I'm just here to help these people out. They're good people, not fat-assed jerks that never do anything for anyone. They're taking food and medicine and bicycles to the people of Nicaragua." But it was difficult to turn the other cheek. "And I want you to keep your fat hands off them."

Comino exchanged grins with his men. Then, he faced Honoré. "*Chingao*," he said with a smirk, "why are you helping the Nicaraguans? You should be helping the people in the *colonias, cabrón*. Why don't you join the Salvation Army? That way you could be part of a real army and we could all see you at Christmas in a blue uniform ringing a bell downtown. Instead you get involved with these weirdos who are trying to destroy the American way of life. You and your family would still be in Mexico starving to death, *cabrón*, if it weren't for America."

Suddenly, Honoré felt dizzy. At first he thought it was a result of his brother-in-law's beer belly, whose curvature resembled a planet he had seen in Tequila's observatory. The gravitational pull always disoriented him, but it was probably the armpits. Comino smelled worse than the gringos.

Then, something nasty occurred to Honoré. "Why are you so fucking ugly?"

Honoré might as well have punched Comino in the mouth. His brother-in-law's face twitched. Beads of sweat broke out. If his face had been light-skinned like Honoré's, it probably would have turned red. Since it was brown, it turned purple.

Comino's mustache shuddered. "If it weren't for my sister or my niece, *cabrón*," he said, "they would have locked you up long ago and thrown away the key. First chance we get, Coyote, we're going to kick your ass!"

Honoré grinned. "You've been trying to do that as long as I can remember."

"But this time no one will save you," swore Comino. "Not even Maruca."

"Leave Maruca out of this."

Comino lowered his voice. "¡*Me la mamas, güey*!"

Honoré replied just as quietly, "Tell your buddies to suck you off, asshole!"

The parish hall door flew open. "I'll drink to that!" said a gringo.

"Ha, ha, ha, ha, ha!" laughed another gringo.

At first they sounded like a bunch of drunken tourists walking out of a whorehouse in Nuevo Escandón, but it was the government agents slamming through the doors of the hall.

"Honoré!" shouted Rex, who stopped to loosen his tie as the other agents headed for their cars. "Hasta la vista, *compadre*," he said with a twang in his Spanish. "We'll see y'all at the bridge tomorrow."

Thirty minutes later, the Commander convened a meeting in the conference room. A painting on the wall caught Honoré's attention when he entered. With tonsured heads and spare beards, friars ministered to the Indians in the courtyard of a church. Franciscan friars from Querétaro had founded the missions in this region, Trotsky had explained, building them all the way to San Antonio. While the Commander chatted with Zuckermann at one end of the conference table, Molly sat beside them, embroidering a blue-and-white Nicaraguan flag. Honoré sat with Trotsky at the other end, wondering whether the window unit would cool off the Commander.

"First," said the Commander, "I want to thank all of you from Escandón for the support you've given us. Now it looks like we'll need you more than ever. Treasury just told us they're going to stop the convoy at the bridge tomorrow. They said it's okay for us to take humanitarian aid to Nicaragua—food, bicycles, medicine—but they cannot allow us to cross with the vehicles unless we pay a deposit insuring that the vehicles return to the United States. Otherwise, we'll be violating the embargo against Nicaragua. Of course, there's no way in hell we can leave a deposit. We simply don't have the money. Besides, the vehicles stay in Nicaragua."

Molly looked up from the flag. "But we aren't just going to give up here in Escandón, are we?"

"Good question," said the Commander, a huge drop of sweat wiggling on his nose. "And the last thing we need is a retreat. This administration would love that." Then, the Commander's face grew serious. "So where do we go from here, gentlemen?"

The door opened. Altagracia entered and sat next to Trotsky. "The bishop," she said quietly to him and Honoré, "got on the phone as soon as he found out about the convoy. He was very upset. They can spend the night here and in the dormitories across the street, but they need to be out of here in the morning."

Suddenly, yelling erupted outside, and a door flew open. In walked a woman, a big woman in overalls, arms thick as salmons. "Where's that asshole Honoré!" shouted Mrs. Savage.

Honoré slowly stood up. "Right here, ma'am."

She lumbered toward him, teeth bared, a fist clenched, cheeks red as a baboon's ass. She got in his face and grabbed him by the collar. "Where the fuck is my husband?"

Honoré was a big man. In fact, he was bigger than Mrs. Savage. But clearly she was stronger than most of the men in the room. "I don't know," he said, blood percolating in his neck.

She tightened her grip. "You get that motherfucker back or I'm gonna give you an ass-whupping! You hear?"

Honoré knew he could probably beat the shit out of this ugly middle-aged truck driver, but his dignity as a caballero from South Texas kept him from it. "What have I done?"

Her breath smelled of mustard, onions, and sardines after a long day on the road. "Ever since you and your good-for-nothin' friend Mesquila—"

"Tequila," Honoré corrected.

"Whatever. Ever since you took him to boys' town, he's never been the same. All he talks about when he's drunk is how happy he'd be if he was screwing some Meskin whore."

"Ma Savage," yelled the Commander, rising to his feet at the other end of the table, "this is a church! A little decorum! Or I'll have you taken into custody!"

She let go.

The Commander walked toward her. "What happened? Where's Uncle Savage?"

She backed toward the door. "He's gone. Left with Tennessee and Johnny Paint. Probably to Mexico."

The Commander rested his hand on her shoulder. "Now calm down. Tomorrow, we have a long day ahead of us. I'll take care of this. Get something to eat."

She stormed out of the room. Honoré straightened his collar and sat down. The Commander returned to his seat. After conferring with Molly and Zuckermann, he turned to Trotsky. "Where were we?" he asked.

Trotsky turned to the Commander. "I suggest you spend the night here. However, if they stop us at the bridge, which they no doubt will, we can't return to the church."

"So what we do?" asked Zuckermann.

"Honoré has a backup plan," Trotsky said.

Honoré looked down the length of the table. "A friend of mine, a wealthy rancher, has a piece of land north of town. Used to be a campground for snow birds, retired folks from up north. Has everything, bathrooms, showers, an office, telephone. I already talked to him."

"Is it safe?" asked Molly.

Honoré frowned. "Of course, it's safe. It's on the highway northwest of Escandón. River Road. But it's not close to the river."

"A lot of snakes?" asked Zuckermann.

"No more than usual."

Molly fanned herself. "Does it have running water?"

Honoré exchanged glances with Trotsky. "Yes, ma'am."

"Clean bathrooms?" asked Zuckermann.

Honoré wished they would shut up. "I think so."

"What kind of place is this?" asked Zuckermann.

Honoré felt everyone's eyes on him. He cleared his throat. "It's a nudist colony."

"No shit!" The Commander slammed the table. "A nudist colony? I'll be damned! This is the first time I hear of a bunch of Vietnam veterans taking refuge in a nudist colony! If we had had something like that in Vietnam, we wouldn't have come back so crazy." He paused suddenly, thoughtfully, fixing Honoré in a gaze. "Does this mean we'll have to run around naked?"

Next morning, vehicle upon vehicle stood in line, drivers in the driver's seat, American flags tied to antennas yawning in a soft breeze, Nicaraguan flags fluttering like white doves. The KMEX and KAOS vans were parked in the street next to the church, and two young men with oily copper arms in white T-shirts wandered about with cameras on their shoulders, accompanied by Conchita Terrazas. Shirley English, on the other hand, was nowhere to be seen. So Honoré wondered whether the latter had taken off with Ty and the Savages across the river. Eyebrows knitted, Ma Savage had been fuming all morning, on the verge of smacking anyone in her way. So Honoré kept his distance, sitting securely in his pickup at the head of the column of vehicles, waiting for the Commander, Trotsky, Zuckermann, and other members of his staff to finish their meeting in the parish hall. Earlier they had decided to postpone the bridge crossing a day or two, giving them a chance to rest and strategize. Then, the Commander asked Honoré to lead the convoy to El Paraíso del Nopal, the campground north of Escandón, where the Governor had promised to meet them.

Pastor Paul walked outside first. With a huge golden cross hanging from a chain around his neck, he looked like a black prophet from the Old Testament, who saw angels and a silver lining everywhere he turned, his white teeth rooted in pink gums when he smiled. He seemed incorrigibly happy. Then Trotsky and Zuckermann came out.

Trotsky headed toward Honoré. "Sorry about the delay," he said as he climbed in the pickup. "There may not be much of a convoy left after the South Texas sun gets done with these northerners. Jack had a fainting spell."

"Is he okay?" asked Honoré.

"I hope so. Molly and Zuckermann are good people, but they don't have the Commander's clout with leftist organizations in the U.S. and Latin America. Without him, none of this would have been possible. And if we lose him now, the whole project might unravel."

At last, the Commander appeared, his blond hair shimmering, looking tall but fragile in the morning sunlight. However, Molly, a permanent sun-drenched scowl under her safari hat, and two Vietnam vets in jungle hats and olive-green fatigues escorted him, prepared—at the slightest wobble in his stride—to catch him.

The Commander halted in the middle of the parking lot. "Okay, let's move out!" he yelled.

Gray and dumb as a hammerhead shark, a TV camera came up to Honoré's window and fed on his face as if he were a lobster—well, maybe not a lobster but definitely a weird-looking sea creature. Why? Because the thought of Maruca, his in-laws, and everyone else seeing him on television made him feel weird. The world became distorted but interesting with the TV cameras around. Maybe Maruca was right. Maybe he should have been an actor. He started the engine.

"Feels like a movie set," he said offhandedly to Trotsky. "All of Escandón must be watching us."

"The whole world is watching."

Slowly, Honoré rolled out of the parking lot. The street led past empty lots overgrown by grass, where government buildings once stood. When the air base was closed in the late seventies, the city bought this land but never developed it. Now young men played soccer here on weekends, kicking the ball across the barren dirt fields as if they lived in some Latin American country. Up ahead, Honoré saw a lot of traffic on Kennedy. When he reached the intersection, the traffic pulled over and let the convoy pass. Honoré turned right and headed across town. At another intersection a young store clerk came out of a drive-thru corner store and watched. Minutes later, they passed a bakery, several Mexican restaurants, a *vulcanizadora* or tire shop, and two gasoline stations. A beautiful young girl Honoré had never seen before stood at a bus stop and waved as if he were part of a float in the annual George Washington's Birthday Celebration parade. A fat gringo in a Cadillac stuck out a muscular white arm and gave him the finger. A block later, headstones and white angels and wooden crosses braided with yellow and white carnations reminded Honoré of all his friends from high school now buried among the mesquite trees and cactus of the cemetery.

"*Pinche* Honoré," they said as he imagined them sitting up and sticking their heads out of their graves. "You think you're hot shit because you're alive. But it won't be long before you are a dead *tlacuache* like us."

Then the convoy passed under the interstate.

At Escandón High School, the scene of some of the most spectacular football games Escandonians had ever seen, with Honoré as the star quarterback and Tequila as a running back, they turned and headed north on Tamaulipas Avenue, a strip full of used car lots, restaurants, and Mexican curio shops. In the front yard of an old house converted into a store, the carved wooden figure of Don Quixote stared at them. At another curio shop, a band of mariachis, made from metal cut with an acetylene torch, held guitars on their bellies as they raised their whiskered faces under wide-brimmed sombreros and even wider mouths. Then they drove past Pizza Hut on the left and Castillo's Mexican Curios on the right. After passing cheap motels and a truck stop, where eighteen-wheelers fed like gigantic prehistoric insects at diesel pumps, they rumbled over the railroad tracks. Wooden fence posts carried miles of barbed wire into the brush country.

Twenty minutes later, he rolled to a stop in front of a ranch gate made from long steel pipes welded together under a sign that read "El Paraíso del Nopal," The Nopal Paradise. In the rear view mirror, the rest of the convoy pulled over.

Trotsky got out, pushed the gate open, and got back in. "Let's go."

Potholes kicked the hell out of the pickup, which creaked and moaned through a cloud of dust. Lizards scrambled across their path, and about a hundred yards ahead, a white-tailed deer ran across the caliche road and leaped into the undergrowth. A chain, gray as a rattlesnake with a big padlock for a head, hung wrapped around two steel pipes at the second gate.

Honoré stopped, looking up and down the length of fence. "Motherfucker told me he'd meet us here!"

"Over there," Trotsky said and pointed.

The stars-and-stripes snapped at the end of a long antenna. Stones clattered against the underbelly of a drab olive-green WWII vintage jeep speeding out of a cloud of dust in the east. A man wearing a military cap stood beside the driver and held on to the windshield, like General McArthur with that famous cap with gold embroidery on its bill shading his face when he reviewed his troops on Okinawa.

"Is this Hollywood or what?" asked Trotsky.

"Oh, shit!" Honoré turned off the engine. "Cuz."

The jeep skidded to a stop on the other side of the gate. The driver—his mahogany face narrow beneath the brim of a straw cowboy hat, a khaki shirt streaked with perspiration—looked as if he had just gotten out of the Mexican army. In other words, very Indian. A new ranch hand, thought Honoré as he and Trotsky climbed out of the pickup.

Then Cuz spoke, like a child, a woman, or a queer, as if one of his vocal cords had been cut, "May I help you, gentlemen?"

Honoré stood before the gate. "We're waiting for the Governor."

Cuz's blue eyes glittered with suspicion as he gazed at the vehicles idling on the road. "Who are these people?"

"Poor folks taking aid to the people of Nicaragua," Honoré replied.

After a long pause, Cuz sneered, "Contras?"

Honoré did not want to debate with an idiot. "Look, just open this gate and direct us to the Governor's ranch."

"This road passes through my property, and no bunch of contras and commies are crossing my land. It would be unpatriotic."

"Sir," said Honoré, suddenly distracted by noise in the west. A squeaking and jangling of loose metal carried through the mesquite, nopal, and huisache.

Cuz glared at Honoré. "Sir *what?*"

Annoyed, Honoré looked up the road that ran along the fence. A cloud of dust gathered as a vehicle barreled toward them. A Land Rover, old and beat-up, rolled to a stop a few yards from the gate. A door flew open.

Hair sparkling like white gold in the sun, the Governor clambered from the old vehicle while the driver, an old man with a cap pulled low across his face, waited. Faded jeans slung low on his hips and cowboy shirt open on his red chest, the Governor walked toward them, keys jingling in one hand.

"Sorry, Comandante," he said, unlocking the gate.

Cuz climbed down from the jeep. "Wait a minute. You know these people?"

The Governor unraveled the chain. "Yeah," he said. "Honoré here is an old buddy. And these are his friends."

"They're contras."

The Governor removed his cowboy hat and scratched his head. "What did you say?"

"I said these are contras."

The Governor put the hat back on. "What the fuck does *contra* mean?" He looked at Honoré. "*Contra*ceptive?"

"It means they're *contra*ry to the interests of our country," said Cuz.

The Governor pushed open the gate. "And what country are you talking about? Texas? The Republic of the Rio Grande?"

Cuz frowned. "The United States of America."

After wrapping the chain around a steel pipe, the Governor stood and gazed north thoughtfully. "Last I heard, so many Meskins have crossed the Rio Bravo that the border moved north of the Nueces, where it should have been in the first place. So South Texas really ain't America anymore."

"What the hell are you talking about? All I know is I can't allow any contras on my property."

Like the wing of an eagle rising against the sky, the Governor's eyebrow took flight above a blue eye, a look that meant only one thing—trouble.

"Did I hear what I think I heard?" he asked. "Our aunt dies. The will hasn't been probated but already you're claiming this is your property? Aren't you being a little goddamn greedy?"

Cuz turned red, swallowed hard, his little blue eyes fidgeting.

Honoré could see why Cuz dressed like General McArthur. For a moment he looked like the general—handsome, grand, and heroic. But then with the cap's long bill shading his face, he looked like a duck.

"Listen, Cuz," the Governor said in a low voice, "Honoré once saved my life. So I told him if he ever needed my help, he'd get it. No matter what. No questions asked. On the other hand, you and your family didn't give a shit when I got shot up in that ambush. So piss off."

Cuz put his hands on his hips like General McArthur. "What about my plane?"

"What about it?"

Cuz, unlike the great WWII general, whined. "You crashed it in the lake. How do I know you won't get me into trouble with these contras? What happens when the FBI finds out they're staying here? My name will be mud in this town."

"Give me a fucking break. It's already mud. It's shit. Which is what you get for fucking the maids."

Cuz stepped back, glanced at his driver, who was cleaning his fingernails with a pocket knife. "I swear by Almighty God," he sputtered before pivoting and tramping back to the jeep.

His driver shifted gears as Cuz climbed inside. Bouncing and shaking, the jeep spun around and headed back up the dirt road.

The Governor pushed open the gate. "He's got a big surprise coming," he said to Honoré. "My great aunt told me I was getting this land. But Cuz and Company want everything. He ain't getting this if I have any say-so."

Jack rabbits leaped from the brush as the Governor led the convoy past cows grazing at the edge of a narrow dirt road that ran through thickets of gray scrub and green cactus. Buzzards floated in the sky like slivers of mesquite in a pool of water.

They drove past old wooden crosses surrounded by a wrought iron fence of an abandoned cemetery and bounced up another hill before dropping into a small valley embraced by low-lying mesquite-filled hills.

Palmettoes fastened to round wooden beams provided shade for the picnic tables around a grill at the end of a pond surrounded by dozens of palm trees.

"This looks better," said Trotsky.

Honoré wasn't so sure. Every time he thought he had stumbled into the Garden of Eden, he had gotten into trouble. There was no telling what evil lurked here.

An A-frame bungalow stood at the end of the road. The Governor's iron hog, with its expensive saddlebags and beribboned handlebars, glittered in front of the A-frame. The old man driving the Land Rover dropped off the Governor at its entrance and then took off down the road. Honoré parked next to the motorcycle while the Commander and the rest of the convoy rumbled past, heading for different parts of the camp, and parked wherever they could find shade. After climbing out of the pickup, Honoré and Trotsky joined the Governor.

"Welcome to El Nopal," the Governor said, as he wiped his brow with the back of his sleeve. "Ain't much, but it's better than nothing."

Trotsky looked at the A-frame. "This is more than we expected."

The Commander walked up from his pickup across the road. "Is this really a nudist colony?"

The Governor frowned. "The politically correct word is 'nudist resort.'"

"Well," said the Commander, "is this really a nudist resort?"

"Not yet."

The front door of the A-frame opened, and out pranced two dazzling long brown legs in red cowboy boots. The young woman's terrycloth robe was so short she was naked from her hips to her boots. However, all eyes converged on the *maracas* jouncing under the terrycloth, as if at any moment the robe might open. The most they got was a glimpse of the upper slope of a breast as she walked past, smelling of soap and perfume.

When she winked at Honoré, he didn't know whether to wink back, look away, or laugh. He glanced at the Commander, who coughed, straightened up, pretending not to see the woman's charms.

The Governor shifted his ass in a swagger. "I asked city council for a permit to build a nudist resort out here, but so far nothing. Word got out, and some preachers opposed it. Cuz back there opposes it. I don't know what the hell's wrong with him. Either he's a *testículo*—I mean a *Testigo—de Jehovah*, or he's a member of the Church of Latter Day Devils."

Everyone laughed.

Then the Governor climbed on the hog and kick-started it. It coughed and farted. The men silently watched the Mexican bombshell hold the robe tight around her hips, slide on the hog, sidesaddle, and cross her lovely leg in front of her. Her buttocks were brown and lovely as two loaves of whole wheat bread settling on black leather. She wore a red thong.

The Governor revved the hog. "You guys need anything," he said, "just give me a holler at the mansion back in town. I'll be there the rest of the day. My little señorita here and I have business to attend to. And listen, Commander, if y'all want to take off your clothes and run around naked, go ahead. I always said the best way to deal with the South Texas heat is buck naked."

He rolled out of the compound, engine coughing and spitting. When he hit the throttle hard, the hog roared down the dirt road, and the glamorous couple looked as if they were zooming straight out of the latest Hollywood skin flick.

"How can he get away with driving around with her half-naked?" asked the Commander. "Up north they'd get arrested."

"His family owns a third of Escandón," said Honoré. "They hate his guts, he hates theirs, but they're family. In Escandón family counts more than anything else, especially if they're screwed up."

Back at the store, when Honoré closed the door behind him and a dozen parrots hanging from wires flew towards him through sunlight from the window, he felt as if he had stumbled into a bird-filled jungle somewhere in Chiapas or Guatemala. In his office he sat down and spread the newspaper on the gray metal desk. On the front page, a photo showed Trotsky and Don Sixto standing alongside the Commander with the pickups, cars, buses, and vans in the parking lot behind them.

"Honoré!" yelled Maruca before barging into the office. "The phone has been ringing all morning."

"Who's been calling?"

She opened a desk drawer and took out some keys. "Your friends from the convoy. They're in jail in Nuevo Escandón."

"Fucking idiots."

She paused at the door. "I'm going to see your mother."

"How is she?"

"The same. One day she feels great and talks like she'll live forever. The next day she swears the room is full of people, that she's talking to your father and angels are fluttering all about."

When Maruca left, he picked up the phone and dialed Sixto's number in Nuevo Escandón. It rang for a long time. He dialed several other numbers, including El Víbora's and La Clínica del Barrio's. Nothing.

Suddenly, the building shuddered. Before Honoré had a chance to put the phone back on the receiver, two six-foot beach balls burst through the door. In fact, the entire house seemed to wobble as his cousins crowded into the tiny office. When Honoré rose from his desk, he found himself face-to-face with two creatures, a total of over six hundred pounds that could crush him any second.

"What the hell are you doing here?" he asked.

"Boss, we need to talk to you."

Honoré didn't like fat people. Not only wouldn't they let you breathe because they sucked all the oxygen out of the air, but they were always throwing their weight around. "Can't you see I'm busy?"

"We need to talk about a job."

"No way, *güey!*" he yelled and pushed them away.

"Ouch!"

"Boss! Please!"

"You hurt me!"

"Pretty please!"

Suddenly, sirens exploded outside. Honoré froze as tires screeched and the sirens wailed. "What the hell is going on?" He peered out the window. "Oh, fuck!"

A pickup flew into the yard amid a cloud of steam and dust. With toothpick-thin arms swinging loosely, Johnny Paint stumbled from behind the wheel while Tennessee stayed in the cab, head thrown back on his seat, mouth open, as if he were dead or dead drunk. In the street, three squad cars, red lights flashing, skidded to a halt. A bunch of fat cops jumped out with guns drawn.

Honoré turned from the window to the hogs. "You motherfuckers want your jobs back?"

"Yeeeeeees," they cooed.

They were such *mamones.* No dignity. No old-fashioned manliness. "Follow me."

In the back room, he took out two AK-47s from a closet. After loading them, he explained how a cross-fire worked. They didn't understand a damned thing, so he pushed the assault rifles in their hands and told them what to do when they saw him raise his arm. Then, knowing that in the next five minutes he might wake up singing with a choir of angels, he stomped down the hallway and walked outside.

"*¡Pinche gringo!*" yelled the cop pinning Johnny Paint to the ground under a knee as he unlatched some handcuffs from his belt.

"Fuck you!" yelled Johnny Paint.

Another cop kicked him in the ribs. "*¡Callate, pendejo!*"

Another cop dragged Tennessee from the pickup and threw him on the ground. "*¡Idiota!*"

Honoré climbed down the porch steps. "What the hell is going on?"

"These assholes are drunk on their asses," yelled Comino, holding a gun to Johnny Paint's head.

"So?"

Comino held the gun steady while another cop handcuffed Johnny Paint. "They crossed the bridge without stopping. This idiot almost ran down a customs inspector."

"Put that thing away," Honoré said, then kneeled next to Johnny Paint. "Where are the women?"

Johnny Paint held his side, moaning. "I don't know."

"Where's your uncle?"

"In the pickup."

Honoré stood. In the back of the truck, he found a six-foot lobster, his face red, pants at half-mast, wet from piss, buttocks white and hairy, one shoe missing, the nails on his toes long and yellow. And he smelled like shit.

"How you doing, Hank?"

Hank rolled over and grinned, saliva dripping from one corner of his mouth. "Man, that Meskin poontang is powerful stuff. You boys ready to go back for some more?"

Comino waved his gun and said to one of the cops. "Drag his ass down."

"No," said Honoré, "leave him there. This is liberated territory. I'll take care of these gringos.

"You're full of shit," said Comino.

Like a heavy wrench, Honoré's right hand curled slowly into a fist that could turn this guy's teeth into dice. "What did you say?"

Comino stepped back, pistol in hand. "I said you're full of shit. If you don't get out of the way, we're taking you in, too."

"Yeah, well, if you don't get your ass off my property, we're going to have a *carne asada*."

"Yeah, with what?"

Honoré raised an arm.

A hog stepped out from the door to the warehouse, a *cuerno de chivo* in his hands. Seconds later, the other hog stepped from behind the south end of the store, a *cuerno de chivo* in his hands.

Honoré lowered his arm. "And your *nalgas* will be the first to fry. One wrong move, and you're a pork chop, *pendejo*."

Comino glared at the hogs.

Honoré knew that fat people don't fuck with each other. They know what they're up against.

"Do you know how much trouble you'll be in for threatening officers of the law?" asked Comino.

Honoré fixed his brother-in-law in a gaze. "Do you know how much trouble you'll be in with your ass shot off? You won't be able to sit down."

An eye flared. "Don't push your luck. You think you can get away with shit because you're married to my sister."

"Well, isn't that the way things are done in South Texas?"

"Okay, men," said Comino, "put down your guns."

One by one the cops put their guns back in their holsters.

"Take those handcuffs off," said Honoré.

The cops looked at Comino, who nodded grudgingly. Then they removed the cuffs, first from Johnny Paint and then Tennessee.

"Motherfuckers," muttered Johnny Paint as the cops stormed out of the yard.

Honoré grabbed Johnny Paint by the neck of his T-shirt and pulled him to his feet. "You got me into hot water with Ma Savage and the Commander, asshole!"

Johnny squirmed. "It wasn't our idea. That fat little boy asked us if we wanted to go, but we said we couldn't. "

Honoré held him tightly. "Bullshit."

Johnny raised a hand. "I swear. Pa Savage wanted to go across. He offered to pay for everything. Now when a Savage wants something, there ain't nothing going to stop him, especially Pa Savage. But that fat little boy—Ty—Pa didn't want him tagging along. Pa's ready to beat the shit out of him until I get involved. I say let's take his ass across to further the cause of peace."

"The cause of peace?" Honoré pushed the blue-eyed savage away. "A piece of ass?"

"Same thing."

Honoré should have let the cops haul him away. "What happened?"

"Pa Savage couldn't get it up."

"So?"

"So he wanted his money back. There's a fight. The cops come. And we all got arrested, everyone except the fat boy, who was locked in a room with two women with the biggest tits I've ever seen. Talk about knockers. White as milk. Nipples pink as strawberries. So this morning when they came to take us to the Calabozo, next thing we know we're in a fistfight with the cops. Then, we make a break for it, get back in the truck, and make a beeline for the US of A. They take potshots at us when we get close to the bridge. U.S. Customs stops us and sends us into secondary inspection, but we high tail it because it looks like nothing is gonna to stop those Meskin cops. So we run over some dumbass inspector's foot. Hope he was wearing steel toes. Then we head downtown, getting chased by a rhino in a cop car."

This guy wasn't as dumb as Honoré thought. "Comino does look like a rhino."

After trying to start the pickup, Tennessee got out, hunkered on the ground, and gazed at the puddle of acid under the engine. "Damned thing is dead. Either one of those Mexican cops plugged the battery when they shot at us or the damned thing cracked when we hit the curb."

"It's an old battery," said Johnny. "It was about ready to croak."

Tennessee stood up. "You'll have to give us a ride to the church," he said to Honoré.

"They got kicked out of the church. They're camped outside of town." Then Honoré spoke to the hogs in Spanish, "Keep an eye on everything. I'll be right back."

"Sí, *jefe*."

Thirty minutes later, Honoré rumbled into camp with Johnny Paint and Tennessee in the cab and Pa Savage in back. He climbed out of the truck, relieved he was finally able to get these losers out of his hair. But when he saw the meat cleaver in Ma Savage's hand as she stormed across the road, he knew he had been right about trouble in paradise.

"Oh, fuck!" moaned Johnny Paint.

Suddenly, everything turned political again. Forget about the Republicans and American foreign policy. Forget about Cuz, snakes, and the heat. Unless Honoré took a stand, Ma Savage would chop off her husband's balls. The convoy would lose its mechanic. In an uproar the media would ridicule what began as a heroic undertaking to help embattled revolutionaries in Nicaragua and call it a Mexican soap opera. If worse came to worse, Meskin poontang would stop the convoy, as the gringos loved to say, all by its lonesome.

Disgusted, he climbed down.

"Mrs. Savage," he said with all the courtesy of a caballero from South Texas as he halted between her and the truck. "I got your husband back, safe and sound, like I promised."

Growling as she stomped across the road, she yelled, "Get out of the way!"

"The convoy needs your husband!" exclaimed Honoré.

She veered to the right. "Get the fuck out of the way, you greaser!"

He jumped to the right.

She swung the meat cleaver at his neck, but he ducked. Maneuvering behind her, he grabbed her arm and kicked out one of her legs. They fell on the dirt road, where they rolled back and forth through the heat waves rising from the sand until she sat on him, a big woman with tits big as pillows and buttocks hard as chunks of Mexican cheese. Sunlight dripped from the mean-looking blade in her hands.

Honoré grabbed her wrist so she couldn't swing the cleaver.

"Get the rope!" yelled one of the Savages.

When Honoré thrust his pelvis hard up against her butt, she flew over him and hit the truck's back wheel so hard that the meat cleaver sliced the rubber, which let out a long, sad, ugly fart.

Tennessee grabbed her from behind, slipped a hairy arm around her thick neck, and pulled with all his might.

Bellowing like a wounded steer at the rodeo in Ft. Worth, she stood up with him clinging to her back and tried to buck him off. He held on tight, his boots flying everywhere as if he were riding the electronic bull at Gilley's. "Whoa!" he cried.

"Ride 'em, cowboy!" yelled Johnny Paint, twirling a lasso above his head.

Then, just as she sent Tennessee flying through the air, the lasso fell around her neck. She grabbed it and yanked so hard with one hand that Johnny, who had dug his heels in the sand, stumbled and almost let go, but as soon as Tennessee got up, the two cousins pulled the rope, which quivered in their white-knuckled hands as they dragged the kicking and screaming woman past a prickly pear.

Honoré sat up. He couldn't believe that this swamp rat from Mississippi had just saved his life. He turned out to be a real cowpoke.

Two skinny women ran from a vehicle parked behind a mesquite tree and grabbed the rope in Tennessee's hands. "Let her be! Can't you see she's just a woman!"

Tennessee let go and stepped aside. "Yeah, well, she ain't acting like one," he drawled.

Johnny Paint wiped his face with the back of his arm. "More like a fucking bull!" "Now, now, honey," cooed one of the women as she removed the rope from Ma Savage's neck and helped her to her feet. "Everything will be all right."

Though looking like a man in bib overalls, Ma Savage sobbed like a little girl with a broken heart. "I hate men! I hate men!"

Boots halted three feet from Honoré. Long legs in faded blue jeans rose to thumbs hooked on the belt buckle below a khaki shirt. "What the fuck is going on?" asked the Commander.

"Nothing, sir," said Johnny Paint.

Tennessee looked at his hands, red and raw from the rope. "We just broke up a domestic squabble."

"No shit."

"No shit," said Johnny Paint.

In the distance a small engine buzzed toward them as the Commander helped Honoré to his feet.

A helicopter flew out of the south. "BP," Honoré muttered.

The Commander turned his attention to the women. "You take care of my aunt. Make sure she keeps her hands off my uncle."

The women pulled Ma Savage to her feet. "Yes, comrade," they said and escorted her inside the A-frame.

The Commander turned to Johnny and Tennessee. "What the fuck is wrong with you? Is that any way to treat a woman?" He glared at Pa Savage. "Sober up Pa Savage and get to work on the vehicles. Keep him away from Mexican women. You hear?"

"Yes, sir."

"Oh, and fix this man's tire."

"Yes, sir."

The Commander gazed at the helicopter as it roared overhead and swung over the palm trees, a blond head sticking out the side and looking down at them through binoculars. The insect-shaped contraption raised so much dust it looked like a tornado had struck before it lifted and flew south. "Idiots," he muttered.

CHAPTER 11
Nothing Personal, Strictly Political

Amid the dust, the smell of exhaust, and the rumble of thirty-some-odd vehicles lining up on a dirt road behind him, Honoré waited in his pick-up. Ahead, the Commander's truck shivered like a feverish old woman as exhaust sputtered from its tailpipe. While Altagracia sat next to Honoré, Trotsky waited outside the door on the passenger's side. Suddenly, something in the sky caught Honoré's attention. A buzzard cruised past the flag pole standing next to the A-frame, whose lights in the windows were out, air conditioners silenced, doors locked. Headed south, the scavenger flew high above the pot-bellied, pistol-toting scavengers in blue. Since the city had assigned the convoy a police escort from Paraíso del Nopal to the international bridge, Comino's buddies sat on their motorcycles talking on their two-way radios, waiting for God-knows-what. When they arrived at the camp an hour before, leather belts and holsters creaking, faces somber behind shades in the bright morning sunlight, they didn't say or do anything nasty to Honoré, but it was obvious from the way they leered they were ready to kick his ass at the first opportunity.

"By the way," said Trotsky as he climbed in beside Altagracia, "Ty Cobb is back."

Honoré fixed Trotsky in a dead serious gaze. "No kidding?"

Trotsky slammed the door. "I guess she didn't want to miss out on the fun. Listen to this. She got some of her friends in Austin and San Antonio to donate a bus full of wheels."

"Wheels?" asked Altagracia.

"Many Sandinistas lost their legs in the war. They can't get prosthetics. So they want wheels, from tricycles or small bikes or lawn mowers, to build small two-wheeler carts. Basically, a slab of wood fastened between two wheels. In fact, one day I was standing outside a hotel in Managua. The Commander and I had just finished talking. I was about to cross the street when suddenly a dozen legless men flew down the hill on the two-wheelers. Amazing. Full grown men flying down the street like children. So when Ty asked me what her friends could contribute in the way of medical supplies, I suggested wheels."

Up ahead, a motorcycle growled. "Time to go," said Honoré and started the engine.

Soon the police escort roared out of the camp, followed by the Commander's pickup. Honoré shifted and then in tandem plunged into a cloud of dust billowing from the desert floor like flour from torn sacks. With dull sun-baked fenders whacked out of shape, chassis creaking and moaning, and loose tailpipes rattling, the vehicles were so old Honoré wondered how they made it across the country or expected to get to Nicaragua. Yet he marveled at how tough and idealistic these gringos could be, willing to drive across the continent and spend days roasting in the sun before traversing Mexico and risking their lives in Central America. At one time he would have done something like this for money or just for the hell of it, but for a noble cause?

"How's the Commander doing?" Altagracia asked.

"Better," said Trotsky.

"What's wrong with him?"

"Sunstroke. But I think it's more than that. He had a fainting spell in Managua when we met with him. That's why I've had doubts about this from the beginning. Molly and Zuckermann and others, too, have wondered if he was up to this trip."

As the pickup bounced and shuddered over the potholes, Honoré kept an eye on the vehicle ahead. "Did Zuckermann leave already?"

"Yeah," Trotsky said. "He's meeting some lawyers in town before they appear in federal court later today."

"I thought all that was unnecessary," said Honoré. "Everyone says the government is bluffing."

"Doesn't sound like they're bluffing," said Altagracia.

"Zuckermann convinced Jack we should take no chances. So we're filing an injunction against the embargo just in case they stop us. As you know, things have a weird way of going south when you least expect it."

Honoré made a face. "Yeah, just like with that crazy gringa who tried to kill me yesterday."

Altagracia shook her head. "Who are these people? The Savages? What a name! What are they doing here?"

"The Commander's relatives," Trotsky said. "They helped the convoy in Mississippi, so he feels obligated. Honoré knows them."

Honoré slowed down as they left the dirt road and turned east on River Road, a smooth ride on asphalt. "My family has done business with them for years. And you're right—they're crazy. They don't care about anything except making a buck. They'll probably abandon the convoy in Escandón."

"I sure as hell hope so," said Trotsky.

As barbed wire leaped from wooden post to wooden post, the names of El Salteador, Gonzales, Las Minas, and Stillwater appeared on signs above ranch gates. Twenty minutes later, the cactus and mesquite sank behind them as the convoy passed hundreds of tractor-trailers parked in rows in the industrial park. The brick veneer homes in the new suburbs spoke of Escandón's booming economy and reminded Honoré of the kind of house Maruca wanted. After rumbling over the railroad tracks, they left River Road and tooled south on the interstate toward Mexico. A green Ford Bronco shot past, the BP agents in the cab—handsome, young, and blond—gazing coolly from behind sunglasses and the brown-faced prisoners peering from behind wire meshing.

Up ahead, a red light flashed.

A black-and-white squad car idled on the shoulder, a fat cop leaning against its side, pings of red splashing on his light blue uniform. Comino lowered his walkie-talkie and studied the passing convoy. For a split second, Honoré and his brother-in-law locked stares. Then Comino appeared in Honoré's rearview mirror, a fat *tlacuache* stroking its black mustache.

"You think he'll give us any trouble?' Trotsky asked Honoré.

Honoré held the steering wheel steady. "No more than usual."

The convoy would cross at the Bridge of the Americas, but instead of taking the direct route, the police insisted they take back streets to avoid downtown traffic. At the Queen Victoria exit, the cops slowed, got off the interstate, and drove along the access road to the International Bank of Nuevo Santander, where they turned west and followed the truck route through an old barrio, a mix of sandstone homes with peaked aluminum roofs, two-storey clapboard homes, shanties in dirt lots, and cars on broken sidewalks. At length, they passed warehouses along the railroad tracks, turned south under the bridge that led to the college, and drove between some hole-in-the-wall cantinas on the left and the train depot on the right. Thickets of mesquite and bamboo hid the Rio Grande from view.

El Rio de las Palmas Mall had been built on the north embankment of the river's flood plain. At its west end stood the Hilton Inn, a squat coffee-can-shaped tower twenty stories high. At its other end, Sears Roebuck, JC Penny's, a local clothing store named Kimberly and Oscar's, the Las Palmas Family Supermarket, and a McDonald's crowded the lane that led to the U.S. Customs compound on Washington Avenue, which cut through downtown.

The Bridge of the Americas stood above the brown water flowing between *carrizo* thickets on both sides of the river, where skinny sunburned

boys floated on inner tubes as they scouted for smugglers getting ready
to cross illegals that morning. On the Mexican side stood the Customs
building, a pile of red bricks with dozens of windows broken during an
anti-government demonstration. The convoy turned north on a street that
took it across the huge parking lot and stopped between the mall and the
river. Since Honoré would not be crossing, he pulled out of the column and
parked a few yards away. A helicopter puttered over the river on routine
patrol. Then Honoré, Altagracia, and Trotsky climbed out of the pickup
and walked toward the column of vehicles.

"We should be able to cross in an hour," said the Commander to the
drivers, about twenty, gathered around him. "Get your papers ready, and
keep an eye out for saboteurs. All we need now is for someone to sneak
into a vehicle and plant some dope."

A veteran wearing a jungle hat raised a hand. "Sir."

"Yes," responded the Commander.

"We've heard all kinds of rumors."

The Commander mopped his brow with a kerchief. "Like what?"

"Like a bomb might be set off on the bridge."

A murmur spread quickly. "Next they'll accuse us of being terrorists,"
said a woman.

"They've already done that."

Trotsky stepped forward. "Bridge officials get bomb threats at least once
a week. It's a tactic smugglers use to distract the inspectors, especially when
a huge load is coming across."

The Commander stood between Pastor Paul and Molly. "Look, just keep
cool—"

"And vigilant," Molly added.

"Pray," intoned the pastor.

"In other words, don't fuck up," drawled Johnny Paint.

Tennessee shoved him. "That coming from a guy who knows all about
fucking up?" He snickered.

The Commander glared at them.

Afterward, Trotsky drew him aside. "We're going ahead. I told Sixto we'd
meet him at the toll booths. If they don't stop you, he'll cross with you into
Nuevo Escandón. But if they stop the convoy, he and his people are ready
for that, too."

"Ten-four," said the Commander.

Honoré led the way to the bridge while Altagracia and Trotsky walked
closely behind, chatting about Zuckermann's court injunction, which

would lay the legal groundwork for similar convoys in the future. At the end of the mall, they turned right and halted a few yards from the toll-booths at the entrance to the bridge. Across the street, a wide, flat aluminum canopy cast a long shadow over the U. S. Customs compound, where officers wearing white shirts with patches on their shoulders and black trousers inspected the long line of vehicles crossing into the United States. At this hour of the morning, few cars crossed into Mexico, so the two southbound lanes were virtually empty. Downriver to the east, the sunrise was the color inside a conch shell glittering on South Padre Island, silver lacquer turning orange and pink.

"I don't see Sixto anywhere," said Honoré.

Trotsky walked to the middle of the street and looked at the bridge. "It's early."

"Should I go look for him?"

Trotsky returned. "No, no. We'll wait. Let's go up the street."

Suddenly, Honoré spotted his favorite FBI agent, chatting with officials on a landing outside the main entrance to the Customs building. "Go ahead. I'll catch up with you in a minute."

Trotsky and Altagracia left.

Then the tall, lanky redhead wearing cowboy boots and a shiny light gray suit broke from his colleagues. After walking through the compound, he trotted across the street to where Honoré stood on the curb. "Can we talk, Tex?"

"Depends."

Rex peered over his shoulder warily. "There are rumors that some asshole may try to blow up the bridge today. A tractor-trailer with fertilizer might be crossing from Mexico. What do you know about this?"

Honoré caught a glimpse of Trotsky and Altagracia walking past the KAOS van parked near the money exchange. "Manure? Sounds like bullshit to me. Or is it horse shit?" He grinned.

"Cut the bullshit. Shit is shit."

"When aren't there rumors that some idiot plans to blow up the bridge?"

Rex glanced at cars stopped at the tollbooth. "That's what I told the new port director. But he still doesn't understand that if he believes half the shit he hears in this town, he's in a lot of shit himself."

"No shit."

Rex's reddish eyebrows fidgeted. "Look, I'm trying to keep things simple. I can't afford for things to get out of hand on this bridge today."

Up the street, Ty Cobb's lover from New England, Shirley English, climbed out of the KAOS van. Tall and willowy in a pink blouse, blue jeans, and cowboy boots, she carried a camera and was followed by a crewman with a microphone on a boom. An anchorwoman in a dark business suit and high heels, Conchita Terrazas, talked to a fat cop.

Honoré turned to Rex. "What can I do?"

"Just tell the Commander to postpone the crossing."

"Too late for that."

Rex swallowed hard, containing the rage in his throat. "The CIA," he whispered, "is here. And whenever those assholes get involved, they fuck everything up. Watch for spies. Their assets are roaming all over the place."

Honoré had heard these warnings before. He yawned. "I gotta go."

"Have it your way," said Rex, "but don't come begging me to get your ass out of Comino's hotel."

Honoré walked up the street, past a tiny perfume-and-liquor boutique and a hole-in-the-wall fruit and vegetable market, to the money exchange.

Shirley knelt before the camera on the sidewalk. "Hi."

"Hi," he said. "Where's Ty?"

The young woman stood up, camera in hand. "She should be here any minute. Why?"

"She's not in jail?"

She frowned. "I don't think so."

"Cops!" yelled a cameraman.

Suddenly, red lights flashed, and a siren wailed as a squad car skidded to a halt across the street. Comino pushed himself out and slammed the door. He adjusted his holster under his belly with both hands before freezing and locking eyes with Honoré. Two other cops, *panzas* swollen above their ammunition belts, waddled over from U.S. Customs. After casting dirty looks at Honoré, the three laughed.

Honoré wanted nothing more than to walk over and punch them in the face. Instead, he looked around for Trotsky, who was walking out of the money exchange with Altagracia.

"What's going on?" asked Trotsky.

"Cops."

"Look!" said Altagracia and pointed down the street at the column of vehicles creeping along from the Rio de las Palmas Mall. "The convoy!"

"Let's see what's happening," said Trotsky.

To keep an eye on Comino and his goons, Honoré stayed behind. The Commander's pickup crawled toward the tollbooths, followed closely by three vans. The rest of the convoy, though hidden by a boutique at the end of the sidewalk, approached from the parking lot. Meanwhile, two officers, a man and a woman in blue uniforms, gold badges on their chests and pistols on their hips, walked from U.S. Customs. Tall, young, and good-looking, the man raised an arm like a school patrol boy at a crosswalk and stopped the Commander's pickup a few yards from the tollbooths with their guard rails.

All at once, loud honking sliced the hot morning. A school bus with "Yellow Submarine" painted across its side rolled toward him, so Honoré stepped away from the curb. After it halted in front of the money exchange, a bunch of white Vietnam vets in combat boots, flak jackets, and jungle hats climbed down carrying anti-embargo placards. Chicanos, their thick black hair tied down with red bandannas, stumbled down the steps, combat boots flying. Next came the Chicanas, black hair long and thick, jeans so low that Honoré couldn't ignore them as they headed toward the bridge.

Suddenly, Honoré stopped in his tracks. "Oh, my God!" he muttered.

Ty Cobb Ramirez, cowboy boots, headband around her head and an Indian choker of bear claws around her pudgy neck, scrambled down the steps. "Ho!"

"Ho?" Honoré asked. "What the ho are you doing here? I heard you took off with the Savages."

She stood next to Honoré, eyes alert. "I called Danielle Mujica. She and some of her friends funded this bus from Austin. What do you think?"

"Did they come only to protest or are they part of the convoy?"

"Who cares? They're here, no?"

Giggles floated through the air like bubbles of shampoo. Suddenly, some gringas marched out of the bus, winged helmets on braided blond hair, gold bracelets on their arms, breasts rolling bralessly beneath the chain mail. Ty checked out the white goddesses' butts as their shapely suntanned legs carried them across the pavement toward the bridge. Thank God, reflected Honoré, they wore T-shirts and thongs underneath.

"Looks to me like they're here to screw things up," Honoré said.

Ty guffawed. "Or just screw."

"Maybe they're spies."

Another bombshell climbed out of the bus. The youngest and prettiest of the girls, she wore denim hot pants and combat boots laced to mid-calf. Braless beneath a T-shirt, she stood on the curb and chewed bubble gum. With long blond braids reaching her shoulders and *maracas* as big as mangos fresh from the fields in the Valley, she checked out Honoré with childlike curiosity.

"Hi," she said in a gooey high-pitched voice, like a little girl.

"Hi," Honoré said. "Welcome to Escandón."

A bead of sweat ran down the slope of a golden breast. "Kinda hot down here, no?"

"Yes, ma'am," he said. "Everything down here is hot."

Ty pinched his arm. "*No mames, güey.* You trying to rob the cradle?"

"Are we in Mexico?" asked the bubble-gum-chewing Viking princess.

"A dumb blonde," Ty whispered to Honoré. "Don't listen to her. All she wants is attention. As if she didn't get enough of it already."

The golden hair dazzled him. "Some people would say 'yes,' " he crooned. "Some would say 'no.' "

The princess poked him in the ribs. "But what do you say?"

Ty grabbed the blonde's elbow. "Come on. Let's go see what's happening."

"Wait, wait, wait!" the girl said, breaking free. She squeezed Honorés bicep, sending a gale of chills through his three lower limbs. "Are Mexican men really macho?"

Ty grabbed her arm again. "He'll only get you in trouble!" she yelled and pulled the bubble-gum-chewing, butt-swinging babe through a flashflood of men's stares. "Coyote, see you later."

If she were a CIA asset, mulled Honoré, then this confrontation between the U.S. government and the convoy was going to be more fun than he expected—or extremely dangerous. Deadly, in fact. He better keep an eye on her. Maybe two eyes.

Not only was the morning heating up, but traffic was beginning to back up in both directions. Cars seethed in plumes of exhaust as they waited for the northbound lanes to clear before heading into town. Southbound cars, though few, had to stop because the confrontation between the customs officers and the convoy blocked the two lanes to the tollbooths. Suddenly, a Mexican driver in the southbound lane, craning his neck to get an eyeful of one of the gringas, slammed his car into the back of a dump truck. Soon Escandón's finest, led by Comino, silver with sweat, sprang into action and surrounded the Mexican. They were about to drag him from his car until they saw the gringas. Lips moist, cheeks twitching, they changed their minds and let the man go so they could attend to homeland security.

Then the chopping of an engine rattled the windows in the money exchange. Honoré spotted something in the sky, buzzing, annoying as a mosquito.

The mosquito grew into a hummingbird with silver wings slashing through glints of sunlight. Moments later, the helicopter swooped down and roared dangerously close to the roof of the yellow bus, sweeping past, circling above Customs and coming back, veering to the right as an agent in the co-pilot seat peered through binoculars at the women. The chopper swept past, came back, and veered again, sharply this time. The agent grasped wildly for something to hold on to, his eyes wide with the realization he wasn't strapped in. Blond hair and shiny black boots tumbled through the air.

Then, bang!

Everyone gawked at the green uniform and black boots on the roof of the Yellow Submarine. "First casualty!" yelled a man wearing a red headband, raising a fist amid the shouts and laughter of the crowd on the sidewalk. "Friendly fire! Hit him right where it hurts! *¡Pendejo!*"

The chopper took off, came back, hovering a few feet above the bus. A rope ladder flew out, but the agent was too dazed to reach for it.

Two cops climbed on the hood of the bus and helped the agent down. An ambulance arrived; then they left, sirens screaming as if warning Escandónians of an imminent air raid. Honoré ran down the street and joined Trotsky and Altagracia on the curb a few feet from the Commander's pickup, where Johnny Paint sat behind the steering wheel while the Commander, his arm on the window, spoke to the male officer. In the van behind them, Pastor Paul rode with Molly, who sat in the driver's seat. Ty and her friends mingled in the crowd gathering on the sidewalk.

"Are these the people from Austin?" asked Trotsky.

Honoré nodded.

"Are they here to protest or join the convoy?"

"Protest." Then, someone across the street caught Honoré's attention. "There's Sixto."

A short sturdily built man, wearing khaki pants, polo shirt, and a beret, worked his way through the traffic exiting the Customs compound and strode past cop cars in the middle of the southbound lanes.

Honoré shook his hand with an iron grip. "We've been looking for you."

"I was waiting for the people from Lucero."

"Don't tell me they drove all the way here to support *la causa!*" said Trotsky.

Sixto removed his hat and greeted Altagracia, "*Buenos días, señora.*"

"*Buenos días.*"

Sixto put his hat back on and turned to Trotsky. "Doña Catarina and her friend, as soon they found out what was going on, drove all the way from Lucero. Brought some allies. They're on the bridge now." He turned to

Honoré. "I heard some of your friends got shot up in Nuevo Escandón. Are they okay?"

Honoré described what happened at the red light district. "It's been crazy."

"*Teatro*," said Sixto with a grin, "*puro teatro.*"

All traffic on the southbound lanes was stalled now, but the crowd of tourists and locals headed to Mexico grew as they stopped to watch from the sidewalk. Members of the convoy climbed out of their vehicles and carried signs back and forth across the southbound lanes while hammerhead-like cameras from NBC, ABC, and CBS swam everywhere. With TV cameras at her back, Conchita Terrazas interviewed Pastor Paul and Molly, who remained in the van. Comino and his men, *panzas* big as watermelons, took positions a few yards from the Commander's pickup and cast ugly glances at Honoré. While Johnny Paint flirted with the shapely female officer holding a walkie talkie to her ear, the Commander, face serious as ever, engaged in friendly conversation with the other officer. The morning lost its freshness as the sun rose in the sky. Faces glimmered. The helicopter returned periodically.

Suddenly, a handful of Vietnam vets carrying posters gathered on the sidewalk and shouted, "Let the convoy go!"

A dozen pedestrians joined. "Let the convoy go!"

Sixto jumped right in. "*¡El pueblo unido jamás será vencido!*"

Members of the convoy gathered around. "*¡El pueblo unido jamás será vencido!*"

"Let the convoy go! Let the convoy go!"

After about thirty long and raucous minutes, a tall, heavy-set Anglo in uniform stepped from beneath the canopy of the U.S. Customs compound, a pair of gold-rimmed glasses on a face white as a marshmallow in the sunlight. After joining the two other officers standing with arms crossed in front of the Commander's pickup, he looked up and down the street. Then he barked orders at Comino's men, who assembled between the Commander's pickup and the protestors on the sidewalk. The TV cameras captured everything.

Finally, the officer walked around the front of the pickup to where the Commander sat. Trotsky, Altagracia, and Honoré got as close as the police allowed, a yard or two away.

"Sir, I am the director of the Port of Escandón," he said, "and I cannot let you cross. You will be in violation of the United States embargo against Nicaragua."

"Sir," said the Commander, his slender red face hanging low, blue eyes lively as fresh water in the heat, "we are taking medicine, food, bicycles, and school materials to the people of Nicaragua. This is a humanitarian mission. What's wrong with that?"

The director crossed his hairy white arms. "Sir, I know what you are carrying. I know why you're here."

The Commander's face was grim as ever. "This is a humanitarian cause. But as lackeys of the current administration, you would not understand that, would you?"

The director's badge shimmered. "I suggest you and your people turn around and head north."

"Sir, we ain't headed nowhere except south."

The director leaned over the side of the pickup, placing a hand on the window. "Think about this. You could save us a lot of headaches today if you just turn your little white hillbilly ass around and head back to the sticks, where you belong."

"You're insulting me, sir!"

The director straightened up. "No more than you and your friends are insulting me and everyone else sacrificing their lives to secure our borders and make America safe."

"Sir, please get out of the way or we'll have to take you with us. I'm sure you don't want to go all the way to Nicaragua on the hood of my pickup."

The director chuckled and shook his head. "All right, boys and girls," he shouted at Comino's men, "it's time to put away the toys. Let's show this asshole the might of the United States government."

The Commander rolled up his window, and Johnny started the pickup. Members of the convoy dropped their signs and jumped in their vehicles. Suddenly, tires screeched, and the director tried to leap out of the way as the Commander's pickup lurched forward and rammed a tollbooth guard rail.

"Ahhh!" yelled the director, hopping around on one foot. "That fucking asshole ran over my toe! That fucking asshole!"

He staggered and fell. Two other convoy vehicles drove past and blocked the lanes to the toll booths.

The female officer shouted in her walkie talkie, "The director is down! Send reinforcements! Now! Yes! Yes!"

Two of Comino's officers helped the director up. On his feet, he yelled, "Get that wrecker down here!"

With lights flashing and tires screeching, the Broncos arrived. Doors flew open as thirty nightstick-wielding BP agents—brown and white men and a handful of women—jumped out of their vehicles and double-timed in a sharp column toward the bridge, young and trim in their dark olive-green uniforms. They stood shoulder to shoulder, forming a cordon between U.S. Customs and the convoy.

As Comino's men pushed the crowd back, Honoré retreated and then worked his way up the street. If he wasn't careful, Comino's men would beat the shit out of him first chance they got. He paused next to some red-faced gringo tourists who had just arrived, wearing straw hats, shorts, and sandals.

"Let the convoy go!" shouted the demonstrators up and down the sidewalk. "Let the convoy go!"

"*¡Viva la revolución!*"

"Let the convoy go!"

Suddenly, a gringo tourist shouted, "Commies, go home!"

"Better dead than red!" another shouted.

A wrecker with a flashing yellow light growled down the street, driven by a man who had to look through the steering wheel to see where he was headed. The wrecker looked familiar.

Then Honoré saw who it was. "Jesus Christ!" he cursed.

After turning the wrecker around and backing up to the Commander's pickup, Tequila jumped out and talked to the officers. Suddenly, he saw Honoré. "Coyote!" he shouted from the middle of the street.

Honoré sneaked past Comino's men but couldn't break through the Border Patrol cordon. "Get that wrecker out of here, *cabrón!*" he yelled.

"*¡No mames, pendejo!* Can't you see I'm working for the United States government?"

Honoré wanted nothing more than to kick this guy's ass. Instead, his cheek quivered violently. Was it his turn to come down with the malady of local yokels—*cara chueca* or paralysis of the face? So he retreated and joined Trotsky and Altagracia.

The director raised a bullhorn to his mouth and squawked, "Sweep these hillbillies away!"

As Comino's men went into action with their nightsticks, glass shattered and tinkled. Two cops flung the Commander's pickup doors open and yanked Johnny Paint out, slamming him against the asphalt and kicking him in the butt before they cuffed his hands behind his back. Then they grabbed the Commander, who laid a supersized cop flat on the asphalt before they subdued him. Outside the van behind them, the cops let go of

Pastor Paul but grabbed Molly, who kicked and clawed until they threw her on the ground and handcuffed her.

"Motherfuckers!" yelled a Vietnam vet on the sidewalk as the cops dragged the Commander away.

A young Chicana screamed at the cops, "Cowards!"

"*¡Cabrónes!*" yelled an old Mexican woman as the cops beat the shit out of Johnny Paint after he bit a cop's hand.

"Let the convoy go! Let the convoy go!"

Sixto yelled to Honoré and Trotsky, "Close the bridge!"

"Let's go!" shouted Trotsky.

Things happened so fast that Honoré lost track of time, and now it was close to noon. All the southbound lanes on the bridge were empty, but in the northbound lanes, cars wobbled in a flood of heat. Hoods opened, and clouds of steam leaped from overheated engines. Behind them, the diesels throbbed, their silver pipes smoking above them as they carried heavy loads in aluminum-walled trailers to the American market. Protestors holding placards flocked like great white birds on the sidewalks and in the streets. Asphalt softened and sparkled like licorice. The air itself became liquid. Below, the Rio Grande slowly slipped east to the Gulf of Mexico.

Honoré ran to the middle of the bridge, where Altagracia was already talking to Doña Catarina and the women from Lucero while Sixto consulted with Trotsky. El Víbora, carrying a placard condemning U.S. imperialism, slapped Honoré on the shoulder as he ran past and told him that things were finally getting exciting, just the way he liked them. The fat dark women who had participated in the sit-in at El Calabozo ran through plumes of exhaust and joined the huddle around Sixto. For a while everyone seemed so happy to be together they forgot the honking cars and the humming engines of diesel trucks and the cursing of outraged drivers. In a blouse and a loose skirt that reached her huaraches, La Morenita joined Sixto, a white-toothed smile flashing against her brown skin.

"Now listen!" Sixto yelled at last. "We're forming a human cordon here, in the middle of the bridge. We're closing the northbound lane. And we're stopping all pedestrian traffic north and south."

"That won't be easy," said Trotsky.

"Just hold hands and don't let go."

Everyone grasped each other's hands and formed a human cordon across all four lanes. Honoré found himself standing next to Sixto as they faced America, where the red-tile roofs of the U.S. Customs compound shimmered under a blue sky. Next to it, a gorgeous white-washed Spanish colonial hotel stood perched on the riverbank, and beyond that rose the Washington Hotel.

"Don't move!" shouted Don Sixto, as vehicles in the northbound lanes came to a stop. "Don't move!"

Powerful as a lion, a diesel hummed behind Honoré. It cleared its throat, growled; then it honked—loud, shrill, restless. The diesel behind it honked. Then, all of the diesels were honking. Above, a helicopter swung low.

On the sidewalks protestors waved their placards. "Let the convoy go! Let the convoy go!"

Nuggets of gold struck Honoré's eyes, melting and scurrying to the edge of his eyelids, down his cheeks. Meanwhile, the bridge swayed under his feet.

"*¡Águila!*" shouted Sixto. "Watch out!"

Honoré didn't understand why Sixto was yelling until the diesel came up from behind, slowly and patiently, heaving and churning, anxious for action. Had it been an animal, it would have bit Honoré's butt. The huge vehicle smelled of rubber, oil, and diesel fuel. In the blink of an eye, it could turn him into a tortilla.

"*¡Águila! ¡Águila!*" shouted Sixto again.

When the diesel nudged Honoré, hard this time, he spun around, grabbed the grill, climbed across the hood, and inched to the side of the cab, where he pulled himself up by the bar holding the mirror. The truck driver glared at him through the open window.

Below, Sixto shouted at the truck driver, "*¡Cabrón!*"

"*¡Tu madre!*" yelled the driver.

The truck jerked forward.

Honoré lost his footing on the side step. He clung to the mirror, then fell, hitting the pavement with his shoulder. Jagged and sharp as lightning, pain shot through his body.

The diesel's tire rolled toward his face until a fat Mexican woman dragged him away by his feet.

He rose on one knee and cursed the driver, "*¡Hijo de tu rechingada madre!*"

Then he scrambled up the side of the truck. Lips thin and purple, the driver sneered at Honoré. "*¡Otra vez, pendejo!*"

Hitting somebody in the face was too much like kissing—too intimate, too personal, mulled Honoré as he secured his footing on the side step. Sometimes the face gave way like mush, but sometimes you hit a hard jagged coral reef and cut yourself on their teeth, so you had to do it again.

He grabbed the truck driver by the collar. "Nothing personal, strictly political."

He swung.

The man's face collapsed like a rubber mask.

Then Honoré flung the door open and pulled the man out.

The driver tumbled to the asphalt, where the women kicked him in the ass. The diesel lurched forward.

"Stop the truck!" shouted Sixto. "Stop the truck!"

Honoré jumped inside the cab, hit the brakes, jammed the clutch against the floor, grabbed the stick shift, and put the truck in neutral.

Don Sixto clambered up the side of the cab. "We have to keep the bridge closed at all costs!" he shouted, his tongue thick and desperate. "Move the truck! Block the bridge! We'll take care of the police!"

As soon as Sixto jumped off and joined the protestors, Honoré turned the enormous steering wheel, plunged the gas pedal, and drove the big rig diagonally across the bridge. Abruptly, he stopped and shifted gears. Metal whined, and people screamed as he backed up. He looked in the side view mirror and backed up. Suddenly, the entire vehicle shuddered.

Honoré stuck his head out the window. The diesel truck behind him had rammed into him, hard. Metal screamed and wobbled as the trailer tottered. Women shouted and ran. The police stood aghast. All of a sudden, the trailer turned over, and its sides came apart. An exploding volcano of brand new television sets sent thousands of pieces of glass across the bridge like molten lava.

"Oh, fuck!" Honoré muttered.

A fire-breathing bull appeared at the window. Standing on the step on the side of the tractor, Comino tried opening the door, but it was stuck. "Open the door, *cabrón*!" he shouted.

Good idea, thought Honoré. In fact, a good push would send Comino flying. Honoré tried, but dealing with a three-hundred-pound animal wasn't easy. Any moment Comino might land a punch on Honoré's face. The door remained stuck.

Honoré pushed hard. Nothing.

He pushed harder. Nothing.

He pushed even harder. Nothing.

When he saw the animal reaching for his throat, Honoré swung and landed a solid punch on Comino's left eye. "Imbecile!" he muttered.

Comino fell.

Another imbecile with a gold badge climbed up on the hood of the cab and glared at him through the windshield. "¡*Otro cabrón!*" spat Honoré.

At length, the cop climbed on the roof of the tractor and reached inside the window. A powerful hand grabbed Honoré's face as if it were about to rip it off like a mask. Honoré bit a finger the size of a sausage.

"¡*A la chingada!*" the cop screamed, howled, and yanked his hand away.

Another cop climbed up and jerked the door open. Two powerful hands grabbed Honoré's leg. He kicked. The man let go, then attacked again. They struggled.

Suddenly, the asphalt looked like a wall of black slag flying toward Honoré. "Fuck!" Flat and hard, the asphalt slammed his face, mauled a shoulder, his arm, his skull. He rolled on his back. A man loomed above him.

With a black eye blossoming like a purple flower, Comino stood dusting off his uniform, first the sleeves, then the seat of his pants, and then his cap, which he put back on. He tossed the handcuffs to one of his men.

"Fascist bastards!" spit Honoré as the cop turned him over and cuffed his hands behind his back.

"Get him up!" shouted Comino.

Two police officers raised him to his feet.

"This guy thinks he's hot stuff," said a cop in Spanish.

Another officer peered at Honoré. "Look at that face," he said.

Comino growled, "He's looked like that as long as I can remember."

"How do you know?"

"He's my brother-in-law."

"Really? In that case, he needs a little warming up."

"He sure does," said Comino with relish, his eye so swollen he looked as if Honoré had jammed a prune in his eye socket. "I've been wanting to do this for a long time."

A knee in the stomach knocked the wind out of Honoré and filled his head with stars and stripes as if he had begun celebrating the Fourth of July early. Next, he felt like an astronaut taking off at Cape Canaveral. In fact, he got a glimpse of the solar system—huge planets in orbit around the sun— until he realized they were bellies.

Curiously, Honoré felt no pain. Each blow to his head, his stomach, his balls felt like an injection of anesthesia, a pinching of the flesh and then numbness. Then, he was back on the ground and getting pummeled from all sides.

Nearby, a bouquet of blood shot from a cop's head. Rolling pins, which the women from Lucero pulled from their purses and brandished like samurai swords, laid out two more cops on the asphalt. A fat dark woman sent another cop flying past Honoré, bouncing off the diesel's tire, and rolling unconscious on the bridge. El Víbora, like a character straight out of a kung-fu movie, landed blow after blow. Trotsky and Altagracia fought as a team. La Morenita fought alone. Honoré tried to get up, but his head spun.

Reinforcements arrived from both sides of the border.

Trotsky went down first. Altagracia stood up against a man the size of a bear, but she too fell, her long skirt back off her white legs. Sixto kicked one of Comino's men in the balls before someone knocked him down and steel-toed black service boots descended on him like a flock of crows. El Víbora, pursued by Mexican cops with pistols drawn, climbed the guard rail along the sidewalk, jumped off the side of the bridge, and dropped into the river. Some Vietnam vets dragged Altagracia and then Trotsky out of harm's way. The fat women, who screamed and kicked and cursed, were the toughest, but they, too, fell under the blows. Sturdy as a branch of green mesquite, La Morenita endured the longest, but she, too, fell.

Ten minutes later, Comino came up and glared at Honoré, who lay with his back on the asphalt. "You piece of shit!"

Two bulls grabbed Honoré under his arms and raised him to his feet. Then they dragged him backwards, toward the Customs compound, as demonstrators jeered and TV cameras poked into the action like dogs sniffing garbage. Amid the broken TVs scattered across the bridge, the diesel stood with its chrome-plated exhaust pipe gleaming in the sun.

"Let the convoy go!" chanted everyone. "Let the convoy go! Let the convoy go!"

Silver bullets shone on a thick black belt under a sagging belly that smelled of bacon and beans as the cops dragged Honoré to the squad car, shoved him in the back seat, and slammed the door in his face. The car spun amid broken glass and burnt rubber; sirens screaming, it sped up Washington Avenue to the county jail four blocks away, where a bunch of faces stared down at him from inside the steel bars on the second and third floors. Like the sound of pigeons taking flight in the early morning, cheers and cries rippled through the air from the prisoners' windows as if welcoming Honoré while jeering at the cops yanking him across the asphalt to the back of the county jail, where more cops played lovely music with their batons on his ribs as if he were a marimba from Guatemala. Arms hurting like hell, wrists sore from the handcuffs, blood hot and salty in his mouth, he stumbled down a dank hall to an office, where they removed the handcuffs and forced him to strip and climb into an orange jumpsuit and plastic sandals. Later, they dragged him up several flights of steps to a zoo buzzing with the sound of running water and the screams of maniacs and potheads.

"*Muy chingon*, right?" muttered one of the cops in his ear. "Well, we're going to see how *chingon* you are here among the *chingones*." The two cops threw him into a cell and locked the door.

All of this was familiar. Though Honoré had never done hard time like the Governor or some of his buddies from the old days, he had been in and out of this jail so many times he didn't understand why people were so unfriendly now. When he was in here for conspiracy, everyone treated him like an old friend, a partner-in-crime, letting him off the hook at the first opportunity because they knew they would get paid off. Like most of his friends in "the business," he had had connections with the district attorney through the DA's father, an old man who held court on his front porch in the El Rincón del Diablo barrio. Now Honoré was just a troublemaker. Worse, he was broke. On the other hand, Trotsky had asserted that all revolutionaries went to jail, so Honoré should feel privileged to be a political prisoner. For a revolutionary, jail was a time of reflection and preparation for a lifetime of action.

A great idea, Honoré thought, until the smell of armpits hit him.

"I want to see the prisoner," growled a familiar male voice.

Honoré sat up on his bunk. Two other cops joined the parade. The smell grew worse.

"Unlock the door," barked Comino.

As the bellies rolled into the cell, Honoré could not restrain himself. "Maruca told me there's a sale on deodorant at ChiChiB."

"Get this asshole off his ass," Comino told one of the cops.

Thick fingers grabbed Honoré's arms and pulled him to his feet. "Well, boss," said the cop, shoving him before Comino, "do we kick his ass now or later?"

Comino smelled so bad Honoré wondered if a *tlacuache* had died in his armpit. But there was no mistaking he had taken a beating on the bridge. With his black eye, he looked like a bull dog. "I get a phone call."

"Correction. Everyone else gets a phone call."

When the cop loosened his grip, Honoré asked, "Where's the rest of the convoy?"

"Downstairs," Comino sneered. "With their Jewish lawyer from New York. What's his name, Fuckerman or Fuckface?"

"Zuckermann," said Honoré.

"Same thing—a fucking Jew. I told them to put you up here," Comino said, glancing around contemptuously, "with the perverts."

Then he came up so close, Honoré could see a bug in his thick black mustache. Maybe a booger. No, a bean. "I want to see a lawyer."

"And where you do you think you're at?" asked Comino. "The United States? Listen up. You've gotten away with a lot of shit. Running guns across the border, smuggling terrorists, insulting my mother, insulting me and my family. Turning our sister against us and running off with her. Your in-laws run this jail, so you're fucked." Now Honoré smelled the bad breath. "You're in the Telaraña County Jail in Escandón, Texas!"

"When I get out of here," muttered Honoré, "I'm going to kick your ass."

"There's only one ass you have to worry about."

Honoré struggled against the cop, who doubled his grip. "I want to speak to my wife!"

"Your wife doesn't want to speak to you. In fact, she asked us to keep you here until the convoy leaves Escandón."

Honoré yanked his arm free. "Bullshit!"

"*Tranquilo, tranqui*lo," said the cop, grabbing the other arm.

"Look, Coyote," said Comino, looming too close for comfort. "That little *jotito* down the hall says you look like his favorite porno star. He begged us to put him in here with you. Not a bad idea. Maybe he should spend the night with you." Then, he whispered in a thick, brackish voice, "Listen carefully, Coyote. You may get out of here alive, but you'll be lucky to get out with your manhood, *cabrón*."

An hour later, the loud voice of a happy gringo—like some six-pack Joe glad to be home after work—echoed off the cement walls and died in an isolated corner of the unit. Some inmates yelled that he should go fuck his mother, but that only made the visitor laugh louder.

"This place smells like shit," Rex said as the guard opened the cell door and let him in. "Mexican shit."

Honoré rose to his feet. "Cut the racist crap."

Chuckling, Rex sat on the bunk. "Aren't you the one who claims white shit stinks worse than Mexican shit?"

"All I said was that white shit was radioactive," said Honoré, closing his finger around a steel bar. "What the fuck do you want?"

The FBI agent loosened his tie and collar. "I need your help."

Disgust gripped Honoré's stomach. "I haven't seen a judge! I didn't get my phone call! I was dragged and beaten and then thrown in here. And you want me to help you? Cut the crap, Rex!"

Rex wiped his face. "What can I say? We live in Escandón, Texas."

"Stand on the side of peace and justice for once in your life. Enforce the law."

Rex removed his jacket, the silk lining shining in a sliver of light from the window, and laid it on the bunk. "If the church couldn't civilize the Mexicans in South Texas, why should I?"

"What happened to the Commander?" asked Honoré.

A streak of sweat darkened Rex's white shirt. "He was released, just before I walked in here, as a matter of fact. Mexican police arrested that guy Trusky, but he got out almost as soon as they locked him up. His wife, however, is in a hospital in Nuevo Escandón."

"She okay?"

"I don't know."

"What about the convoy?"

"They're back at the camp."

Honoré then remembered something he heard from Trotsky a long time ago. "Are your colleagues in the KKK?"

A twinkle appeared in the agent's eyes. "Who else would give a shit about this lousy border? Most gringos don't want to be assigned here. To come out here, you have to be a crusader. The KKK is the last of the crusaders. Have you heard about the evacuation plans of the *Escandón Morning Times*?"

"No."

"For your information, South Texas is considered lost territory in case of a foreign invasion. The newspaper's staff would retreat to San Antonio, the last line of defense. Only a crusader would want to defend lost territory."

"Are you KKK?"

Rex grinned and then bowed his head in frustration. After clearing his throat, he cast a glance at Honoré. "How did you get involved with these losers, these Vietnam-vets-turned-revolutionaries? Don't you know what a mess this tinhorn commander made? Traffic has been paralyzed for hours. On top of that, we've been on the national news every day since the convoy arrived. Now it's every hour. You especially. That was quite a performance, punching that guy in the face on national TV and then turning over that trailer and blocking the bridge with hundreds of Sony television sets."

Honoré raised an eyebrow. "National TV?"

Rex nodded. "The incident is a sensation in Europe. The Cubans are protesting. You made the people in Washington look like a bunch of assholes, but now my phone is ringing off the wall. On top of that, the director of the port of Escandón—another fanatic, an anti-communist nut, a mad bull when he sees red—says the convoy will cross into Mexico over his dead body. And the Commander is threatening to drive all the way to Washington and close down Pennsylvania Avenue just like y'all closed down the Bridge of the Americas."

"So what do you want from me?"

The agent's eyelids crinkled. "Get them out of my hair."

Honoré rolled his eyes. "Sorry, I can't help you."

"Talk to the Commander."

"Why me?"

Rex's chin was as square as the toe of a construction boot. "He won't talk to us."

Honoré faced this so-called defender of the free world. "This is a humanitarian cause. You're a fucking overpaid cop. I'm not betraying the people of Nicaragua."

The FBI agent picked up his coat and stood. "How the hell you get into these situations is beyond me. With a brother-in-law like Comino, who needs enemies? He runs this *calabozo* like you run your store. But there's more money in pot than in pottery. Man, what a setup. Must be making plenty of dough."

The steel bar felt cold in Honoré's hand. "What about what happened on the bridge? Isn't that a federal offense?"

Rex paused, grinned. "All that happened on the Mexican half of the bridge. So it's not under our jurisdiction. And there's something else. Those TVs you scattered across the bridge? They were full of cocaine. This may turn out to be the biggest drug bust in the history of the war on drugs, and that alone can get you out of serving time in a federal penitentiary. But don't count on it 'cause Escandón, Texas, sure as hell ain't the United States of America. I don't know what it is, but it ain't that. So look, Tex, I need a decision today, tonight, now. What do you say?"

Pot smelled the way it always did, like shit. And that's how Honoré felt in this iron house, where men screamed like baboons swinging through a jungle infested with clouds of marijuana, day and night. All he wanted now was to close his eyes, swollen big as oranges, and forget the pain and exhaustion in his arms and legs.

Instead, a guard came to his cell. "Let's go."

Though fat like the rest of the cops in Escandón, this guy was a simple soul who didn't harass Honoré and had enough sense to wear deodorant. He guided Honoré past a cell throbbing with young womanish men in pink underwear, skinny and angular with faces slick with sweat amid the funky smell of sweat, piss, and God-knows-what else. They climbed down several flights of stairs and then headed down a musty hall. Fat cops peered from inside a tiny office. Some were brown; some were fair-skinned. All knew him. He felt stupid in an orange jumpsuit and plastic sandals.

The guard took him down another hall and opened a door. "In here."

Two chairs stood around a plain wooden table, and a bare light bulb hung from the end of a cord. A wire enmeshed window looked out on the brick building next door. Sunlight flowed into the room like slender ribbons of pasta before untangling on the cement floor.

Suddenly, the door flew open and in walked Maruca, tight pants hugging the usual deadly stuff.

"What are you doing here?" he asked.

She rushed to him. "What happened? My God, your face."

The smell of roses caught him by surprise. "Did your brother send you?"

She touched his cheek, delicately. "Yes, he called me and told me you were in a lot of trouble."

"And what else?"

"Are you okay?" She touched the knob on his forehead where the toe of a boot had landed.

"Ouch!" He grabbed her hand. "Yes, I'm okay. Relax. It's nothing."

She withdrew, looking at his orange jumpsuit and then the bare light bulb and chairs in the dreary room. At length, she sat at the table. "Comino said you had become a terrorist. Said you and your friends were plotting to blow up the bridge."

He sat opposite her. "Call the Governor."

Maruca frowned. "That slob. Why can't you call him?"

"Because your fucking brother refuses to let me see a lawyer or make a call."

She touched his hand. "He says you committed a federal crime, says you'll be in prison for the rest of your life."

Her fingers sent a tingle throughout his body. "There is no such thing as a federal crime in Escandón. If there were, your brother and your entire family would be in Leavenworth."

Her eyes watered. "You broke your promise. You told me you would quit all of this. But the minute Trotsky calls you, there you go again. And now here you are, locked up. Your face beaten to a pulp. They could have killed you. When is all this going to stop?"

"When is *what* going to stop?"

She wiped a tear. "This craziness!"

"Craziness? When haven't we been surrounded by craziness? When?"

"All I want is peace and quiet—a normal life."

Exasperated, Honoré shot to his feet and walked to the window. The wire meshing reminded him of the oppression most Escandonians lived in. "A normal life?" he asked, looking at the street below. "Poor, chaotic, drunk, coked-up, ignorant, afraid, sick people in this town can barely speak English or Spanish. No one understands them. Most eat too much or drink too much. All my friends from high school, the ones still alive, are missing a toe, a foot, or a leg. Diabetic. And they're all missing a brain."

"Like you?"

He saw a fat woman waddling across the street. "Hamburgers, French fries, malts, candy, pizza—everywhere you turn, you find fat maker. Now *that*," he said, crossing the room and stopping inches from her, "should be a federal crime!"

Startled, she said, "What are you talking about?"

"Fat people are like alcoholics—the most selfish, self-centered people on earth. Liars. Cops arrest drunks and dope fiends and wife beaters and burglars every day in this town. They should arrest fat people."

A question mark sprouted on Maruca's face. "Who would guard them? All the guards are fat."

"But fat is legal. Pot is not. Booze is legal. Heroin is not. Bullshit is legal. Honesty is not." He glared. "And then you blame me for becoming a revolutionary? For trying to find some self-respect?"

"How are you going to find self-respect by hanging out with a bunch of losers? Trotsky is crazy. Sixto is crazy. These hippies are all crazy."

He laid his hand on her shoulder. "Those people, that ragtag bunch of revolutionaries standing up to Goliath . . . are worth admiring. They may all be a bunch of fools, but at least they try to stand up for something. Unlike the *tlacuaches* that inhabit this fucking border town."

She pushed his hand away. "My brother says it's useless."

"Your brother is useless."

She glared at him with moist shiny eyes. "Your daughter hasn't been able to sleep since the convoy arrived. She dreamed you got killed in some jungle."

He returned to his chair. "I already told you. I'm not going to Nicaragua."

"We just took your mother to the hospital."

"What happened?"

"She fell and broke a hip."

"How?"

"She got stoned and then tried to walk. She fell."

"That's it—I'm going to kill the hogs. Butcher them and hang them in the store window like *cabrito*."

"They had nothing to do with it. She got stoned on her own. Said she read pot was good for arthritis." Maruca got up, a bit wobbly, wiping her eyes, the smell of fresh soap and young flesh engulfing him as she walked around the table. "Ah, baby."

When her leg touched his elbow, she reminded him of the meaning of freedom. The laughter of his daughter and home cooking and the delights of that old battlefield on her bed. As her fingers ran through his hair, touching his scalp and caressing it, chills ran down his back, down his legs, to his toes, numbing him. He closed his eyes.

"Let's leave Escandón, baby," she whispered, as if pouring sweet honey in his ears. It streamed down his arms to his heart. "I know how unhappy you are here."

He didn't open his eyes. "Where can we go?"

"San Antonio, Houston, anywhere."

Then, just as he ran his hand along the back of her leg, the door flew open, and two fat cops, with black leather ammunition belts and holsters and pearl-handled pistols strapped about their waists, waddled in. "Visiting hours are over."

"Wait," said Honoré, his entire body awake.

A uniform stood next to the Maruca. "Ma'am, it's time."

"Thank you," she said.

The other cop held the door open for her. Worried, she looked at him one last time before departing.

The first cop grabbed Honoré's arm. "Let's go."

"I can't get up," Honoré said.

The other cop came around the table. "Why not?" he asked.

"I have a cramp."

The cop stepped back and peered at Honoré. "Don't give me that shit. You're okay."

Honoré tried to stand up, couldn't. "In a minute! Give me a minute!"

"No! Let's go!"

All at once, both cops picked him up and dragged him out of the room. "Stand up!"

Women weakened men. No one understood that better than interrogators, even Comino and the other Escandón police. Maruca had come to offer some kind of support and instead had given him such a cramp that the cops had to carry him up several flights of stairs, sweating and puffing and groaning all the way back to the zoo.

Upon seeing his condition, the *jotillos* sneered and whistled, "Come here *papacito. Aquí te curamos.*"

"*¡'Ta bien buenote el cabrón!*"

"*¡Qué envergadura!*"

Devastating. Overwhelming. This was what Trotsky called American totalitarianism at its worst—or rather, its best. Don't bother, it said. Things don't matter anyway. There's nothing you can do. Man lives by bread alone. Nothing is worthy of personal risk. Abandon the convoy. Abandon Nicaragua. Let the government do what the hell it wants. Abandon the revolution. Buy a television and feed your dong.

He lay on the hard mattress as the house of iron cooled, creaking and screeching as it settled in for the night. "Saltpeter," he thought amid clouds of marijuana. "I should have drunk a dozen malts of saltpeter."

At length, he fell asleep.

When he woke up, it was dark. But something was happening in the next cell.

"*¡Cállate, cabrón!*"

Then, there was a thud.

"No! No!" It was the voice of a young man.

Another thud. "On your knees, *cabrón!*"

Honoré rolled toward the wall. He didn't want to see this. Nonetheless, the voice reached him, a voice from Nicaragua or Guatemala. He could do nothing. It wasn't his problem.

Suddenly, against his will, Honoré shot up.

In the next cell, two cops with nightsticks stood over a prisoner on his knees and in handcuffs. One of them held his head back by the hair while the other unzipped.

"Suck it!" said the cop.

"*Ándale, puto,*" said the other cop. "Taste some Chicano sausage."

One minute Honoré was sitting on the bunk; the next he was flying across the cell and grabbing the cop's neck through the steel bars and pulling as hard as he could. "*¡Déjenlo, cabrones!*"

The cop choked. "Ahhhhhh!"

The other cop grabbed Honoré's arm. "Let him go, *pendejo!*"

The first cop, coughing and wheezing, broke away. "Who's this sonuvabitch?"

"Comino's brother-in-law."

"Why did they put him with all the *jotos*?"

"I don't know. Maybe he's *joto.*"

Honoré gripped the bars as if he could tear them apart. "Fuck you!"

The cop grinned at him. "*Muy chingón*, right? Well, let's find out."

The two stepped into the hall, locking the door behind them. "I saw him on television. He's a communist. He smacked that guy on the face."

Standing before Honoré's cell, the cop tapped his nightstick on a steel bar. "Oh yeah? Since this guy is out trying to save everyone else, let's see if he can save himself."

"What if he bites off your dick?"

The cop slipped the nightstick between the steel bars. "Well, in that case, we'll have to go in through the back door, no?"

Suddenly, the door down the hall screeched open. "What the hell's going on?" barked the guard. "Get out here! We need some help downstairs. We just got an army of wetbacks."

As soon as they were gone, Honoré collapsed on the bunk, his head on a pillow, his legs stretched out, his eyelids heavy as mountains beneath a rosy thunderhead in his dreams. But the moans and groans of men banging each other wouldn't let him sleep for a long while.

The next morning, the cement walls glistened in sunlight as if buckets of water had been thrown on them the night before. The steady rush of water in the showers carried away the screams and cursing and laughter. Was he dreaming? He heard footsteps in the hall. He rubbed his eyes. Keys rattled.

Honoré's door swung open.

The Governor stood tall in his boots, looking around the cell. "Ain't nothing like the good ole days. Feels like home."

Honoré sat up. "How did you know I was here?"

The Governor checked out the toilet. "Saw you on TV."

"My wife didn't call you?"

The Governor positioned himself before the toilet and unzipped his fly. "Maybe she did, maybe she didn't."

"So why did you come?"

Water gurgled. "To get you out. What else?"

"How the fuck did you do it?"

The Governor finished and then zipped up. "Do what?"

"Spend eight years in the federal penitentiary?"

The Governor washed his hands in the sink. "Did I ever tell you one time we asked ourselves that same question—what we lacked in the pen? We decided only one thing."

"Pussy."

"Nope." The Governor dried his hands on a towel. "Cars."

"What about pussy?"

The Governor slipped the towel back on the rack. "We had all the sex we needed, and then some. Most of it was better than pussy."

What a lowlife, thought Honoré. Queers scared the shit out of him, but no one scared him like the Governor.

"Let's go."

"What?"

"I said let's go."

Honoré looked at the guard outside the cell and then at the Governor. "Are you sure?"

"Is the pope Catholic?"

As they walked past cells overflowing with drooling baboons, the Governor said, "You know what I enjoy about coming down here? The guards say 'sir' to you."

After going down several flights of stairs, they reached the ground floor. While the Governor waited in the hall, Honoré went into the booking unit, where fat cops watched TV in a cubicle behind walls of thick, wire-en-meshed windows. One got up and spoke through an opening in the glass to the guard escorting Honoré. Nearby laughter and yelling poured from the tank, a cell crowded with drunks and wife beaters and homeless gringos. Honoré took his personal belongings from the metal tray handed to him through an opening under the window, and he signed a receipt. In anoth-er room, Honoré climbed out of the orange jumpsuit. With each piece of clothing he put on, he felt better, as if he were putting on the mask of his real identity—his pants, his belt, his wallet, his shirt, his socks, his boots.

Suddenly, the door flew wide open, and there stood a black-eyed Sas-quatch in uniform. "What the hell is going on here? Who authorized his release?" yelled Comino at the top of his lungs.

"The Governor," said the guard.

Comino looked around, his good eye glaring beneath an arched eyebrow, a gold tooth gleaming. "*¿Quién chingados* is the Governor?" He crossed the room and grabbed the guard by the collar. "The governor of Texas?"

"I guess."

"The governor of Texas has no jurisdiction in Telaraña County!" Comi-no yelled in the man's face.

Cops with drawn nightsticks packed the room. "Arrest this man!" shouted Comino.

A cop looked first at the guard and then at Honoré. "Which one?"

"The prisoner, *pendejo!*"

The cops were about to pounce on Honoré when someone yelled from the door, "Hold your fucking horses!"

Comino froze, an eyelid twitching. The cops stepped aside.

Tossing a gold coin in his hand, the Governor swaggered into the room. "Remember me?"

Comino's mouth fell open. "What the hell are you doing here?"

"Heard a friend was in trouble."

"Coyote hates gringos."

A mischievous look blossomed on the Governor's face as if he were about to reveal a great secret. "If the Comandante and I have anything in common," he said, "it's that we both hate Meskins."

The black mustache quivered on Comino's lip. "No fucking piece of white trash comes in here and tells me how to run this place. This ain't goddamn Hicksville, Georgia."

The Governor shifted his weight. "No, but it might as well be, with all the Meskin rednecks we have down here. My old man always told me there were more rednecks in South Texas than in East Texas." He looked around at the cops, fat and ugly and vicious. "Now tell these beaners to vamoose."

Comino took a deep breath, looking as if he wanted to punch the Governor. Instead, he ordered all the cops out of the room.

"Muchas Garcias—or is it gracías?" said the Governor—then got in Comino's face. "Remember what happened to the sheriff?"

Comino shifted uneasily.

"Well, I'm proud to say," said the Governor, "I don't do those things anymore. Now I pay people to do them for me. Today I went by your new house before I moseyed out here. Very nice. Looks like a huge wedding cake. Business must be good. A lot of dope coming through." He tossed the coin and caught it without taking his eyes off Comino. "Now either you escort us out of this dump right now or you're driving home tonight to Hiroshima."

As a great silence settled in the room, Honoré remembered how some Escandonians lorded it over other Escandonians simply because they worked behind a desk or wore a uniform or had a Ph.D. Yet the minute you put them next to a gringo, they shit in their pants.

As if his lips had to be pried open with a Bowie knife, Comino muttered, "*Pinche* gringo!"

The Governor grabbed Comino by the collar. "One more thing, beaner. You know who runs this town? In Escandón, the Meskins work for the gringos. So as long as you're throwing your weight around and messing with my friends, I'd just like to remind you who owns the land and the banks and your ass." He let go of Comino. "*¿Comprende, amigo?*"

Then, the Governor led Honoré out of the room.

After marching down a long hall with a water-stained ceiling and weak yellow lights and tiny offices out of which stared fat cops behind silver badges on blue uniforms, they entered a lobby, where federal agents in cowboy hats, shiny three-piece suits, and cowboy boots stood and watched them walk through the frosted glass doors.

Outside, the air was scorching, the sunlight dazzling.

"Where to?" asked the Governor.

"The store."

The Governor climbed on the motorcycle first and then with a quick hop awoke the animal. Honoré climbed on behind him and hooked his heels on the foot pegs. The Governor swung around and headed down the street through scarves of heat untangling in their faces. The Governor's hair blew in the breeze. He stopped at an intersection, where Pastor Paul and Vietnam vets carried placards denouncing the U.S. embargo against Nicaragua. Holding on to both handlebars, the Governor turned north on Tamaulipas Avenue, and when he whacked the engine with a flick of the throttle, the hog roared.

CHAPTER 13

La Rubia Superior

Arms outstretched and hands nailed to a wooden cross, the crucified Christ hung on a wall facing a flock of brightly painted birds suspended from the ceiling by wires. On the other wall, He hung on a cross of rusted metal. On the wall next to the door, He was a figure woven from straw with a red ribbon tied around his waist. In prints of the Savior, he was a white man with blue eyes, brown beard, and long brown hair that fell to his shoulders, who looked more like a high school beauty queen than a thirty-two-year-old Semite nailed to a cross by Roman soldiers. Why Honoré's customers, gringos and Mexicans alike, found consolation in this crap or bought it was beyond him, despite Trotsky's theorizing.

These clichés, Trotsky explained, were an effort to make sense of the world around us, to comfort the dying and console the grieving. Such icons helped people live with the belief that, if they behaved on this earth and did pretty much what the Church asked of them, they would die and go to heaven. Above all, the icons told them that the world had meaning, that life was worth living, that things mattered. Honoré wanted to believe in these clichés, having been brought up a Catholic, and sometimes he did. The important thing, though, was that they sold well.

The phone rang. "Castillo's Mexican Curios," he said.

"Feeling any better?" asked Trotsky.

"The swelling has gone down. And I'm back at work. How's everything going?"

"Spooks everywhere."

Honoré's eyes wandered outside the window. "I hear you."

"Guess who's back in town."

There was not much traffic. "Who?"

"And pissed."

"Dr. Olivia de la Ó?"

"Yep."

Honoré glanced at his watch. "What about this afternoon? Are we still going out to the camp?"

"I'll call you."

As soon as Honoré hung up, he spotted a cop car cruising by. No telling who might be in it. Of course, he was used to it. The convoy had now been in town for two weeks, and there seemed to be no end in sight.

On televisions everywhere, the grim sunburned handsome face of Jack

Halligan, the Commander, denounced the international terrorist policies of the administration. In a daily demonstration at the bridge, Sixto brought together protestors carrying placards and banners from both sides of the river. At the mall in north Escandón, members of the convoy carried signs and banners challenging the embargo and stopped passersby to tell them about the Nicaraguan cause. Some onlookers smiled or raised their fists in solidarity, but most just stared and then went home. Along the interstate near Castillo's Mexican Curios, a handful of old farts, with bellies round as porcelain bedpans and hair just as white, carried posters denouncing U.S. imperialist policies in Latin America. Pastor Paul delivered sermons on peace and justice for third-world nations at every church where he could finagle an invitation while Zuckermann and some local attorneys pleaded their case before a federal judge

Not to be outdone, Cuz appeared on local television regularly. First, he denounced the convoy because it passed through what he considered his property, even though his and the Governor's portion of their late aunt's estate had not been settled. Subsequently, he denounced the Governor's proposal that a nudist resort be constructed at Paraíso del Nopal. Lines of vehicles—journalists and tourists from out of town and sympathizers from Escandón—crowded River Road, day and night. Helicopters flew low over the camp. Men in dark cars with long antennas and tinted windows parked on the road outside the encampment.

Then, just as Honoré was getting back to work, the damned phone rang again. He picked it up.

"Tex, I hate Mexicans!"

Honoré sat back and grinned, swinging his boots up on the desk with a leather-on-wood thump. "Welcome to the club, Rex."

Nasal and twangy, the voice was a fiddle with strings about to break. "I want to get out of this fucking town! That's all I ask. Get me out of this fucking town!"

Outside, afternoon sunlight boiled. "Well, then pray, and pray hard."

"Believe me, I pray all the time."

"Then try turning the other cheek."

The voice boomed. "I want this convoy out of town now! Not next week, not tomorrow! Now! Gringos have been keeling over and sent back home up north and then they've been on the phone protesting to their congressmen in Washington. One of the assholes is the son of a powerful senator."

"It wouldn't happen to be the senator who got you kicked out of Washington?"

Silence.

After a while, Honoré said, "How can I help?"

"I want to talk to the Commander."

Honoré removed his boots from his desk and sat straight, wondering how much longer he would have to put up with all this shit. "He refuses to talk to you."

"Is it true he's been sick?"

Honoré hung a smile from a corner of his mouth. "No, he's all right. They're ready to hold out all summer and longer if necessary."

Now the voice grew thick but gooey as oil or molasses or diarrhea. "Tell the Commander this: all they have to do is cross at night, one by one, as tourists. One by one. No political statements. No fanfare. No signs. Remove the slogans from the vehicles or cover them up. They're just traveling into Mexico. That's it. Keep your mouth shut. Don't tell them I told you. Just do it. I'll make sure the right people are on duty at the bridge."

Honoré's chair creaked. "That's it?"

"That's it."

It was too good to be true. "What about the asshole?"

"Which one?"

In the street outside, a cop car cruised through waves of heat. "Comino—he and his men have been tailing me."

"There's not much I can do right now. First, get these gringos out of town. But watch your back. Comino is dangerous. A raging bull. I'm afraid he might have a stroke any day now. Eats like a pig."

"Looks like one," Honoré said.

Trotsky drove. No one followed them, but it was hot as hell. The ride was long but smooth. Upon leaving the asphalt behind and bouncing along an uneven dirt road, Honoré coughed as the jeep gorged on dust. At the camp a veteran had tied the flag Molly had embroidered to a rope and raised it on a flag pole next to the A-frame, where journalists had set up a phone tree and reports of the latest developments went out every day to all parts of the world. Trotsky parked next to a thicket of prickly pears. As Honoré climbed from the jeep, he put a hand over his sun-blasted eyes and squinted at what was beginning to look more like a junk heap of abandoned pickups, vans, and school buses than an outpost of revolutionaries. Faces red as baked ham, the gringos sat or lay in whatever shade they could find, drinking ice-cold water or splashing it on themselves or walking around with wet towels on their heads, their bellies glistening with rivulets of water. Those with money or credit cards were holed up in cheap motels on the strip not far from Honoré's store. Others were already considering jumping on the next bus out of town. While a buzzard flew high above, the Nicaraguan flag hung lifeless atop the flag pole.

"This may be the last hurrah of the American left," Trotsky muttered.

Honoré wanted to ask him what he meant, but they were already standing outside the A-frame. When the door suddenly opened and Tennessee, melancholy as ever, emerged. "The Commander was just asking about you," he said.

"How he's doing?" Trotsky asked.

"So-so."

"The troops?"

"Losing a lot of people."

According to reports, Ma Savage had been arrested for assaulting a Mexican woman in a dive downtown. The police dragged her to the county jail, where she beat up four Mexican women, after which she was transferred to the state mental hospital on the base—not far, in fact, from the church where the convoy had arrived. In the meantime Johnny Paint, who had been hauled away on the bridge, was still locked up at the county jail and would be there until he was transferred back to the federal penitentiary in Mississippi.

"So what happened to your aunt?" Honoré asked.

"They let her out of the looney bin," he growled, "on the condition that she get the hell out of town. So I arranged for one of the vets to drive her and Pa back home."

"We've lost our mechanic?"

"Afraid so."

"And you?"

"I cain't go home unless I'm ready to do ten years in the pen. So I'm headed for Acapulco, Mexico."

Suddenly, a VW van jounced into sight, chassis creaking and squealing in a cloud of dust, engine purring as it cruised past. It stopped down the road under a mesquite tree, where the bubble-gum-chewing Viking princess climbed out of the driver's seat, a tight ass in shorts, tits wiggling beneath a loose blouse. Buttocks flowed and ebbed as combat boots carried her to the yellow school bus, where she joined her friends from Austin.

Tennessee, face glistening, looked at a buzzard in the sky and wiped his forehead with the back of his arm. "I'm going into town for some R&R. I need to get out of his fucking heat. Some cold ones would do me a lot of good. Any place you recommend that's cool and quiet? Maybe with some hookers?"

"Try the Lazy Mex," Honoré said. "Just down the street from my shop."

"See 'ya later, alligator."

Trotsky then led the way into an atmosphere thick with sweat and cigarette smoke cooled by air spewing from the window units. Veterans and journalists sat around two long vinyl-topped tables and manned the telephone tree, faces red and swollen as if they were tomatoes in a pot of boiling water. The Commander rose from a chair between Zuckermann and Molly, who greeted Honoré and Trotsky briefly and then returned to an animated conversation. The Commander led Trotsky and Honoré past a wall covered with maps of Texas, Mexico, and Central America, to a small room in back, where a desk with a telephone had been set up next to a bunk. After apologizing for not feeling well, the Commander lay down on the bunk and rested his head near a small window unit. Honoré and Trotsky sat on folding chairs across from the bunk.

Honoré wondered if he should warn the Commander that if you spent too much time in front of an air-conditioner or in a cold room and then stepped into the heat, you might be struck down by *cara chueca*. Endemic to South Texas and Escandón in particular, the disease grabbed half of your face and left it paralyzed. But since the people who got *cara chueca* were either ugly or *pendejos* or both, Jack might be immune.

The Commander stretched his legs and propped up his head on a bed roll. "How does anyone survive in this hellhole?"

"You get used to it," said Trotsky.

"We're either gonna cross soon or retreat."

"Replacements are flying in from all parts of the country."

"I know, I know. But the minute they step on the tarmac," muttered the Commander, "they panic. Can't breathe. Leave on the next flight. Can you blame them?"

"We might have a solution," Trotsky said.

"Oh, yeah?"

"An FBI agent offered to cross the convoy."

The Commander rose on his elbow. "No shit? Can you trust him?"

"Like a lot of other government officials down here," said Honoré, "he was sent to Escandón as punishment. Used to be stationed in Washington. A cushy job. Then, he got drunk and screwed a senator's wife, got demoted, and sent here. He's been trying to get out ever since."

Streaks of sweat forked across the Commander's khaki shirt as he lay back. "That's the way things are in a colony."

"The convoy brought everything to a halt," added Honoré. "So he wants the convoy out of Escandón as soon as possible. He's afraid that if something else goes wrong, the bureaucrats in Washington will blame him. The port director is his enemy."

Sweat oozed out of the Commander's matted brown hair and trickled down the side of his face. He paused and then sat up.

Trotsky peered at the Commander, whose face looked like a pork chop on a hot skillet. "Sir, are you all right?"

"Sure," said the Commander as he slowly stood up. "I'm okay."

His blue eyes were glassy as if dipped in oil. All of a sudden, his mouth sagged, and he weaved from side to side. He held on to the back of a chair. Then his combat boots flew into the air as he flopped over. A puddle of red flesh, blond hair, and two blue eyes bubbled on the floor.

It was dark by the time they left camp. Zuckermann drove the van while Molly accompanied a delirious Commander in the backseat; Honoré and Trotsky followed in the jeep. Honoré explained that not only did he need to pick up some money at the store, but he wanted to make sure things were locked since Maruca had reported seeing a car parked outside and a strange woman snooping around. After crossing the railroad tracks, the two vehicles pulled up side by side, windows rolled down, at a traffic light where River Road intersected Tamaulipas Avenue. Trotsky explained he would join them at the hospital after dropping off Honoré.

"Cool," said Molly.

But when Trotsky and Honoré arrived at the store, everything seemed okay. No phantom car. No strange woman. In fact, no one even followed them.

"Where's the restroom?" asked Trotsky.

"Better use the one in the warehouse. But watch your step. My cousins leave all kinds of shit lying around. The light switch is on your left."

As soon as Honoré unlocked the front door, the phone rang. He rushed inside. "Hello," he said.

"When are you coming home?" asked Maruca.

"I'll be there in a few minutes. I just dropped by the store to check on things. By the way, when did you see the strange woman?"

"I didn't. One of the hogs saw her."

"Why didn't you tell me that in the first place?"

"I don't know. I've been so busy with your mother I can't remember everything."

"How is she?"

"We're waiting for some test results. She's doing better. She may not need surgery. How are things at the camp?"

His gaze wandered outside, where the red, blue, and yellow of neon lights ebbed. "Not good. The Commander fainted, and they had to take him to the hospital. Every day the heat wipes out more people." Suddenly, a strange car parked behind Trotsky's jeep. A woman, thin as the Christ woven from straw with the red ribbon tied around his waist, climbed out. First, she studied Trotsky's jeep. Then, she looked at the store. When she entered the yard, he recognized her. "*¡Chingada madre!*"

"*¿Qué pasa?*"

Honoré felt his hand shaking. "*¡El pinche diablo!*"

"Who?"

"I'll call you right back." He hung up and headed out of his office.

As he stomped down the hall to the front of the store, a woman screamed outside, "*¡Auxilio! ¡Auxilio!*"

Waves of heat flooded the night as he threw open the door and clambered down the porch steps. All elbows and knees, Olivia sat on the dirt before the cast iron bull, looking like another one of the artifacts for sale, like the wooden Don Quixote down the street. A Chicana Doña Quixote.

He kneeled next to her. "Are you okay?"

Wearing a pantsuit, sleek and black as a tuxedo with the shiny *zapatos de charol*, the kind of shoes flamenco dancers wear, she rubbed her side. "That bull gored me," she moaned. Then she grabbed a sword on the ground. "I tripped on this."

"Sorry," he said, "I should have turned on the lights."

"Where's Trotsky?"

He helped her up. "Trotsky?"

She pointed the sword at the jeep. "That's his, isn't it?"

Something in the warehouse rumbled. She froze, looked around. Someone moaned. Then, the unmistakable detonations of farts. Poor Trotsky.

Brandishing the sword, she wheeled and stormed into the darkness leading inside the warehouse. Honoré ran after her. "Hold on!" he yelled, grabbing her by the elbow.

She yanked her arm away. "Don't you dare lay your filthy hands on me!"

"I just don't want you to fall again. Let me turn on the light," he said and hit the switch on a nearby wooden post.

Olivia gasped as she looked around.

Eyes and ears big as pans, a six-foot Mickey Mouse welcomed her with a huge smile and open arms while Donald Duck hung from a wire in the ceiling, leering. Hands white as toilet paper and eyes blue as Texas bluebonnets, a blond Cinderella looked at Olivia as if she had found a long-lost childhood friend. Manufactured in Nuevo Escandón, the six-foot tall papier-mâché piñatas were the latest craze in Austin, Dallas, and Houston, selling better than the clay pots, crucifixes, or anything else in the store. The gringos loved them.

"Would you like to purchase a *piñata*?" he asked, unable to think of something better to say while trying to buy some time.

"What do you think I am? An idiot?"

"No, ma'am."

Something squeaked. A toilet flushed. Water sputtered and vomited, swallowing itself in huge gulps. She ran to the restroom. "There you are, you liar!" she yelled as she pulled open the door.

"What the hell?" said Trotsky, standing with his pants midway down his thighs. He grabbed the door and shut it.

She banged the sword on it. "You made me a laughingstock of my political enemies! You interfered in my personal life! If it weren't for you," she screamed, "Ty wouldn't have ended up in *la zona* with a bunch of whores!"

When she stopped battering the door with the sword, it creaked open, and Trotsky stood there, dignity intact as he tied his belt. "None of this was my fault," he said solemnly.

"Then whose fault was it?"

Honoré spoke up. "That drunk from Berkeley."

"Pigs!" she yelled, raising the sword like an anorexic Joan of Arc. "Male chauvinist pigs!"

"Listen, goddamit!" Trotsky said, stepping between her and Honoré. "Ty knows what she's doing. She's not a child. She asked Honoré to take her to *la zona*. And she offered to help us with the convoy. She got some Grupo Femenil women to cook the food at the church. She and Mujica got us that school bus in Austin. Which is more than you've done for us." Trotsky took out a handkerchief. "Olivia," he said, calmly wiping his face, "I've always felt that if we joined forces we could accomplish more. That's why I asked Honoré to talk to you. All I wanted was to get some help for the women in Lucero."

She brandished the sword dangerously close to Trotsky's face. "Listen, there isn't one Chicana in this country that respects a Chicano. Men like you and this piece of shit here." She pointed the blade at Honoré. "Do you hear me? Not one!"

Mickey Mouse, Donald Duck, and Cinderella stared happily as Olivia cast the sword aside and stormed out. Honoré and Trotsky looked at each other, shook their heads, and then followed her into the yard, where they watched her speed away, tires squealing.

Honoré reached for the sword, bent but not broken, which had fallen beneath the scrotum of the cast-iron bull. "For a while there," he said, "I thought she was going to cut off *your* balls."

Trotsky stood next to him. "Crazy bitch—you never know if you're dealing with a woman, a man, or a nut."

They headed toward the jeep. "What if the Commander has to be hospitalized?" Honoré asked.

They stopped at the curb's edge. "Molly and Zuckermann asked me to consider taking command. I told them we should see how the Commander does. If push comes to shove, I'll do it." Trotsky pulled his keys from a shirt pocket. "The only thing pending is the mechanic. We lost Pa Savage. I don't want to drive across Mexico without a good mechanic. What about Sixto or his son?"

Honoré cast a glance at a lowrider speeding by. "They got the hell beat out of them."

"What about your friend Tequila?"

Honoré fidgeted. "That guy's an idiot. He sided with the feds on the bridge."

"An idiot mechanic is better than no mechanic."

"Yeah, but this idiot in particular doesn't have a trustworthy bone in his body."

"No? Well, then can we appeal to a different bone?"

Sword still in hand, Honoré sighed and felt like he was getting sucked into a black hole. Again. "What did you have in mind?"

"An ICBM."

Cars splashed through pools of headlights clear as tequila. Suddenly, the goons popped up in Honoré's rearview mirror. When he stopped at the traffic light at the intersection of Kennedy and Gonzalez, just a few blocks from home, a white unmarked car with a chrome-plated spotlight and a long antenna at its back pulled up next to him on the driver's side. A fat-cheeked motherfucker rolled down the window, one of Comino's undercover men, brandishing a shotgun.

At home Honoré stormed through the kitchen into the back room and threw open the glass gun case.

As he took out an AK-47, Maruca confronted him. "What's the matter?"

He walked past her. "I'm going to kill some motherfuckers!"

"Stop! Wait! You've gotten a bunch of calls! The FBI, Zuckermann. . . ."

Cuerno de chivo in hand, Honoré looked deep into her wavering eyes. "A man's gotta do what a man's gotta do." Then he strode out the front door.

The phantom car was parked across the street, windows rolled up, the engine running. Stopping a few feet from the tree trunk left by the hurricane, Honoré locked and loaded the man-eater. He then strode across the street to let it do some man-eating.

The driver started the engine. Amid the shriek and smell of burnt rubber, he sped down the street and careened around the next corner.

"*¡Hijos de su rechingada madre!*" cursed Honoré.

Back inside the house, he left the AK-47 on the dining room table and went into the restroom to wash. Eyes fierce but exhausted over sagging cheeks reminded him he was getting ugly. He wiped his face.

In the kitchen he opened the refrigerator, took out a cold one, and cracked it open. "Bastards," he muttered and drank.

Maruca, standing next to the stove, looked at him. "What's wrong with you? Look at what the convoy is doing to you."

He took another slug. "It's not the convoy. It's what Escandón has done to all of us. We can't think. We can't act. We don't know what's going on in the world, and we don't give a shit."

Bonita walked into the kitchen. "Oh, hi Dad," she said, thick glasses above her nose, braids touching her shoulders.

"Bonita," said Maruca, "would you please clean the table in the dining room?"

"Sure," she said and left. "Dad," she called from the other room, "is this rifle loaded?"

"It's not a rifle."

"Well, whatever it is, the gun. Is it loaded?"

"Yes."

Honoré put his beer on the counter and walked into the dining room. He picked up the AK-47 and carried it to the den where he stood it against the wall. Afterward, he went back for his beer before returning to the dining room, where he sat at the head of the table.

While Maruca served him some *milanesa*, he announced, "I'm thinking of going to Nicaragua."

Maruca held a knife in mid-air. "What?"

"Trotsky may be taking over as Commander. He needs help. I'll probably be gone a week."

When the phone rang in the kitchen, Maruca left to pick it up. "Your mother."

Honoré got up. "*Bueno*, señora, what's up?"

"I'm dying, *hijo*."

He raised an eyebrow. "Are you sure?"

"That's what the doctor says."

"Let me talk to him."

A strong male voice poured out of the phone. "Yes, sir."

"Is my mother dying?"

"Yes, sir. In a matter of days, two at the most."

"Are you sure?"

"Listen, what do you think we do at this hospital? Read tea leaves? Play with ouija boards?"

Honoré gritted his teeth but kept his cool. "Let me talk to her."

Doña Pánfila's voice was fragile as a yellow leaf in a desert breeze. "*¿Qué?*"

"Look, mother, I have to be out of the country for a few days. Can you wait till I get back?"

After a long silence, the old woman cleared her groggy voice. "On one condition."

"What's that?"

"If I'm going to die, I want to die at home. In my bed, at home."

"Deal."

Honoré parked in front of Tequila's Hi Tech Shop, a compound of tin-roofed wooden shacks built on the upper slope of Coyote Creek, which emptied into the Rio Grande, several blocks downstream. Sheets of corrugated tin slanted above the cars that filled the shop like shoes jammed in a closet. Everything seemed black, burnt, and evil-looking—the oil stains on the cement floor, the piles of worn-out tires, and the hoses thick and long as bull snakes—as if the shop were a junkyard in hell. That included the seven-foot-tall tin mariachi Honoré had given him in exchange for a favor two years ago. It sang with a whiskered wide-open mouth while wrought iron fingers held a guitar on a belly cut from scraps of rusted tin.

He headed inside the garage. Walking past a car above a pit in the ground, he halted, struck by the chilling sensation that someone was looking at him. Yes, in this junkyard everything looked evil—except for the lovely angel gazing at him from the wall. "*Disfrute con una rubia superior,*" said an ad on a calendar for Cerveza Superior, while a blond woman with big maracas in a bikini smiled at him.

"*Yo sigo siendo el rey,*" crooned a strong male voice somewhere below Honoré. Suddenly, the voice stopped as metal struck metal. Then, it started again, "*Con dinero y sin dinero . . . yo sigo siendo el rey.*" It stopped again, and a head the size of a soccer ball dipped in dirty oil popped up from the grave-like pit beneath a car. "Is that you, Coyote?" rasped Tequila.

Honoré crouched. "Looks like you can never get out of that black hole."

A hammer banged against metal. "I thought you were in jail."

"I was."

"So? Looking for a place to hide?"

"We need help."

"No way, José."

Honoré stood up. "Then I've gotta go."

Tequila peeked from under the car. "No, wait," he said and then disappeared before climbing up the steps at the end of the pit, grinning and wiping his hands on a red piece of cloth as he emerged. "Did you hear the one about the cannibals and the airplane crash?"

"*Por favor*, no stupid jokes."

"Wait."

Then, Honoré remembered he was here on a secret mission. He shouldn't take Tequila's stupid jokes so personally. "Go ahead. But don't take forever."

"A plane crashed in a jungle," said Tequila. "All the passengers died, except one. Two cannibals from a nearby village, a father and son, discovered the crash site. While looking for watches and money among the bodies, they found a white woman, most of her clothes torn off, her legs white and long, big white tits, the kind you like."

"Please leave me out of the joke."

Tequila grinned. "Anyway, the son said, 'Papá, you and me take woman home. We cook and eat her.' So, the father checked to see if she was alive. She was. She opened her eyes, which looked like jewels, blue jewels. The father shook his head, 'No, *mijito*, we take white woman home, and we cook and eat your mother.'"

While Tequila laughed uproariously, slapping his thigh and stumbling against the poster of La Rubia Superior, Honoré wondered why his old sidekick was so stupid or spent so much time on stupid jokes.

But that didn't matter right now. "We need you to look at some vehicles," Honoré said.

Tequila wiped tears from his face with the red cloth. "No, no, that's all I need now—to be running around with a bunch of queers, terrorists, and Jews."

Honoré was ready to wallop him. "Who told you that?"

"Your brother-in-law. Who else?"

Honoré seldom saw red. Usually, a flash of white light blinded him. This time he felt as if a geyser of red blood had exploded between his ears before he grabbed Tequila by the collar and threw him against the car. The hood slammed shut, missing the soccer-ball-shaped head by an inch.

"Olivia is right!" yelled Honoré. "You and your *carne asadas* and beer bellies and *movidas* and stupid jokes. You and Comino and the men who run this fucking town and the caciques and the priests turn my stomach. You stand for nothing. You've never had a fucking idea in your head. You eat too much. You fuck too much. You talk too much."

Tequila yelled. "¡*Ya 'stuvo*! You're killing me!"

Honoré threw Tequila on the ground, held him down by the neck and squeezed hard though it was difficult because Tequila's neck was thick and sturdy as a tree trunk. But Honoré's fingers were big and powerful. "That's right, I'm going to kill you, motherfucker!"

All of a sudden, a VW bus rumbled into the mechanic's shop up front, spewing smoke and gasping like a lawn mower on its last leg. Honoré let go and stood.

Tequila, rubbing his neck, staggered to his feet. "¿*Qué pasa, compadre?* You've always been loco in the *cabeza*, but now it looks like they're going to have to lock you up. Some coca, some Mary Jane, and some pussy will calm you down."

As Tequila headed toward his office in back, Honoré wondered whether he had made a big mistake in plotting with Trotsky to get an ICBM involved. With a nut like Tequila, there was no telling what might happen.

With blue eyes shimmering amid blond braids, the girl turned off the engine of the gray metal junk heap that looked as if it had survived the bombing of Beirut. The door creaked open. Honoré caught his breath as first one sun-toasted leg and then another slid to the ground. Long legs in khaki shorts and a white silk blouse filled with fresh *maracas* made it impossible *not* to look at her.

"Señor," she began in a sonorous morning voice, the voice of a young woman who had just climbed out of bed. "Trotsky sent me." At length, she recognized Honoré. "Oh, hi. You're the nice man from the bridge."

"Yes, ma'am," said Honoré, clearing his throat. "Did Trotsky tell you what this was about?"

She blew a bubble and popped it. "He said we need a mechanic, that we can't leave because we're out of mechanics."

Honoré glanced to see if Tequila was nearby. He wasn't. "Did he tell you what you might have to do?"

"Well, he just asked me if I was willing to do anything for la causa."

"That's it?"

"Yes, sir."

Then, the smell of soap and female sweat drew him, and he noticed the black pin in her earlobe, which he wouldn't mind nibbling. In fact, the ICBM was already affecting him where God had made him a three-legged creature. He better get out of here as soon as possible lest he end up being a nuke's collateral damage.

"Coyote," said Tequila as he came around the front of the Volkswagen bus—he halted and stared at the young woman, an eyelid twitching. "*¡La rubia superior!*" he gushed, grinning like a slice of watermelon. "Welcome."

A deadly smile broke across a set of ivory white teeth as she cooed in perfect Spanish, "Can you look at my Volkswagen?"

Tequila's eyes hovered between his ears like bumblebees looking for honey. "What's wrong with the Volkswagen?"

"The tail pipe is broken."

Tequila glanced at Honoré. "Your tail pipe is broken?"

"Yes."

Tequila pulled Honoré aside. "Why did you bring her?"

Honoré whispered, "I didn't. If you don't believe me, I'll ask her to leave."

"No, no," said Tequila and then walked over and knelt behind the Volkswagen. He stuck his head under the bus, but his eyes were drawn to Sugar's curvaceous calves. "This won't take long. I just need to move the car."

When he tried to get up, he couldn't. He stayed kneeling on one leg as he explained that his back had been giving him trouble. Eventually, he stood up, whistling as he limped past Honoré and then climbed in the car, which he backed out of the garage and parked in the street. With a grin that grew bigger by the minute, he returned and climbed in the van and moved it over the black hole in the floor. Moments later, Sugar descended into the pit with him.

"I'll be at the hospital," said Honoré to Tequila.

"Bye," she cooed.

"*Hay te wacho,*" said Tequila.

Then, just as Honoré was climbing in his pickup, he heard what he thought was a pack of dogs barking down the street. He stopped, listened carefully, looked down the street. No, they weren't dogs, and the noise was not coming from the street. It was the sound of a man turning into a howling dog.

PART 3

Honoré didn't want to leave. But he had to, having given his word. So he came to say good-bye. After dumping his duffel bag on the porch, he walked inside the house his father built for his mother thirty years ago and headed down the hall to her bedroom, where he found her lying in a brass bed amid silver rays of sunlight from the window while Maruca wiped her forehead with a towel. On the wall across the room, a handsome man wearing a cowboy hat smiled from the depths of an old black-and-white photograph in a gold frame; it was his father, in his early forties. At the foot of the bed, the *coronas* of flowers bound on wire wrapped in leaves reminded Honoré of all his friends whose funerals had been like *quinceañeras*, parties for fifteen-year-old Mexican girls coming of age, and everybody got drunk on their asses and fired AK-47s at the heavens as if taking on God Himself.

"Look at all the flowers!" he said.

With petals in fist-sized whorls of pink, white, and yellow, the flowers smelled fresh from the garden. In fact, they smelled so delicious, so suggestive, he forgot his dear old mother and God when it occurred to him the flowers looked like tits. Then he thought of pussy. Young and clean-shaven. Pink or white, wrapped in folds of flesh.

Doña Pánfila raised her head from the pillow. "Is that you, Honoré?"

The smell of bad breath and old feet brought him to his senses. "Sí, señora," he said, stopping next to Maruca. "I came to say goodbye."

"Why?" Doña Pánfila squawked.

The older she got, the more she confused him. "Why did I come to say goodbye?" he said.

"No. Why the flowers?"

He held her fingers, fragile as old *carrizo*. "Your family loves you."

Eyes gray and gooey as fresh oysters, Doña Pánfila yelled, "What did you say?"

He got close, raising his voice. "I said your family and friends sent all these flowers because they love you!"

Doña Pánfila rolled her head back and forth. "No, they don't! They just want to see me dead!"

Maruca moved a strand of gray hair from the old woman's sun-toasted face. "How can you say that, Doña Pánfila?"

For an old woman on her deathbed, her voice was strong. "Today everyone wants to rush things, especially the young, who think they're going to live forever." She caught her breath. "Flowers should be sent after someone dies, not before. Get rid of them!"

Suddenly, Bonita breezed into the room and stopped at the foot of the bed. "Look at all the flowers! They're gorgeous!"

"Would you please put them in the bedroom at the end of the hall?" Honoré asked.

"No, no!" said Doña Pánfila. "The trashcan."

Bonita frowned. "But they're so beautiful!"

Cartwheel-like, Rig and Cachetes rolled into the room carrying huge pizzas, red with pepperoni and yellow with cheese. "We got everything you asked for," said Cachetes, short of breath.

Rig, cheeks rosy as candy apples, raised a liter of A & W root beer. "They didn't have Barq's, but we got this."

In a matter of seconds, everyone except Honoré held a slice of pizza. Maruca lay hers on the bed so she could help his mother sit up, but Cachetes grabbed it and swallowed it in two sickening gulps.

"I don't understand these doctors," muttered Doña Pánfila, propped up against the headboard, a slice of pizza in her hand. "If they know you're going to die, why do they tell you not to eat what you want?"

Maruca wiped her mouth. "It's for your own good."

"Well, if I'm going to die, why can't I have a little fun?"

Honoré squeezed her hand. "You're not going to die, señora."

She slapped his hand. "¡*Muchacho malcriado!* Now you're making fun of me!"

Outside, a horn honked.

"I gotta go," said Honoré and turned to his cousins. "Keep an eye on the store. Maruca's in charge. No messing around."

Next to Honoré, Cachetes chomped on a piece of pizza. "Okay, boss."

Rig burped. "Don't worry, boss. We'll make sure Doña Pánfila is happy. She might even have some fun while you're gone."

The hogs glanced at each other and giggled like fat girls. Annoyed, Honoré poked a belly dense as a huge sponge.

"Ouch!" said Rig.

"No messing around. No red eyes. You hear me?"

"Yes, sir," said Rig.

The horn honked again.

"I gotta go," said Honoré. "Remember your promise, señora."

"What if God sends the Archangel Gabriel for me?"

He rubbed her hand. "Mother, *por favor*! Would you please wait till I get back?"

She gripped his fingers. "I'll try. But I'm not promising anything. Now get out of here before I change my mind! Go play with your friends! And get back before your father comes home!"

Suddenly, he felt like he was back in grammar school, a little boy getting ready to go out and play cowboys and Indians with his friends down the street until his father's photograph on the wall reminded him that all that happened long ago and any day now his mother would be up there with him among the angels, chatting with La Virgen de Guadalupe and Jesus Christ.

The honking started again so he kissed his mother's forehead, hard as a chunk of Mexican brown sugar.

Bonita stopped him at the foot of the bed, glasses on her light-skinned face, frizzy hair glowing in sunlight, and her pink lips greasy from the piz-za. "Mom is right. I don't think you should go on this trip."

He embraced her. "I'll be all right, honey."

Tears filled her eyes. "Dad, please don't go."

He hated this, leaving his little girl. He never wanted to abandon his family the way his father left his mother and him when he got into trouble in Sabinas Hidalgo. So after kissing Bonita, he stalked out of the bedroom, eyes moist, swearing this would be his last mission. Maruca followed him down the hallway, where he picked up his duffel bag; then he walked out the front door into the porch's muggy air. He waved at Tequila in the Volkswagen van parked across the street under a tree as big as the one knocked down by the hurricane. Sugar was with him, but Honoré couldn't see her from here.

Maruca, thick black hair pulled over her ears and tied in a bun at the back of her head, slipped her arm through his. "There's another storm coming."

After eyeing the dark clouds gathering in the south, he put down the duffel bag and slipped an arm around her waist. "Ah, baby, don't worry."

"I can't help it."

He kissed the side of her head. "This is the last time I do this. I mean it. I'll be back in a week. I'm going with friends. Trotsky is going. We have a lawyer."

She trembled in his arms. "Bye."

He let go and picked up the duffel bag. "*Hasta la vista, chula.*"

"Be careful."

Tequila told Honoré to drive because he didn't want to deal with customs officials when they crossed into Mexico but more likely because he wanted to spend time with Sugar. Honoré agreed and then drove across town while Tequila and Sugar nuzzled each other in the front seat like lovebirds. Their giggling annoyed him.

At Trotsky's house, the couple climbed in the back seat while Trotsky sat up front with Honoré. Lightning flashed among the boiling clouds. A clap of thunder shook the world as he drove across the Bridge of the Americas, and a strong wind flung silver needles of water against the windshield. It seemed the thumping wipers would wipe away the bridge, but the bridge poured right back into view through the smeared glass.

"I can't believe," said Honoré to Trotsky as they passed a slow-moving eighteen-wheeler, "that just a few weeks ago we were in the middle of a battle on this bridge."

"How long to get through customs?" asked Sugar.

"An hour at most," said Trotsky.

The four-lane-wide pavement carried them beneath a two-storey, bunker-shaped Mexican customs building squatting on sturdy round cement columns. Honoré turned right and parked between two buses resting like huge caterpillars with windshields for eyes and the names of their destinations—Monterrey, Saltillo, Mexico City, and Oaxaca—on their brows. Skinny, brown-armed kids thrust small boxes of Chiclets at them as they entered a brick building with high and narrow metal-framed windows. Dozens of tourists stood in line to get their visas.

Tequila smiled and hummed a tune like a man in love as they got in line. In fact, next to the blond goddess, Tequila looked like a prickly pear cactus in full bloom as valentines spun around his ugly head.

Suddenly, a woman standing nearby hissed at her bald male companion. "What are you looking at?"

"Shut up!" he said.

"Then stop staring at that gringa!"

No other vehicle crossing that morning was searched so thoroughly. In fact, the buses and their throngs of passengers came and went while the inspectors took their time checking out every inch of the Volkswagen as they looked for guns or drugs. But Honoré suspected they were making things difficult so they could feast their eyes on Sugar, who looked as if her blue denim shorts had been jam packed with fresh cabbage heads and her silky pink blouse filled with scoops of ivory pudding so sensitive they quivered beneath the Mexicans' slightest glance. When she bent over to tie one of her shoelaces on her U.S. Army combat boots—showing plenty of muscle as she flashed the curve of inner thigh—everything came to a standstill.

Two hours later, Honoré pulled out of customs. As they drove down Nuevo Escandón's main street, they passed curio shops and el mercado with its *zarapes* and piñatas hanging under canvas canopies. They rolled past the first plaza and then the second, where they turned left and drove along a narrow street abutted by tin roofs sustained by walls of swollen wood painted many times over. The wind died down as Honoré parked a block from Don Sixto's shop, and then they walked along a street crowded by the convoy's pickups, buses, and vans, which had crossed during the night in accordance with the FBI agent's instructions—singly and without fanfare.

Vets—in combat boots, khaki pants, white T-shirts, and jungle hats—stood guard outside Sixto's shop, their tattooed white arms thick and hairy, faces dead serious. A crowd of white-haired elderly folks gathered around Pastor Paul, who looked like a big ever-smiling black prophet among a bunch of jabbering pot-bellied snowmen. Trotsky led the way past the Mexican journalists scribbling on yellow notepads, through the gate and inside the yard. After walking past unattended cars with their hoods open, they entered Sixto's office.

A turban of gauze on his head, Sixto reclined in a wooden swivel chair behind his desk while La Morenita stood behind him. "*¡Felicidades!*" he yelled and rose to his feet. "You got the convoy across. You beat Uncle Sam."

Trotsky shook his hand. "Don't thank me. Honoré arranged all that."

Honoré gripped Sixto's hand. "I suppose you won't be going with us."

Sixto sat down. "If I hadn't neglected the shop here all this last year, I would."

El Víbora sat on a box, a cast on his leg, crutches lying on the floor at his feet. "*¡Qué suerte!* You go to Nicaragua, and we remain political prisoners in Escandón!"

La Morenita, her hand on Sixto's shoulder, spoke up, "Where are you staying in Oaxaca?"

"Iglesia de los Descalzos," Trotsky replied.

"I wish I could go with you. But God sent me to take care of this man," she said and then kissed Sixto on top of his head.

Sixto patted her fingers. "This woman is a true *guerrillera* for putting up with an old man like me."

Everyone laughed.

Meanwhile, Molly stood next to the Commander, who lay on a litter. Amid streaks of gray exploding in brown hair, she fixed Honoré in a stare. "We were wondering where you were," she said.

"We got delayed at customs," responded Trotsky.

"Well, we can't afford to lose more time," declared Zuckermann, who wore white tennis shoes and khaki cutoffs.

The Commander rose on an elbow. "The important thing is that you're here and we're ready to go."

Trotsky crouched before the Commander. "How are *you*? We've been worried about you."

"Fine, just fine," he said. "The doctor said I'd make it to Nicaragua."

Molly made a face. "That's not true. In fact, you left the hospital AMA."

"AMA?" asked El Víbora.

"Against medical advice," explained Zuckermann, in English and then in Spanish.

"I'm afraid soon you'll be MIA," said Molly.

"Or KIA," said Trotsky.

"Isn't that the best way to die?" said Don Sixto. "Like a man."

"Or a fool," muttered Molly.

"Or a *guerrillero*," said La Morenita, surprising everyone that she understood some English.

Suddenly, thunder rolled and shook the building. "What about the storm?" asked Trotsky. "A hurricane, even this far inland, can bring flash floods. The highways lack good drainage. I say we wait a day."

"Sixto, what do you think?" asked the Commander.

Sixto's chair squeaked. "Depends on how bad it gets," he said. "Last year flash floods covered the highway south of Sabinas Hidalgo with boulders. One lane was washed away."

"But once we reach the *altiplano* around Saltillo," argued Zuckermann, "we'll be okay. Besides, we're running out of money."

"I say we go now," said the Commander.

"You should have no problem at the checkpoint," said Sixto. "I already talked to my *compadre*. He took care of everything. He will be there when you go through. Just present your documents—and that's it. If you have any problems, call me."

After everyone hugged and shook hands like family before departing after a long holiday together, the Commander told Zuckermann he was ready to leave. Two Vietnam vets carried him out on the litter like a wedding cake on a wooden slab. Cameras flashed like small bolts of lightning as journalists photographed him when the veterans set the litter a few feet from the bus; then they asked him questions about the American embargo against Nicaragua. The wind picked up.

Zuckermann caught up with them outside the bus. "You and Honoré," he said to Trotsky, "will drive the Commander's pickup at the head of the convoy. The Commander will ride with me and Molly in the bus. We'll be right behind you."

Trotsky glanced at the bus. "The one from Austin?"

Zuckermann nodded. "Yep. It's in pretty good shape."

"Which of the women are going with us?"

"Just Sugar." He then pushed the bus's glass-paneled door open. "I want to show you something."

Several rows of seats had been removed behind the driver's seat, and now a short wave radio, a CB, and walkie-talkies crowded a narrow wooden slab supported by a tool box at one end and a squat metal file cabinet at the other.

"We've set up a communications network," explained Zuckermann, "between here and Nicaragua. Just in case."

Trotsky looked at everything. "Good."

On the other side of the bus, a wheelchair stood folded next to a bunk that extended from the door to the seats still intact. "This is the Commander's bunk," said Zuckermann.

Three rows of seats bulged with backpacks and sleeping bags and a small canvas bag and a red purse. At the back of the bus, Honoré spotted dozens of small rubber wheels with spokes, the kind he had seen on children's bicycles, and others taken from abandoned lawn mowers.

"One more thing," said Zuckermann to Trotsky, glancing suspiciously over both shoulders. "Sugar," Zuckermann said quietly, "may be CIA."

Trotsky exchanged doubtful glances with Honoré. "Well, I've always said the real ICBMs in the Cold War were women."

Honoré smiled.

Zuckermann didn't. "If she is CIA, she'll try to stop the convoy. Or discredit us."

Trotsky adjusted his eye patch. "Not likely, if she's anything like the CIA I knew in 'Nam."

"Yes," said Zuckermann, "but their stupidity can be lethal."

Outside, Honoré found the journalists taking photos of Sugar as if she were a movie star, lights flashing, tongues drooling. If Tequila hadn't been there to keep the men at bay, God knows what the pack of ravenous dogs would have done to the poor darling with the deadly denim-packaged twat. As if that weren't bad enough, the Commander and Molly began arguing like husband and wife over some medication he had forgotten to take until two vets carried the tall gringo with lanky legs and sharp elbows inside the school bus. Seething, Molly followed. The wind rocked the bus. Lightning flashed.

Trotsky turned to Honoré. "I'll get the Commander's pickup."

"What about our duffel bags?"

"Leave them in the van," Trotsky said and took off with Zuckermann.

Suddenly, Honoré heard footsteps approaching from behind. "Hey, Honoré," drawled a hillbilly.

Honoré turned and faced a gangly bird with long arms and sad blue eyes. "Tennessee!"

A smile flickered. "Guess who else is here."

Johnny Paint stumbled out from behind the bus. "Hey."

"How did you get out of jail?" asked Honoré.

Johnny Paint's eyes rolled wildly as if he were skateboarding across a glacier of cocaine. "I don't know what you did to that guy Comino. The minute I mentioned your name, his whole face twitched and beads of sweat big as beans popped out all over."

"No shit?"

"No shit."

"What did you tell him?"

"Just that I needed to call Castillo's Mexican Curios. The next thing I know a guard is escorting me out of the jail."

The wind howled. Nonetheless, Honoré took off, the school bus behind him, followed by thirty-eight more vehicles, moseying along a narrow street as they headed out of Don Sixto's barrio. At length, they crawled past a plaza, whose palm trees were lashed by the wind as people scurried for cover. Upon reaching the main street, he turned south and passed more curio shops with huge vases and Roman columns on the sidewalk under canvas canopies. After a cannonade of lightning, the wind flung spears of water. On the outskirts of town, Honoré approached the intersection where the highway connected with the highway to Piedras Negras.

The walkie-talkie squawked. "Hello," Trotsky said. "Roger." He handed the walkie-talkie to Honoré.

"Hello."

"*Ya estufas*," said Tequila. "I'm done."

Honoré kept his eyes on the road as wind-borne water lashed an eighteen-wheeler with the force of a bullwhip. "*¿Cómo que ya estufas?*"

"I want to go home."

"*No mames*. Why?"

"I don't know how to swim."

"Don't you think it's about time you learned?"

"I miss my kids."

Honoré looked at Trotsky and shook his head.

"What's the matter?" asked Trotsky.

"He's thinking about deserting."

"Let me talk to Sugar," said Trotsky.

"Trotsky wants to talk to Sugar," said Honoré.

Trotsky said, "Listen, honey. Thanks again. If not for you, we might not have a mechanic. Yes, ma'am. Good. We can't afford to drive through Mexico without a mechanic. So do what you have to. If necessary, use handcuffs. You know what I mean. And from now on, report directly to me."

Soon Honoré found himself in a long line of tractor trailers that looked like a caravan of woolly mammoths headed south for the winter. Since an eighteen-wheeler had broken down up ahead, they were stuck in traffic for about thirty minutes, creeping forward through blinding sheets of rain until Honoré got off the highway and took the access road. At the next intersection, some eighteen-wheelers looked like women—with dainty, penciled feminine eyes for headlights and glittering with chrome. Others were macho—plain and square, with a no-nonsense look, tough, angry. Three brand new trucks, which resembled fine cats with whiskers and narrow eyes, swept past on shiny wet tires, chrome-plated bumpers looking like expensive necklaces.

A huge black tidal wave waited on the horizon. "Doesn't look good," Honoré muttered.

"Where's the hurricane expected to make landfall?"

"Veracruz."

A lake appeared. Honoré slowed down. As the water swallowed the pickup, Honoré feared the engine might die. He passed one stalled car, then another, with passengers inside, water half way up the door. Then he hit a pothole and sank, but the pickup kept moving, engine humming, breathing. In the rearview mirror, the yellow bus lumbered through the water, followed closely by the rest of the convoy.

An eighteen-wheeler threw a cascade of water on Honoré's windshield, darkening the cab as if it were evening, but gradually the wipers swept the water away. He saw a bird. No, a fly.

It buzzed past his nose. "*¡Pinche mosca!*"

It landed on Trotsky's nose. Trotsky rolled down the window. The creature flew outside. Then, suddenly it stopped raining.

Sunlight changed the beads of water on the windshield into sparkling jewelry, which burst and trickled down the glass like sad afterthoughts. Honoré felt what he had always felt at such rare moments—that there was hope, hope for the convoy, hope for him. That there might even be a God. So he kept the faith and kept moving through the churning water, slowly. At long last he saw landfall as the highway rose majestically out of the foam, the asphalt black and shiny like the back of a whale emerging from the ocean.

"Praised be the Lord!" sneered Trotsky.

Soon they picked up speed and left the pools of water behind. Old adobe houses snuggled among thickets of mesquite and cactus. A dog, its tongue sticking out of its stiff muzzle, lay dead on the edge of the pavement. Ten kilometers later, Honoré slowed down as they approached soldiers manning a machine gun behind a pile of sandbags. Others stood guard with assault rifles strapped to their shoulders, olive-green helmets on their heads, one of whom waved a red flag. Another swaggered to the edge of the highway as the convoy approached the *retén*, a checkpoint protected by an aluminum canopy on steel girders while a small aluminum building stood on the shoulder.

Honoré stopped, rolled down his window, and handed over Trotsky's and his documents. "*Buenos días.*"

The soldier opened a passport. "Where you headed?"

"Nicaragua," said Honoré.

Another soldier—a sergeant, by the look of the stripes on his arm—stopped next to the soldier examining the passports. "Where do you plan to cross into Guatemala?" he asked.

"Tapachula."

The soldier handed the documents to the sergeant. "Look at this."

Tall and light-skinned, the sergeant looked at the documents and then at Honoré. "Where were you born?"

"Escandón, Texas."

"You're an American?"

"Yes, sir. Why?"

"Because we're looking for someone who looks like you. But from Guatemala. Step down. We'd like to ask you a few questions."

Honoré and Trotsky climbed out of the pickup and stood on the pavement as the sergeant examined the documents. Two or three other members of the convoy already stood outside their vehicles as they watched cars and trucks amassing behind the convoy. An eighteen-wheeler blasted its horn.

Zuckermann approached. "What's going on?" he asked.

Trotsky replied, "They think Honoré is someone else."

"What?" asked Zuckermann. "Why?"

Honoré lowered his voice. "It's probably just some excuse to get a *mordida.*"

Zuckermann glanced at the officers. "I thought Don Sixto made arrangements. Should we call him?"

"No, wait," said Trotsky. "Here comes someone else."

A middle-aged customs officer in a cap, raincoat, and boots approached from the building at the side of the highway. "What's the problem?" he asked.

"Comandante," the sergeant said, "look at this."

The Comandante looked at the documents. "So?"

"This could be the terrorist we're looking for."

Perplexed, Honoré glanced at Trotsky. Meanwhile, Zuckermann was about to say something until Trotsky shook his head. Having dealt with Mexican officials before, Honoré assumed they were up to their old tricks again—namely, shaking down people for some extra cash.

But the Comandante must be Sixto's contact. Even the way the Comandante stood looking at the passport, confident and bullish as he tweaked his mustache, reminded Honoré of Don Sixto. They were about the same age. Then lightning struck the distant horizon.

The Comandante looked at the threatening sky.

Annoyed by the honking of the vehicles, the sergeant cast an ugly glance at Honoré and then said to the Comandante. "So what are we going to do?"

Then, as if a huge fiery sickle had been flung against the desert, the lightning struck nearby, and an earth-shattering boom shook the aluminum roof. "That was close," the Comandante said. "Last year lightning struck one of my compadres. It didn't kill him, but it left him staring out a window for the rest of his life, drooling like a dog."

Exasperated, the sergeant asked, "What about these hippies?"

"What about them?"

The sergeant looked down the length of the convoy. "They're revolutionaries."

Zuckermann could no longer contain himself. "Sir."

The Comandante turned to him. "Yes."

"May I speak?"

"Yes, of course," the Comandante replied in English.

"Sir, we're carrying humanitarian aid to the pueblo de Nicaragua. We're all Americans."

The Comandante seemed to take a special interest him. "So where are you from?"

"New York."

"Ah, sí. I love New York. Excellent food. And the women—"

But the honking drowned out his voice, and the sergeant nudged him. "Excuse me. Can we talk?"

Though the officers withdrew a few feet away, Honoré could still hear just about everything they said.

"So what do we do?" asked the sergeant.

The Comandante slapped him on the back. "Compadre, when the hell hasn't there been a revolution going on somewhere in Mexico? It's a national pastime, like fútbol. Let them through. They won't harm a fly."

The sergeant lowered his voice. "Have they paid the quota?"

"What quota?"

"You know."

"A *mordida*? What are they going to pay with? Just look at them."

Lightning flashed again.

His dark face deeply creased by the years, the Comandante stared at the horizon. "I hate it," he said solemnly, "when there is revolution in the heavens."

"So what do we do with these assholes?"

"Let them go."

God designed a stained glass window that vanished as soon as the windshield dried. After leaving the puddles behind, the convoy rolled into the desert, past the little towns of Santa María, Las Penas, Vallecillo, and La

Peinada. All were familiar to Honoré because his father's family was from
here and because he made this trip at least once a week with Tequila in the
old days. Along with the Governor, they transported millions of dollars
worth of pot from here to the border. In fact, the dark gray mountains
looked unusually familiar, as if he had just been here the day before; then,
as they drove into a small town, past trucks parked in clumps at the gas
station at its outskirts, he felt eerie. Tequila, the Governor, and he almost
died in a shootout with a local gang on this street. Now he spotted two men
in a car parked along the highway. They could be *federales* or gangsters.
Same thing.

"Sabinas Hidalgo," Trotsky muttered.

When Honoré drove past the car and saw white hair on the men and a
kid in the back seat, he breathed a sigh of relief. Everything was cool. Yet
not until they drove out of town did he relax. "My father got killed here in
a gunfight over a woman. We would have lost the store if it hadn't been for
my mother. Later, my friends and I used to pick up stuff here and transport
it to Escandón. I haven't set foot in this place in years."

Suddenly, the walkie-talkie squawked. "It's Tequila," said Trotsky.

Honoré put the walkie-talkie to his ear. "What?"

"Remember?"

"Remember what?"

"The good old days."

"What about them?"

"Pussy and pot."

"And potshots."

Gray clouds boiled along a dark mountain ridge that looked like the
smooth spine of a charging bull as the wet asphalt carried them south.
Curve after curve, they crept past chunks of unearthed rock jutting from
the face of the cliffs, probably the most dangerous stretch of highway
between Nuevo Escandón and Monterrey, where the last hurricane had
washed out parts of the highway.

Thirty minutes later, Honoré looked in the rearview mirror. A cloud of
steam poured from the nose of the Yellow Submarine like a white parachute unfurling in the wind. "Trouble."

Trotsky glanced in his side mirror. "I thought that bus was in fairly good
condition."

Suddenly, a crevice appeared several yards ahead. In Honoré's lane.
He hit the brakes. Slowing down, he steered around the cave-in, dark and
narrow as a freshly dug grave left by flash floods. After parking, he climbed

out, along with Trotsky, and they walked to the edge of the four-or-five-feet-wide abyss that separated the pickup from the bus. Chunks of asphalt and the dirt that once sustained it had collapsed into the ravine skirting the highway. Honoré looked across the highway at a steep cliff whose red earth lay exposed like a raw steak freshly cut while boulders studded the slope like fat brown sheep.

"Look at that," said Trotsky. "If we had driven into that, we would never have made it to Monterrey."

They hopped over the crevice and headed toward the bus, where Johnny Paint and Zuckermann joined them. The radiator sizzled like an overheated pork chop while a murky cloud of steam unraveled across their faces. Drivers climbed out of their vehicles and stood on the highway, stretching arms and legs.

Then Tequila showed up, eating a banana, finishing it in one gulp, throwing the peel on the highway. Fucking ape, thought Honoré.

Tequila opened the hood and let the steam clear.

"I thought you said it was in perfect condition when we left the border. What's wrong?" Honoré said.

"Nothing," said Tequila, pulling a rag from his back pocket. "You know how women act up when they reach a certain age. They heat up. This bus is menopausal." He grinned.

Zuckermann made an ugly face. "I'm going to check on the vehicles, make sure we haven't lost anyone."

Trotsky accompanied him.

In the meantime, Tequila wiped his hands on the rag and leaned against the fender. "Let me tell you a story," he said to Honoré. "One Sunday I agreed to take my wife to see her mother."

Honoré's hand trembled. "What the hell does your mother-in-law have to do with this bus?"

"The same thing your mother has to do with it. You wouldn't be here if it weren't for her. None of us would. So show some respect for mothers."

Johnny Paint nodded. "I hear you, brother. Mothers are important."

"Anyway," Tequila said, "my wife asked me to fix her car because it had been overheating. On the day we set out, I still hadn't fixed it. I even forgot to put water in it. Sure enough, we weren't long out of Escandón when the damned car started overheating. Like a weak, hysterical woman, my wife began crying. Since I'm a mechanic, there's nada I don't know about cars, I told her. She didn't believe me. So as soon as the car cooled down, we started it again. We took off. When it got hot again, we stopped, let the engine cool off. The trip took about three-and-a-half hours, but we got there. It's the same with women. You just let them cool off. Otherwise, they'll cut off your balls and send you to the dog house."

Honoré thought about punching him in the face. "Are you saying we have to let the engine cool off until we get to the next town?"

Tequila dropped his arms to his sides. "That's what I have always admired about you, Coyote," he said with a smirk. "Not only are you taller and better looking than me, but you might even be as smart as me."

Johnny Paint giggled. Honoré could stomach a lot of bullshit, but he couldn't take ridicule from idiots like Tequila, so he considered wiping the smirk off his face with his knuckles. But just as he was getting ready to let him have it, lightning struck the mountain above them like a machete. Sizzling and white and sharp-edged, it sliced the air, struck the earth, and made it tremble. The smell of sulphur reminded Honoré of where he might end up if he killed Tequila.

No problem. A man had to do what a man had to do. And he would have done it had not a slew of rocks suddenly broken loose like dozens of chunky footballs, which came tumbling down the side of the cliff.

"Fuck!" yelled Johnny Paint. "A landslide."

"*¡A la chingada!*" shouted Tequila.

Amid a thick cloud of rocks and dirt, a boulder the size of a Volkswagen Beetle rolled toward Honoré, who scrambled out of the way at the last second. Stumbling, he fell and hit the pavement hard. Moments later, he sat up, nose and cheekbone hurting like hell, swelling as if he had grown a mango on his face. A second too late—and he'd be hamburger. Rolling between Honoré's pickup and the Commander's bus, the boulder had missed both by a few feet before plummeting into the ravine.

"Where's Tequila and Johnny Paint?" asked Zuckermann, who came running. He helped Honoré to his feet.

Honoré sniffed the air. "What smells?"

"Look," said Zuckermann, pointing at the ground behind the Commander's pickup.

Just as in the cartoons Honoré had grown up watching on American TV, the figures of a gringo and a Mexican lay flattened, side-by-side, on the highway. Blond hair, pink face, eyes covered with dirt, mud, and stones— that was Johnny Paint. Black hair, a fat brown face, an oil-stained brown finger—Tequila.

Trotsky halted at Honoré's side, breathing hard. "What happened?"

"Bad luck," Honoré said. "The bastards dove into the gully before the boulder rolled over them."

Tequila sat up, dirt spilling from his face. "*¿Qué onda?*"

"*¡Pendejo!*" Honoré said.

Trotsky helped Tequila up while Zuckermann helped Johnny Paint dig his way out.

Tequila brushed himself off, spitting dirt. "Thought I was dead, right?" he smirked. "Well, let me tell you something, Coyote. *Cosa mala nunca muere.*"

Soon after the veterans cleared the highway of debris, Honoré took off in the pickup. More washouts appeared. So Honoré took it easy, skirting them. Then it was a smooth ride for several miles. After two stops to let the bus cool down again, they reached the top of a hill and from there coasted into a valley, where a squad of young men on bicycles waited for them on both sides of the highway. After Trotsky spoke to them, the cyclists escorted them into Ciénega de Flores, a tiny Spanish colonial town with a plaza and a church at its heart. Well-wishers lined both sides of the highway and waved flags.

"This is the part I love the most," said Trotsky. "*El pueblo.* They're the reason we're fighting."

In Ciénega de Flores, the local support committee welcomed them in a café famous for its *tacos de huevos con machacado.* Members of the convoy, including the Commander and his staff, went inside while Honoré and Trotsky talked with the locals, who were flattered to be part of this humanitarian effort and wished they could accompany the convoy to Nicaragua. Tequila didn't waste any time in removing the radiator from the vehicle or disassembling it and determining that it was so clogged from rust that it needed to be replaced. The locals offered to provide a used but still functional radiator they had salvaged from a school bus that had been in an ugly accident farther down the highway earlier that year. Miraculously, they explained, no one died.

Chatter and laughter burst from the café as Johnny Paint and Tennessee shambled out the door. "Great tacos!" said Johnny as he wiped his mouth with the back of his hand.

"I'll be inside," Honoré told Tequila. "Call me if you need me."

In the restaurant, Vietnam vets and white-haired elderly couples sat at wooden tables covered with red table cloths throughout the smoke-filled room. After striding past some women and Sugar, who smiled at Honoré, he headed to a far corner, where Trotsky and Zuckermann sat across from Pastor Paul, Molly, and the Commander. A waiter came over, and Honoré ordered.

Clearly, the Commander was feeling better, sitting straight with his arm on the table, no longer perspiring, eyes focused and lively, a ring in his voice. "Man, what a trip!" he said. "Can you imagine where we'd be if the vehicles got caught in that landslide?"

"Dead ducks," said Zuckermann.

"You better believe it," said Molly.

Pastor Paul fiddled with the gold cross in his fingers. "That's what happens," he said, his voice deep and resonant as if speaking from the pulpit, "whenever you try to do something good. Satan will be there to stop you."

"We just got to keep moving," said Molly.

Pastor Paul nodded solemnly. "Amen to that, sister."

"I'm just glad we're out of the heat," said the Commander. "Monterrey and Saltillo will be cool."

"Where we staying in Saltillo?" asked Pastor Paul.

"At the agricultural college," said Zuckermann.

"In fact," said Trotsky, "Buena Vista is just down the highway from the college."

"Never heard of it."

Trotsky explained, "After Matamoros fell, the Americans took Monterrey while Santa Ana advanced from the south. At Buena Vista, Santa Ana defeated Taylor but then turned back. Some say Santa Ana sold out to the gringos. Today, it's an unmarked battlefield, a reminder that at one time there was pride in Mexico as a nation."

Molly slammed her beer bottle on the table. "I have a great idea."

"Shoot," said the Commander.

"In Mexico City we take a wreath to Chapúltepec Park. What do you think?"

"Let's do it," said the Commander. "With a bit of publicity, maybe we could arrange a press conference, too."

Though happiness filled the restaurant, Honoré caught the first faint whiff of trouble drifting from a nearby window. However, no one else at the table seemed to notice, so he ignored it and began eating the famous tacos of *machacado con huevo* and drank coffee with cinnamon from a clay mug.

Fifteen minutes later, he knew there was trouble. When he stepped outside, he was pleased to see that a new radiator had been installed in the bus. Then the smell of shit, good shit, from Acapulco, led him around the restaurant to an arroyo. Standing behind a thicket of prickly pears, he listened.

"So you've worked with Honoré?" Johnny Paint asked, his southern twang taking wing in the fresh mountain air.

"Yep," Tequila said. "Made lots of money. Then he almost got his ass blown off. The Russian saved his life, and he's never been the same."

"The Russian?"

"Trotsky."

"Is he really a Russian?"

"No, just another dumb Mexican like the rest of us."

"Man," drawled Tennessee. "This is good stuff. Where'd you get it?"

"Acapulco," said Tequila.

"You got connections down there?"

"Yep."

Johnny Paint spoke up, enthusiastically, "We're headed down there ourselves."

"I thought you guys were revolutionaries," said Tequila.

"Revolutionaries, my ass!" said Tennessee. "You think we're loco in the *cabeza*? The Commander's our cousin—but that's it. He and his friends are the ones loco in the *cabeza*."

Johnny Paint slurred his words. "Crazy motherfucker. When he got back from Vietnam, they locked him up. After he got out, he got involved with that dyke, Molly. Ugly as shit. She don't like us. In fact, back in Escandón she was ready to turn us over to the FBI."

"Man, this shit hits the spot," said Tennessee. "Why don't you come with us to Acapulco? Bring that bombshell with you."

"Sugar?"

Johnny strung out his words with the high-pitched twang of an electric guitar. "Yep. She looks like she gives good head."

Tequila held a smoking toke between his fingers. "She swallows."

Crosses with flowers and ribbons marked the places along the highway where people had died in auto accidents, and as Honoré took a sharp curve, he glimpsed at the bottom of an arroyo a blue cockroach with tires for feet, windows broken, streaks of rust on its side—no doubt, the bus that provided the new radiator. He marveled that the Mexicans hadn't bothered to remove it, but that's the way they were.

Gray clouds boiled with a silver light that spilled across the mountains as Honoré sped across the floor of a long, flat valley at the end of which lay Monterrey.

"Ah, *la sultana del norte*," Trotsky said, as he gazed through the windshield.

"The *what*?"

"The Spaniards first named this 'El Valle de Extremadura.' Now it's called 'El Valle del Oriente.' Monterrey is known as 'La Ciudad de las Montañas' and 'La Sultana del Norte.'"

Honoré glanced at Trotsky. "How do you translate Monterrey? 'King of the Mountain' or 'the Mountain of the King'?"

"How about the 'Royal Mount'?"

Honoré grinned. "Why?"

"Because Uncle Sam is doing a great job of fucking La Sultana del Norte in the ass."

Honoré laughed.

On the outskirts of Monterrey, the convoy got off the highway and took the road to El Viejo Chaparral, past huge long warehouses and buildings and telephone poles and men, women, and children waiting on the muddy shoulder for a bus. Soon Honoré found himself in a long line of eighteen-wheelers going in both directions on the two-lane road, bumper to bumper.

"Turn right here," said Trotsky as they approached an intersection. Several long city blocks and traffic lights later, he announced, "We're lost."

On the side of the road ahead, a man—lean and dark under a straw cowboy hat—stood on the muddy shoulder.

"Pull over by that man," said Trotsky.

As the pickup rumbled to a stop, Trotsky rolled down his window. "*Buenas tardes, maestro.*"

"*Buenas tardes,*" said the man. "*¿En qué les puedo servir?*"

"How do we get to El Viejo Chaparral?"

After the man finished explaining in Spanish, Zuckermann popped up at Honoré's window. "What happened?"

Trotsky switched to English. "We got lost. Tell the Commander we're going ahead. Wait here. We'll be right back. Otherwise, we'll be driving in circles."

Several traffic lights later, Honoré drove along a cobblestone street lined with the façades of colonial homes painted royal blue, emerald green, and fuchsia. Stone benches from another era rested under trees rich with leaves that cast shadows on the plaza's sidewalks.

"There it is," Trotsky said and pointed at a high wall.

Honoré parked across the street from a gray six-foot cement wall with a metal gate. Among the trees in the yard behind the wall stood the red two-storey house with black iron grates on its windows.

They climbed out of the pickup and stood in the middle of the street.

"Trotsky!" yelled a man.

Trotsky looked past Honoré. "Manuel!"

A short dark man wearing a baseball cap stood at the gate. "*¡Bienvenidos!*"

He led them through the gate into a dirt yard shaded by gigantic trees with long gnarled arms. A wing of dormitory-like rooms along the back wall held several bunks, where some members of the convoy could spend the night. Two bathrooms had running water. Most of the pickups and vans could park in the yard, Manuel told them, but the buses would have to stay in the street. Revolutionary slogans, alongside the names of men and women disappeared by the Mexican government, covered the inside of the wall.

"We were disappointed," said Manuel, "when we found out they had stopped you on the border. We had hoped for a big event in the plaza downtown, coinciding with a protest against the government."

"It's been hell," said Trotsky. "One of the buses overheated, and we were caught in a landslide."

Manuel pivoted, "This way."

They followed a path of flat stones through a thicket of broad-leafed green plants to a heavy wooden door, which Manuel opened. Inside, iron grillwork on the windows shed slats of gray sunlight on the wooden floor. From a black and white photograph on the wall, the narrow, light-skinned face of a young man stared at them. Dressed in a dark suit, a white shirt, and a gray tie, his black hair nicely combed and shiny on a compact skull, he looked like a professor, a lawyer, or a physician.

"Who's that?" asked Trotsky.

"Dr. Téllez's son," said Manuel. "Disappeared in the seventies during the dirty war."

"My aunt told me about him," Trotsky said. "How's the doctor?"

"Very sick."

"Any chance of seeing him?"

"I don't think so. He's with his family."

"My aunt told me about this place. Is it true you have a secret hiding place for guns?"

A telescope stood on a tripod on a rug next to a brick column that rose to the ceiling. Manuel set the telescope aside and pulled open a door in the floor. "Let me show you. Because as soon as everyone else arrives, it'll be impossible. You have time?"

"Sure," said Trotsky.

Manuel climbed down the narrow stairs into the basement and turned on the light. Then Trotsky and Honoré descended beneath the house. A light bulb hanging on a wire from the ceiling lit boxes of handbills and posters stacked against the moist cement walls. A shaft, wide enough for a man to climb up on the metal rungs in one corner, led upstairs.

The man's voice jumped at them from all sides. "That is the escape route. It goes to the roof."

"Have you ever had to use it?" asked Trotsky.

"Twice."

Trotsky gazed at the beams supporting the ceiling. "My aunt has been here many times. She's a great admirer of Dr. Téllez and his family. She helped Fidel Castro and Che Guevara smuggle guns into Cuba. I've heard a lot about this place, but this is the first time I see it."

While the two men talked about the history of the Téllez house, Honoré checked his watch. "It's getting late."

"Yeah," Trotsky said. "We better get back."

So they climbed out of the basement and walked out of the house. Twenty minutes later, they returned with the convoy.

"This looks nice," said the Commander as he slowly walked off the bus followed by Molly and the vets. They disappeared inside the gate.

On the street, Zuckermann asked Manuel, "Where's the convoy support committee?"

"We were planning a reception," Manuel explained, "but the hurricane ruined all that. Members of the convoy support committee will be here tonight. Let me show you where you'll be staying."

Trotsky gazed up the street and then said to Honoré, "Oh, my God. Look at this."

In boots and tight jeans, Sugar walked behind two vets carrying Tequila on a stretcher.

"Put him down," Honoré said and then waited for the vets to leave. "What happened?"

With two B-52 bombers wiggling, Sugar spoke like a little girl complaining about a younger brother. "He got stoned. He said he was going to abandon the convoy. He wanted me to go with him. I tried to talk him out of it. One moment he's happy, the next he's crying like a baby. I had to knock him out."

Groggy and confused, Tequila rose on an elbow and stared at her ass. "What a knockout!"

Honoré glanced at Trotsky. "I'll take care of this."

Trotsky led the bubble-gum chewing bombshell to the house. Once they were out of sight, Honoré grabbed Tequila by the collar. "Get off of that stretcher."

Tequila stood up. "*¡Pinche vieja!*"

Honoré held him by the collar, face to face. "We need to talk, *compadre*."

"I want to go home."

Honoré's hands shook. If Trotsky had not insisted on bringing this jerk along, Honoré would have sent him packing. "What?"

Sweat flew from Tequila's cabbage-shaped head as he tried to pry Honoré's hands loose. "*Ya estufas.*"

Chills ran up and down Honoré's spine like electricity sizzling across a broken circuit board. "You fucking idiot!"

Suddenly, Tequila, who never cried for anything or anyone, wept like a little girl. "I miss my little ones," he squealed.

Disgusting, thought Honoré. Why couldn't men act like men anymore? "Bullshit," he said.

"No, I mean it. I miss watching TV and eating hamburgers with them. I miss my boy, Tercero."

Honoré's voice trembled. "I'll make a deal with you. Get us to Mexico City, and I'll find a mechanic to replace you there."

Then, the real Tequila perked up, eyes widening in reflection, and announced, "No dice."

Since there was only one way to deal with sentimentalists—with more sentimentality—an idea popped into Honoré's head. One of Tequila's passions was singing like a mariachi as he had done for Honoré outside Maruca's window many years ago. If he could get this guy to Mexico City, maybe he could trick him into accompanying the convoy to Nicaragua. Breathing more easily, he spoke as sweetly as he could, like a daddy to his little girl. "Look, *compadre*, how about if I take you to Plaza Garibaldi? You've always wanted to sing with a good mariachi band. I'll arrange for you to sing with the best mariachi band in all of Mexico."

Tequila's face lit up. "Are you serious?"

"Dead serious."

"Then I can go home?"

"Yes."

Late that afternoon, newspaper reporters and TV cameras roamed through the compound, and representatives of various leftist groups crowded in the living room, where the Commander, Molly, and Zuckermann gave speeches thanking the Mexicans for their support and condemning the U.S. embargo against Nicaragua.

At length, the Mexicans spoke.

A flat-chested woman wearing horn-rimmed glasses on a face jittery with triangular expressions ranted against the Mexican government's fraud and corruption. A short, dark-skinned Mexican man—face stern, voice deep-throated as a bullfrog's—blasted the damage to the environment caused by unregulated industrialization in Monterrey. A light-skinned Mexican man, tall as a giraffe feeding among tree tops, bemoaned the fate of companions who had been disappeared by the government. He himself had been disappeared and described in eerie detail how his testicles had been fried. Since then, he suffered pain whenever he sat down. Afterward, Pastor Paul, a halo about his head, led everyone in a prayer and gave thanks to God Almighty for delivering the convoy from the clutches of Satan on the Texas-Mexico border and bringing them to the Mountain of the King.

"This is wonderful," beamed Molly at everyone afterward. "Thank you for your support."

"In solidarity," said the flat-chested woman, "we can accomplish anything."

The man tall as a giraffe approached Trotsky. "The march of history is on our side. Either we deal with social inequity, or we perish."

Trotsky nodded. "Too bad we didn't make it in time to support your anti-government demonstration."

That evening Honoré was surprised by how exhausted he was when he climbed in his sleeping bag in the now empty living room, where Trotsky and Zuckermann would join him later. Despite the laughter and chatter in the yard outside, he fell asleep right away.

In the middle of the night when he awoke, he found Zuckermann and several veterans asleep on the floor.

Trotsky lay curled on his side in a sleeping bag, moaning like a wounded dog. "No, no," he muttered. "Nicaragua. I said Nicaragua."

After scrambling to his feet, Honoré found the bathroom in an adjacent room. When he returned, he slid into his sleeping bag, dozed off, and toppled back into a dream about Maruca and Bonita and cooking *carne asada* on a hill that overlooked the Rio Grande. Suddenly, he fell in the river. He floated along as if he were on an inner tube. Then he thought he had become a fish pleasantly carried away by the water. Then he thought he had become a log as he sank to the bottom, drowning. He tried to wake up, couldn't, couldn't breathe either. Worse, his neck hurt as if he were tangled in weeds. He forced his eyes open. Trotsky was on top of him, strangling him.

"What's going on?" shouted Zuckermann from across the room.

"You fucking gook!" shouted Trotsky. "You motherfucking gook!"

Honoré couldn't break the iron hold. Zuckermann jumped up and wrestled Trotsky to the floor.

Shaking, his forehead glistening with sweat, Trotsky sat and blinked at Honoré. "What happened?"

"You were choking him," said Zuckermann, breathing hard.

"You okay, bro?" asked a veteran.

"I need some fresh air," said Trotsky.

Honoré, rubbing his throat, followed him outside, where like a great silver-plated monocle the moon peered through heavy clouds, and they walked out of the compound and down the street, where cobblestones shone as if made of silver. At the plaza they sat down on a bench.

"Sorry," said Trotsky.

"No problem."

"Something about this trip has awakened old demons. The Commander reminds me of a guy I knew in Vietnam. A first-rate officer. A good man. Got his head blown off in front of me. His teeth hit my face."

Honoré was shocked to see the dark side of a man whose strength and conviction he had long admired.

"I can smell them," said Trotsky after awhile. "The sweat. The grime. The shit. I can see them. The helmets, the flak jackets, their eyes. I hear the choppers. The explosions. They've been waiting for me, they tell me. Why aren't I with them? They're ready to leave on the next patrol. That's when I heard the noise. Maybe laughter. It could have been anything. In the dream a gook attacks a buddy. I attack the gook."

The clouds abandoned the moon. A dog barked, and thunder rumbled in the distance. Honoré could not imagine what it had been like, what happened in Vietnam to men like Trotsky and other vets on the convoy. All he knew was that they were haunted.

"We were like brothers," said Trotsky. "More than brothers because your life depended on what the man next to you did. We lived each day as if we were going to die. When you live with that assumption, it's amazing what you're capable of. You don't think. The enemy is out there to kill you and your buddies. Men, women, and children—they're all the same. The enemy. That's why so much shit happened. After your buddy's head explodes in your face, it's easy to go into a village and kill everyone." He shook his head and stared into the night. Eventually, he turned to Honoré. "You better get some sleep."

Honoré stood up. "You coming?"

Trotsky's black-patched gaze wandered as if he had spotted something in the distance. "Someone's got to guard the perimeter."

Back on the highway the next morning, they headed west toward Saltillo, skirting the green mountains that crouched together like dogs with their snouts in the clouds, remnants of the hurricane that came undone north of Veracruz last night.

"I haven't seen the mountains this clean and fresh in a long time," said Trotsky, his one good eye bloodshot from lack of sleep. "Usually, the entire valley is filled with white dust and smog. The white scars on the mountains are from strip mining by *la cementera*."

However, it was slow going because stretches of the new highway were under construction. Detour after detour took them past dump trucks, tractors, and machines digging into the earth amid plumes of dust. The convoy wound past makeshift jacales of mesquite limbs tied together, where short brown women wearing aprons and huaraches sold *tacos de barbacoa* and tortas while young men sold everything from pictures of Christ and the Virgen de Guadalupe to owls tied to their wrists with leather thongs. At a Pemex gasoline station dozens of boys and girls, their brown and dirty faces, their hair coarse and black, boxes of pink and green Chiclets in their hands, surrounded the gringos, who delighted in all the attention, their red faces beaming as they laughed and talked loudly. Pastor Paul smiled at the children who peered at his huge black fingers as if they were freshly unwrapped chocolate bars. On the outskirts of Saltillo, the highway took them past transmission towers holding electricity-laden black cables and then great warehouses and factories and a building that looked like a turtle.

"By the way," said Trotsky, "last night Sugar was in the bus going through some papers."

"So what do we do?"

"Nothing. Just keep an eye on her." The walkie-talkie squawked, and Trotsky raised it to his ear. "Yes, sir."

Honoré kept his eyes on the highway.

"Okay," said Trotsky and listened for a while. "No, I understand. Yes. I'll call my aunt as soon as we get to Matehuala."

Trotsky put down the walkie-talkie. "We're bypassing Saltillo."

"Why?"

"He doesn't want to lose another day on the road. Wants to get to Mexico City today."

South of Saltillo, the pounding on the cracked, uneven highway was so bad that Honoré thought he might lose control of the vehicle and slide into oncoming traffic if he tried to pass the eighteen-wheeler in front of him. Besides, he couldn't, not yet, since a long line of trucks approached in the other lane. Meanwhile, he crept along the bumpy highway for dozens of miles behind a tractor-trailer carrying logs. Then Zuckermann called on the walkie-talkie and asked why Honoré hadn't passed the truck and Honoré said it was too dangerous, but he would at the first opportunity.

Suddenly, the road ahead was clear, except for a tin can in the distance wobbling on waves of heat, growing by flickers. An eighteen-wheeler. Honoré shifted down, hit the gas, and pulled into the left lane, bouncing from wrinkle to wrinkle on the dry asphalt. When they were halfway around the trailer, the pickup coughed, chugged, and lost speed. The oncoming truck blasted its horn. An overwhelming desire to will the pickup into flight turned his stomach into a pretzel. All at once, Honoré found himself and Trotsky suspended, dreamlike, on the center line between the gigantic logs on the lumber truck on their right and thousands of pounds of metal and rubber hurtling past on the shoulder on their left.

Nothing happened.

"Man," said Trotsky, his good eye dreamy as a coin dipped in oil, "that was close."

Honoré sped along the meshed wire fence dividing the six-lane *periférico*. As if full-blown ads had been cut from the pages of *Vanity Fair* and erected as billboards on both sides of the loop around the city, the white faces of young men and women greeted the bumper-to-bumper traffic with gorgeous smiles. On the side of a three-storey building, a gigantic woman in a bikini, her hair blond, her breasts delicious scoops of vanilla ice cream, teeth sparkling like jewelry made from white onyx, arms and legs long and supple, welcomed the convoy to the monstrous city. *La rubia superior*, Honoré mulled. Always *la pinche rubia superior* messing with your head. And then the smell hit him. He didn't know where it came from, through the floor, from the sewer, but the smell of *aguas negras* assaulted him like a huge ugly iguana that wrapped itself around his face and sent a shit-caked tongue up his nose. Then the smog crept inside the cab and scraped the back of his throat.

"I don't see how the Commander will survive here," said Honoré. "I can barely breathe."

Trotsky nodded. "The smell of Mexico City is the smell of *caca* and *cabrones*."

Iron rods stuck out of a cinder block wall in a shanty perched on the side of a brown hill. More shanties lined a dirt road that plunged into a pool of water where gaunt dogs drank while children kicked a soccer ball across a vacant lot. Like tiny sharp-cornered dice, a handful of tightly packed houses clung to another ridge. A few miles later, dozens of cables hung between steel towers, and white vapor rose from a factory into a gray sky. In a park on the other side of the highway, young men and women sat on cement benches among trees whose black trunks had been painted white but looked as if they had barely survived the disaster that had befallen the rest of the city.

The walkie-talkie squawked. "Yes, sir," said Trotsky, gazing out the window. "No, we're not far. Yes, sir. Everything is ready. We won't have to look for motels. Some people will stay with friends, others with the Quakers. Some can stay in the vehicles. There's a bathroom and a shower. And there are some cheap *pensiones* nearby. My aunt has taken care of everything."

Many unfamiliar names and a few he recognized flew past Honoré's window. Cementera La Tolteca. La Costena. The orange letters of VIPs.

The gigantic letters of GIGANTE. Tenayuca. Polanco. Bano y Garcia Lopez
Funeral Home. Holbein. Churubusco. Ron Bacardi. Claiborne. Apple-
ton Estate. When Trotsky pointed out La Plaza de Toros Mexico, Honoré
couldn't tell whether it was a giant turtle shell or a football stadium. In the
distance, skyscrapers stood amid the gray haze covering the valley that had
once been a lake.

"Get in the right lane," muttered Trotsky, his attention on the street
signs, which flew past like green parrots. "We exit at Division del Norte."

In brown uniforms, black jack boots, and helmets, cops sat on motorcycles on the side of the highway. The Mexicans called them "*tecolotes*"
because not only did they look like them but they pounced like owls on
rabbits and rodents. More traffic merged onto the highway. Like giant
metallic cockroaches, cars and trucks squealed and groaned and farted
and screamed through thunderheads of gray and yellow smog. Then, just
as Honoré was about to change lanes, a car zoomed past, horn blaring like
a trumpet on doomsday, missing Honoré by inches. His heart slammed
against his throat; he swallowed hard and kept swallowing hard until he
found himself chewing the exhaust of *camiones* as he exited. Watching the
convoy's vehicles in the side mirror, he took the access road and rolled to a
stop before a wall with a mural of Spanish conquistadors holding a cross.
The roar and hum and breath of the biggest city in the world made his head
hurt.

"Churusbusco," said Trotsky, "takes us to Coyoacán."

Several Mexico City blocks later, Honoré smelled something wonderful. A thicket of pines and poplars rose behind the wall enclosing Parque
Viveros, where the day's light slid across green leaves like golden wings
and fresh air mixed with the smell of tacos and the laughter of children on
the sidewalk. A young man with black hair reaching his shoulders saluted
the convoy with a raised fist. After passing a metro station, Honoré turned
right into a narrow street and crept past cars parked along the sidewalk
amid chirping birds. A few tree-lined avenues later, iron-grilled façades of
colonial houses stood side by side on a cobblestone street turning blue in
the evening light.

"Two blocks down and then right," said Trotsky.

Honoré eased up on the gas and slowed down, making sure the convoy
vehicles were still behind him. He turned right. After cruising past cars
parked on both sides of the street, he spotted a thin figure waving at them.
Dressed in khaki pants and shirt, face sunburned and white hair matted
beneath a straw hat, a lanky old man stood on the sidewalk. The brick wall
behind him was tattooed with slogans—"No to Impunity!" and "Down

with the PRI!" Honoré pulled over, and Trotsky got out. After the man pushed open a metal gate, Honoré drove into an empty dirt lot framed by brick walls two stories high and parked next to an unfinished building, half cinder block and half wood, which could have been an office or a tiny apartment at one time; it stood next to a garage with a corrugated steel roof over an oil-stained slab of cement. He climbed out and waited for the bus, which, too big to park anywhere else, coughed and died in the middle of the lot.

"What a nightmare," said Zuckermann, jumping from the yellow contraption. "I didn't know if we were going to make it through that traffic."

Molly, lips pale as milk, joined him. "How can anyone breathe in this hellhole?"

"At least here the air is fresh," said Honoré.

"Where?" she asked.

"Here, in Coyoacán."

Molly scowled at the brick walls. "Well, you could have fooled me."

"How's the Commander holding up?" asked Trotsky.

"Okay as far as I can tell," said Zuckermann.

Molly turned to Zuckermann. "Would you make sure the vehicles are all here and accounted for?"

"Sure," he said.

With the help of the parking lot attendant, Zuckermann directed traffic and assembled the pickups and van along the walls so the buses could be accommodated in the middle of the yard.

In the meantime, the Yellow Submarine shuddered, and shoes scraped the metal steps as Tennessee and Johnny Paint helped the Commander climb down. Smelling of sweat, he wobbled on his feet and then did something strange. Listing to one side, he stuck his finger in his right ear, as if something had gotten stuck in there, and he tried to get it out, though probably it was just itching from too much wax or dirt.

"Let's get you to a doctor," said Trotsky.

After removing his finger, the Commander steadied himself with a hand on Molly's shoulder. "Doctor, my ass."

"That's exactly what we're worried about," said Molly. "Your ass."

The Commander, eyes glassy, didn't look any sicker after crossing the border. But there was still no telling what effect Mexico City might have on him.

"I've made arrangements for you and Molly to stay in a pensione down the street," said Trotsky.

The Commander shook his head. "What kind of revolutionaries are we if have to stay in motels?" He glared at everyone. "Tourists, American tourists—that's what."

"Well," said Trotsky, "I'm sending for a doctor."

"I told you. I don't need no goddamned doctor."

"Trotsky," said Molly firmly to the Commander, "is only doing what's best for the convoy. We can't afford for you to croak between here and Nicaragua. I'm the one who requested the doctor. Trotsky's aunt lives here— she can get a good doctor on a moment's notice. And cheap. Once we leave Mexico City, we won't have that kind of support."

The Commander fixed Trotsky in a blue-eyed gaze. "Some of us are staying with the vehicles."

"In that case," said Trotsky, "stay in that small building. It has a bathroom and a shower and can serve as your headquarters. If you change your mind, you can stay at the pensione. It's cheaper and nicer than a hotel. And the food is great. I've stayed there many times."

"Where are you staying?"

"My aunt's," said Trotsky.

When Zuckermann returned, he reported that none of the thirty-nine vehicles had been lost in the crazy Mexico City traffic. "However," he added, "the vehicles are old. Some are on their last leg. We may lose some between here and Nicaragua."

The Commander rubbed his ear. "Not as long as we have a good mechanic. Look, if we managed to travel from all parts of the United States to the border, I don't see why we can't make it to Nicaragua in one piece."

As soon as all the vehicles were parked, the convoyers gathered around the Commander, who reviewed the list of camp chores and duties. Then he asked Trotsky to provide everyone directions to the pensione. Molly added that a doctor would come by in case anyone wanted to see him.

"And remember," said the Commander, "we're scheduled to visit Niños Heroes Monument tomorrow morning. So be here by 9:00 a.m., at the latest. I know how tired you are, so get some rest. Trotsky made arrangements for the media to be there. As soon as we're done, we leave for Puebla."

After night fell, the parking lot attendant turned on the lamp at the gate and another on a telephone pole behind the bus while some vets built a fire that flung eerie shadows on the walls. Other members of the convoy set up their cots under a tarpaulin slung between tent poles. The Quakers showed up in pickups, and some people left with them. The rest walked to the pensione down the street, carrying their backpacks and duffel bags. After reminding Honoré of his promise to take him to Garibaldi Plaza, Tequila disappeared among the vehicles with Sugar. While Trotsky accompanied the Commander inside the building designated as the new camp headquarters, Honoré helped Pastor Paul and some veterans set up a kitchen in the garage.

About an hour later, Honoré noticed the bus's flat front tire, so he walked across the lot and checked the other tires, which were okay. However, a puddle of water stood beneath the engine, so he got down on one knee. The radiator was leaking. When he scanned the length of the underside of the bus, he froze. In a triangle of light cast by the telephone pole, something moved. Like a thick rubber band stretching and then pulling, a muscle rose and fell beneath the sparkling flesh of a gorgeous leg as Sugar slipped off her panties. Then, Tequila showed up. First, he stuck his nose in her *maracas*, which spilled across his face like smooth mounds of Mexican cheese. Next, they began kissing like teenagers. When she pushed him away, he went down on his knees, grabbed her foot, and began kissing her toes. When she kicked him in the face, he fell and rolled like a pig, laughing.

When Honoré tried to stand, the gila monster in his jeans wouldn't let him. He waited. He couldn't get Sugar's leg out of his head. One minute passed. He thought about the trip, about the treacherous mountains around Monterrey, but the mountains turned into *maracas*. Desperately, he tried to focus on the landslide, but the boulders turned into *maracas* bearing down on him. Two minutes passed. Then he imagined Dr. de la O. He rose to his feet without a problem.

"What's the matter?" asked Trotsky, stepping around the front of the bus.

"Nothing. Why?"

"You look like you can barely walk."

"Just my knee. An old football injury."

Trotsky directed Honoré to a spot near the gate that offered some privacy. "Zuckermann and the Commander," he said quietly, "told me about a plot to stop the convoy. Possibly tonight. That's why the Commander, Molly, and some veterans are spending the night here. They asked me to stay, but I need to meet with my aunt. Can you stay?"

"I promised Tequila I'd take him to Plaza Garibaldi."

Trotsky gazed thoughtfully at the shadows of devils dancing cast by campfire on the brick walls. "That place is dangerous."

"I'm trying to convince him to accompany us to Nicaragua."

Trotsky looked directly at Honoré. "Okay, I'll talk to Zuckermann. He wanted to spend night at the pensione, but I'm sure he'll stay."

As soon as Trotsky left, Honoré moseyed around to the back of the bus. "Tequila!"

Tequila stepped from among the vehicles, smiling. "What's up, *jefe*?"

"The bus has a flat. And the radiator is leaking."

"No big deal. We'll fix that in the morning."

"No, tonight."

"What about Garibaldi Plaza?"

Suddenly, several yards away pigtails gleamed like golden braids of a German field marshal's uniform. Shapely bronze legs were on full display in shorts and tight-fitting blouse as Sugar climbed out of the van. She smiled, then sashayed out of sight.

"*Aye, mamacita*," Tequila murmured. Licking his chops, he turned to Honoré. "What about Garibaldi Plaza?"

Honoré skewered him in a gaze. "Not until the bus is repaired. One more thing. Now that this gringa has turned you into a pig, I don't want you acting like one. No smooching in public. And keep your nose out of her *maracas*."

Tequila licked his chops like a raccoon in a garbage can. "Why? Do you like them?"

Honoré grabbed him by the collar. "*No mames, cabrón.*"

"Okay, okay, okay."

Honoré shoved him away. "And tell her to put on some clothes."

Arm in arm like middle school kids, Tequila and Sugar traipsed along the sidewalk while Honoré and Trotsky followed close behind like mama and papa. Though Sugar had changed into a light denim jacket, jeans, and cowboy boots, Honoré had a tough time not looking. Even the heels of her boots provoked him. At the end of the block, they turned left into the long dark shadows flung by trees across the cobblestones and cars whose windows caught bits and pieces of light shaped like goldfish.

"The metro isn't far," said Trotsky to Honoré. "Just a few blocks. It'll take you directly to Garibaldi Plaza."

As they strolled past an idling car, its lights off, a whiff of marijuana oozed from the glow of a tiny cigarette in the half-opened window.

"*¡Qué buenota esta la gringa!*" a man growled.

"*¡Mirale las nalgotas!*" said another inside the car.

"*¡Qué chichotas!*"

"*¡Mucha vieja, poco hombre!*"

Trotsky stopped. "*¿Qué?*"

The man rolled down the window several inches and stuck out the barrel of a *cuerno de chivo*. "*¿Qué qué, cabrón?*"

Trotsky raised his hands and backed off. "*Disculpe, maestro. Tranquilo, todo tranquilo.*"

Before the AK-47 could unleash its flesh-eating white tongue, coyotes began wailing. They were sirens, approaching fast. Somewhere tires shrieked. An engine accelerated. Then, more sirens, this time coming from the opposite direction. Firecrackers popped in rapid succession. The deadly AK-47, suddenly a frightened squirrel, took refuge inside the car, which farted and spit, before skidding across the cobblestones. A bullet whizzed past Honoré's head.

"*¡A la chingada!*" Tequila yelled. "Run!"

Ramming into Honoré by mistake, Sugar stumbled and fell. "Oh, my God!"

At first Honoré thought she had been hit. But after seeing her sit up on the sidewalk, no blood anywhere, *maracas* lively as ever, he pulled her to her feet. "Let's go! Let's go!"

Now Honoré felt like a frightened squirrel himself, boots stomping on the cobblestone, chest heaving, dry mouth gulping air, as they ran through pools of light spilling from windows. At the end of the block, they galloped around a corner, then down another street, running through a cone of light cast by a street lamp, then loping along a brick wall. He stopped next to a tree, puffing. The others joined him, coughing and breathing heavily as they crouched behind a black sedan shiny as a polished casket. In the distance, cars came and went, honking; a siren wailed. Then, just as they peeked over the hood of the sedan and up and down the street, a window on the passenger's side exploded in Honoré's face like a bucket of water thrown against a wall, spewing shattered glass against his cheeks.

"They're behind the car!" yelled a man down the street.

More cars showed up amid a chorus of sirens. "What the hell is going on?" asked Trotsky.

Chotas versus *narcos*? *Narcos* versus *narcos*? "Who knows?" Honoré muttered, knowing that in Mexico it was impossible to tell the difference between the bad guys and the good guys.

"They think we're *narcos*!" said Tequila.

When the AK-47's started barking at each other from cars at both ends of the street, their tongues long and white in the night, Honoré yelled, "Keep your heads down! We're in a crossfire!"

A bullet whizzed past Honoré's nose and punched a hole the size of a fist in the black sedan.

"¡A la chingada!" cursed Tequila, standing up and giving the shooters the finger.

Honoré grabbed him. "Get down, you idiot!"

"¡No chingues!" Tequila yelled and then jumped on the tree trunk like a squirrel or a monkey or a gorilla, thrusting himself up with his hands and knees, until he perched on a branch, turned, held out his hand, and dragged Sugar after him.

More gunshots sent a bullet whizzing through Honoré's hair, giving his scalp a hot caress before punching a hole in the sedan. The next thing he knew he had also become a squirrel or a monkey or a gorilla clambering up the tree, Trotsky right behind him. After groping through a thicket of leaves and branches, he crouched on the wall, legs dangling over the edge, looking for Tequila and Sugar in the dark. All of a sudden, the cold bony hand of death slapped him in the face. At first he thought he had been shot—but, no, it was a branch let loose by Trotsky. Honoré lost his balance, fell. And as he was falling, he realized that any second now he would break his neck but that it was taking unusually long to hit bottom. Then, thud! The ground was hard. As the night grew thick with the smell of gunpowder, Honoré wondered whether he was paralyzed. In fact, he felt as if his butt had been shot off.

Then, Trotsky landed on top of him.

"Ah," Honoré groaned.

Trotsky rolled off. "Sorry, man!"

Honoré didn't know how long he lay there in pain, but it felt like a long time. Meanwhile, the bursts of gunfire were so loud that he thought the shooters might climb over the wall any second.

Trotsky muttered, "There's a light over there."

Honoré sat up. Hard volcanic rock bit his knees as they crawled toward the light, which soon gave shape to shrubs, palms, cacti, and trees. He grew suspicious. Every time he had this sensation, it had meant trouble. The lush garden smelled too good to be true.

"Look," whispered Trotsky.

A floodlight on the ground illuminated a red flag hanging from a pole that rose from a rectangular white stone column several feet high whose base stood among century plants, palms, and flowers. A hammer and sickle were inscribed on the stone.

Trotsky stood and dusted off his hands. "The tomb of Leon Trotsky," he said quietly.

Honoré stood up—straight. He realized again that bullets are less debilitating than boobs. "Who?"

"Leon Trotsky, the famous Russian revolutionary."

Suddenly, dozens of leaves rained on them as if a flock of birds had crashed into the trees. The racket on the other side of the ten-foot wall was unbearable as AK-47's sent bullets flying everywhere.

"We better hide," said Trotsky.

A faint light glowed in one of the buildings across the courtyard. "Look," said Honoré.

"Come on," said Trotsky, leading the way along the flat volcanic stones toward some French doors with glass panels where they saw the light. Then the shooting stopped. Voices floated in the night like butterflies. A girl giggled.

"¡Idiotas!" Trotsky muttered and flung the doors open. "What the hell are you doing in here? How did you get in?"

"We walked in," Tequila said. "Someone left the door unlocked."

Honoré followed Trotsky inside and stood behind Sugar, who smelled of sweat, soap, and freshly cut grass. "Are you okay?" he whispered.

She nodded.

Then Tequila said, "My butt hurts."

"Shut up!" said Trotsky as gunfire erupted again. "Lower your voices. Turn off the light."

At one point Honoré was certain the killers had climbed over the wall or broken inside the wall some other way. At length, the shooting stopped, and the cars left. When either Tequila or Sugar turned on the light, Honoré found himself standing a few feet from a cluttered desk with a chair. The wooden floor creaked underneath as Trotsky walked past, crossing the room slowly, cautiously, stopping behind the chair and peering at the books, papers, pens, inkpots and a magnifying glass on the desk. Tequila and Sugar remained by the French doors gazing at a bust of a man on a wooden stand.

"Who's this guy?" asked Tequila, poking his finger in the man's nose.

Sugar giggled.

"Leon Trotsky," muttered Trotsky.

"No wonder they call you Trotsky. You look like him." He wiped his finger on Sugar's shoulder.

She slapped Tequila.

Meanwhile, Trotsky gazed at the newspapers, the name *Pravda* inscribed in Russian letters, lying in shallow piles on two small tables set against a stucco wall where a pale green map of Mexico hung. "I came here many times with my aunt," he said. "She loved the place, said it was like going to church. It inspired her, strengthened her faith in mankind. She would have given anything to have known the real Trotsky."

"Is Trotsky your real name?" Sugar asked.

"Maybe it should be Snotsky," Tequila whispered to her.

Annoyed, Trotsky fixed her in his gaze. "Trotsky was the name of a jailer in Odessa where the real Trotsky was incarcerated."

"Odessa, Texas?" asked Tequila. "Honoré and I spent a night in jail there. Remember? With the Governor."

Trotsky sighed. "Odessa, Russia. His real name was Bronstein. His father was a wealthy Jewish farmer."

"Is that why they call you Trotsky?" asked Sugar.

"What do you mean?"

"You're Jewish, right?"

Trotsky glared at Tequila and then at the girl. "My friends in Mexico City used to make fun of me. It's a joke. In some circles, to be a Trotskyite is not a good thing. My real name is Juan Sanchez Trusky."

Tequila examined the bust of Trotsky. "So how many Trotskys are there?"

Sugar stood beside the bust. "I need to pee," she said.

Trotsky pointed at a door in back. "There's a bathroom through that door."

As she turned, one of her *maracas* hit the stand. "Oops!"

"Watch it!" Trotsky yelled, lunging in time to catch the bust in his arms, which he cradled as if it were his own head. "Don't touch anything! Nothing in this room has been moved for more than forty years!"

Tequila and Sugar moved out of the way, sidling past Honoré, disappearing in back, while Trotsky put the bust back on the stand. "This office," he said, returning to the desk, "is the same as the day he was killed. Trotsky's wife refused to change anything. We're standing in a living photograph of history."

"Why did they kill him?" asked Honoré.

Trotsky's eyes settled on the objects on the desk. "He criticized Stalin.

So Stalin sent an agent named Mercador to kill him. It happened here. At this desk. With a mountain climber's pick axe. In the head."

"So the revolution killed him?" Honoré said.

Trotsky, his good eye weary as it wandered about the room, nodded. "You could say that."

Suddenly, giggles profaned the silence.

"What are those two idiots doing?"

In the next room, Honoré found Tequila and Sugar on a bed, wrapped in each other's arms, cleavage showing, boots dangling off the end, smooching. "What the fuck?"

"*Cómo qué*—what the fuck?"

"Get out of there."

Sugar sat up and buttoned her blouse. Her *maracas* were so big that even after she had buttoned the blouse they wobbled as they tried to nose their way out. Tequila stretched and yawned.

Honoré grabbed him by the arm. "I said get out of that bed, now! Didn't Trotsky tell you not to touch anything?"

Standing up, Tequila broke away. "*¡Ya estufas!*"

Honoré waited for the two to storm out of the small bedroom, where the great revolutionary and his family must have slept. When he returned to the office, he found Trotsky in the chair snoring loudly, his arms and face on the desk, black hair thick and long. Tequila and Sugar stood just outside the French doors.

Honoré crossed the room.

Trotsky raised his head, his one good eye bloodshot.

"Are you okay?" asked Honoré.

Trotsky slowly pushed himself out of the chair. "Sorry, I was wondering what it was like to sit here. Couldn't help it. Next thing I know, I'm asleep."

"The coast is clear!" yelled Tequila through the open doors.

Trotsky pushed the chair under the desk. After checking that everything was in its right place, he walked around the desk cautiously. "We better go."

Honoré headed toward the French doors, but all of a sudden Trotsky halted. "Wait," he said and then crouched on the floor. "Look at this. In all the years I've come here with my aunt, I never noticed this. It's red."

"Why would anyone paint a floor red?"

Trotsky wiped a board. Slowly he raised his hand and contemplated the dust on his fingers as if he were about to cross himself with holy water. "Red is a symbol of defiance. The blood of angry workers. The price we must pay for social change."

Sombrero upon sombrero bobbed upon a pool of black mustaches and white-toothed grins. In embroidered jackets and leggings with silver clasps, the mariachis played guitars, bird-like violins, and golden trumpets along the walkways intersecting the grassy gardens of Plaza Garibaldi, where couples sat on antiquated benches under lanterns of yellow light. Clusters of balloons on strings held by an old dark-faced man wearing a straw hat and plastic pennants strung on wires overhead produced a feria-like quality. Like a black and white llama moving by slowly, a young man carried a pile of *zarapes* on his shoulder toward a mother playing patty cake with her daughter. At the back of the plaza stood buildings from another century, archways on the first floor, rows of canopied windows on the second, and the neon-lit billboards for Cerveza Corona on the roofs. Honoré wished Trotsky had accompanied them, but he was exhausted and had gone to spend the night with his aunt in Coyoacán.

Then Honoré recognized the two-storey-high façade on his left. "There's the Salon Tenampa!" he yelled above the din of the music and took the lead.

The doors swung open on smoke tremulous with voices and trumpets. White-shirted waiters poured drinks behind the neon-lit bar on the left while arches framed two sides of the barn-like room on the far right. Pennants with the red, white, and green of the Mexican flag hung from wires stretched above the heads of a band of mariachis with guns in holsters and ammunition belts around their waists. They entertained the men and women, mostly Mexicans and a handful of gringos, who packed the long wooden tables sparkling with bottles.

Honoré looked around for a place to sit. Nothing as far as the eye could see, not even in back where the stairs led to the second floor.

Then Tequila yelled, "Over here!"

Tequila led Sugar by the hand into a nebula of smoke and sat at a table. Honoré plopped in a chair next to her, and she turned to him with such a delicious smile that he feared falling into her cleavage if he looked too long.

Tequila stood and waved at the waiter. Then he sat, rubbing his hands. "This is a dream come true. I wish my mother was here."

"Why?" asked Sugar. "It looks like just another Mexican cantina to me. Big, noisy, a lot of smoke."

A waiter in a white shirt and black trousers came over. "*Bienvenidos al Salon Tenampa. ¿Qué gustan tomar?*"

"*Maestro*," said Tequila, his arm around Sugar, "tell us about Garibaldi

Plaza and this cantina. My little gringa here loves Mexico and Mexicans and wants to know all about us."

Like a soldier snapping to attention, the waiter straightened with a shudder that ran the length of his body. "Plaza Garibaldi," he said with the gravity and pride of a Mexican patriot, "is named for Giuseppe Garibaldi, not the Italian hero but his son, who was a *teniente coronel* in Pancho Villa's army. All the great stars of *el cine mexicano* have come here. Pedro Infante especially. As you can see, there are paintings of him as well as *el charro cantor* Jorge Negrete. There are paintings of Agustín Lara and the queen of ranchero music, Lola Beltrán. Several movies were made here."

"My mother loved Mexican movies," Tequila said to Sugar. "She loved Pedro Infante. She had posters of all his movies in her bedroom."

"Now what can I get you to drink?" asked the waiter.

"Cuba libre," said Sugar.

Tequila removed his arm from Sugar. "*Un submarino*," he said, meaning tequila with Tecate, salt, and lime as a chaser.

Honoré ordered a light beer. "*Una rubia superior.*"

When the drinks arrived, Tequila picked up his shot of tequila and whiffed it. "Mmm, smells great!" He added, relishing the moment, "My mother always wanted to come here. One day I promised her I'd bring her to Garibaldi Plaza and the Salón Tenampa, but she died weeks before we could make the trip."

"You were in jail," said Honoré.

In a tear-filled far-away gaze, the shot of tequila between his oil-stained fingers, Tequila said slowly, "Yes, I've always felt bad about that, failing my little *mamacita*." He wiped a tear from his cheek with the back of his other hand. "But here I am tonight, and I carry the spirit of my *mamacita* in my heart, so let's drink to her memory. May she rest in peace."

The glasses clinked in mid-air.

Afterward, Honoré set down his glass and waved at the waiter across the room. "*¡Maestro!*" he yelled.

The waiter came over. "*Diga, usted.*"

"*Otro round.*"

"*Seguro que sí.*"

Honoré didn't miss a beat. "And tell the mariachis that our friend here is another Pedro Infante."

The waiter cast a doubtful glance at Tequila. "*¿En serio?*"

"*En serio*," said Honoré, standing up and moving with the waiter out of earshot. "Can you do me a favor?"

"Depends."

"I promised my friend that one day I would have him sing here with one of the best mariachi bands in Mexico."

The waiter's face became stern. "You're right about one thing. This is a good mariachi band, one of the best in Mexico. But you're wrong if you think they'll want to accompany a *pendejo*, especially tonight that we have some very important guests from Acapulco."

Honoré reached inside his pocket and took out a wad of pesos. "Here take this. Just one song."

Huffily, the waiter left and came back. "No way. The captain doesn't want to disappoint his guests."

Out of cash, Honoré didn't know want to do next until he spotted the captain sneaking a peek at Sugar from across the room. "Look, tell the captain that if he wants to meet a beautiful young gringa I can arrange it for him."

The waiter shook his head. "You're loco in the *cabeza*, señor."

"Then, give me back my money."

"Okay, okay."

After speaking to the captain, who nodded and smiled at Honoré, the waiter returned and reported that the mariachis would be happy to accompany Tequila, but for just one song.

Honoré returned to his table. "Guess what?"

Tequila removed his arm from around Sugar. "What?"

"The mariachi captain has invited you to sing."

Smiling broadly, rubbing his hands, Tequila got up and joined the mariachis in the middle of the smoke-filled, high-ceiling raucous room, falling right in with them as if he had known them all his life. The mariachi captain removed his wide-rimmed sombrero, embroidered with flowers of gold filigree, and handed it to him. Another mariachi offered a narrow blue and red *zarape* with white tassles at the ends. After cocking the sombrero on his head rakishly and throwing the *zarape* over a shoulder, Tequila took the microphone.

Suddenly, a powerful male voice rose above the hubbub and paused in mid-air as everyone quietly waited to see what he would do next. His voice banked, swooped, took flight, Tequila shaping every word that carried, aloft, a song about love, with the skill of a magician, a poet, or a man inspired by a beautiful woman.

Women might find this savage too short or too brown or too fat or too stupid to jump in bed with him, but from the way some gorgeous light-skinned women who had just entered the cantina with male companions stopped to gawk, clearly Tequila could seduce any of them with his voice.

"*¡Otra! ¡Otra! ¡Otra!*" everyone screamed when he finished in a crescendo of applause.

And he didn't disappoint them, pausing only to take a gulp of beer before launching into the next ballad.

"Isn't he wonderful?" asked Sugar, her hand alighting on Honoré's knee. "Oh, I love Mexico. The men are so manly. They're so passionate. They sing and they dance like movie stars. They make love like teenagers. Are you like that?"

Honoré kept his eye on Tequila. "No."

"But you're so good-looking and big and strong," she said. "Yet you're so serious you're frightening." The hand crawled dangerously close to where God had made him a man. "Are you really like that?"

Blond, blue-eyed, and big-boobed, she looked too good to be true. Now she sounded too good to be true. "Who are you?" he asked abruptly.

"What do you mean?"

The hand sent tingles up his leg. "Why are you on this convoy?" he asked.

"It's fun."

He grabbed her hand just as the serpent uncoiled in the Garden of Eden. "Tell me the truth."

She smiled and removed her hand. "I thought it would be a nice way to explore Mexico."

"I hear you're government property."

The blue eyes grew dead serious, the muscles in her jaw tightening, as she acquired a certain womanly dignity of someone entirely different behind the mask of a dumb blonde. But she caught herself and slipped right back into her little girl's voice. "What do you mean?"

"You know what I mean."

Amid the applause sweeping the room, she raised her voice. "You don't trust me? You think I'm a spy?"

"That's what they say."

"But how could that be?" she cooed in his ear, placing her hand on his knee again. "It's men who spy on me."

He removed her hand gently. "Can we talk about this later?"

"About what?" she asked, deadly gorgeous blue eyes caressing him moments before she grabbed him in the crotch. "This?"

Something sprang to life beneath his jeans, and he held her wrist. "Cool it."

She sat back in her chair, smiling. "Too late."

Tequila removed his sombrero with a flourish and bowed. After the applause died down, he said, "This is my last song. My mother's favorite. It reminded her of my father, may he rest in peace."

First, he took a shot of tequila and quaffed it with a beer. Then his voice vigorous as ever, his posture robust and dignified beneath the sombrero and *zarape*, he sang *"Sigo siendo el rey"* with such passion and aplomb that when he finished, people whooped and banged on the tables.

When he removed his sombrero and bowed like a movie star, the crowd rose to its feet and applauded. A long line of women formed and asked the short fat dark-skinned Meskin from the Texas-Mexico border, a Chicano in faded jeans and scuffed cowboy boots, for his autograph. He signed whatever they brought him, a napkin, a handkerchief, the palm of a hand, a brassiere. Eventually, he returned the sombrero and *zarape* to the mariachis.

"Ya estufas," he muttered as he plopped back in his chair, coughing and clearing his throat. *"Agua, agua, maestro,"* he said to the waiter, who brought him a glass of water. After sipping it, he wiped his face and opened his shirt, his chest shiny as rawhide dipped in oil. *"¡Qué chinga!"*

Sugar slipped her arm through his. "You were wonderful!"

Tequila turned to her with a wily grin. *"¿Te gusto, güerita?"*

She nodded like a little girl, a strand of blond hair falling across her forehead. Tequila brushed it aside with surprising tenderness. "Later I'm going to give you something you're going to like even more," he said.

"You were great, *cabrón*," admitted Honoré, reluctantly.

Tequila picked up the shot of tequila. "I love Mexico City. This is the life. Mexicans know how to live. If it weren't for my little ones waiting for me at home, I would die here." He raised the shot glass toward Honoré. "And, Coyote, I want to thank you for this. None of this would have been possible without you." He nudged Sugar with an elbow. "Coyote here is an old friend, a real friend, the best of friends. Isn't that right, Coyote?"

"Yep."

Tequila raised his glass. "To our friendship."

Everyone toasted.

The waiter arrived with a red metal tray filled with drinks. "Courtesy of Pedro Infante's fans," said the waiter.

"Me?" asked Tequila.

"Sí, señor," said the waiter as he cleared away the empty glasses and bottles. "We haven't had such a performance in many years."

When the waiter returned later with a second round, Honoré objected, "No more. We won't be able to finish them. Send them to the mariachis."

"*No mames, güey,*" slurred a cross-eyed Tequila.

Honoré glanced at his watch. "It's late. We have a long drive tomorrow."

"*No chingues, cabrón.* Things are just getting interesting."

"Where's the restroom?" asked Sugar, scooting back.

"*Maestro,*" Tequila yelled across the room, "where's the restroom?"

The waiter pointed at the back of the cantina.

As soon as Sugar left, Tequila picked up a lemon. "Here goes, *cabrón.* I'm going on a cruise in my *submarino.*" He bit the lemon and took a slug of tequila. Then he grabbed the red can of Tecate and gulped it down as if he were putting out a fire in his belly. He belched and wiped his mouth with the back of his hand. "This has been one of best nights of my life. Booze, music, and *una vieja bien buenota.* What else can a man ask for? All I need now is a *tokesito.*"

"We leave for Oaxaca tomorrow, *pendejo.*"

"Well, I'm not going."

"Then the gringa stays with me."

"*No mames.* She was part of the deal."

Suddenly, something distracted Honoré. He couldn't tell—there was a huge crowd—but he thought Sugar had stopped to talk to someone. "I already told you. She's government property."

"You mean your property, *mendigo.* I'm telling your wife."

Honoré slammed the table. "Mind your own fucking business. You bother my wife or anybody else in my family, I'll personally sink you in a barrel of acid in Tamaulipas."

Tequila downed another shot of tequila. "*Ya, ya, por favor.* Stop exaggerating."

Sugar stormed back. "A bunch of assholes just grabbed my ass!"

Tequila jumped to his feet. "Who?"

"Sit down, you idiot!" said Honoré, rising.

"Tell me who! Where?" he said, staggering toward the crowd. "No one's gonna fuck around with my woman!"

Honoré led him back to the table and pushed him in his chair, where he submerged like a submarine, eyes growing tiny as a cucaracha's, until he lay with his face on the table, snoring loudly as a horse farting.

Honoré looked around. "Keep an eye on this guy."

"Where you going?"

"The restroom."

The path to the back of the cantina was crowded, but he got through without incident, edging past the gorgeous light-skinned women who had

walked in earlier with their companions and now sat at a table. In the restroom he brushed against a stocky man on the way out. Dressed in a black
suit, with black whiskers on his cheeks, a ponytail down his back, the man
paused at the door and glared at Honoré, who noticed a pistol beneath the
man's coat. Then the man left.

Amid the stench of limes and Pinesol in the urinal, Honoré considered
the possible dangers posed by the stranger, clearly a thug or a *narcotraficante*. When he was done, he washed his hands.

Afterward, as he worked his way back to the table, someone growled.
"There goes that *pendejo*. Thinks he's *bien chingón*."

"*Mucha vieja, poco hombre*," cracked another.

Amid tumbleweeds of cigarette smoke rolling from a table, Honoré
halted. The gorgeous light-skinned women and their companions were so
absorbed in each other's conversation that they didn't even bother to look
at him. Then, at a nearby table, he spotted the men in black suits with black
glasses on solemn faces. A diamond shone in the teeth of the man Honoré
had seen in the restroom as he leaned back on his chair and gave Honoré a
fuck-you-make-my-day smirk.

Honoré returned to his table. "We better get out of here."

"Why?" said Sugar. "What's wrong?"

Honoré hailed the waiter and asked for the bill.

"Everything is paid for," said the waiter. "But captain wants to talk to
you."

"Tell him I'll be right back. I need to get this guy out of here before he
causes any more trouble."

The waiter left and spoke to the captain, who cast an ugly glance at
Honoré until one of his mariachis engaged him. Upon returning, the waiter
helped Honoré hoist Tequila to his feet. At the door, Honoré was glad to
get out of the smoke, happy to breathe fresh air, but when the siren wailed
from the cop car parked in front and arrows of red light turned the waiter's
white shirt pink, he wondered what the hell was going on.

"Not again," said the waiter.

"What the matter?" asked Honoré.

"Another police raid. The second one this week. You better get out of
here. Sometimes these things turn ugly." Then the waiter ducked inside.

"Get a taxi," Honoré said to Sugar.

Suddenly, the wall spewed dozens of stone chips on his face. When
more gunshots tore through the night and bullets hit the wall, one thud after another, he ducked, pulling Tequila and Sugar to the ground. Someone
was firing from a car in the street. They looked like cops, but he wasn't sure.

"Oh, my God!" she cried and sat up in a pool of water.

"Come on!" Honoré stood up and grabbed one of Tequila's ankles. "Help me with this guy!"

"I pissed on myself."

"So fucking what! Let's get the hell out of here!"

Sugar stood. Next, she grabbed Tequila's ankle, and together they dragged him around the side of the building. After pulling him to his feet and holding him between them, they stumbled toward the back of the plaza, where she stepped on a dog that charged into the night squealing like a pig. She fell; Tequila flopped on the ground. After Honoré helped her up again, they dragged him along a tree-lined promenade toward a back street. More gunshots echoed among the old buildings, and sirens screamed from every direction. When they paused at the corner, they spotted a hotel down the street, an old three-storey mansion with iron grates on high narrow windows. The entrance to the lobby was open.

"We need a room," Honoré told the clerk, a broad-shouldered man with a long gray face.

He wore eyeliner and spoke in a woman's voice. "They're all taken. But we have a storage room on the third floor."

"Does it have a bathroom?" asked Sugar.

"Yes."

Honoré pulled out a wad of dollars from his pocket. "We'll take anything."

Honoré and Sugar carried Tequila up a flight of metal stairs that screamed and bonged. After lugging him to the third floor, they headed down a hall, the dank walls and linoleum floor lit by a yellow bulb hanging from a wire. As they hauled Tequila through the musty dust-laden shadows of another century, they passed a couple—an old white-haired gringo and a shapely young Mexican woman in a short red dress. Someone snored in a room. In another room a woman moaned. In a third room someone giggled. In a fourth room, mattress springs churned. In a fifth room, someone farted like a burro.

"There it is," said Sugar and pointed at a door at the end of the hall.

Honoré took out the rusted three-inch key from his pocket. "Here. I'll hold this idiot."

Inside, mannequins lay stacked on top of each other like bodies in a concentration camp. Wigs hung from pegs on a wooden stand. In a corner stood a sewing machine, and on the sewing machine lay a box of tools with a hammer and a saw. Chairs, bedsprings, mattresses, typewriters, lamps, coffee tables, and a desk crowded the gloomy room with high ceilings. An empty coffin didn't make sense. A mattress on the floor did. A door led to another room.

Honoré dumped Tequila on the mattress. "You two sleep here. I'll sleep in the next room."

In the adjacent room, large mirrors with ornate gilded frames stood against a wall lit by the glow of a neon sign on the building across the street. A stack of curtains lay on a coffee table while a dusty old sofa sagged in a corner next to a window that opened on the street below, where sirens ebbed. Then Honoré found the bathroom and walked in, surprised to find hot water when he turned on the faucet in the shower. Cheap hotels in Mexico usually didn't have hot water, and if they did, it came out in a trickle. He stripped and jumped into billows of steam. But just as he was beginning to enjoy the warm water on his face and shoulders, the smell of trouble wafted into the bathroom. He peeked from behind the curtain.

"Can I come in?" asked Sugar at the door. Smoking roach in hand and wearing a white T-shirt that covered everything except her shapely thigh, firm and muscular and shiny as a flank of roasted pork, she sat on the toilet.

He closed the curtain.

"Sorry," she said. "I couldn't hold it."

Another whiff of mota reached Honoré. This was becoming dangerous. "How's Tequila?" he asked, warily.

"Died and gone to heaven," she said, releasing the pot-laden words, slowly. "This is good shit. You ought to try some." As if floating on a cloud, she hummed "Lucy in the Sky with Diamonds." She sucked on the roach some more, filling the bathroom with the smell of the Sixties. "Is something wrong, Honoré?"

"No."

She pulled the curtain aside. "Then why are you acting like this?"

"Acting like what?" He closed the curtain.

"Like you don't like good shit."

If her pigtails didn't shine like woven gold and remind him of a friend's sister who was young enough to be Honoré's daughter, he would do what he had done in the past to the women who adored him. In the world of whores, *cantinuchas*, and red light districts, undoing a young woman didn't matter because there nothing mattered. But in this world, the world of history, real history, as Trotsky put it, it was different. If he jumped into bed with this angel, he might abandon everything—the convoy, the revolution, Trotsky, even Maruca and his daughter. He knew himself too well.

She pulled the curtain aside amid strings of smoke seeping from the roach. "I can give that gila monster just what it needs, honey."

He closed the curtain.

She opened it again, blue eyes smiling.

He yanked the curtain again.

She wouldn't let go. "C'mon, Coyote."

Suddenly, the door banged open.

Tequila crashed inside, hitting the wall, then straightening up, wobbling in front of Sugar who sat on the stool as his trousers fell to the floor. Groaning, burping, and farting, he stood still for a moment as he prayed to the Virgen de Guadalupe and then pissed, the sparkling yellow stream spattering this way and that as he staggered.

"Shit!" Sugar yelled, jumping to her feet. "You're pissing on me!" She pushed him away. "Fucking asshole!"

Tequila slumped against the door and then collapsed on the floor, where he lay with his mouth open, arms spread, jeans down to his knees, dick limp and wooly as a bat asleep on his belly. Honoré turned off the water and pulled a towel from the wall. Next, he wrapped himself in it and stepped out of the shower. Honoré grabbed Tequila by the ankles and dragged him to the room in front. As he rolled him onto the mattress, Honoré's towel came undone and fell to the floor.

He picked it up, wrapped himself in it, and returned to the bathroom. "That's what you get for hanging out with a bunch of Meskins," he said to Sugar.

"Don't laugh! It's not funny!" she said and sat back on the toilet.

He touched the side of her face.

Closing her eyes, she took his hand and held it against her cheek. "Oh, Coyote, you're so strong."

"Sugar," he said gently, "we need to get some rest. We have a long day tomorrow. Why don't you take a shower and hit the sack?"

"You sound just like my daddy."

He untangled his hand.

Upon returning to his room, he sat down on the couch near the window and listened to the water run and Sugar sing in the shower. He glanced across the room and saw himself in the ornately framed mirrors from another era, his face that of a regal Spaniard, a viceroy or a conquistador, light-skinned, distinguished with an even jawbone and nose and dark eyes, just like one of the paintings Trotsky had shown him by that Spanish painter El Greco or maybe the face of a bullfighter on posters announcing a bullfight in the Plaza Mexico. So if he was a descendant of the Spaniards as his mother always reminded him, why was he fighting for the Indians and mestizos of Mexico and Central America? An Indian like Tequila should be doing that.

The bathroom door swung open and a triangle of yellow light stretched across the floor. "Coyote?"

"What?" he said.

She didn't lunge. She didn't hit him. She didn't try to bite him. She didn't grab anything. She just stood there, a naked gringa steaming in a trapezoid of light, gorgeous as the *rubia superior* on the side of the building when they were entering Mexico City but without the bikini, nipples moving about like two loose eyes trying to outstare him. After taking one last drag on the roach and exhaling snake-like streams of *mota* before tossing it on the floor, she sat down beside him on the couch and slipped her hand on his inner thigh. He grabbed her hand, held it, then removed it slowly as his gila monster yawned, raised its head, and looked around.

Her mouth was lopsided. "I love your peepee."

He grabbed her hand again. "Not now."

"Let me suck your peepee."

She pushed her long hair out of her face. A *maraca* appeared in profile beneath her raised arm, supple and fresh, converging in a nipple hard as a pink gumdrop. On the other hand, like freshly baked loaves of bread, her thighs were hot and smelled good.

"Do me a favor, Sugar," he said as he ran his fingers through her hair. "Make sure Tequila stays with the convoy. Make sure he arrives in Nicaragua. If you do that, you can have all the peepee you want. Can you do that for me, baby?"

"If you promise to let me suck your peepee," she oozed, with a thick-lipped pout.

"In Nicaragua."

She shook her head. "Tonight, right now."

She paused, opening her mouth as if to say something else. Instead, she swayed, eyes rolling back in her head. Suddenly, she froze and let out a long sigh before tumbling to the wooden floor, where she lay on her back, arms far flung, breasts flattened against her ribcage, and legs spread wide open so that her pubic hair sparkled in the light from the bathroom like the blond beard of some Viking crossing the North Sea.

"What do you do," the Governor asked him once, "when they put the red snapper in your face?" Drunk on his ass, Honoré didn't know what to say. "Don't touch it," the Governor advised. "Don't look at it. And don't go near it. Above all, don't smell it."

After carrying the gorgeous gringa to the room in front, he deposited her gently on the mattress next to Tequila and covered both of them with curtains. Next he returned to his room, where he opened the window and then climbed into his underwear and T-shirt and stretched out on the sofa in a stream of fresh air that carried him out of the musty room. He felt as if he were falling backwards into a well or a tunnel or a black hole and kept falling until he woke up in front of his house in Escandón.

"I'm home," he said as he entered the front door.

"How was your trip?" asked Maruca, standing in her white bathrobe, her hair wrapped in a towel.

"Great," he said.

"We missed you."

"Dad!"

A young girl with braids and thick glasses ran into the living room and flung her arms around his neck. Smelling like the newborn she had once been, she kissed the side of his face. And as the muscles in his arms and legs loosened and his breathing relaxed and he was carried away by the sweet mists of sleep, he kept hearing his daughter's voice, "Dad! Dad! Dad!"

CHAPTER 16
Oaxaca, Zaragoza, and La Mesilla

Gray, soft, and radiant as a pigeon's wing, a triangle of light fell across the wooden floor. At first Honoré thought he was back in Texas as he lay at the edge of the sofa until the honking of cars and the sound of men's voices coming through the open window reminded him of the Tenampa Bar and the police raid. He rose on an elbow in the fresh morning air and looked around—he was in a hotel room in Mexico City. Then he glanced at his watch. It was late. Tequila and Sugar should be up by now. Well, maybe not—they had gotten drunk, stoned, plastered out of their minds. Probably still asleep.

He sat up, stood, and pulled on his jeans. After buckling his belt, he walked shirtless and barefoot into the bathroom.

Scrawled in red lipstick on the mirror, he read:

> *¡Hay te wacho, pendejo!*
> —Pedro Infante

"Fucking asshole!" Honoré muttered and then took a piss.

Where the hell were those two idiots? And why did they leave without telling him? Maybe they were downstairs or at some nearby café eating breakfast and might be back soon; maybe they went back to the convoy in Coyoacán. Or were they up to no good? He flushed the toilet, turned on a faucet in the washbasin, and flung water on his face. He dried himself with a towel still damp from the previous night.

One crazy night.

He tramped back to the sofa, picked up his shirt from the floor, and slipped it on. Then, he thought about Sugar. Was she really a spy? CIA? Was all this her idea? As an ex-*narcotraficante*, he was used to craziness, but at least then he was paid good money for doing crazy things. Besides, he was getting too old for this stuff. Maruca was right. He needed to think about the future, his future, the future of his family. Oh well, in a few days he would be back home. He pulled on his socks and boots.

In the lobby he asked the clerk, "Did you see a man and a gringa leave this morning?"

Tiny, blond, and slender with the delicate leaf-shaped ears of a Chihuahua dog, the young man sitting behind the reception desk did not look up from the comic book in his hands. "No."

"Did you see anything strange or unusual?"

The clerk sat back thoughtfully, ears turning pink in the morning light, eyes watery and blue. "I see strange and unusual things all the time, señor. A comet that predicted the end of the world. An earthquake we thought was the end of the world. And corruption that convinced us that, no, the world would not end any time soon. Is that what you mean by 'strange and unusual'?"

Honoré thought about grabbing this imbecile by his shirt and slapping him around. Instead, he took a deep breath. "Well, did you see a car or strange people?"

"A car was parked outside."

A phone sat on the counter. Honoré pulled his wallet from his back pocket and rifled through it for a list of telephone numbers. "Well, was there anything unusual about the car?" he asked.

The clerk laid the comic book on the desk. "A Lincoln Continental. Usually I don't see Continentals around here."

Honoré found what he was looking for. "Did you see anybody in the car?"

The clerk stretched his arms and yawned. "No. The windows were up, tinted." Suddenly, he froze. "Oh, wait. Yes, I did see somebody. A man. He looked like he was eating a diamond."

Honoré's hand trembled with anticipation. "Really?" he said and then handed the clerk a five. "May I use your phone?"

The clerk stared doubtfully at the tip. "Don't take too long."

Honoré picked up the phone and dialed. "May I speak to Señor Trotsky?"

"*Un momentito, por favor,*" said a young woman.

Trotsky's voice was fresh and lively as the morning air seeping from the street through the lobby's open door. "Hi. Good to hear from you." He lowered his voice. "I was worried, though. I called camp headquarters, and they said you didn't show up last night."

Honoré told him about the Salón Tenampa and the police raid. "I think Tequila went back to Texas," he added. "Took Sugar with him."

Trotsky's voice surged. "Why would she want to go back to the border with that idiot? The only reason she's taken an interest in him is to get to you."

"Well, she was a bad little girl last night."

"What happened?"

"Nothing. But what I had to deal with wasn't easy." He chuckled. "I deserve the Order of Lenin."

Behind him, metal clanged. A woman giggled. A man coughed. The scuffle of feet grew as a couple came down the stairs. Honoré turned around. An old white-haired gringo with a pale freckled face and a dark-skinned young woman with breasts smooth, shiny, and bouncy as two bowls of flan. She wore a slit skirt, and there was plenty of muscle in that leg.

"By the way," Trotsky added, "Last night Johnny Paint and Tennessee went to meet some friends at Plaza Garibaldi. Did you see them?"

The woman's slit skirt opened. "No," said Honoré. "Why?"

"They're not back. They might have hooked up with Tequila."

The woman glanced at Honoré as her swinging hips carried her gorgeous butt out the front door. "So what's the plan now?" Honoré asked.

"Well, the convoy is headed to Chapultepec, and the Commander wants me to pick up a wreath of flowers in Tepito. You're not far from there. I'll pick you up in a few minutes."

The wreath sprouted dozens of eyes. But they weren't eyes. They were sunflowers, whose dark brown disc-shaped dilated pupils amid clusters of bright yellow petals peered at Honoré as he helped Trotsky carry them to the taxi parked behind the Mercado Tepito, a conglomeration of tarpaulin-covered stalls and tin-roofed buildings selling everything from incense, candles, and flowers to pirated music and drugs. When the two men raised the wreath onto the roof, the flowers dangled like suns springing from a galaxy of green leaves wrapped around a base of stiff wires. After tying it down with twine, Honoré climbed in the backseat with Trotsky.

"Chapultepec," Trotsky snapped at the chubby middle-aged Mexican behind the wheel. "And make it quick."

The driver started the engine. "Yes, sir," he said looking at them in the mirror, sneaky eyes above jowls beaded with sweat. "We'll be there in a Mexico City minute."

Honoré knew that look. He had seen it in Tequila. Most Mexicans had it. If he and Trotsky weren't careful, this *chilango* was going to rob them. "How much?" he asked gruffly.

The driver offered a reasonable price, but Honoré was still suspicious, especially when the cab backfired, belching like a drunk and engulfing them in a cloud of exhaust that poured in through the open windows. But soon the idiot got the car running smoothly, and they lurched ahead.

Winding through one narrow crowded, trash-strewn street after another, the driver honked at pedestrians and bicycles until the taxi was speeding down a wide boulevard. Honoré stared at a giant sword raised against the sky, an ultra-modern skyscraper of shiny glass—La Bolsa Mexicana. The Mexican stock exchange. Then they cruised along a tree-lined boulevard, whizzing past the golden statue of an Indian in the middle of an intersection.

"Cuauhtemoc," shouted the cab driver over his shoulder, "the last emperor of Mexico."

"You sound like a professor," said Trotsky.

The driver smiled. "No, I'm simply *un diabolico*."

"Diabolic?" asked Trotsky, glancing doubtfully at Honoré.

"A diabetic."

Trotsky laughed. Honoré stared out the window.

"Some of my *compadres*," added the driver, "are professors, but they drive cabs because teachers are paid nothing in this country. Anyway, after diabetes unmanned me, I started reading books. Much more satisfying than women. *Pinches viejas*, they drive men crazy. Maybe that's why we lost the Mexican-American war."

Trotsky chuckled. Honoré's distrust grew as the cab stopped for a red light at an intersection clogged with people and cars.

Long yellow teeth in a greasy face painted black and white grinned at Honoré through the window. Then the wiry figure in a body suit with bones sketched in white paint and with a beer bottle in one hand and a lighter in the other raised the bottle to his lips. When he blew the liquid into the air, he flicked the lighter, and a tongue of fire jumped from his mouth.

Soon the traffic light turned green, and the taxi took off.

"Chapultepec," shouted the driver over his shoulder at Trotsky, "is a monument to Mexican heroism. You're familiar with our history. Yes?"

"Yes," said Trotsky, gazing out the window indifferently.

"We Mexicans may be poor, but we're not cowards. Several cadets jumped off the top of the castle rather than surrender. One of them with the Mexican flag wrapped around him so it wouldn't fall into enemy hands. The gringos said we were stupid because we fought until we could no longer fight. And we're still fighting!" yelled the driver as he slammed on the brakes. "Look!"

Posters and banners plastered with slogans such as "Down with the dictatorship!" and "*¡No chinguen!*" and "*¡El pueblo unido jamás será vencido!*" danced above hundreds of men, women, and children marching down the avenue, past the front of the taxi. A fifteen-foot puppet of Uncle Sam—a top hat above a sharp nose and a long white beard, a blue jacket, and trousers of red and white stripes—led a string of bronze-skinned *danzantes* wearing headdresses of feathers and filling the sky with the thumping of drums. More puppets followed. A blond gringa with a pink face, blue eyes, and red lips smiled at Honoré. A mustachioed man in a black tuxedo resembled a Latin American dictator.

Trotsky slumped back in frustration. "That's a lot of people."

"I assure you, señor, it'll clear up soon."

Honoré leaned forward. "Why don't you just drive through them?"

The driver turned around, an eyebrow hoisted above a bloodshot eye. "And orphan my children? Mexicans are a brave lot. But they can also be mean and crazy. Remember at one time we practiced human sacrifice. Ha, ha!"

Suddenly, the taxicab shuddered as a drunk stumbled into its front fender on the passenger side, hair a mess, a wrinkled white shirt open down the middle of his shiny brown chest, dark trousers rumpled, big toes sticking out from huaraches. He unzipped and pissed on the front tire like a dog.

"*Hijo de tu re-chingada madre,*" muttered the driver, throwing open his door and jumping out.

With a mixture of surprise and contempt, Honoré watched the driver run around the cab and punch the man in the face, knocking him down. As the drunk crawled away, pants bunched around his knees, buttocks sizzling in the Aztec sun, the driver kicked him in the ass.

"*¡Pendejo!*" the driver cursed as he climbed back in the car.

Honoré tapped him on the shoulder. "Look, *jefe,*" he said, "how much longer are we going to be stuck in this traffic?"

"Depends on Washington," the driver said, wiping his hands on a handkerchief. Then he held up his hand and rubbed his thumb and finger together.

Honoré wanted to clobber the sonuvabitch. Nonetheless, he reached in his pocket and found a few dollars. Trotsky checked his pockets and handed over a wad of pesos.

"Let me see," said the driver as he peered at the money in Honoré's hands, smiled, and then took it. "Roll up your windows."

In fits and starts, the cab took off. Plunging into the crowd, it sent people screaming, feet flying, butts twirling, panties showing, and tongues lolling. A banner fell across the windshield, but the driver forged ahead through the screams and taunts until the banner tore in half. A pretty girl spat at the window inches from Honoré's face. Thousands of hands banged on the cab, and a tall man dropped his pants and pressed his butt against the window on the driver's side. As the demonstrators rocked the taxi from side to side, Honoré felt the same fear in his gut that he had under the mob of lesbians in Escandón. But soon they plowed past the last of the demonstrators and the driver turned on the wipers to clear off the spit, feathers, flower petals, and handprints. Then they cruised along another boulevard, turned onto a tree-lined street, and slowed as they approached the pickups, vans, and school buses parked by the entrance to Chapultepec Park.

Molly, Zuckermann, and a handful of white-haired geezers stood on the sidewalk. As soon as Honoré and Trotsky got out and untied the wreath, the cab took off.

"Oh, my God!" said Molly as she examined the mangled sunflowers. "What happened? There's nothing left."

"We got caught in traffic," said Trotsky.

"A demonstration," Honoré added. "Turned ugly."

"The cab driver robbed us," said Trotsky.

"Robbed?"

Trotsky shrugged. "Extortion. Robbery. Seduction. It's all the same when you're dealing with assholes."

Honoré helped Trotsky carry the mangled wreath to the end of the promenade, where the convoyers mingled in front of a statue of a woman holding her two sons at her side. Several feet in back stood a row of stone columns, each dedicated to the young cadets who sacrificed themselves in defense of Chapultepec Castle, a European-style palace straddling the hill beyond the trees.

The Commander looked around. "Where's Tequila and Sugar?"

"No idea," said Trotsky, who then quietly explained what happened at the Tenampa.

The Commander rubbed his right ear. "Traveling without a mechanic is risky. Johnny Paint and Tennessee are gone, too."

"How'd the press conference go?" Trotsky asked.

"We begged the media to wait, but they were in a rush to cover a car pileup on the *periférico*. Without the wreath we couldn't do the honors."

Suddenly, engines hummed in the parking lot as two super deluxe buses rolled to a stop. Cameras hanging from their necks, Japanese tourists climbed out of one, pointing at the stone columns and chattering about God knows what. German tourists descended from the second bus, straw sombreros on their blond heads and white feet in huaraches. They looked like gringos but sounded like Nazis.

Short, brown, and skinny, a tour guide puttered across the asphalt. "Are you the Americans we heard about on the radio?"

A stocky fraulein approached. "Dese volks," she said in a thick German accent, "fight das Amerikanisch government on die Brücke. Ve vatched it on das TV in die airport."

Her husband, thin as a reed and bald, with rimless glasses on his red face, stood beside her. "Ya, das ist gut ve lost da var. Be Amerikanisch ist das Problem. Ach, I vouldn't vant to be Amerikanisch."

"Why?" the guide asked.

"Vy? You don't know vy? Ve fight dose Amerikaners. Dese Japaners fight dose Amerikaners. Even you Mexikaners fight dose Amerikaners. And see now dese Amerikaners fight Amerikaners. Vat's da matter vit dem Amerikaners dat day alvays fight vit everyvone?"

The guide chuckled. "This is the side of Mexico tourists never see," he said with delight. "May we take pictures?"

The Commander removed his finger from his ear. "Sure," he said. "Take all the pictures you want."

The guide noticed the microphone. "Will you give a speech?"

Molly glanced at the Commander. "What do you think?"

"Might as well," Jack said. "Now that we have an audience."

A man wearing a loud Hawaiian shirt and shorts trudged from behind the buses as Molly picked up the microphone. His hairy legs reminded Honoré of old man Savage.

"What's going on here?" the gringo muttered.

"Shhhh," the woman behind him hissed.

Molly glared at the man and fidgeted with the microphone before plunging ahead. "The Mexican-American war," she began in a tremulous voice, "was the first foreign war fought by the United States." She stopped and took a deep breath as the tourist guide translated, first into German and then Japanese. "Not all Americans supported it."

The gringo lowered his camera. "What's this shit?" he said.

His wife, her face round and white as a communion wafer, nudged him. "Hush," she whispered.

"No one talks about my country like that!"

She grabbed his elbow. "Come on!"

He jerked his arm loose. "Let's hear what else these idiots have to say!"

Molly, now flanked by two stern-faced Vietnam vets, continued. "Henry

David Thoreau, Ulysses S. Grant, and Abraham Lincoln opposed the war. Lincoln said, 'I had a horror of the Mexican War. We had no claim on Mexico. I am always ashamed of my country when I think of that invasion.' "

"Bullshit!" the heckler yelled.

This time his wife hooked her arm through his and tugged. "Now, now, sweetie, that's no way to act in public. Let's go look at the museum. They say Juarez's coach is there."

The heckler's face reddened. "America, love or leave it!"

No longer smiling, the tour guide addressed his companions and said something in each of their languages. Almost at once, everyone followed him toward Chapultepec Castle, cameras clicking and flashing amid a welter of foreign words Honoré did not understand. Meanwhile, a blond, blue-eyed, seven-year-old German girl stayed behind, lips pink from eating a *raspa*. Next to her stood a Japanese boy, about the same height, cross-eyed behind steel-rimmed glasses, like a smart kid in middle school, holding a dripping snow cone. Their parents chatted nearby. Honoré felt strange, but most of all he felt sorry for Molly.

"And so it is in this spirit that we bring this corona of lovely flowers," said Molly, glancing doubtfully at the mangled sunflowers. "We are taking humanitarian aid to the people of another embattled country. But as we pass through Mexico, we want to honor the 'heroic children' of Chapultepec Castle. And by doing so, we want to convey the message that not all Americans support the imperialist foreign policy of a strong nation against its weaker neighbors."

"Bullshit!" the gringo yelled from the gate leading to the castle and gave them a big, pale finger.

Men, women and children waited to cross the highway. Others gathered at a bus stop. Some waved. At one point, construction forced the convoy to stop or take detours along dirt access roads because the metro was being extended to the suburbs. The convoy traveled east toward Puebla and passed hundreds of shanties sewn together along dirt streets by dark birdless cables sagging between utility poles. An hour later, Honoré steered the pickup past a hill shaped like the back of a huge armadillo that had just taken a shit—the Chalco city dump. The stench was so bad Honoré thought he had driven into a cloud of gas from the city's sewer system. A young couple with an infant in its mother's arms stood on the shoulder and waved.

"How anybody can live in this hell is beyond me," said Honoré.

"They've been doing it for a long time," Trotsky said matter-of-factly as he stared out the window. "People can survive under the worst of circumstances. In the United States, we forget this."

Honoré held the steering wheel steady. "Did the Commander get to see the doctor?"

"Yes, he's feeling much better. Some problem with his prescription. High blood pressure."

Honoré glanced at Trotsky. "Something wrong with his ear?"

"Why?"

"At Chapultepec he kept putting his finger in it."

"The doctor called my aunt this morning, said the Commander was stubborn and uncooperative. The doctor did what he could. This is why I've had doubts about this convoy since Managua."

"What does Molly say?"

"She's fed up with him."

"I'm sure she's glad the Savages are gone."

"Who isn't?"

The smell grew. If anything was going to kill the human race, reflected Honoré, it was shit. If not human shit, then nuclear shit and all the other shit dumped in the atmosphere. Just a few years ago in Mexico City, they reported shit storms, in which feces-laden rain cascaded from thunderheads above the sprawling city. He didn't believe it, but it was true. And the ugly truth was always funny. Suddenly, bus after bus boomed past, followed by trucks and cars, a motorcycle. Exhaust fumes mingled with the smell of shit.

Gradually, a mountain range rose on the horizon. Two volcanoes, Popocatepetl and Ixtachihuatl, looked like a man and a woman reclining with white-handkerchief-like snow caps on their faces as they dozed. After crossing the Valley of Chalco under a blue sky, the convoy entered pine-covered foothills and gained altitude. In Honoré's rearview mirror, the convoy vehicles followed in a ragged procession. Zuckermann drove the Commander's bus.

"So what happened at the Tenampa?" asked Trotsky.

"Supposedly a police raid. But in Mexico that could mean anything, rival gangs settling scores."

"Of course."

"Tennessee and Johnny Paint may be headed south," said Honoré. "I heard them and Tequila talking about Acapulco. Probably hooked up with some *narcotraficantes* and headed there. The thing is, though, Tequila wanted to go home. He missed his kids. But that guy is so crazy you never know what he'll do next. Especially with Sugar involved. But if she's out to stop or discredit the convoy, she's going about it the wrong way."

Trotsky adjusted his eye patch. "CIA people are looney tunes. Can't tell the difference between them and cartoon characters. But then, of course, that's true of most people today."

In Puebla they stopped at a Pemex. Trotsky climbed out of the pickup. "I need to talk to Zuckermann," he said.

As Honoré got out and stretched his legs on the oil-stained cement, sunlight fell across the spotted faces of vitamin-deficient children who thronged him with boxes of Chiclets. After telling the attendant to fill up the pickup, he stalked through the smell of gasoline to the stench of the restroom at the back of a whitewashed building. Five minutes later, he headed outside, to the public phones in front of smudged windows. The silvery air was fresh and crisp. After the buzz of repeatedly cut-off telephone connections, an international telephone operator put him through to the United States. First, he called home. No answer. Then he called the store. Again, no answer. He hung up and walked back to the convoy.

"There's a tropical storm forming off the Pacific coast," Zuckermann reported as Honoré joined him and Trotsky in front of the Commander's bus. "As long as it doesn't become a hurricane, there's nothing to worry about."

"We'll be okay between here and Oaxaca," said Trotsky. "But near the isthmus, it could get ugly."

Zuckermann pulled a notebook from his back pocket and scribbled something. "Did you get a hold of the priest?" he asked without looking up.

"Yes," said Trotsky. "I called him from my aunt's house. He's made all the arrangements. We're staying at La Iglesia de los Descalzos tonight."

Zuckermann put away the notebook. "Let's check on the troops."

Honoré followed the two men along the line of thirty-nine vehicles waiting to refuel, here and there stopping to talk to the elderly folks, who took photos of each other in T-shirts and Bermuda shorts. While the veterans checked the oil and water in their engines, others made sure bicycles and boxes of medical supplies were tied securely on the roofs of their vehicles. On the way back, they found Molly and the Commander chatting outside the bus.

"How you doing?" asked Trotsky.

The Commander smiled. "Much better. It's cool now. Fresh air. Thanks for the doctor."

"Glad to help."

"Everyone's relieved to be out of Mexico City," said Molly.

An hour later they were ready to leave. The vehicles were refueled, tires in good shape, motors running smoothly. "We'll take the detour through Puebla," Trotsky said as they clambered aboard the pickup. "The loop is under construction. Just follow the signs."

They passed churches with heavy wooden doors, mansions with domes adorned with Talavera tiles, and buildings with iron-grilled windows—all signs of New Spain. In the shadow of a heavy dark stone cathedral, young couples sat on benches and gazed at the passing convoy. Two long city blocks later, they drove past crowded tables under stone arches that went from one end of the block to the other. Some people waved.

"I love Mexico," said Trotsky, waving back. "I've always loved Mexico. Probably because it's not my country." He looked at Honoré. "There's always an exaggerated quality in the love of a country not your own. The romanticism of the ex-pat."

"Why don't you live here?"

Trotsky gazed at the people in the street thoughtfully. "If it weren't for my wife, I'd have left Texas long ago."

Waves of carbon monoxide unleashed by the slow-moving line of cars and trucks gagged Honoré as he worked his way through narrow streets, but soon traffic thinned out south of the city. "Here we go," he muttered as he got back on the highway.

According to a sign, Oaxaca was 363 kilometers or about 200 miles away, which didn't seem like much until a huge bus lunged around a sharp curve, reminding him it was 200 miles of dangerous highway. In Atlixco he slowed down and crept past the plaza surrounded by trees. On the outskirts, clouds of steam sprang from the hoods of two trucks behind Honoré. They tried Tequila's trick of driving and stopping so the engines could cool down until they got to the next town, but they ended up burning out the engines. After Zuckermann proposed salvaging the vehicles, the Commander sent Honoré and Trotsky to find a local mechanic. The mechanic told them that he could help them if they waited a day or paid him an exorbitant fee, upon which the Commander decided to abandon the trucks. After unloading boxes of medical supplies and packing them in the other vehicles, they took off again.

As they headed south, the highway wound through curve after curve—dozens of them, hundreds, it seemed—past slopes bristling with organ cactus. The sun weakened on the horizon, a gold doubloon releasing its last rays of light amid pink clouds.

"Take it easy," warned Trotsky as the truck plunged around a bend.

From his window, Honoré looked down a steep grade into craggy ravines that hurtled past. He shifted down. Then he heard geese honking. But the geese were not geese. In the side mirror, he saw the Commander's bus in the left lane. It passed, honking wildly. In the driver's seat, Zuckermann gripped the steering wheel, eyes wide, face pale as death.

"Brakes on the bus are out!" yelled Honoré.

When they came around the curve, the bus was gone. Honoré pulled over, the other vehicles stopping behind him. Honoré and Trotsky jumped out and ran to edge of the road. And sure enough, thought Honoré, there it was, wheels in the air hundreds of feet below. A yellow bus.

"My God," groaned Trotsky. "Molly. Zuckermann. Jack. It's over." His voice caught in his throat. "Fucking CIA."

Everyone halted at the edge of the highway, panting. "Oh, my God!" cried a woman.

"Fuck!" said a vet.

Pastor Paul arrived, galloping. He halted, stunned, gripping his gold cross in a huge black hand. Then he crossed himself and prayed.

Someone yelled in the distance, a man standing on the edge of the highway at the next curve. He waved his arms over his head.

"Look," Honoré said and nudged Trotsky.

Trotsky looked at the man, then at the bus, and back at the man. "How the hell?" he said and smiled. "Zuckermann!"

Everyone ran toward the Jew. Honoré caught up with them just as Pastor Paul and the vets started yelling jubilantly and pointing at the yellow bus, which had made it around the curve and crashed into a thicket of cactus on the side of the highway.

"How's the Commander?" asked Trotsky, breathlessly.

"Fine," said Zuckermann. "Everyone's fine."

"We thought you went over the edge."

"We almost did."

"There's a bus at the bottom of the ravine. A yellow bus. Come look."

"No shit?"

"No shit."

Spanish galleons carried silver plates through the rays of the moon by the time the convoy was back on the highway. While the thunder and lightning suggested a battle erupting on the horizon, Trotsky dozed and the voices of singers from La Epoca de Oro—Jorge Negrete, Agustin Lara, Pedro Infante, Tonya la Negra, and Libertad Lamar—beamed in from a distant radio station, reminding Honoré not only of Plaza Garibaldi and the Salon

Tenampa but of his father and mother and how at one time both were
happy and the family was happy and the children had played in an arroyo
that emptied into the Rio Grande. Things had been so much easier then
as they ran barefoot in the hot, dirt streets of the barrio and so much fun
when friends and cousins returned from working in the *pizcas en el norte*
and they played cowboys and Indians or went fishing and swimming in the
Rio Grande.

Suddenly, sheets of light unrolled in the left lane. The roar of a truck
passing, its gutted mufflers bellowing and barking, was as deafening as an
AK-47 going off.

Trotsky bolted upright, rubbing his good eye. "Where are we?"

Honoré turned down the radio. "Halfway there."

Trotsky rolled down the window. An organ cactus stood silver-tipped in
the moonlight. "Look at that moon. Reminds me of Isla de Mujeres. Ever
been there?"

"Off the coast of the Yucatán Peninsula, near Cancún?"

"Right."

"No. Just to Merida."

"The Spaniards found so many images of a moon goddess there that
they named it 'Isla de Mujeres.'"

Few men were like Trotsky, always full of interesting information and
surprises. Passion. Ideals. At times Honoré felt he knew him better than
his own father, but the more he learned about him, the more mysterious
he became. Not only did Trotsky come from southern California, but he
belonged to a different generation. Well traveled and highly educated, he
lived in a different universe.

"After I returned from the war," said Trotsky, his face lit by the dash
lights, "I ran into a bunch of friends from high school. Rich kids who
avoided the draft. The girls were gorgeous. Blond hair, blue eyes. California
girls. They went to Berkeley pretty normal but came back hippies. They
invited me along to Mexico. To Isla de Mujeres. We spent nights on the
beach, stoned on our asses. The sun toasted us. We ate *tamales de iguana*
or turtle eggs for breakfast in my friends' bungalow and slept the rest of the
morning. At noon we ate fish cooked over an open fire on the beach. My
friends paid off the police. They loved us."

The headlights of an oncoming car sliced through the darkness. Then a
bus with "Puebla" on its plaque above the windshield roared past, followed
by several more cars moving bumper to bumper. In the mirror the convoy
of vehicles followed slowly like moons strung out on the highway winding
through the Mexican night.

"One morning," said Trotsky, "I stood on the beach at sunrise. A throbbing bloodshot eye peered at me from the edge of the ocean, as if asking, 'What the hell is wrong with you? You may travel to the ends of the universe on pot and women, but there always comes a time when you must come back to earth.' The surf was heavy. The ocean, monumental. The water washed up to my feet. I was lucky to be alive."

Trotsky spoke like a poet, but he was a soldier. And though there was much Honoré didn't understand about him, he felt nothing but respect for Trotsky's surviving Vietnam and then trying to ease his conscience by helping people in a poor country. Unlike the men in his own family.

"Soon I realized," said Trotsky as he rested his arm on the back of the seat, "I wasn't a Mexican. No matter how well I spoke Spanish or how much I knew about Mexico, I would never be a Mexican. In a corner of my heart, I still felt that emotion I felt as a schoolboy saying the Pledge of Allegiance. No matter how hard I tried yanking it out of my soul, I was an American. A gringo. So I told my friends I was headed back to Mexico City to enroll in the American university. They were headed for Guatemala. To start a hippie commune near Santiago de Atitlán. One Sunday morning, I left on the bus."

Hundreds of moon-lit curves gobbled the hours. While long lines of traffic slowed them down, steep grades hurtled buses and trucks past them. Some vehicles overheated, and so they had to stop. After cooling down, the engines coughed as they were started up; soon they were humming as they undertook the trek again. The last curve brought them to a ridge with thousands of lights below.

"Oaxaca," said a green-and-white sign on the side of the highway as Honoré sped past.

Soon, they entered the outskirts. After driving along several narrow unfamiliar streets, Honoré found La Iglesia de los Descalzos, a church nestled among huge trees in one of the poorest barrios in Oaxaca, where Don Pedro, a short, bald priest in an ankle-length cassock, welcomed them. After parking the vehicles in a courtyard behind the church, members of the convoy trekked into a basketball gym with broken windows and walls unpainted for years. They unrolled their sleeping bags on the cement floor.

"Welcome! Welcome!" said Don Pedro, puttering around and shaking everyone's hand. "The restrooms are over there. If you need anything, let us know. We will serve breakfast in the morning." He turned to the Commander. "This way, this way, to my office."

"Go ahead," Honoré said to Trotsky. "I'm exhausted."

The next morning he joined Trotsky and the others for breakfast amid long blades of sunlight skewering the windows.

Don Pedro sat midway down the crowded table from Honoré as he addressed his guests, face rugged and serious as sun-baked granite. "Americans are a fine people. When I lived in Boston, I saw Americans' passion for social justice. As long as they're informed, they do the right thing. But often governments lie to their people." His eyes swept across everyone's face; then he intoned as if he were blessing them. "The convoy to Nicaragua is the other face of America. That America will always be welcome at La Iglesia de los Descalzos."

A cobblestone street took them past the balconies of mansions with grated windows and thick wooden doors, past the façades of churches gorgeous with angels and saints carved in stone. On the outskirts of Oaxaca, magueys, yucca, and ocotillo stood in silvery morning light. Long-limbed jacaranda trees bearing lovely pink flowers stood along the highway. Organ cacti raised their pipes along curve after curve of asphalt snaking through the mountains.

Three oncoming trucks painted red, green, and yellow, tassels on the sun visors inside their windshields, reminded Honoré of *matachines*, brightly arrayed dancers he had seen in church courtyards throughout Mexico. They, too, wore tassels on their headdresses' visors.

Three hours later, Honoré could still not see the Pacific Ocean. But as they left the mountains behind and descended to the flat terrain below, he felt its presence grow. Not only did palms toss in the breeze sweeping the brittle asphalt carrying the convoy to the coast, but the air, like a hot tongue, licked his face. An old man riding a donkey on the side of the highway held his hat with one hand.

A bridge took them over the Rio Tehuantepec. It was early afternoon, and Honoré was hungry.

Soon they reached the outskirts of Zaragoza, about thirty minutes from the ocean. Muddy streets guided them past heaps of trash as a Volkswagen taxi picked up a couple from the narrow sidewalks and sped off in a cloud of exhaust. Signs on haphazardly shaped modern buildings crunched together announced a hotel, a restaurant, a pharmacy, and a clothing store. Like a flock of white doves, hundreds of papers flew from an overturned trashcan.

"Did you see that?" said Honoré, watching the papers fly overhead.

Trotsky cleared his throat. "It's always windy in Zaragoza. With that storm brewing in the Pacific, it'll only get worse."

At the end of a cobblestone street, the whitewashed walls of a beautiful church stood among trees lashed by the wind. Next to it, a monastery-like building occupied the rest of the block.

"There it is," said Trotsky. "La Casa de la Cultura."

Honoré parked a few feet from a canopied entrance, wide enough for a car to enter. The rest of the vehicles parked in the street, where the soggy wind ran back and forth like a crazy kid excited by the arrival of new playmates.

"Welcome to Zaragoza," said Jorge, a stout brown man with thick glasses and an infectious smile. He stood in a courtyard bounded on four sides by arches festooned with bright red banners.

"So this is the famous Zaragoza," said the Commander, looking at the banners.

Jorge laughed. "You mean the infamous Zaragoza!"

"Yes, yes," said the Commander. "I've heard about this place. The women. The Zapotecs. Acción Campesina. Your brave struggle for social justice. The first community to triumph against the dictatorship." Then he turned to members of the convoy. "And these are my countrymen. We know that what we're carrying to Nicaragua is meager, but we also know we're sending a powerful message to the world—namely, that American patriots, real American patriots, object to our country's terrorist foreign policies."

"Welcome, welcome," said Jorge. "Let me show you where you'll stay."

The Commander, Molly, Trotsky, and Honoré followed him to a room with wooden benches, which looked as if monks had once prayed or studied here. Next door, dark wooden beams sustained the roof above cots lining the stucco wall. Windows faced the street. Most of the convoy members would sleep here. Jorge apologized that he didn't have enough cots for everyone. Molly said there was no need since they had sleeping bags and were used to sleeping on the floor or the ground. Jorge then showed them a small office with a wooden desk, a telephone and a typewriter; it would serve as camp headquarters.

Zuckermann caught up with them. "Some of the vehicles need repairs," he confided quietly to the Commander.

The Commander turned to Jorge. "This is our lawyer, Pinchas Zuckermann."

"Welcome," said Jorge, shaking Zuckermann's hand. "We're here to help you in any way we can."

The lawyer was all business. "Thank you."

"We had some problems on the way," added the Commander. "Lost two vehicles. Almost lost a third one. Also, we lost our mechanic."

Jorge said to Zuckermann. "Come with me. One of my staff will help you find a mechanic."

Honoré tapped Jorge's elbow. "Señor."

Jorge halted. "Yes."

"May I use your phone to make a collect call to the United States?"

"Of course," Jorge said.

After everyone left, Honoré, much to his surprise, got through to Escandón.

"Dad!" The girl's voice was sweet.

"How are you, *mi'ja*?" he said.

"Dad, Mom's been worried to death. Are you okay?"

"Yes, I'm fine. Let me talk to your mother."

Maruca's warm voice filled his ear. "We heard about the storm in the Pacific. Everyone's been calling—the Governor, Señora Cuervo, *The New York Times*, the FBI, your mother."

"How is she?"

"Same as ever. Where are you?"

"Zaragoza, a small town on the coast. Tomorrow we head south to Tapachula. On the Mexican-Guatemalan border.

"Why haven't you called?"

"I have, but either you weren't home or I couldn't get through. I'll call you when—" The line went dead. "Fuck!" He redialed. Nothing.

Outside, the wind howled. He tried once more. Maruca answered.

"Hello. Sorry about that," he said.

"How long will you be gone?"

"I'll be back next week."

"I've been watching the news. All kinds of horrible things are happening in Central America. I can't sleep at night. And Señora Cuervo calls me every day to ask about Tequila. Your mother is driving me crazy."

Outside, the wind screeched. "You've never worried about me like this before."

"This is different. I feel like a dark shadow has fallen over the house. A curse."

Honoré thought about the owl. "Stop watching the news."

"Bonita wants to talk to you."

"Hey, Dad. When you coming home?"

"Next week, *mi'ja*."

"Can you come to the volleyball game? Misty and I are playing. We're playing a team from San Antonio."

Comino came to mind. Why, he didn't know, just did. "How you getting along with Misty?"

"Fine. Why?"

"Has she said anything about me?"

"No. Not really. She just asked where you—."

The line went dead. He tried to get through again but couldn't. Outside the wind sent shudders throughout the building. Hunger set in.

After members of the convoy unloaded their belongings and set themselves up in the rooms, they lined up in the dining hall. Food tray in hand, Honoré stood before three women from Oaxaca serving dinner. The two young ones giggled and smiled as they tried to keep their eyes off him while the middle-aged woman with streaks of gray in her black hair surveyed the hall as she made sure that everything ran smoothly.

Then he joined Jorge, the Commander, and Trotsky at a long table near the entrance. The wooden door rattled as the wind lunged at it like a pack of rabid dogs.

"In Mexico nothing surprises us anymore," Jorge said. "The whole country is a powder keg. It's just a matter of time before it blows up. Soon we may have to surrender our sovereignty in a fire sale."

The Commander fixed Jorge in a gaze. "What do you mean?"

"Mexico is so indebted to the Americans that they already see it as real estate. Already they have their eyes set on the isthmus. But our party won the elections, and we're going to fight until we turn things around."

"Well, that's why we're here," said the Commander. "The fight is happening on many fronts. Mexico, Guatemala, Nicaragua—"

"El Salvador," said Trotsky.

"But it can easily take an ugly turn," Jorge added. "The criminal element. The mafia. They've always been around. With the decline of the PRI, they might get out of control."

Trotsky glanced at Honoré. "Can it get any worse? Tons of drugs cross into the United States every day."

"Which reminds me," Jorge said and then turned to Honoré. "We saw you on TV. The confrontation on the bridge. I saw you punch that cop in the face."

Honoré lowered his spoon. "It was hell."

"We didn't think you'd make it."

"We didn't either," said the Commander. "North of Monterrey we were almost swept off the highway by a landslide. In Mexico City, there were rumors that the CIA was going to sabotage the convoy. On a highway north of Oaxaca, the brakes on my bus gave out."

The door swung open. The wind swooshed a young dark-skinned woman into the hall. No one except Honoré paid her any attention. In an embroidered red blouse on square shoulders, thick black hair tied back over fine ears, shiny red lipstick as if she had put it on her thick lips moments before stepping inside, she reminded Honoré of Frida Kahlo. And in some strange way, Don Sixto's La Morenita. She approached the table, carrying a basket.

Teeth white and smooth as onyx, the girl pulled back a cloth to show the basket's contents. "¿*Tamales de iguana?*" she announced.

Trotsky removed a tamale wrapped in a thick brown greasy leaves. He took one, unpasted the leaves, and took a bite. "Mmm, delicious."

"You like them, yes?" asked the girl, who couldn't keep her eyes off Honoré as she explained that her mother was the best cook in the state of Oaxaca and that sometimes she got requests from as far away as Mexico City. Right now she was sick and couldn't work. "I'm helping her until she gets back on her feet."

"Let me look at those tamales," the Commander said.

Trotsky turned to him. "I wouldn't advise it, sir. I'm used to eating in the street, but you may not be."

"Looking never hurt."

After examining a tamale wrapped in thick brown greasy leaves, the Commander returned it. "What else do you have?"

She took out a plastic bag full of ping pong balls. "Turtle eggs."

"Turtle eggs?" said the Commander, and he reached for one.

Trotsky spoke up, "Sir, are you sure?"

"I can eat anything. I've got a cast iron stomach."

Jorge waved the middle-aged Oaxacan woman in the serving line over. She arrived, drying her hands on her apron. "Yes, sir?"

"Doña Petra, would it be too much to ask you to cook some eggs for our guests?" said Jorge.

After casting an ugly glance at the girl, the woman addressed the Commander gravely, "Welcome to Zaragoza, sir. We're a proud people. And our greatest pride is hospitality. This won't take long."

The Commander smiled. "Gracias, señora. I've heard about your town's wonderful customs."

The girl handed the turtle eggs to the woman, who gave her another ugly look before walking across the hall to the kitchen. Then, as the men returned to the subject of American exploitation of Mexico, convoyers at the other tables finished their meals and trickled out of the hall. The girl stood a few feet from Honoré, watching everyone quietly, listening, waiting.

Ten minutes later, the middle-aged woman returned with the turtle eggs in a bowl, soft-boiled ping pong balls. "Here you go."

"Show us how you eat turtle eggs," said Jorge, pouring *agua de jamaica* from a pitcher into a plastic cup.

"Very simple," she said, taking an egg between her fingers and punching a hole on top with a knife, then raising it and squeezing the yolk into her mouth. After swallowing, she took a slug of *agua de jamaica*. "This should be done with tequila."

The Commander grinned. "Next time."

The woman smiled at last. "Yes, next time."

Then the Commander took an egg between his fingers and punched a hole on top with a knife, squeezed out the yolk, and chased it with a slug of *agua de jamaica*. "Give me another one."

Trotsky frowned. "Take it easy, Jack."

Suddenly, the door swung open again. The wind blew Zuckermann inside. "We found a mechanic. Drunk on his ass. But he'll do for the time being."

The Commander stood, wiping his mouth. "Señora, thank you so much. Now I can brag that I tasted Zaragoza's famous cuisine."

She bowed with a smile on her otherwise grave dark face. "Always glad to be of service."

"Si, señora," he said, smiling, and then left with Jorge.

Suddenly, goose pimples sprouted on Honoré's neck as a hand plowed through his hair, fingertips massaging his scalp, splitting his hair into tendrils of tingling that relieved the weariness of days on the road and sleepless nights on the floor or the sofa in Mexico City. The tender loving care of a woman felt so good that the buzz soon spread to where God had made him a two-legged creature.

"*¿Qué pasó, papasote?*" the girl whispered in his ear.

The woman spun around. "*!No chingues!*" she hissed. "You've taken all the men in town. Leave some for the women."

The girl withdrew her hand. Then, as if removing a Halloween mask from her face, she changed, and her voice deepened. "Doña Petra is jealous now! Look at her. Doesn't she look like an old man dressed as a woman? You should see how she treats her husband."

The woman addressed Honoré and Trotsky. "In Zaragoza we say you can tell a civilized society by how much they love their *putos*. We have a long tradition of honoring ours. They have been at our parties. But some of them, like this one, are after all the men. Others want to replace the women."

Honoré felt his face turn red. *Putos*? This lovely girl was a man? Impossible!

"Can I help it," asked the manly girl, picking up the pail and wiggling his ass like a woman as he turned away from them, "that I was born with the heart of a woman, the dick of a macho, and the asshole of a puto?"

The next morning, thunder rolled across the heavens. Inside the office serving as the convoy's headquarters, Honoré closed the door on the howling wind and joined the Commander, Molly, Trotsky, and a handful of other drivers studying a map on the desk.

"We're taking the Pacific route to Tapachula," the Commander said, running the tip of his pen along the Pan American Highway, south along the coast. "We cross the river here into Guatemala."

Suddenly, a door flew open, and the wind leaped inside and spit on their faces. "Bad news," said Zuckermann breathlessly.

The Commander looked up.

"The storm washed out the bridge in Tapachula," Zuckermann said.

"That means only one thing," said Trotsky.

"We have to turn inland," said Zuckermann.

"Yes, but once we cross into Guatemala," Trotsky said, pointing at a dark green region on the map, "we'll be in guerrilla territory. The military will think we're taking supplies to the rebels."

"Doesn't matter," said the Commander, folding the map. "They'll think that regardless of the route we take." The wind slammed the building, and he looked at the ceiling. "We better get moving."

Long silver needles struck the courtyard as everyone trekked outside the office. The Commander, Molly, and Zuckermann walked ahead, joining members of the convoy and Jorge at the entrance to Casa de la Cultura. Amid much laughter and happy faces, everyone exchanged farewells, Jorge kissing Molly on the cheek, Honoré shaking Jorge's hand.

When thunder exploded, the Commander yelled, "Mount up, people!" Everyone ran.

Trotsky rolled down his window and waved at the well-wishers standing in the entrance to Casa de la Cultura while Honoré started the truck. After creeping through a gray sheet of water, they turned at the corner. Three long city blocks later, they reached the outskirts and headed out of town. Visibility was so poor Honoré drove slowly on the highway. Finally, they reached Zanapetec, south of which he turned east. Then the convoy headed toward the mountains, where the cactus came out of hiding as the rain-filled galleons in the sky moved north.

About noon the skies grew bright and clear, and an hour later they were rolling through the green hills around Tuxtla Gutierrez, the capital of Chiapas, where they ate lunch and refueled. The Commander didn't eat. A gas attendant warned Honoré about army checkpoints on the road to San Cristobal, but said if they took the route to Comitán, they'd have no problems. Honoré told the Commander, who ordered them on to Comitán. Traveling along a valley hedged by a mountain range on their left and river on their right but no traffic for miles, they expected to reach the Guatemalan border by nightfall.

Up ahead, a flag unfurled like a bullfighter's red cape. Helmets glimmered above the olive-green fatigues of soldiers holding assault rifles. Honoré slowed down.

The soldier with the red flag approached the idling pickup. "Would you please step down?"

Honoré and Trotsky got out. Zuckermann peered at them from the bus, and the rest of the vehicles idled on the road.

"Your papers?"

Another soldier, stocky and muscle bound, evidently an officer, swaggered from behind the sandbags, the pistol in his hand sleek and oily as if the gray metal were the flesh of a lizard. He stopped a few feet in front of Honoré and took a handful of silver bullets from his pants pocket. "Do we know each other?" asked the officer, casually.

Honoré watched the barrel, which occasionally pointed at him like a gray finger with a tiny mouth at its end. He had the strange sensation that he was looking at a man about to perform an intimate act, like copulation or summary execution, in public. "No, sir."

The soldier with the red flag kept his eyes on the road behind them. "Sir, a car is headed this way."

The officer studied Honoré. "You look familiar." Then he asked the soldier, "Doesn't he look familiar?"

The soldier eyed Honoré. "Like a famous Mexican actor."

The officer closed the chamber in his gun. "Or someone the police are looking for."

An engine brayed in the distance, tires squealing. "Sir," the soldier said again.

The officer stuffed the pistol in its holster and then looked up the road coolly at the car hurtling toward them. "On your feet, men! Let's give these idiots a Mexican greeting!"

Two soldiers ran into the middle of the road and fired warning shots into the sky. The car bore down on them, so the soldiers knelt and aimed. The members of the convoy ducked behind the trucks.

"What the hell?" muttered Trotsky.

The stench of burning rubber jammed the air as the car skidded to a stop a few feet from Honoré and Trotsky, powerful engine rumbling, silver wheels sparkling on brand-new tires, dark and thick as oil, windows tinted, throbbing with rock and roll music inside.

"Put down those fucking guns!" the officer yelled at the soldiers as he walked around to the driver's side of the car. "You should know better, *compadre*," said the officer to the driver behind the dark windows, "than to be speeding down these country roads. What if you hit a cow or horse? And what the hell are you doing this far south? Last I heard you were in Texas."

Honoré couldn't see the driver from where he stood, but he smelled the shit-like stink of pot amid the blast of rock and roll. The driver said something.

The officer grinned.

Then a window on Honoré's side of the car slid down a few inches. Like loud obnoxious crows soaring out of a thick cloud of pot smoke, the sound of "Born to be Wild" roared through the window. A fist sprouting one finger appeared, a fat brown oil-stained middle finger. Suddenly, a blond head popped up, with dazed blue eyes, then disappeared, giggling, behind the rolled-up window.

Honoré thought that finger looked awfully familiar.

Abruptly, the officer yelled. "Clear the way! This car has diplomatic immunity." He slammed the roof with his hand. "Get the fuck out of here, *compadre*, before we all end up in *el calabozo*!"

The tires screamed, and the car shot down the road.

"Fucking Tequila," Honoré said.

Trotsky raised his eyebrows. "Shhhh."

"What?" barked the officer, marching toward Honoré.

"Nothing, sir," said Honoré.

The officer halted a few feet in front of Honoré and Trotsky—eyes suspicious and mischievous as ever—before yelling, "All right, men. I want a thorough search of these vehicles. Check everyone's papers. These guys look like subversives."

An hour later, the soldiers waved them through the checkpoint and south toward the border. The road ran parallel to a mountain range on their left. Had Sugar joined forces with the *narcotraficantes*? wondered Honoré. Was she hatching a new plot to stop the convoy or discredit it in the eyes of the international press? What about the bus they almost lost north of Oaxaca? Did she sabotage the brakes? Despite Trotsky's suspicions, Honoré remained unconvinced she was a CIA asset. Too stupid. Crazy. Or had Tequila simply abandoned the convoy and gone back into the business with his newfound associates in Acapulco? And where were Johnny Paint and Tennessee?

"Slow down," said Trotsky as they sped past a thicket of cacti on the side of the road and toward a sharp curve. "There's a fork up ahead, and I don't see any signs. Let's ask him." He pointed to a man near the road.

Honoré pulled onto the shoulder before a gaunt dark-skinned campesino standing in front of a wooden shack. His limbs seemed to have been cut from mesquite.

"Which road goes to Comitán?" Trotsky asked the old man.

"Both."

"Which is the better road?"

The man removed the straw hat and scratched his head. "Neither."

"Which one should we take?"

A smile brightened his face. "Either. One is just as bad as the other."

Thirty minutes later, they were climbing the foothills, winding through curve after curve until the temperature dropped and Honoré's ears popped. A black-haired woman with a shawl about her shoulders stood by the side of the road, holding a small boy's hand. Sunlight glowed on the tile roofs as they sped down the main street of a small town. Then the road dipped and curved and rose and dipped again. They passed through another town. About an hour later, they arrived at an intersection with the highway from Comitán to Guatemala. Honoré pulled into a Pemex station on the corner.

While Trotsky walked toward the Commander's bus, Honoré, standing on oil-stained cement, watched a wiry boy with dusty black hair and a lizard's round eyes remove the cap from the gas tank. "Did a black car come through here?" Honoré asked him.

"Yes," said the boy as he inserted the pump's nozzle.

"Which way did they go?"

"South."

"Did you see the people inside the car?"

"No, not really." He smiled. "Only *la rubia superior*."

The gasoline smelled like an octane-enriched fart. "*¿Cómo qué 'la rubia superior'?*"

"*Pues una gringa*," said the boy, a wad of pesos in his hand and white teeth on his eager face. "What a doll! As soon as I save enough money, I'm headed to the United States. I'm going to get my hands on a gringa if it's the last thing I do. Gringas are the most beautiful things God created on this earth."

As soon as the vehicles were refueled and everyone used the restroom, they headed south on a narrow highway. An hour later, they arrived at another fork in the road, where one signpost directed them toward Tapachula, several hundred miles to the south, while the other one pointed east toward La Mesilla, a short distance. Honoré turned east.

"That's Guatemala up ahead," said Trotsky, as they plunged into the green vegetation.

The mountains, round and surly as the rumps of big bears dozing back to back, lay in a mist seething with sun-lit quicksilver that chilled Honoré. Even though Mexico was dangerous, it was familiar. But he had never been to Guatemala and had heard about it from refugees crossing the border into Texas. Nothing but horror stories about the Guatemalan army.

Dark gray galleons in the sky threatened to unleash a barrage of water as they followed the winding road. After cruising past a sign that said, "Ciudad Cuauhtemoc," Honoré slowed down. At a checkpoint in the left lane for travelers coming from Guatemala, Mexican soldiers stared at the convoy as it lumbered past. A few yards down the road stood a small building with large glass windows above which hung a sign that said, "*Aduana.*"

"I thought Ciudad Cuauhtemoc was a city," said Honoré. "It's not even a village. It's just customs. How far to the border?"

"Two or three miles."

The road plunged into vegetation screaming so loudly with birds that it felt like a jungle. Sharp curves slowed them down. Then as Honoré passed a garbage dump, the view opened on ramshackle buildings pushing against each other while clinging to the edge of a shallow ravine—tin roofs on raw cement blocks, windows without screens or glass panes, and dark girls staring from doorways. The pavement turned to dirt, and the pickup shuddered as the tires splashed through water-filled potholes.

"La Mesilla," muttered Trotsky.

Honoré pulled to the side of the dirt road and stopped. Behind him, the rest of the convoy did the same.

Everyone gathered around the Commander's bus. He looked weak and tipped his head like someone trying to get water out of his ear.

He straightened up. "We cross early in the morning, about two or three. So get your papers ready. Get rid of all political literature. If they find a flyer or a book they think is subversive, they'll confiscate everything, and that'll be the end of it. That includes the Bible. Stay close when they go through your things. Make sure they don't plant anything on us."

Shadows ran across the road and hid behind old cars squatting among weeds where the sun's orange afterglow ebbed. Unlike the border between Texas and Mexico, there was no border patrol or immigration officials or dogs or helicopters or cameras everywhere you turned. A crossing gate equipped with a black and white arm and a counter weight separated Mexico from Guatemala. But as Honoré looked at the mountains, dark green with thousands of trees under a blood-streaked sky, it was difficult to tell where one country ended and the other began.

Honoré didn't believe in ghosts. Yet he could not shake the suspicion that, among the flashlights bobbing in the hands of the rifle-toting teenagers in fatigues, a lot more was going on around him than he could see at three in the morning. Across the border in La Mesilla, buildings stood in shadows and laughter echoed while a cumbia throbbed from a cantina somewhere. Suddenly, a lightning bolt flashed across the sky. A loud clap followed, then several seconds of thunder. Honoré, whose passport was already stamped, stood by the pickup and waited for Trotsky, who, along with the Commander and Zuckermann, was still clearing Guatemalan customs.

A soldier appeared. With a helmet much too big for his slender five-foot frame, he looked too young—about fifteen or sixteen—to be carrying an assault rifle strapped to his shoulder. "We're almost done checking the vehicles, *jefe*," he warbled in Spanish like a tropical bird.

He reminded Honoré of a Guatemalan refugee he had helped cross the Texas-Mexico border about a year ago.

" 'Guatemala,' which means 'land of trees,' " the refugee had said, "is a land of ghosts." In the highlands, he explained, entire villages had been destroyed, families murdered and buried in common graves, priests killed, nuns raped. Rats were stuffed in women's vaginas while captured guerrillas were stripped naked and then hung from trees into pools of lime until their skin peeled off. A Mayan woman, an activist who had protested human rights violations for years, had been tortured, raped, and shot. After dismembering her body, the soldiers buried her remains under a tree and pissed on them. Were these ghosts or spirits now inhabiting the lightning-skewered night? Or was it all in Honoré's imagination?

A drop of rain struck his cheek as another soldier, short and sturdy, approached. "*¿Ya mero, Tito?*" the man barked.

Tito's voice was sweet as a girl's. "*Ya mero, Sargento.*"

A cocked red beret on his head, stripes on his sleeve, and a pistol in a holster on his hip, the sergeant reeked of booze. His eyes were wild and bloodshot, cheeks drenched in sweat. "Looks like they emptied the insane asylums in California. Any commie propaganda?"

"No, *jefe*."

"Not even a Bible?"

"No, *jefe*."

"You and your buddies will escort these gringos to Guatemala City. You're in charge. You hear?"

"Yes, *jefe*."

"Take the jeep. And if you run into that bastard Ladino," he growled, "tell him he hasn't paid me. I risked my life, the lives of my men, for that pimp. If it weren't for me, he wouldn't be where he is today."

"He's crazy, *jefe*. He won't listen to me."

The sergeant lowered his voice. "Look, just find out where he lives in Guate."

The boy's helmet wobbled. "Yes, sir."

Then it began to sprinkle. "Now get the hell of here!" yelled the sergeant.

Fistfuls of water pounded the roof. Squealing and moaning, the windshield wipers flapped back and forth. Ahead, Tito's jeep cut a swath through the downpour while Honoré followed at a safe distance, the glare of his headlights polishing the long slender silver reeds of water striking the pavement. In the sweep of the lights, ferns and shrubs swayed like spirits on the side of the Carretera Interamericana, which would take them through the highlands, past Huehuetenango, then Quetzaltenango, and on to Guatemala City.

"How far to Guate?" asked Honoré.

Trotsky glanced at him. "About 160 kilometers."

The red glow of the jeep's tail-lights electrified the water streaming across Honoré's windshield as Tito braked occasionally on a steep grade, so Honoré slowed down. After they crept through several dangerous and nerve-wracking curves, the road evened out, and Honoré relaxed a little. He thought about Maruca and Bonita. His mother. He even thought about his cousins, those buffoons, and smiled. He couldn't believe he missed them. Or Escandón. Several miles later, the rain stopped abruptly. When the two men rolled down their windows, the crying and hooting of animals, the bristling of limbs, and the dripping of water filled the night. A string of lights poured into the side mirror as the convoy rumbled through the dark. The moon, magnificent as a silver coin, glittered on the wet asphalt.

"Fresh air!" said Trotsky.

Honoré checked his watch. "The sun should be up in an hour or so."

"This looks like 'Nam," said Trotsky at last, his voice thick, black eye patch lit by the dashboard's glow. "Sometimes the VC came out of nowhere, invisible. Then, an AK-47 and a flash of light." He shuddered. "The next day, sunlight. A beautiful country. And the stench of bodies, the buzz of flies. The smell of war is the smell of shit." He paused. "When I got wounded, the gringos thought I was a gook in an American uniform and left me for dead." He stared out the window and laughed. "Until a Chicano spotted me."

As they rode quietly for several miles, Honoré thought about Tequila and how, along with the Governor, they had been involved in a lot of shit themselves. In fact, Honoré was lucky to be alive, but none of their experiences compared with what Trotsky suffered in Vietnam.

When the first hint of light appeared in the east, Trotsky asked, "Can you feel it?"

"What?"

"The eeriness."

In the faint light, the mist unraveled. "I felt something ever since La Mesilla."

"The ghost of Alvarado."

"Who?"

"Pedro de Alvarado, the Spanish conquistador."

Though Honoré's mother had always reminded him that he was a Spaniard, not an Indian, he never understood what it meant to be "Spanish," only that he had light skin and was tall for a Mexican. He had heard about them all his life, but they lived in a faraway country. God knows who they were or why it was important to be like them.

"If he were alive today," Trotsky said, "he'd be on the cover of *Gentleman's Quarterly*."

"Why?"

"He was handsome, athletic. The Indians called him 'tonatiuh'—'the sun'—because he was blond," said Trotsky. "After the fall of Tenochtitlán, Cortez sent him to conquer Guatemala. Like Cortez in Mexico, he turned the Indians against each other and defeated them in Quetzaltenango. Then, he enslaved the population, and for five hundred years Guatemala has been a chamber of horrors."

The light grew.

Up ahead, a lone figure—a shapely young woman, wearing a black skirt and bright red shawl around her shoulders and holding a bundle on her head—walked barefoot along the highway. She reminded him of Sixto's Morenita. And women like her throughout Mexico. Brown, silent, mysterious. He even thought of Maruca, who was dark like them. Soon daggers of sunshine cut the mist into loaves of white bread steaming among hills dense with trees. Carrying a machete, a man walked along the edge of the highway in rubber boots while the woman followed him. Honoré could not imagine where they were headed out here in the middle of nowhere, but they were going somewhere, maybe a nearby village.

"When I came to Guatemala looking for the hippie commune," Trotsky said, "I wandered into a monastery. Inside I stopped before a stone monument. The names of three people were inscribed on it: Pedro de Alvarado. His wife. And Bernal Díaz del Castillo, who wrote *The Conquest of New Spain*. Nearby, a set of stairs took me underground to a small cellar-like room, where dozens of candles crackled on a wooden slab covered with wax. A Mayan altar. I stood there dumbfounded."

"Why?"

Trotsky hesitated. "Because the spirit of these people is still alive."

Patches of blue sky appeared as the sun prowled among the green hills. The road swerved to the right, then dipped, turned to the left, and dipped again. As they swung around a curve and plunged between two steep wooded slopes, spectacular cliffs rose on both sides of the road.

"Guatemala is beautiful," said Trotsky, "but it's a beauty that hurts."

Cars, trucks, and buses stood in a line along the highway while men, women, and children sat, stood, talked, or played under the pine trees as if they were on a picnic and expected to be there the rest of the morning. When Tito's jeep slowed down, Honoré hit the brake, and the two vehicles rolled to a stop in the shadow of a blue bus with chickens in wire cages on the roof. Up ahead, behind a pile of sandbags, soldiers milled about a machine gun poised like a giant insect. Honoré turned off the engine.

Tito, carrying his assault rifle, jumped out of his jeep and walked up to Trotsky's window. "An alert. Guerrillas. Probably nothing. I'll see what's happening."

"How long will it be?" asked Trotsky.

"Thirty minutes," said Tito. He smiled. "Or several hours."

Trotsky opened his door. "More like hours."

The scent of pine enchanted Honoré. While Trotsky headed toward the Commander's bus, Honoré stood in the middle of the highway and absorbed the spectacle of trees in the gorgeous valley, where the voices of the men, women, and children carried like butterflies. Trotsky was right. What a beautiful country! Maruca and Bonita would love a picnic here. Who knows? Maybe one day—when the Cold War was over—he could bring

them. Then, a smell reached him. Something burning. A dirt road, about
fifty yards away, skirted the woods before connecting with the highway.
Above the woods, a column of smoke rose while a buzzard circled lazily
about. Probably nothing to worry about. Still he felt weird, like when he
first felt the presence of ghosts. Meanwhile, the veterans—with shoulder-
length hair, fat bellies, and red faces—stretched and yawned on the highway. Some soldiers with rifles strapped on their shoulders like musical
instruments marched past, talking and laughing like kids.

Outside the Commander's bus, Honoré joined Trotsky and Zuckermann. "How's he doing?" Trotsky asked.

"Not well," Zuckermann said.

"What's wrong?"

"Dizzy spells. He's dehydrated. Those turtle eggs may have gotten to
him."

"But he was okay when we left Zaragosa."

"Who knows? It could be a virus. Maybe the water."

"Has he been taking his medication?"

"I hope so, but you know how stubborn he can be. He needs to see a
doctor soon."

Trotsky looked down the length of the convoy. "Where's Tito? Maybe
he'll get us past this checkpoint."

Suddenly, the bus creaked, shuddered. The Commander—pale, unshav-
en, hair loose, a wild look in his eyes—appeared on the steps of the bus.
"Incoming! Incoming! Gooks everywhere!"

"What's the matter, Jack?" yelled Zuckermann.

Then Jack clambered down. "Get the men out of here!" he screamed,
pushing Honoré aside and staggering toward the dirt road. "We're under
attack!"

Inside the bus, Molly shouted, "Stop him! He's gone crazy!" She scam-
pered down the steps.

When she leaped to the ground, Zuckermann grabbed her by the arm.
"Stay here! We'll get him!"

"Jack! Jack!" shouted Trotsky, running after him. "Where you going?"

Honoré yelled at Zuckermann. "Stay with her!"

Midway to the road, Trotsky caught up with the Commander and
jerked his arm. Halting, the Commander turned and pushed Trotsky away.
When Trotsky grabbed his arm again, the Commander punched him in the
chest and knocked him down. Moments later, the Commander was gone,
running across the road and disappearing into the woods.

As soon as Honoré reached Trotsky, he pulled him to his feet. "You okay?"

"Yes. C'mon!"

Trotsky and Honoré stopped at the edge of the woods. The smell of burning garbage lingered in the pine-scented air.

"Jack!" yelled Trotsky.

Nothing.

A narrow path led into the dark pine. Ten minutes later, Trotsky stopped. "Jack!"

A bird screamed.

Honoré stood before a vine thick as a sewer pipe as he peered at the undergrowth. "He couldn't have gotten far."

"Shhhh! Listen!"

Wings fluttered. A dog barked. High in the trees, birds shrieked. Voices floated up from the highway. After three long minutes, Trotsky pushed through the dense undergrowth again and found a path lit by beams of sunlight.

Then, something stopped Honoré in his tracks. "Oh, God!"

Trotsky sniffed the air. "Smells like something dead."

Honoré crawled under vines, halted when a snake slithered toward him. But it wasn't a snake, just a lizard with a long pointed tail scampering into the shadows. Honoré stood up.

The smell grew worse.

Several yards away, they stumbled upon a ravine, where buzzards flew in and out of the gray murk of smoke rising from a garbage dump below. But Honoré still could not tell where the ugly smell was coming from until he saw a pair of buttocks in a small clearing. A body, a white body, pants down to its knees, shirt flung back across its shoulders, face flat on the ground.

Trotsky ran. "Jack?" He rolled him on his back.

The Commander blinked and groaned. "Mike?" the Commander mumbled.

"No, it's me, Trotsky."

"Mike, there's gooks everywhere."

"Jack, we're in Guatemala."

"Did I get hit?"

"No," said Trotsky. "Well, at least not by gunfire."

He stunk, worse than anything Honoré had ever smelled. Nonetheless, after hoisting his pants to his waist, Honoré grabbed one arm while Trotsky took the other, and together they pulled their friend to his feet. As they stumbled over vines and got slapped in the face by low-hanging branches, they reached the ravine again.

A blast of wings filled the air. The men halted.

Buzzards settled on the garbage, closing their huge wings as if wrapping themselves in capes, and became tiny bald-headed men in gray suits waddling on skinny leathery legs among the tires, clothes, shoes, cans, boxes, and broken bottles. Suddenly, a scrawny dog with yellow eyes and a long pink tongue scrambled onto the trash. In an explosion of feathers, the buzzards scattered. Then the dog pushed his nose in the rubble and froze as Honoré watched closely. The dog jerked something out of the trash with its teeth. It looked like a gray lizard or a frog hanging from its mouth. But no, it was a human hand.

At first it sounded like target practice. But when Honoré saw people running and ducking, diving, and cowering among the vehicles while smoke rose amid the crackle of machine gun fire, he knew this was no target practice. In fact, the gunfire was so loud and overwhelming and frightening he forgot how badly the Commander stunk.

"What the hell is happening?" Trotsky growled.

Puffs of smoke rose from the highway and trees near the machine gun nest. "The guerrillas are attacking," Honoré said.

As they lurched forward with the Commander, he stumbled and dropped to his knees, but they hoisted him up and pulled him along, his boots dragging in the dirt. They scrambled across the highway and took cover behind the Commander's bus, where Molly and Zuckermann huddled on the ground as bullets whizzed overhead. Behind them, the convoyers crawled under their vehicles. Bullets hit doors and fenders with stone-like thuds, windows exploded, and glass tinkled. An officer yelled a command, and the soldiers opened up with machine gun fire.

"Stay here. I'll go look for Tito," Honoré said to Trotsky.

Keeping low, he inched toward the deafening explosions. In the middle of the highway, he crouched behind the bullet-riddled flat tires of Tito's jeep. Three boys in uniform lay asleep on the pavement, side by side, their rifles in their hands, their olive-green uniforms neatly pressed, new boots catching slivers of sunlight.

"Fuck!" muttered Honoré.

But there was no blood or wounds that Honoré could see, and he couldn't tell if one was Tito because they all looked alike. Suddenly, machine gun fire punched three holes in the side of the jeep inches from his face, and a fourth shot ricocheted next to one of the boy's heads, spewing chunks of asphalt on his cheek. An eerie stillness cloaked them.

They were dead.

The shooting ceased abruptly. Then, around the front of the jeep, Tito scrambled with two friends, who gripped rifles reeking of gunpowder.

"I thought you were dead!" said Honoré.

"No," Tito said and crossed himself, breathing hard. "By the grace of God, I'm still here, but we better go before He changes His mind." He turned to his companions. "We're taking the back road. Get everyone in the vehicles. Turn those buses around. We're leaving the jeep behind. I'm riding with this man up front. You bring up the rear vehicle. Now go!"

"Yes, sir," said one of the soldiers, and they ran along the trucks and buses, barking. "In the vehicles! Everyone! Let's go!"

Honoré and Tito darted to the bus, where Zuckermann and Molly pulled a delirious, mumbling Commander toward the door.

"Anybody hit?" Honoré asked.

Molly looked frantic as she struggled with the Commander. "No. We're okay."

"Okay, let's get moving!" said Zuckermann as he followed them inside the bus. He climbed into the driver's seat, closed the door with a lever, and fired up the engine.

"Where's Trotsky?" asked Honoré.

"He's coming," Tito said.

Honoré ran to his pickup, which, thank God, had no flat tires. However, the windshield on the driver's side was cracked so badly it was impossible to see through the dense spider web, so Tito, standing beside the truck, knocked out the glass with the butt of his rifle before he joined his men in the middle of the two-lane highway and helped the drivers turn the buses around.

When Tito returned, out of breath, he and Trotsky climbed in the pickup, but no sooner had Honoré started the engine than explosions sent bullets flying overhead. The thumping of the machine gun filled the air with the smell of gunpowder. Honoré spun the truck around and headed to where the highway intersected the dirt road.

In the rearview mirror, the Commander's bus and the rest of the convoy bounced and rattled in tandem. After passing beneath the column of smoke, Honoré hurtled over a hill, wind blowing hard in his face through the empty windshield. The gunfire sounded familiar, like firecrackers on the Fourth of July, but he knew better. This was deadly stuff. He negotiated curve after curve, refusing to slow down until the gunfire subsided. When it was a faint echo, he eased off the gas and pulled to the side of the road.

"Okay," said Trotsky as they climbed out of the pickup. "Let's check out the damage."

Tito took off running. Honoré followed Trotsky, who stopped outside the Commander's bus as Zuckermann clambered down the steps.

"How's the Commander?" asked Trotsky.

"Not well," said Zuckermann. "He needs a doctor. Soon."

"Or a priest."

"The pastor will do."

"Speaking of the pastor," Honoré said and pointed at the van behind the Commander's bus, "look at that."

Clasping the gold crucifix on his chest, the pastor kneeled next to the van's front left tire as he mumbled a prayer with eyes closed. He did not seem to be hurt as Honoré approached him, but there was no telling.

So Honoré squatted before him. "Sir, are you okay?"

The pastor opened huge bloodshot eyes. "Look at this, son." He held up the cross. It had a dent in it. Then he opened his shirt. "Tell me if that is not a sign from God!"

The man was so black it was difficult to tell, but when Honoré looked closely there was no mistake the crucifix had stopped the bullet and left a bruise in the shape of a cross on his chest.

"Ahhhhh!" yelled a man several vehicles down the highway.

"Sounds like someone needs help," said Zuckermann and then ran. Trotsky and Honoré followed close behind.

Teeth chattering, hands trembling, a vet lay beneath his pickup where apparently he had taken cover. "Medic! Medic! I've been hit!"

"We'll take care of him," Trotsky said to Zuckermann as he and Honoré helped the man crawl from under the pickup.

"Okay," said Zuckermann and departed.

All of a sudden, two other veterans, grizzly, in white T-shirts and fatigues, showed up. "Someone get hit?" asked one of them.

"No, no," said Trotsky. "Just a little battle fatigue."

"Beg to differ, sir," said the vet as he pointed to blood on the ground. "This guy got shot in the ass."

The other vet interjected, "We'll take care of him. A butt plug'll stop the bleeding."

"Fuck you!" screamed the wounded man. "Give me some morphine, asshole!"

Suddenly, a woman, a few vehicles down the convoy, boomed through the shot-out window in her bus. "Why'd we take this route?"

"Right through guerrilla territory?" the husband added.

Honoré exchanged glances with Trotsky, who shouted, "The bridge in Tapachula is washed out!"

"We should have stayed in Zaragoza," she said loudly. "Plenty of support there. We could have waited until they fixed the bridge."

"Ma'am," Trotsky said soothingly, "the Commander's done the best he can."

Soon Zuckermann returned with a report. "Sprained ankles. Road burn. Three broken fingers from getting slammed in a door. An ear shot off. A woman's breast burned on a hot muffler when she took cover under a bus. Some elderly folks scared shitless. Not only are they blithering idiots, but their blood pressure is out of control. Tires and a gas tank punctured. Plenty of bullet holes. A bunch of shot-out windows. It'll be rough at night, with mosquitoes and all. And some people are threatening to turn back. We may have a mutiny on our hands."

Nothing could be done about the shot-out windows, but they could replace the flat tires with spares. An hour later, the convoy was back on the road.

Tito, who claimed to know this part of the country like the palm of his hand, explained that this roundabout route would eventually get them back to the main highway safely. "The guerrillas got a lot of support from the villages, but the army has done good in the last year. We made the highway safe."

"Until today," added Trotsky.

"Yes, until today, but that's just the way it is. You never know what's going to happen. Those guys that got hit were from my village. I know their families. Now I'm going to have to tell them what happened."

"So how'd you get dragged into this?" Honoré asked.

The helmet cast a shadow on the boy's face. "I joined. My father cried when I told him, but it was the only way to help him with my brothers and sisters. We are many in my family—and poor. Besides, I wanted to defend my country from the communists. But it's been hard. The discipline is very strict. It's for our own good. Most of the commanders are good people. They treat the soldiers with respect. They don't make us do crazy things. But others treat us bad. Like this Ladino."

"Who?" Trotsky asked.

"He's weird, looks weird. His mother was Mayan, his father a Spaniard. You can see it in his face and on his chest."

"What do you mean?"

"There's a line down the middle of his body. Really weird. He's half brown and half white."

"Sounds like a chimera," said Trotsky.

"A what?" asked Honoré.

"A chimera. Somebody with two sets of DNA. If he was born with male and female genes, he might have male and female equipment." Trotsky looked at Tito. "Does he?"

The boy shook his head. "I don't know. I don't want to know. He's nuts. He was a very good soldier. Very loyal. So the Americans sent him to train in a special school—I forget the name—in the United States."

"The School of the Americas?"

The boy gripped the rifle barrel. "Maybe. Anyway, after he came back, he thought he was a gringo. Couldn't eat our food anymore. Wanted to eat steak and mashed potatoes, hamburgers and French fries, but he had to eat what we ate. Beans, squash, tortillas. He still thought he was better than us. Marched us for days without stopping. Wouldn't feed us. I'm very proud we protect our country, but this guy is crazy. Everyone says so. Especially his victims."

Wind filled the cab of the pickup as it plunged past pine trees. Soon the ravine opened into a valley. Eventually, the convoy limped into a village of whitewashed houses with red tile roofs surrounded by volcanoes dark and hostile as bulls on their haunches. Women in black dresses and red shawls and with bundles on their heads walked along the streets. A church appeared at the end of the plaza, where children kicked a ball. Two blocks later, they turned up another street between walls smeared with slogans: *"¡No a la discriminación! ¡Justicia a los asesinos!"*

The gun barrel weaved in Tito's hand as he peered through the empty windshield. "El Pueblo de los Brujos," he said. "That's what we call it, but its real name is El Pueblo de Burgos. Slow down. There's an empty lot down the street. An old building fell down during an earthquake. They haven't cleared the rubble, but it's okay."

"Is there a doctor here?" asked Trotsky.

"Yes," said Tito. "A good one. He helped me and my friends. Helps everybody. The guerrillas, too, unfortunately. That will get him killed one day."

Honoré parked on a cobblestone street. Then he joined Trotsky and Tito on the sidewalk and watched the vehicles rumble into the empty lot and park among piles of rubble covering what remained of a terra cotta floor.

At the far end stood a wall with a window that framed a volcano in the distance.

Honoré looked at Trotsky. "What's next?"

"First things first," Trotsky said. "Let's get everyone to the doctor. We'll take the Commander and the wounded vet in the van. The rest can come in the pickups."

Tito wiped his forehead with the back of his hand. "The clinic is not far."

From the moment everyone crowded into the clinic, the screech and screams of birds pierced the open window while the jungle's wet breath delivered fat mosquitoes that had everyone slapping their arms and grumbling. While Tito and his men remained outside, Trotsky, frustrated that the doctor was taking so long to get there, paced up and down. According to the nurse, he left the night before to some village on an emergency call but should return soon. Across the room the Commander—pale, feverish, and delirious—swayed in a rickety metal chair, but Molly and Zuckermann, who stood guard at his side, kept him from collapsing. In an adjacent room, the nurses attended to the vet shot in the butt. Honoré stood near the front entrance to the waiting room, intrigued by the zigzags on a wall.

A woman limped past and sat down in a chair next to the veteran with the missing ear. "I'm ready to go home," she said.

"Well, let's see if we get out of this alive," he said.

Another woman said, "What I'd give for a nice hot shower back home."

"I miss my dog," said the first woman.

"Where the hell is that doctor?" grumbled the veteran, standing up and pacing back and forth before the zigzag-covered wall. Then he sat down.

As Trotsky joined him, Honoré said, "Look at those cracks."

Trotsky examined the wall. "Ever been in an earthquake?"

"No."

"Feels weird. Reality moves. Then, it cracks, and everything around you comes crashing down."

Molly approached. "It's been more than two hours since we arrived."

Suddenly, in the next room, a door opened and slammed shut. Then footsteps. "What?" yelled a man in a frightening voice. "Gringos? My hands are full with women dying in childbirth, children starving, men crippled by bullets and machetes—and they bring me gringos? What do they think this is, a resort town? Why didn't they take them to Quetzaltenango?"

The gray-haired women and some of the vets exchanged worried looks.

Suddenly, a small man in his late forties stood at a back door, two nurses behind him. With gold-rimmed glasses on a grim face and closely cropped black hair, he could have passed for a Japanese or Chinese general, but Honoré assumed that like the nurses he was Guatemalan.

The doctor raised an eyebrow. "Hippies."

Honoré's blood began to boil.

"Americans, yes?" he said to everyone. "Sorry to be late. We're short on staff." Then he added, "We'll do what we can."

"Thank you, doctor," a woman said.

The doctor stopped before a fat gringo in a chair and examined a flesh wound in an arm that looked like a woman's freckled thigh. He looked at the woman with broken fingers and said something; she smiled. A man handed the doctor his ear, which he checked carefully. Shaking his head, he gave it back to the man, who threw it in a trash can and stormed out. Another woman pulled up her skirt, and the doctor gazed at a white leg that looked as if it been smeared with lipstick but had, in fact, been scraped by a bullet.

At length, he spoke to the nurses. "Let's clean these wounds."

Standing before the Commander, now slumped in his chair, he said to Zuckermann, "Take this man into the examination room."

Zuckermann signaled Honoré and Trotsky.

The smell of shit and sweat and urine and unwashed genitals was so bad that Honoré wanted to puke as he and Trotsky helped Zuckermann carry the Commander to a table in a room down the hall—actually, a maternity stretcher with stirrups and leather straps and manacles. On the floor the nozzle of a water hose stuck out from the crack in the restroom door. Several medical instruments lay on a counter top with a washbasin next to a gray metal cabinet heavy with boxes of medication.

The doctor sniffed the air. "Would someone give this man a bath?"

"Like now?" asked Molly.

The doctor glared at her. "Yes, like now."

"Doctor, is this necessary?" Zuckermann asked.

The doctor raised an eyebrow. "Do you want me to attend to this man or not?"

"Yes, of course."

"Then take off his clothes. Oh—and strap him down."

Zuckermann balked. "Like a woman?"

"Is he going to have baby?"

"No," said Zuckermann.

"The last time I had to deal with a crazy gringo, he attacked my nurses. I won't take any risks. We're understaffed as it is."

Honoré stepped out of the way and let Zuckermann and Trotsky do the honors. Long white legs stretched the length of the table and a sturdy chest with scars from knives or bullets rose and fell as they tied him down. Tufts of hair stuck out from the armpits, and a thicket of hair sprouted around a pair of low-hanging pink balls. His dick was surprisingly small.

The nurse picked up the water hose from the floor. Then the doctor grabbed it, and she turned it on, full blast.

As the doctor hosed the gringo down like a horse, the Commander shuddered and heaved. "What the hell?" he bellowed, struggling to break loose from the straps around his chest. "Molly! Zuckermann! What's this asshole doing?"

The hosing stopped as quickly as it started. Though shivering like an idling old pickup, the Commander was lucid now, eyes wide open. The nurse left and returned with some frayed towels and a flimsy torn gown. After Zuckermann and Trotsky unstrapped him, Molly dried him and then helped him into the gown.

The doctor sniffed the air again. "All right, now we can talk," he said to Molly and Zuckermann. "How can I help you?"

Zuckermann stood next to the Commander. "He's been having fainting spells. Diarrhea. Night sweats. Talking out of his head. Can't sit up for any length of time. We're afraid he won't make it to Guatemala City. Or back home."

The doctor took a wooden tongue depressor from the cabinet. "Sit him up."

After Trotsky and Zuckermann helped the Commander up, the doctor stood before the blue-eyed giant. "Open your mouth and stick out your tongue," he said.

He inserted the depressor.

After checking the back of the throat, he stuck a thermometer between the Commander's teeth. Putting two fingers on the gringo's wrist, the doctor kept an eye on his watch and checked his pulse. Then he pulled a stethoscope from a jacket pocket and listened to the heart and lungs. Once done, he took out another instrument, an ophthalmoscope, and peered at the Commander's bloodshot eyes. "Well, at least you're not having a stroke."

After removing the thermometer, he took an auriscope from his other pocket, turned on its light, and checked one ear and then the other. "Hm-mmm. How strange. I haven't seen anything like this in years."

"What is it, doctor?" asked Molly.

"You spend a lot of time outdoors?"

Water glistened on the Commander's face. "No more than usual."

"Where have you lived?"

"Minnesota, Tennessee. . . ."

"How about Vietnam?" said Molly. "He spent two years in Vietnam."

"Infantry?" the doctor asked.

The Commander nodded.

"Contract any disease there?"

"Nothing major."

"Bullshit!" erupted Molly. "He almost died. I should know. I've been his nursemaid for years. What did you see, doctor?"

The doctor ignored her. "I assume you're never been diagnosed with cancer?"

"No," the Commander replied.

"Cancer of the ear?" asked Molly, thunderstruck. "Is that why he's been getting dizzy?"

"No, of course not!" The doctor paused thoughtfully. "We can rule out cancer, but there's always the possibility of a gastrointestinal infection."

"What about the ear?" she insisted.

The doctor turned to the Commander. "Lie down."

The Commander reclined on the maternity stretcher, his toenails dry, long and yellow. His feet smelled.

"Now face your friends, sir. Yes, that way. Thank you."

The Commander, with his butt toward the wall, gazed at Honoré, Molly, and Trotsky with the look of a frightened kid in elementary school. Behind him, the doctor slipped on a latex glove while the nurse approached with a small stick in her hand.

"Just relax," the doctor said. "This won't hurt a bit."

Then he reached behind the Commander and did something that sent shudders through the long white legs. "Ahhhhh!" yelled the Commander. "Ahhhhhh!"

The doctor peered over the Commander's shoulder. "What's the matter? You like that?"

"Hell, no!"

The doctor withdrew his hand. "Well, I can understand. On top of everything else, you have hemorrhoids. Big ones. They feel like oysters."

Honoré watched with disgust as the doctor peered at the peanut butter on his finger, which he then smeared on the stick held by the nurse. After removing the glove, he walked to restroom and washed his hands. Upon returning, he said, "Further tests will be required. You're lucky because I just received a shipment of medications and instruments from the United States. Thanks to the charity of some missionaries." He looked at the nurse. "Draw some blood." He turned to Molly and Zuckermann. "By the way, can one of you go find that man who lost his ear and tell him I need to see him? I would hate to see him get a bad infection."

"I'll go," said Zuckermann.

The doctor smiled at last. "Thank you."

As soon as the doctor and Zuckermann left the room, the nurse strapped tubing around the Commander's arm. With his back on hard metal, he turned to Trotsky with glassy eyes. "It never ends, does it?"

Trotsky stood next to him. "What never ends, sir?"

" 'Nam."

The Commander closed his eyes as the nurse stuck a needle in his arm. " 'Nam," he said. "After a while, it sounds like 'mom.' "

The nurse removed the needle and wiped his arm with gauze and left the room.

"An airplane flies out of San Diego," the Commander said, "with a bunch of good-looking boys straight out of high school." He stopped, eyes half open, swallowing hard, clearing his throat as if some food got stuck in his gullet.

Molly stood at his side, preoccupied.

"A year later," he continued with difficulty, "the plane returns with the body bags in its belly—the lucky ones." He fell silent. At length, he said with the voice of a man wanting to cry but no longer able to, "I rode with the frogs, lizards, and turtles. That's how badly burned they were."

Molly touched his arm. "Jack, it's okay."

But the Commander, whose mind was elsewhere, looked up at Trotsky, whose dark Indian-like appearance was so different from that of the tall and lanky, blond and blue-eyed gringo. "Niggers, greasers, and honkies," he said. "In 'Nam we were family. We fought together. We died together."

Trotsky rested a hand on Jack's shoulder. "I hear you, Commander. I hear you."

"Then we came back," he said. "We joined the anti-war movement to keep from going crazy."

Trotsky leaned close to him. "And that's why we're here, sir."

"Jack," said Molly, no longer whispering.

"What?"

"We're in Guatemala, not Vietnam."

"Guatemala, Vietnam—what's the difference?" And then the Commander was fast asleep, snoring like a horse.

An hour later, the doctor returned. "Good news. We've attended to everyone. Just give us another thirty minutes to take care of a few loose ends, and you'll be ready to go." He opened the cabinet and took out some small boxes of medication, which he left on the counter, and then walked to the examination table. After taking the auriscope from his pocket, he prodded the Commander.

The Commander awoke, startled. "Where are we?"

"Guatemala," said the doctor.

The Commander sat up. "What's going on?"

"Hold still," he said, standing next to the Commander. "Just double checking something."

The doctor turned on the auriscope's light and checked one ear, then the other. Moments later, he checked the first one again, mumbling, "Hmmmm. I still can't believe it. I haven't seen anything like this in a long time."

"What's up, doc?" asked the Commander.

The doctor stepped back, putting the auriscope back in his pocket. "You have the biggest army and the best doctors in the world," he said. "And they couldn't tell you what's wrong?"

"What's the matter, doctor?" asked Molly.

"There's an insect in his ear."

"Alive?" said Molly.

"No, of course not," he said. "But it's releasing toxins. It should have been removed years ago. This is the worst case of malpractice or neglect I've seen in my life." The doctor took the medications from the counter and handed them to Molly. "These will control the fever, dizziness, and diarrhea. But once he gets back to the States, he needs surgery. Guatemala City isn't far. You should fly him back to the states from there."

"Do you mean," Molly fumed, "we had to travel all the way to Guatemala to find out what's wrong with you?" She turned to the doctor. "He has a bug in his ear all right. He doesn't hear a damned thing I tell him. This man hasn't seen a doctor in years. "

The Commander touched her elbow. "Now, now, Molly."

"We need a decision," she said. "Are you going to follow the doctor's orders or not?"

The Commander let his mind clear. "We'll decide in Guatemala City."

Birds screeched and shrieked in the trees while Honoré and Trotsky stood before a red cross painted on a wall outside the clinic. Much to Honoré's surprise, the doctor didn't charge them a cent. To top it off, since the clinic had just received a shipment of up-to-date textbooks and equipment donated by hospitals in New England and delivered by Jesuits in Boston a few months before, he donated several boxes of outdated medical textbooks and used medical instruments for the people of Nicaragua.

"The guy turned out to be okay," Honoré said to Trotsky.

Members of the convoy loaded the VW van and two pickups while Tito and his men stood guard down the street. "You never know what people are really like," Trotsky said. "Beautiful women turn out to be monsters. Heroes become cowards. Criminals, Robin Hoods. Saints, assassins."

Tequila, Comino, and others came to mind. "Or just plain idiots, who'll never be anything but idiots."

After helping the Commander and the limping vet into the van, Zuckermann approached Trotsky. "The stuff donated by the doctor has taken up all the space. We have to leave some people. We'll come back for them later."

"No need to leave anyone behind," Trotsky said. "Take all of them. Honoré and I will walk back to the parking lot. It's not far."

"Are you sure?"

Honoré handed Zuckermann his keys. "Here."

"I can send for you," Zuckermann added.

Trotsky shook his head. "No. We'll walk."

Then Tito came over. "Everyone ready?"

"Yes," said Zuckermann.

"What about you, sir?" Tito said to Trotsky.

"We're walking back."

Tito glanced at his men already in the jeep. "You can ride with us. It'll be crowded, but it'll do."

"We'll be fine," insisted Trotsky. "Go ahead."

"Don't get lost. This is a dangerous neighborhood," said Tito.

Meanwhile, Zuckermann ordered everyone into the vehicles. After he climbed in the van, he took off behind Tito, followed by the two pickups; they lumbered down the cobblestone street and disappeared around a corner.

Honoré glanced at Trotsky's black patch. "Something you said in Escandón has been bothering me."

Trotsky turned toward him. "What?"

"You said this convoy to Nicaragua was the last hurrah of the American left."

Trotsky chuckled. "I was just thinking aloud when I said that. It was a moment of despair, battle fatigue if you wish. Who knows what history holds in store for us?"

Honoré hesitated. "What if we're wrong?"

"Wrong?"

"About this, about what we're doing. Revolution. Nicaragua."

Trotsky's black hair shone in orange sunlight. "Look, the Commander said it best. It never ends. After a while, 'Nam' begins to sound like 'mom.' It's never ended for me." His voice grew edgy. "History," he added slowly, gravely, in his most professorial manner, "is not Hollywood. History is ugly, absurd, surreal, stupid, comic. One day a man is your friend. The next day he's your political enemy. Sometimes everything and everyone seems wrong." He paused, his one good eye moist. "My friends died in 'Nam, but that's not the worst of what happened. So either I do this, trying to help the people of Central America, trying to make peace with my past, maybe healing one day, or I blow my brains out. The people on this convoy may be a bunch of idiots, but we're idiots trying to do the right thing, the humane thing, the noble thing."

Honoré wished he hadn't brought this up, but he had no choice. "I have no business on this convoy. I'm here mostly because I wanted to pay you back for getting me out of a bind. And because for a while I thought I could be like you. You and your friends are good people. You believe things could be better. Me—I'm like Tequila. We never believed in anything. In fact, we're ex–small-time narcotraficantes. Criminals. We're the real idiots."

"Criminals?" asked Trotsky, anger seething in his voice. "In that case, we must ask who isn't a criminal today. Smuggling drugs is nothing compared to what the masters of the universe in New York or Washington do to make it possible—and necessary—to smuggle them." Trotsky put his hand on Honoré's shoulder. "All I know is you've done very good work for us, for *la causa.*"

Honoré felt the weight of Trotsky's hand. "Yes, but I've never really believed in *la causa.* I've tried, but I'm not a revolutionary."

"That's why I want you to go to Nicaragua," said Trotsky, his brown face with its Indian-black hair, a face that might have been carved on the side of a pyramid in Guatemala. "In Nicaragua you will see the spirit of one of the most beautiful revolutions of our times. In Nicaragua you will become a true believer."

CHAPTER 18
El Caballero y El Cabrón

Cobblestones made walking difficult, so Honoré and Trotsky took it slowly as they approached the church at the foot of the hill. Children's voices rose and fell as they kicked a red ball across the plaza, scaring white pigeons into sudden flight. There wasn't a soldier in sight, and the air was fresh. Though the village was beautiful, Honoré had no desire to live here. Instead, he was surprised by how much he missed Texas—plain, arid, hot Texas—and looked forward to calling his wife and daughter when he got to Guatemala City. In a week or so, he would be back at work at his mother's curio shop, and his life would return to normal.

At the foot of the hill, the street evened out. But because the cobblestones were so bumpy, Honoré and Trotsky advanced along a narrow sidewalk skirting the plaza, where the children now ran toward a woman sitting on the church's front steps.

Suddenly, Honoré halted. "Look at this."

Trotsky stopped as well. "I can't believe it," he moaned.

A young white woman sat on the church steps while girls in orange blouses and long black skirts ran their fingers through her golden hair, the boys crouching in front of her and gazing at her bare legs.

"I don't need another headache," said Trotsky. "Take care of this."

Honoré's blood boiled. "Okay." As soon as Trotsky left, he strode across the plaza.

The boys stepped out of the way the moment they saw him while the young woman, eyes half closed, sat enjoying the girls' attention. Upon seeing him, the girls let go of the golden braids and stood quietly. Making no effort to keep her mini-skirt down, the white girl gave him an eyeful of what had enthralled the boys. The cleavage provided by her loose-fitting pink blouse reminded him of the dangerous night in Mexico City. He gave the children a few pesos and shooed them away.

As soon as they were gone, he turned to Sugar. "What are you doing here?"

In a daze, she muttered, "Waiting for Tequila." She paused, gulping. "He took off with his friends. The Mexicans."

Honoré joined her on the steps, eyes on the children as they gathered at the end of the plaza. "Where are the Savages?"

She leaned against him, her head on his shoulder, drooling. He pushed her away, gently. "Where are the Savages?" he asked again, louder.

She forced her eyes open. "Acapulco."

"And Tequila?"

Her eyes heaved in a tempest of blue. "I don't know. He said he had to take care of some shit. Some stupid deal. He didn't want me to go, said it was too dangerous. So he left me here. Said he'd be right back."

"How long ago?"

"An hour, maybe more."

She might be CIA. But Honoré could not help his instincts as a caballero from South Texas and feel pity for a lady in distress. "I can't believe he left you in this condition."

She put her hand on his knee. "What condition, honey?"

The sound of a motor carried across the plaza. Soldiers gripping assault rifles rode in the back of a truck headed up the street.

He stood, taking her by the hand. "We better get out of here."

She refused to budge. "Wait."

"What?"

"Promise me one thing."

"What?"

"That I can ride with you."

"No. You're riding in the bus with the Commander."

"Why?"

Slivers of rage ran up and down his body. "Don't fuck with me. Or Trotsky. Or his friends, do you hear? And next time I see Tequila, I'm gonna beat the shit out of him. Put on some jeans. Put on some panties. Cover those tits. We're in the middle of a war."

She grabbed his fingers with both hands. "Listen, baby. I'll do whatever you want if you spend just one night with me. You promised in Mexico City. Please, *pretty please.*"

"Get up," he said.

As Honoré plunged the pickup into the cool shade-mottled depths of a ravine, it seemed as if they were driving along the floor of a garden, passing thickets of black tree trunks, ferns lazily hanging in mid-air, and sneaky vines, until the sun unrolled sheets of light among the trees and a valley opened like a breath of fresh air blasting through the broken windshield. Several miles later, the highway curved and then plummeted into another valley. They cruised along for about an hour before spotting a line of vehicles sparkling in sunlight up ahead.

"Checkpoint," Trotsky said.

Soldiers tiny as middle-school kids, though much older, waved red flags as the convoy came up behind a stopped blue-and-white school bus with dozens of suitcases piled on top. Sandbags were stacked neatly around a machine gun manned by two teenagers in olive-green uniforms. On the left side of the highway, more soldiers guarded some prisoners standing in a row, gagged and blindfolded. One dumpy figure, his hands tied behind his back, looked alarmingly familiar.

Tito climbed out. "Don't worry," he said. "These guys are my friends. I'll be right back," he said and took off.

In the side mirror, Honoré watched members of the convoy climb out of their vehicles, including Pastor Paul, who yawned and stretched his arms in the middle of the highway. His gold cross shimmered.

Tito returned. "Ten, fifteen minutes, and we're done."

"Are you sure?" asked Trotsky.

He grinned. "Like I told you, these guys are my friends. We were in basic training together."

"Tito!" shouted a soldier from the other side of the highway.

Tito spun around, the smile suddenly gone. "Oh, brother!"

Large brooding eyes under an even brow, a black mustache on fair skin, a fine nose and mouth, a tall, powerful body—the soldier walking toward them was no teenager. In fact, he looked like a movie star. At first, Honoré thought he was looking at himself in a mirror. But, no, the man really did not look like Honoré. It was simply that beautiful people were often surprised and pleased to find each other in such an ugly world. Not only was the soldier younger than Honoré by at least ten years, but he seemed to wear a wrestler's mask under a red beret, one moment looking like a Spaniard or a gringo as he approached the pickup, and the next, looking like a Mayan as he passed in front of the truck. But it wasn't a mask. A fine line running down the middle of his face divided it in halves.

"Well, look who's here," the strange-looking soldier said. "My old buddy, Tito."

Tito came to attention and saluted him on the passenger's side of the truck. "Glad to see you, sir."

Ladino stopped outside Trotsky's window. "What the hell are you doing with these hippies?"

"Serving my country, sir." Tito saluted again.

"About time." Ladino glanced at the broken windshield. "We heard about the shootout up the road. Three guys hit. Too bad. And I see that your vehicles have been all shot up. Too bad. War is sad, very sad. But a man has to do what a man has to do. And a man must serve his country. At ease, soldier."

"Thank you, sir," Tito said. "There have been a lot of rumors. I feared you were dead or in jail."

Ladino laughed and then scoffed, "They came after me. Made all kinds of accusations, paid off some judge to arrest me, throw me in jail. But I got out. Now I'm an officer, and all my enemies are dead."

"I see."

Ladino took a white glove from his back pocket and slipped it on his right hand, slowly, as if wanting to make sure everyone saw it. "The guerrillas killed them. I never get my hands dirty." He glanced at the other convoy vehicles. "What are these hippies carrying?"

"Medical supplies mostly. Some computers and electronic parts."

"No guns?"

Tito shook his head. "No, sir."

"Are you sure?" asked Ladino, a suspicious eye on Trotsky.

"We inspected the vehicles in La Mesilla."

"Bullshit. The sergeant there was drunk on his ass with some *puta* when we called him."

"He wants to talk to you, sir."

"Oh, really?" he said with a grin. "Everyone wants to talk to me. What do they think I am—a movie star?"

"A lot of people say you look like one."

"Don't give me that shit!" Ladino grimaced. "With this half-baked face? What the hell does the sergeant want? Money?"

Suddenly, he froze as he looked at Honoré through the broken windshield, beckoning the soldiers across the highway with a wave of his white glove before he walked around to Honoré's side of the truck.

Two soldiers carrying assault rifles approached at a trot as Ladino swaggered up to Honoré. "Welcome home, Comandante," he said with surprising chumminess as he pulled a pistol from his holster. "We've been waiting for you."

Honoré looked at the .45's smiling bore. "Me?"

"Please step down," Ladino said and opened the door.

An assault rifle probed the air within inches of Honoré's nose. Another soldier slung his rifle on his shoulder and spun Honoré around, pulling his arms behind him and tying his hands with what felt like women's stockings, elastic and smooth with a fine grain.

Tito accosted Ladino. "Sir!"

"What?"

"Can we talk?"

"About what?"

Trotsky jumped out the passenger's side of the truck. "What's going on?"

Ladino confronted Honoré, Hollywood hunk to Hollywood hunk, braggadocio in his eyes. "Good trick. Trying to sneak back into the country. What do you think we are—a bunch of *pendejos*?"

Sunlight deposited streaks of gold on Trotsky's black eye patch. "What's this about? Why are you arresting him?"

Ladino barked an order at the soldiers across the highway. "Bring that prisoner over here!" He pointed at the row of blindfolded prisoners. "No, not that one! The other one! The one who smells like shit."

"Yes, sir!" they yelled.

Honoré's jaw dropped as Tequila, gagged with a woman's stocking and hands tied behind his back, was dragged across the highway.

"Do you know this asshole?" Ladino asked Honoré.

Tequila stood before them. He made a face, mumbling and grunting through the nylon.

Honoré grinned at how stupid Tequila looked. "Yes. He's our mechanic."

"That's what I thought. Where there's smoke, there's fire. The minute I saw this dipshit, I knew it would be just a matter of time before *you* showed up—and so here you are, just as I expected. Both of you."

Voices drew near. Two vets carried the Commander on a litter, followed by a worried Molly and Zuckermann. Others climbed out of their vehicles while Pastor Paul marched with the gold crucifix glimmering on his chest. Stern-faced, Tito stood nearby, waiting for an opportunity to intervene.

"What's this all about?" demanded the Commander in Spanish, propping himself up on his elbow. The Vietnam vets—vests thick with emblems and medals, arms full of tattoos—stood alongside him.

"These two men are under arrest," said Ladino, more agreeable and respectful now that he was surrounded by gringos, speaking English better than expected—and proudly.

"They're not even from here," the Commander said.

Ladino pawed the ground with the tip of his boot and shook his head. "I can't believe this," he said to Honoré. "All of Central America knows who you are, but these gringos don't?"

The Commander raised his voice. "They're Americans!"

Ladino fixed a gaze on Honoré. "Well, I see you've done it again, tricking these gringos into believing your lies. Everyone tricks the gringos, but the gringos love it because in the end they always win."

"What are you talking about?" Trotsky asked.

"Silence!" yelled Ladino.

Big black tires with teeth chomped on dirt as a military truck rolled to a stop on the shoulder, and half a dozen boys with man-eaters in their hands jumped down. One wrong move, thought Honoré, and the Americans would, in a flash of gunpowder, be turned into a smorgasbord of melted cheese, burnt toast, and cooked goose. Honoré had been in situations like this before. Playing it cool was the only way out.

"The government of Guatemala," the Commander explained in an even tone, "has guaranteed us safe passage from here to the Honduran border. All our papers are in order."

Bitterness clouded Ladino's gaze. "And you believed the government?"

"Sir," said Zuckermann.

Ladino turned. "Who are you?"

"This man's lawyer."

"A lawyer? Really?"

"Really."

"Then shut up."

A gigantic black shadow fell across the asphalt. "Sir."

"And you?"

Pastor Paul's eyes bulged in a face black and shiny as a combat boot, the gold cross on his chest shimmering. "I am the spiritual leader for this mission."

"Ahh," said Ladino, looking at him from head to toe. "You're also a big ugly nigger."

"I beg your pardon."

"Shut up!" he yelled and leveled the .45 at the gold crucifix.

Pastor Paul stood there cross-eyed as if he had just been punched in the head, his faith in God wavering. Then he withdrew, babbling or praying.

"Sir," Molly said.

"¡Otra vez! God, these gringos love to talk," muttered Ladino, as he stared at the woman confronting him. "And who are you?"

"A woman."

He grinned. "Well, that's a surprise. For a while there I thought you were an old man. If you were worth looking at, you might be worth listening to. So shut up!" He waved her away with the barrel of the .45.

As if she had just slammed against a glass ceiling, Molly stood cross-eyed, too, and then stomped away. Meanwhile, Honoré wanted to slug this swashbuckling two-faced Guatemalan freak.

"Where was I?" Ladino turned to the Commander and Trotsky. "Oh, yes—now let me tell you who these men are: criminals, guerrillas who have terrorized the people of Guatemala and Central America for years. Dangerous men. They change disguises and names, and now they've changed their accents!" A terrible past flung shadows across Ladino's divided face. "Many friends are dead because of these bastards. Veterans in the mountains of El Petén claim they cannot be killed. They survived ambushes and two executions. Worse than guerrillas, they're *brujos*!"

Zuckermann returned, easing between Trotsky and Ladino with greenbacks in his hand. "Is there any other way we can handle this?"

Ladino came within inches of the lawyer's nose. "Do you think I would sell my country for a few pieces of gold? Do you think I'm a Jew or what?"

Zuckermann turned pale. "No, señor. I just thought we could—"

"Give me that!" Ladino wrenched the money from Zuckermann. "Don't show off money in a poor country. It'll get you killed, imbecile." He turned toward the Commander. "You better go. These two stay with me."

"We're not leaving without them," said the Commander.

Ladino slipped the money in his shirt pocket. "Then I'll have to confiscate these vehicles."

"On what grounds?" asked Zuckermann.

"Smuggling terrorists into Guatemala."

Trotsky glared at Ladino. "This man has a family and a business in Escandón, Texas. His wife and daughter depend on him. His mother is old and dying. And this one"—he pointed at Tequila—"is his neighbor. A mechanic. And he came along to help with the vehicles. They know nothing about or have anything to do with what's going on in Guatemala."

"I don't give a shit," said Ladino.

"Take me," declared Trotsky.

Ladino looked him up and down. He laughed. "Get out of the way."

"You're not taking them."

Slowly, as if he were getting ready to caress Trotsky's face with his white glove, Ladino raised the .45 to the black eye patch. "Either you get out of the way, blind man, or I'll turn you into a piece of shit right now."

Tito came up from behind Trotsky and nudged him. "Don't worry, sir," he whispered. "Drive into Guatemala City and ask for Lionel Rubio at the Ministry of Defense. He'll connect you with people who can help."

"See what I mean?" said Ladino, sweeping the Commander and Zuckermann in a fierce gaze. "They've been doing this for years. They're very good at it, tricking people into believing what they want them to believe. Here they're known as El Caballero y El Cabrón. The handsome one is "El Caballero." The ugly one is "El Cabrón." We call them "CaCa" for short. Funny, no?"

"Shit," Honoré mumbled.

Ladino slapped Honoré on the back, laughing. "Very good! We need a good translator."

From the moment the soldiers dragged Honoré across the pavement, lifted him on the truck, and sat him down with his hands tied behind his back next to Tequila, he felt his life moving backwards. There was no future. In fact, as the army truck pulled away, followed by a jeep with Ladino and two soldiers in it, Honoré felt how the tin men must have felt the day they were packed in the back of a trailer in front of his store before they were driven north to be turned into scrap metal.

"Pinche Coyote, see what you've gotten us into!" yelled Tequila above the wind and noise of the truck rattling along a dirt road. The barbarian had chewed through the woman's stocking gagging him.

Honoré raised an eyebrow. "Me?"

"Yes, you."

"Where the fuck have *you* been?"

"You tell me. You tricked me into coming on this trip."

The road carried them into the jungle. "Why the hell did you take off with Sugar in Mexico City?"

"I ran into some old friends from Acapulco. They offered me a deal I couldn't refuse. We were going to invite you, but then one thing led to another. We got stoned, and before we knew it, we were in Acapulco. You know how crazy *la vida loca* gets."

The wind eased as the truck slowed down. "What are you doing in Guatemala?"

"My friends have connections in Guatemala City. But then that madman, Ladino, stopped us. The guy's weird. What's wrong with him?"

Honoré could see Ladino in the jeep behind them. "Trotsky says he's a chimera."

"A what?"

"A chimera. A freak with both a prick and a pussy."

"No shit?"

"No shit."

"Anyway, he let the others go. Said I was a *brujo*."

The truck picked up speed again. "And your friends didn't help?"

"No, Ladino scared the shit out of them. They took off and left me here. So how do we get out of this?"

The jeep fell so far behind that Honoré could barely see it. "Tito."

"Who?"

A vulture soared overhead. "Remember Tito?" Honoré asked in English. "The soldier standing behind Trotsky when Trotsky confronted Ladino?"

After some thought, Tequila nodded.

"Okay, well, Trotsky told me he said not to worry. He and Ladino were in basic training together. Tito told Trotsky to go see the minister of defense."

"But this guy Ladino is nuts. What if they shoot us? What if they kill us?"

More vultures appeared, sleek and gray. "Metamorphosis."

"What?"

"Metamorphosis."

"What's that?"

The truck bounced over a pothole. "Pretend you died."

Tequila made a face. "Why don't we pretend *you* died?"

"You want me to explain what metamorphosis means or not?"

"Okay."

"Pretend you were run over by a truck."

Tequila's head turned sharply. "No, let's pretend *you* were run over by a truck."

"Forget it."

"Okay, okay, *ándale pues*, a truck runs over me. What then?"

Honoré sat up, the wind in his hair. "Okay, so a truck runs over you and you die. Then they put your body in a coffin. They take you to the church and the priest blesses you, and then they take you to the cemetery. In the cemetery they lower you into the ground, and after some time passes, you become dust. The dust becomes dirt and you become grass."

Tequila nodded.

"Then a cow comes along, okay?"

Tequila nodded.

"And the cow eats the grass, okay?"

Tequila nodded again.

"Then you go into the cow's stomach. The cow shits on the grass and you become manure. You feed whatever is growing around. You become a flower. And then I come along and see the flower and say, 'My, how you've changed.' That's metamorphosis."

Hair ravaged by the wind, Tequila stared out the back of the truck as if trying to make sense of this. "Okay," he said. "Let's see if I understood you. How about this? Let's pretend *you* died."

Honoré sat back, rested his head against the cab, and closed his eyes. "I don't want to talk anymore."

"But I want to make sure I understood you, Coyote."

"Okay, okay," said Honoré, his head rolling gently from side to side as the truck rumbled along.

"Let's pretend that an airplane ran over you."

Honoré opened his eyes. "Airplanes don't do that."

"I know, but we're pretending, no?"

Annoyed, Honoré shook his head. "Okay."

"So you die and they put you in a coffin and then they take you to the church. They bury you in a cemetery, where you become dust."

"Okay."

The jeep caught up. "Then you become grass and the grass grows and a cow comes along and eats you."

"Okay."

A chain rattled somewhere. "Am I getting it right?"

The buzzards were gone. "Yes."

"Okay, then the cow takes a shit on the grass. Is that right?"

"Right."

"Then I come along and see the shit, and I say, '*Chingao, vato*, you haven't changed at all.' "

The next morning, a hammer struck metal. Something clinked. Then it clanked. A generator coughed and backfired. Outside, young men laughed. Somewhere a radio spoke, and the sound of rock and roll drifted through the window, open but secured by steel bars. Gray sunlight permeated the room, where a single light bulb at the end of a cord glowed over a table flanked by two chairs. Amid the whitewashed walls, dank cement floors, and the stink of days-old urine, Honoré thought he was in a restroom in the red light district in Nuevo Escandón until the chatter of birds reminded him that this was not Texas or Mexico.

He pushed himself from the floor. "How did you get into this mess?" he asked the pale, unshaven mug in the mirror on the wall.

He thought of the tree in front of his house in Escandón. Then Maruca and Bonita. He wished he were there with them, talking and eating breakfast and reading the *New York Times* as he got ready to go to work. What was his mother doing today? Was she even alive? He thought about the Governor, who could not help him here. He even longed to see his fat cousins.

Heels struck pavement. A boot squeaked. Keys jangled, and the wooden door swung open. In walked Tequila, gagged with a red bandana and hands tied behind his back, as Ladino and two soldiers with assault rifles slung over their shoulders escorted him.

Ladino's uniform was fresh, a red beret cocked to one side. "Sit him down," he commanded.

The soldier pulled a chair from the table and pushed Tequila into it. With dark sneaky eyes, Tequila peered around the room while Ladino took out a cigarette and offered it to Honoré, who took it though he hadn't smoked since he got off pot.

"Please have a seat," said Ladino.

Honoré sat down in the chair across the table from Tequila.

Ladino fired up Honoré's cigarette with a silver lighter and then lit one for himself.

They inhaled and exhaled, two handsome men looking at each other as if they had just met on a Mexican *telenovela*. Nonetheless, Honoré couldn't forget he was in the room with two maniacs. If Tequila opened his mouth and said some *pendejada*, he would get both of them killed.

Tequila mumbled something through the bandana.

"Remove the bandana," the Commander ordered the soldier.

After taking several deep breaths, Tequila perked up, "*Jefe*, can I have a cigarette?"

After pivoting on shiny boots, Ladino stood over him. "Did I give you permission to speak?"

Tequila peered from behind the dark rings on his eyes. "Sorry, *jefe*. May I speak?"

Ladino spoke through a tangle of smoke. "If I ask you a question, will you give me an honest answer?"

Tequila smiled. "Yes, of course."

"How about you?" Ladino said to Honoré.

Honoré nodded skeptically.

"Good," said Ladino, "that way I won't have to slap the shit out of you." He pulled out a cigarette as well as the lighter and handed them to one of the soldiers. "Light this for him."

The soldier stuck the cigarette in Tequila's mouth and lit it.

Ladino faced Honoré. "Do you think I enjoy making people suffer?" He paused thoughtfully. "No, not at all. But once you taste the pleasures of evil, you don't want to give them up. Like with booze or drugs, the hangover is horrible. The high can be so high that when you crash you want to blow your brains out. The taste of evil is the taste of power—you always go back for more." A clanking outside interrupted him, so he walked to the door and looked out. Then he returned, stopping in front of Honoré. "Nonetheless, it gets old. What doesn't get old is love of country and duty. Loyalty to friends. Oh, and *truth*." He paused and watched Tequila take a puff and then another. "Okay, that's enough. Let's get down to business."

"Wait, sir," said Tequila.

Raising an eyebrow contemptuously, Ladino watched Tequila take another puff. As soon as the soldier removed the cigarette and crushed it under his boot, Ladino addressed Honoré, "Who killed General Moncada?"

Honoré looked Ladino in the face. "I don't know who General Moncada is."

Ladino kept his cool. "Which guerrilla group organized the assassination? Everyone knows you were involved. Have they returned to Guatemala City? Is that why you were headed there?"

"We're Americans," said Honoré. "We don't know what you're talking about."

Ladino took out the white glove from his back pocket and slipped it on his right hand. "I thought you said you were going to cooperate?"

"Didn't you ask for an honest answer?" asked Honoré.

"So this is not going to be easy." He nodded at one of the soldiers. "Bring the chair."

The soldier left and returned, stringing out wires attached to long, thin clamps with tiny teeth in them. Then he left and brought a simple wooden chair, which he placed in front of the table. Leather straps with buckles hung from the armrests like tongues with rings in them. A hole had been cut in the woven hemp seat as in the Mexican potty chairs Honoré had used when growing up. Outside, the generator hummed a happy tune.

"We'll start with the Indian," said Ladino. "Maybe that'll loosen the Spaniard's tongue when he sees what he's in for."

The soldier propped his assault rifle against the wall. After untying Tequila, he escorted him to the chair, where he pulled down Tequila's pants and underwear before sitting him down so that his private parts passed through the hole snugly, dangling. Then the soldier strapped Tequila's legs and wrists with the belts.

Tequila's butt fidgeted as the soldiers peered at his balls. "*Órale,* what are you doing?"

Ladino flung his cigarette on the floor. "We're inspecting you, *pendejo.* If you're a woman in disguise or a *joto,* we'll have to deal with you differently." He paused thoughtfully. "*Jotos* and women require plenty of sugar cane."

"*Jefe,*" squeaked Tequila.

"*Jefe* what?"

"May I ask you a personal question?"

Ladino froze. He studied Tequila's mug. "You know you're really ugly." He grinned. "And ugly people are usually stupid. But who knows? You might be smarter than you look. Shoot."

"Your *partes nobles.*"

Ladino arched an eyebrow. "My *what*?"

"You know, your private parts."

Ladino shook his head and watched the soldier untangling the wire on the floor. "What the hell are you talking about?"

"Is it true you have both a peepee and a pussy?"

Ladino let his eyes wander above a reluctant grin. "I knew it. Sooner or later, you bastards would try fucking with my mind." He approached Tequila, cautiously. "Why?"

"I heard you're a camera."

"A what?"

Honoré would have kicked Tequila, but he was out of range. "Shut the fuck up, you idiot."

Tequila ignored him. "A camera. Someone with a peepee and a pussy."

Ladino circled the two prisoners, walking around the room, past one soldier and then the other, coming up behind Tequila. "Chimera, you idiot. Don't you know English?"

"Chimera. That's right."

At length, Ladino added. "That's not a bad idea, you know. A man wouldn't need a woman, and a woman wouldn't need a man."

"Yeah."

"No more war between the sexes," added Ladino, moving slowly past Tequila.

"Men could have babies."

Ladino halted on combat boots black and shiny as eggplant. "Disgusting!" he screamed in Tequila's mug. "Are you making fun of me? Listen, imbecile, I'm macho as any self-respecting *guatemalteco.* Just ask my women in Guate. You'll never meet more satisfied women. No, I don't have a pussy, you pussy! And I don't want one! I have more than enough sugar cane."

The generator died, and one of the soldiers went outside. After a while, the light bulb glowed again, though weakly, and the soldier returned. The generator coughed loudly, expired. The light went out again.

Tequila listened intently to the failing machine. "Sir, I can help. I fixed a generator on a yacht in Acapulco a few days ago."

"Shut up!" blurted Honoré.

Ladino regarded Tequila, cautiously. "Untie him."

As soon as the soldier untied him, Tequila stood, pulling up his underwear and pants and tying his belt. Then, rubbing his wrists, he followed the soldier outside.

"Now tie this man," Ladino said to the other soldier.

The soldier led Honoré to the electric chair. He pulled his underwear and pants down around his ankles and pushed him in the chair. Honoré's private parts dangled through the hole as the soldier secured the belts around Honoré's arms and legs.

Rifle slung on his shoulder, the other soldier returned. "The generator will be running in a few minutes."

Ladino turned to Honoré. "Now I am going to ask you again. Who killed General Moncada?"

"I don't know what you're talking about."

Ladino put the bore of the man-eater to the corner of Honoré's eye. "I've heard all kinds of stories about you and your friend. I never thought that one day it would fall to me to save my country from two of the worst criminals Central America has known. I heard you outwitted the most skilled interrogators—some even lost their minds afterward, or that you tortured the torturers. One man went blind. Another could never get an erection again. And the last one died of diarrhea. Shit himself to death." All of a sudden, he halted, listened. The generator belched, coughed, backfired, so he stormed to the window. "What's taking so long?"

Outside, Tequila shouted, "¡Ya mero, jefe! ¡Ya mero!"

Ladino returned. "And you, get ready!"

"Yes, sir!" said one of the soldiers.

Ladino slowly circled Honoré. "People here are ignorant and super-stitious. Indians, mestizos—they're all the same. Once you get people to believe in saints, heaven and hell, and God, they'll believe anything, even revolution. I believe in nothing except what I can see or touch or taste or smell." He halted, holding the .45 steady—admiring the man-eater in his gloved hand as if it were an expensive piece of jewelry. "This is the only world there is or ever will be, which is why I still don't understand why people like you convince those fools to give up their lives for a lost cause."

Outside, the generator suddenly hummed powerfully as if it had recovered from pneumonia, no coughing or wheezing. The light bulb glowed, and on a radio somewhere rock and rollers rocked and rolled. Honoré despised Tequila.

"Check the electrodes," said Ladino.

When the soldiers tapped the electrodes together, sparks flew.

"All right," said Ladino. "Who will do us the honor? Who will fry us some eggs?"

The soldier handed his man-eater to the other one. "What do you want me to do, *mi capitán*?"

"Inspect the prisoner."

The soldier got on his knees with the electrodes in his hands, his butt sticking out as he peered under the seat. In the meantime, Ladino, confident as a man about town at a nightclub, took out another cigarette and tapped it. Then he lit it and watched the smoke unravel.

"I can't believe it!" said the soldier.

"What's the matter?" asked Ladino.

"This man has the balls of a bull."

Ladino grinned. "Good, good. So you are the man we've all been looking for. All newspaper reports say that El Caballero has big balls. They also say he has a scar in the shape of a hammer and sickle on his left testicle. Do you see anything like that?"

"Yes, mi *capitán*," said the soldier. "He has a scar."

"Check it carefully."

The soldier probed one of Honoré's testicles with the fingers of an expert dentist, nudging the sack of seeds gently.

"*Capitán*," said the soldier. "The scar is small. I can't tell if it's a sickle. The only thing that looks like a hammer is his *pito*."

"Are you sure?"

The soldier raised his head. "Would you like to inspect it yourself, *jefe*?"

Ladino recoiled. "No, no," he said and flicked ashes on the floor, his eyes wandering about with exasperation. "I'll ask you one last time. Who killed General Moncada?"

Honoré shook his head. "I already told you. I don't know what you're talking about."

"All right," said Ladino. "Let's give him a *toquecito*. Let's see what those balls are made of."

Honoré closed his eyes as the electrodes' metal teeth bit into his testicles, gently at first, then hard—harder. He couldn't think of anything but the teeth and the electrical shock that would turn his genitals into a bad breakfast—overcooked eggs and a charred sausage. Instead he felt a strange and sudden vibration under his feet.

He opened an eye.

Dust fell from the ceiling, and the light bulb swung slightly. "What was that?" asked the soldier.

"Nothing," Ladino said. "A tremor."

Ladino approached Honoré. "Where were we?"

Honoré didn't want to scream. But he remembered how bad he felt when he got kicked in the balls on the football field and then lay on the grass in front of hundreds of gringos in Houston, nauseated and sickened, until he pulled himself to his feet. No one cheered, and ultimately his team of brown runts from Escandón lost the game to the team of white and black giants.

Another tremor. Outside, the generator coughed, farted, quit. The light bulb expired.

Ladino bent down so his face was inches from Honoré's. "Who killed General Moncada?"

"Sir, I already told you I'm not from here. I'm an American. I never heard of General Moncada."

A white dove flexed its wings. Then it leaped, flying high. Honoré heard his teeth grind, his skull falling apart amid an explosion of stars as the dove slammed into his face. At first it didn't hurt. Then it hurt a lot. Then his face went numb.

"Ah! Ah!" yelled Ladino as he held his gloved hand, swelling so badly it looked like a white balloon with fingers. "Oh, my God!"

A soldier came to his assistance. "What happened? Did he bite you?"

"Look at my hand. This was supposed to happen to his face, not my hand. It feels like I punched the wall."

The soldier pointed the assault rifle at Honoré. "These guys are *brujos*. They have magic powers. They can make anything happen. Even hurricanes and earthquakes."

"Bullshit!" barked Ladino.

"Sir!" shouted the other soldier.

"What?"

Dust fell from the ceiling as the ground shuddered again. "Sir, let's get out here!"

Though the rafters screamed and moaned as the walls wavered and a crack ran down the side of the building, Ladino yelled, "We stay here until we get the truth out of this terrorist!"

"Sir, these walls will kill us!"

Outside, the soldiers screamed and yelled until something crashed—maybe a building—and the racket gobbled their voices. All of a sudden, a rafter fell and missed Ladino by inches. "Untie the prisoner!" he commanded at last.

"*Sí, mi capitán*," said the soldier.

Ladino ran to the door and barked. "Get the trucks ready! Call ahead! Tell them we're coming!" He returned as the soldier unclipped the electrodes from Honoré's balls, untied the leather straps, and yanked him to his feet. "We cannot take any more chances con *estos cabrones*! Let's get out of here before we're all killed."

Honoré never felt better as he hoisted his pants and tied his belt.

A Salvadoran poet wrote that if the natives of Central America were good at anything, it was dying. So many of them had died for so long during the Spanish conquest under Pedro de Alvarado and later under American imperialism that dying was no longer a challenge. In fact, the more they died, the stronger the ideas for which they died became, and that's why the heavens are filled with stars, eternal symbols of the martyrs of Central America. At first, Honoré had been intrigued by such stories, but he always felt he didn't understand or appreciate them as well as Trotsky, who loved to tell them. Now he felt he understood them less.

In fact, as he rode in the back of the truck with a soldier and Tequila, his suspicion that he had no business in this strange world of Latin American politics was confirmed when he smelled something ugly. "*¡No chingues!*"

"What? What did I do now?" said Tequila.

"You let out a fart."

Unlike some of their other friends in school, Tequila was usually careful about farting in public, but when he had eaten too many beans or was scared, he could let out deadly ones. One time Tequila cut a big one in class, and an entire wing of the school had to be evacuated.

Tequila cut another one loose, a loud one.

"What's that?" asked the soldier before getting a whiff. Then he cried, "*¡Dios mío!*" and fell off the tailgate when the truck bounced over a pothole.

Behind them, the jeep swerved abruptly, barely missing the soldier on the ground and flew off the road into a ditch, rolling over. The truck skidded to a halt, and the driver jumped out. With the help of the fallen soldier, he pulled other soldiers from the overturned jeep and then Ladino.

"What the hell happened?" Ladino yelled as he stumbled to his feet.

The fallen soldier pointed at Tequila. "That idiot farted."

The soldiers laughed.

"So?"

"So it was worse than chemical warfare. And I didn't have my gas mask."

The soldiers laughed again. "What the fuck is so funny?" yelled Ladino.

"Nothing, sir."

"I almost got killed!"

The jeep had to be abandoned. So Ladino climbed in the cab, and the rest of the soldiers rode in back with Honoré and Tequila. The road wound past slopes dense with trees and then up and down through fields of maize until a volcano appeared in the distance. Up ahead, Honoré spotted a roof that nestled among the trees. Soon they arrived at a compound of white buildings with red tile roofs, the yard jammed with army trucks and jeeps. Two young men were setting up a TV camera and some campesinos had gathered.

"Capitán," asked the sergeant in charge, "why is this happening? Who are these two men? And who ordered the television crew here?"

"I did," retorted Ladino. "That's who."

"But, *jefe*, this is no place or time to be filming anything. We're on full alert."

Red beret cocked on his head, Ladino stared at the sergeant. "Do you know who these men are?"

The sergeant did not waste more than a glance. "A couple of hippies. One looks like a gringo and the other like a Mexican. And both of them look crazier than my crazy aunt."

"That's what they want you to think, sergeant. But these men are the infamous El Caballero and El Cabrón."

"In that case, shouldn't we take them into Guate?"

"Why?"

"The High Command wants to interrogate them."

Ladino glared at the sergeant. "Every time we've handed these idiots to the High Command, they've escaped. I've been waiting too long to let them slip through my hands now."

None of this made sense to Honoré as the soldiers marched him and Tequila down a narrow path to a clearing below the houses and tied them to two wooden posts at the end of a soccer field. There was no way out.

Ladino barked again. "Get those cameras ready!"

"But why here?" asked the sergeant.

Ladino regarded him with utter disdain. "They murdered my good friend, El General Eusebio Moncada, who was like a father to me. A great Guatemalan patriot. This *finca* once belonged to General Moncada."

"Yes, I know. He used to bring his mistresses here. Why on national television?"

Ladino shook his head impatiently. "We want the nation to witness the end of these two murderers. We don't want to leave any doubt about what happened to El Caballero and El Cabrón."

A camera approached Ladino on the shoulders of a young man. "How close do you want us to get?" he asked.

"Close enough to get a good shot of their mugs."

A glass eye stared at Honoré. "How's this?" asked the cameraman.

"Do you want your head blown off? "

Ladino addressed a squad of soldiers. "Take your positions." Then he approached Honoré. "You will not be blindfolded. No last minute cigarettes. The last time you were allowed to smoke, the cigarette blew up in an officer's face and killed him. No diversions, no rescues this time. Third, no last words. You already said too much."

He turned to a soldier. "Gag them! That way we won't have to hear their screams when they turn to shit."

The soldier jammed a red bandana in Honoré's mouth and tied it behind his head. He did the same to Tequila. Meanwhile, a jeep racing through a cloud of dust honked. The honking increased, urgent, shrill. Dust strung out like sheets on a wire behind the vehicle careening along the dirt road; someone waved a white piece of paper from inside. Midway across the soccer field, the jeep rolled to stop. A soldier jumped out and ran toward Ladino.

Breathless, Tito halted. "We just received this message from the minister of defense."

Ladino studied the message. "So?"

Tito grinned triumphantly. "So let them go."

"Arrest this man!"

Two soldiers grabbed Tito's arms.

"Ladino," yelled Tito, as they dragged him away, "you're crazy! You'll get us all killed!"

Ladino walked up to Honoré. "Your friends in the convoy saw the American ambassador in Guatemala City, and the American ambassador talked to the minister of defense. They say you are not El Caballero y El Cabrón. He has ordered me to release you." He slowly crushed the paper.

"But I will not defraud my country or betray General Moncada. You may or may not be who you say you are. I don't care. And I don't care what the American ambassador or the minister of defense says. Tomorrow your faces will appear on the front pages of the newspapers in Guatemala and the rest of the world, and the people will know that a fatal blow has been dealt against the red menace in Central America. And if we've executed the wrong men, that's fine. We execute the wrong men all the time. It makes finding the real ones easier because they think we stopped looking for them. But we haven't, and when we catch them, we'll execute them. In the meantime you'll do." He smirked. "Besides, I don't like either of you."

After making sure the cameras were in place, Ladino stepped out of the line of fire. "Ready!" he shouted.

Beads of sweat sprouted on Honoré's forehead as the man-eaters were leveled at him by the soldiers in olive-green uniforms, boys with brown skin and black hair who had grown up in the shadows of volcanoes, boys like the ones he played football with in high school. In fact, Honoré felt like he was back in Escandón, in the last quarter of a football game, as he and Tequila awaited the last kickoff.

"Aim!"

Suddenly, Honoré's eyes burned, and he smelled something weird. He felt lightheaded.

Ladino coughed. "Fire!" he shouted at last.

But nothing.

The stink grew.

Ladino weaved in his boots, overwhelmed. A soldier dropped his rifle and ran. Another collapsed and lay twitching. All of a sudden, Honoré smelled the *caca*—and, oh, did it smell bad, like an open sewer with a lot of chili peppers and rotten beans and dead *tlacuaches* pouring out of it. And he turned to where it was coming from, to Tequila slumped on the wooden pole with his head hanging to one side, his eyes closed, dead. Suddenly, an eye opened. *¡Pinche tlacuache!* Playing possum! Well, was he dead or wasn't he? The eye closed, and he slumped further. Then he opened his eyes, stood up, and after finding a more comfortable position slumped again.

Honoré spit out the bandana. "Cut the bullshit, Tequila!" he yelled. "Are you dead or not? Make up your mind, *cabrón!*"

Ladino, holding a handkerchief to his face, pulled out a .45 automatic and fired in the air. "Get back here, you assholes, or I'll shoot you for desertion!"

"We're under attack!" yelled one.

"Haven't you smelled *caca* before?" shouted Ladino.

"Not *caca* like this!" said the soldier. "This is mustard gas!"

Ladino put the .45 to the soldier's temple. "Come to attention or die!"

The soldier came to attention. And except for the soldier twitching on the ground, the firing squad reassembled, faces distorted by pain and disgust. Ladino barked another order, and the soldiers raised their man-eaters to their shoulders.

"Ready!" shouted Ladino.

This is it, thought Honoré as he straightened against the pole and refused to look at Tequila, who still had not decided how he was going to end his life. Outraged, Honoré stared at the bores of the man-eaters. He was not a revolutionary, but he would not faint or cry or shit in his pants.

"Aim!" commanded Ladino.

In the sky a bird appeared. With such a huge wing span, it could not be a buzzard. Maybe it was an airplane. No, it couldn't be that either. It was a bird. A big one. It seemed unusually familiar.

"Fire!"

Like a string of firecrackers Honoré and Tequila used to pop before they grew up and discovered women, before they began smuggling dope across the Rio Grande and got into so much trouble, the man-eaters belched smoke. At first the bullets sounded like a flock of buzzards tearing through the air as everything slowed down, as if in a dream. In his mind Honoré saw only one thing—a woman, Maruca, running toward him, her black hair flying and brown face shining in the tropical sun. Then, the bullets struck, but there was no pain. And so as he fell into the stream of history, he was not afraid.

PART 4

The Governor lowered the flag. In fits and starts, it slid down the pole as he pulled the rope while Trotsky watched from where he stood in front of the A-frame. Three weeks earlier, in a frenzy to cross the border in the middle of the night, members of the convoy had packed their things at the last minute but forgot the flag Molly had embroidered. The Governor unhooked it, folded it neatly, strode across the yard, and gave it to Trotsky. The hog's chrome-plated muffler sparkled like a silver spur in the sunlight as they walked through the gate. Altagracia waited inside the air-conditioned jeep, which hummed as if it were praying.

After the Governor shut the gate, Trotsky said, "Thanks for everything. I'm sorry we caused you and your family so many problems. I know you took a lot of heat during the siege."

The Governor locked the gate. "We've been through worse. Besides, Honoré was a good buddy. Helped me a lot when my family wouldn't have anything to do with me." He reached in his back pocket and took out an envelope. "By the way, here are the bills. Phone, water, and electricity."

"Thanks," said Trotsky, slipping the envelope in his pocket. "Is it true your family came down here at the turn of the century?"

The Governor pushed his cowboy hat back. "Yep. Bank robbers. Used to kill Meskins. Now we just fuck 'em." He grinned. "No offense."

"None taken. Mexicans can be real nasty."

"You better believe it," he said. "I just lost the Battle of the Alamo."

"How so?"

"I'm getting married in two weeks. A girl from Matamoros."

"The one I met here? Honey?"

"Yep."

"Well, congratulations."

The Governor scraped some dirt with the heel of his boot. "Honoré could be a real motherfucker, saying all kinds of weird things. Usually, we didn't make sense because we were so coked up or drunk on our asses. He used to blame the gringos for everything. But I asked him where the Meskins would be if it wasn't for the gringos?"

Trotsky, grinning, could not help but add, "And where would the gringos be if it wasn't for the Meskins?"

The Governor gazed thoughtfully at Trotsky, eyes blue as Texas bluebonnets. Then his voice cracked, as if he were about to say something nice about Honoré but couldn't. He removed his hat and wiped his forehead with a red handkerchief. "Anyway, I was going to ask Honoré to be the best man at my wedding." His eyes grew shiny. "Sorry. Men don't cry, my old man used to say, and I ain't about to start." He threw his hat back on. "Anyway, that's my story, and I'm sticking to it."

Then he moseyed over to the hog, the heels of his boots hooking in the dirt, jeans low on his hips. He swung a leg over the motorcycle and climbed on. With a single jump, he brought it to life. It coughed, farted. As soon as the roar of the engine settled down, humming smoothly as a dishwasher, the Governor rumbled down the dirt road.

"*Hasta la vista, amigo*," he yelled.

Inside the jeep, Trotsky said to Altagracia, "What a weirdo."

"Honoré was kind of weird himself."

Trotsky started the engine. "How so?"

"Like he wasn't there all the time. I never felt he was one of us."

"That's what he told me the last time we spoke." Trotsky shifted gears and headed down the dirt road through a cloud of dust. "But you got to hand it to him. He tried, he really did. He got us out of some difficult spots when no one else would help."

The jeep heaved and jerked over an arroyo. At River Road, Trotsky eased onto the asphalt, which glistened like a steak on the grill. As he picked up speed and headed toward Escandón, he felt the tension with each fence post, each car that passed, each sign that showed he was getting close to Escandon. He still had not seen Honoré's family since returning from Guatemala, and he did not look forward to it. Yes, Altagracia had gone to see his wife, who had already heard about everything on TV, but he needed to go see her himself. Since he couldn't bear the idea of returning to Escandón without making every last effort to find Honoré and Tequila, he had spent days in Guatemala, knocking on office doors, at the ministry of defense, then the American embassy, the Spanish embassy, on whatever door would open. Everyone promised to meet with him or consult a higher up, but nothing came of it. Then he returned to Burgos, looking for Tito and the doctor, but they were gone. Some said the doctor and his staff had joined the guerrillas in the mountains, others that they had been disappeared by a right-wing death squad led by a strange-looking soldier who wore a white glove. And now everything felt as if it had never happened, that Trotsky had only dreamed it one night after a drunken binge.

"So how is the Commander doing?" asked Altagracia.

"A Cuban doctor in Managua removed the insect from his ear, so now he's doing well. Didn't lose any of his hearing. In fact, it got better. He and Molly are organizing new convoys, some to Cuba."

"And the bimbo?"

Trotsky kept an eye on the on-coming traffic. "She disappeared in Tegucigalpa, Honduras, but was later spotted naked and stoned on a beach in Isla de Mujeres with a high-ranking officer of the contras and two gringos. After Zuckermann returned to New York, he confirmed what everyone suspected all along—Sugar was a CIA operative."

"Wow."

"She was after Honoré. She really had the hots for him. When she crossed the line between sex and politics, she lost sight of her mission, which was to sabotage the convoy."

"He never gave in to her?"

"Not that I know of."

"What about Tennessee and that other guy—"

"Johnny Paint."

"Yes."

"Hiding out somewhere in Mexico."

Fifteen minutes later, he rattled across the railroad tracks and took Tamaulipas Avenue into town. At a truck stop, long lines of tractor-trailers rested and fed after long hauls across the country. A man and a woman, whom he could have sworn were Ma and Pa Savage, drove past in a truck jam-packed with tin men—knights in shining armor—but he couldn't tell for sure. The tin men had become so popular that now most curio shops on the main drag sold them. Escandón looked like the staging ground for armies of crusaders invading the north. Near Pizza Hut, he slowed down and then parked in front of Castillo's Mexican Curios.

He had been through this before, when he visited the families of all the men in his platoon who had died in Vietnam. "Are you sure," he asked Altagracia as he opened his door, "you don't want to go inside?"

With the slender light-skinned face and dark eyes of a flamenco dancer, she looked absolutely lovely in an embroidered orange blouse he bought for her in Nicaragua. "No," she said, "I'm not feeling well. Besides, if your friends are going to spend the night at the house, I need to get back and have the food ready. Don't take long."

He strode across the yard, walking past the bull whose horns gleamed in sunlight as if the beast was ready to gore him. He climbed the steps to the porch and entered the store, where he encountered an owl on a wall—a beautiful owl made of porcelain, about three feet tall, painted red, green, and yellow.

"*Buenos días,*" said Maruca, rising from behind Honoré's desk, which had been moved into the showroom. Now it stood among a flock of parrots hanging on wires.

"Please don't get up," he said.

She remained standing. "Can I get you something to drink? It's very hot outside."

"No, thank you. I don't have much time. There's a press conference today at the federal courthouse, and I'm already late. I just got back from Guatemala, and I've been meaning to come by."

A beautiful woman—that's how Trotsky remembered her, a dark, sultry woman with long black hair, long legs, and a voluptuous body. Today she was beginning to look like a widow, large almond-shaped eyes and sensual lips swept by waves of grief that left her skin dry and deposited streaks of gray in her hair.

"Sorry I didn't come by sooner. I didn't want to come back until I did everything to find him."

"Your wife told me."

"I'm truly sorry about this."

Seized by emotion, she sat down. "My husband," she said after a while, "was a very stubborn man. He always did what he wanted to. I never liked his working with you. But it was worse when he was smuggling drugs. We all miss him very much. When I married Honoré, my mother told me, 'You've lost your mind.' I didn't care. I fell passionately in love with him. He was such a handsome man, just like his father."

"And brilliant."

Her voice sounded as if she had suddenly come down with a bad cold. "I always told him he was a frustrated actor. Now he's a ghost. He haunts me everywhere I go. At night it's very bad. He shows up in my dreams. Then, I wake up and he's not there. I wander about the house in the dark as if he's waiting for me in the shadows. He used to joke around that he could never kill me because I would haunt him the rest of his life. And that's what's happened to me. I see his gun cabinet in the back room and remember the days he took Bonita hunting."

She lowered her head and wept.

He wanted to say something. He did not know what to say, wanted to wake up from this nightmare.

Then a back door at the end of the hall opened, and in ran Bonita, pigtails flying and thick glasses overflowing with puddles of morning light. "Mom, Mamá Grande wants to go home. She says she doesn't feel good." She froze. "What's wrong, Mom?"

Maruca wiped her eyes. "Nothing," she said, groggily. "Tell her to wait. Tell her to lie down in the back room. Rig and Cachetes haven't shown up, and I can't leave the store unattended."

The back door opened again. An old woman, cane in hand, entered and then crept along the hall. Smelling of old hair and flesh, she elbowed her way past Trotsky. "*Hijita*," she said to Maruca, "I don't feel good."

Maruca's voice cleared. "As soon as Rig and Cachetes get here, I'll take you home. Right now get some rest in the back room."

Doña Pánfila peered at Trotsky.

"This is Señor Trotsky," Maruca said.

The old woman nodded. "Yes, I remember you. Honoré's friend. Were you with him when he died?"

"No."

Her eyes were liquid, not from weeping but from years of seeing too much. "Is it true he might not be dead?"

"I don't know. I hear rumors, but I don't know what to believe."

Bonita put her arm around her grandmother. The girl's eyes were large, dark, and soft behind the glasses, and her hair was thick and black as her mother's. An even jaw and the shape of her fair cheeks reminded Trotsky of Honoré. "Sir," she asked, on the verge of tears, "will we ever see Dad again?"

This is why Trotsky didn't want to come here. "I don't know," he said.

"*Hijita*," said the grandmother to Bonita, who wiped her eyes with the back of her hand, "one day we will all be together again. If your father is dead, you will see him in heaven. All of us will be there, even Señor Trotsky. That's what I was taught as a young girl, and that's what I've always believed, and that's what I believe today. Don't cry, baby. We don't know why things happen the way they do, but Our Lord and Savior Jesus Christ does. Isn't that so, Señor Trotsky?"

Trotsky paused on the porch. All of a sudden, his bad eye began to itch, and so he reached beneath his patch and rubbed the eyelid, wondering—or trying to remember—what life had been like with two eyes. Maybe it was that simple. If he weren't half-blind, he might not be a disgruntled veteran, might not be so angry, might see things clearly.

After adjusting the patch, he thought about his conversations with

Honoré amid the parrots or as they walked past thick wooden doors dismantled from convents and monasteries in Mexico or stood among the rows of tin men. Honoré's questions haunted him, questions about whether Trotsky might be wrong, whether his vision and struggle for peace and justice in Central America was foolhardy. Then he remembered how the Nicaraguans had received them after the convoy crossed the border between Honduras and Nicaragua, blue-and-white Nicaraguan flags waving and voices full of hope, shouting, "*¡El pueblo unido jamás será vencido!*" or "*¡Hasta la victoria, Comandante Sandino!*" as they accompanied them into drab and beleaguered Managua, its heroic spirit guarded by black metal silhouettes of César Sandino erected on hilltops throughout the city. Right or wrong, he understood the Nicaraguans' struggle for a better life, for justice, for democracy. For dignity. They could not be wrong about that.

Altagracia honked. After climbing down the steps, he walked past the bull and headed across the yard. In the jeep he buckled his seat belt and started the engine.

"How did it go?" asked Altagracia.

He checked for oncoming traffic. "Okay, I guess. You know how these things are. You can never say the right thing. So you say what you can."

He pulled out and headed south on Tamaulipas.

A black wrought iron fence enclosed the yard of another Mexican curio shop on the corner, where he stopped at a traffic light. Amid a jungle brimming with vases, wooden chairs, and wrought iron figures, a band of mariachis held guitars, a cello, and violins as they serenaded a man with long slender arms and legs, sitting on the ground with a lance in one hand and a saucer-like helmet on his head. But it wasn't a man at all; it was a wooden sculpture of Don Quixote. The tin mariachis had rusted and turned a reddish brown.

"One day, the Mexicans," said Trotsky to Altagracia as he waited for the light to turn green, "will make sculptures of Che Guevara, Fidel Castro, Lucio Cabanas, César Augusto Sandino, and José Martí. Then, they'll ship them to these curio shops and sell them to the gringos, and they'll take them home and display them in their living rooms like trophies of the Cold War."

She leaned her head against the window and sighed. "Sometimes you can be so cynical."

"Kitsch," he muttered bitterly. "An imitation of an imitation of an imitation. We're all kitsch."

"You always talk in riddles. What does that mean?"

"It's impossible to be original."

When the light turned green, he made a left. Then, a right onto the highway, which took them south. Up ahead, the Mexican flag rose like a giant plumed serpent above downtown. When he saw the congestion of eighteen-wheelers waiting to cross into Mexico, he took the exit and turned right on Washington Street. After a few blocks, he drove past the Washington Hotel on the left and the federal courthouse on the right. He circled the plaza and parked in front of the monument to the war heroes, with its array of metal helmets around an eternal flame and the names of all the Escandonians who had died in World War I, World War II, Korea, and Vietnam. Across the street the federal courthouse stood like a Greek temple with giant columns built from gray stone among fat palm trees. On its steps journalists gathered around the Commander, Molly, and others.

"I don't see Zuckermann," muttered Trotsky, opening his door and climbing out. "Maybe he left early. He had a plane to catch back to New York."

Altagracia climbed into the driver's seat. "How long will you be?"

"Give us an hour."

"How about two?"

"Okay."

As soon as Altagracia departed, Trotsky strode through stares of three fat cops wearing sunglasses and reclining against the patrol cars parked down the street. He wondered if he should have brought a sack of bananas to placate these gorillas. According to Altagracia, Comino and his buddies were so disgusted that the convoy had sneaked across with the help of the FBI agent that they had a *carne asada* at Comino's house and got plastered. Comino fell asleep in front of an air conditioner. When he awoke and went back outside in the hot sun, he had a mild stroke, coming down with what Honoré called *cara chueca*, the disease of *pendejos* in South Texas.

And sure enough, there he was—Comino, looking as if he had just slammed headlong into a wall. "Buenas tardes," said Trotsky.

Comino spoke out the side of his mouth. "Buenas tardes."

Trotsky headed toward the courthouse.

All of sudden, a ghost appeared. Trotsky cringed. This was the last place he had expected to see Dr. Olivia de la Ó, but there she was, wearing a long green skirt with a belt of turquoise and silver as if she were a squaw from New Mexico, the latest chic among Chicana feminist writers. She had always wanted to be Frida Kahlo, but she lacked Kahlo's good looks, artistic talent, and passion for men. And she had never really suffered. Chicano revolutionaries like her might one day be included among all the other post-Cold War figurines to be sold in Mexican curio shops, but they might not fetch the same prices.

"Trotsky," she said.

"Dr. de la Ó."

She offered a cold, bony hand. "I'm very sorry about what happened to your friends. I heard about the press conference. I wanted to show my support."

Often he wished to could go back to the old days when he didn't bother about her feelings and told her exactly what was on his mind. Now that the feminist movement had taken hold in Escandón and some women supported her, including Altagracia, he had to watch his tongue, knowing that an off-color joke, an offhand or politically incorrect remark—anything—could put them at odds. He understood the necessity of the feminists in South Texas. Men here could be—in fact, were—real assholes. Still he wished things were different. Perhaps one day he and Dr. de la Ó could respect each other enough to be able to work together. But right now it was impossible. The Cold War was not over.

"How is Altagracia?" she asked.

"Fine," he said.

"I heard she got hurt on the bridge."

"She's feeling better, but her headaches haven't gone away."

Suddenly, a car skidded to a stop across the street in front of the monument to the fallen American soldiers. After killing the engine, Ty threw open her door and climbed out, wearing jeans, a short-sleeved khaki shirt, and boots. Tercero, glasses askew on his face, followed. Both helped Señora Cuervo out of the car before the three crossed the street together.

"Ty!" cried Olivia.

"Olivia!" said Ty.

"So good to see you!" said Olivia as the two embraced like long-lost lovers. "I knew I'd find you here. You look great!"

Ty introduced Tequila's wife and their son.

"*Mucho gusto*, señora," said Dr. de la Ó, extending a hand.

Señora Cuervo, her face long and sad, did not bother to shake her hand. "*Mucho gusto*."

Trotsky then took Señora Cuervo's hand in both of his. "Señora, I'm very sorry about what happened to your husband."

Tears filled her eyes. "Is it true he was a victim of mistaken identity?"

"Probably."

Tercero tapped Trotsky's arm. "Sir?"

Trotsky let go of Señora Cuervo. "Yes?"

"Was my father with Señor Castillo?"

The boy's bespectacled look reminded Trotsky of himself when he was the same age. "Yes."

The boy's eyes floated in a pool of refraction. "Apá and Señor Castillo were good friends. They were like brothers. They grew up together. Señor Castillo and I were going to talk about astronomy one day, but we never got a chance."

A TV van parked in front of the courthouse.

"My aunt is an astronomer," said Trotsky, then laid a hand on the boy's shoulder. "Maybe you should meet her the next time she's in town. I could call you. How's that?"

"Great, sir! Can Ty come along? She's my apá's cousin."

Trotsky glanced at Ty. He still couldn't stand her. "Sure."

A reluctant smile floated on her lips. "Yeah, I'll grill some hamburgers and we can invite Mr. Trotsky over. What do you think, Mr. Trotsky?"

"Sure," he said, watching the TV crew walk past.

Señora Cuervo grabbed the boy by the arm. "Let's go. I want see what these people have to report about your father."

But Tercero broke free and said to Trotsky, "Sir, do you know what a black hole is?"

Trotsky grinned. "Yes, they swallow light."

"Light can't escape from them, right?"

"Right."

Tercero's voice was crisp as a bird's in the morning. "Does that mean we'll all disappear in a black hole one day?"

"Probably, but not for millions of years."

"That's what I tell my friends at school. But they don't believe it. They believe angels will save us. What do you think? Do you believe in angels, sir?"

"Shut up!" his mother ordered, grabbing him again and dragging him toward the courthouse.

Trotsky smiled. "Bright kid, no?" he said to Ty, who gazed at Tercero as he toddled alongside his mother.

"Yeah," she said, "but he can be a pain in the ass, just like his father."

"I better go."

Ty stopped him. "Trotsky."

He turned to her. "Yes."

"Is he really dead?"

"I don't know. People disappear all the time. Thousands have disappeared. No one knows what happens to them. Sometimes they show up. Sometimes they don't. And no one really gives a shit."

Ty's eyes moistened. "I really liked Honoré. I miss him. He's probably the first man or woman who understood me. I could talk to him. I owe him an apology, but I guess it's too late. Anyway, I needed to tell someone."

Trotsky still didn't like her. Nevertheless, he patted her on the shoulder. "I don't know what to tell you, except maybe 'thank you.'" He glanced at the crowd of journalists. "Look, honey—"

She scowled. "Don't call me 'honey.' I'm not a little girl."

He tried not to smile. "Sorry, comrade."

"That's better."

Then, as he walked toward the smattering of journalists on the courthouse steps, Trotsky suddenly felt a man gazing at him from beneath a hat slanted across his mustachioed, sunburned face. Shoulders square and posture strong as a bull's, the man could have been a reincarnation of Pancho Villa as he appeared in a black-and-white photo of the Mexican revolution. Next to him stood La Morenita, wearing a white blouse embroidered with roses like those of the women from Oaxaca and a loose cotton skirt that reached her huaraches. An Adelita.

Trotsky halted. "Don Sixto! You're alive and kicking!"

Sixto broke from amid the journalists. "I told you it's impossible to kill a Mexican." He embraced Trotsky.

Trotsky let go and then shook La Morenita's hand. "¡Buenos días!"

"Shhhh!" said Molly, who stood beside the Commander, sunlight on her chapped lips. She wore a T-shirt, faded jeans, and tennis shoes.

"We'll talk later," Trotsky said to Sixto in a hushed voice.

Trotsky joined the Commander, who was being interviewed on the courthouse steps. Though Jack had not gotten rid of the stooped shoulders and probably never would, he looked a lot healthier. He was clean-shaven, steady on his feet.

"Now that the federal court in Escandón has ruled in favor of the convoy to Nicaragua," a journalist said to him, "where do you go from here?"

The Commander's blue eyes glittered in sunlight as he faced the TV cameras defiantly. "More convoys will cross the border, here and in the Valley. This ragtag army of crusaders for peace and justice in Central America brought the issue of the embargo against Nicaragua before the eyes of the American people. They sent the message to Washington that not everyone supports our country's foreign policy."

Another journalist yelled, "Tell us about the two men executed in Guatemala. Who were they, and why were they killed? Were they from Escandón?"

"We've received nothing but conflicting reports," said the Commander. "The Guatemalan government said they executed two terrorists who escaped from a maximum security prison in Guatemala City. They were, in fact, two members of the convoy, originally from Escandón, Texas, mistaken for terrorists. The Guatemalan government insists there was no mistake, and to prove it, they filmed the execution. But they refuse to release a copy. Other reports are that the execution was botched at the last minute. Guerrillas attacked, and the two men escaped. Leaks of a secret CIA report claim that they were smuggled into Nicaragua and are now hiding out in Cuba."

"What do you think happened?"

"I don't know."

"What can you tell us about Honoré del Castillo?"

"Not much." He glanced at Trotsky. "Why don't you ask this gentleman here? He was a good friend of his."

The clear, round, metallic eye of a camera on a young man's shoulder descended upon Trotsky. Another camera twinkled in the sunlight. Someone thrust another microphone in his face.

"Sir," said the journalist, "what can you tell us about Honoré del Castillo?"

Trotsky looked directly into the camera lens—an eye without an iris or blood vessels or even an eyelid, cold and undaunted and merciless as the eye of a shark. Behind that lens were millions of eyes looking at him in living rooms from one end of the country to the other. They were his old enemies: the capitalist and imperialist foes who had funded the low-intensity conflict in Central America, supported the embargo of Nicaragua, mined the Gulf of Fonseca, and sprayed sheets of dengue over Managua. Not only had they sent the Marines into Latin American countries to protect their interests and set up dictatorships to do their bidding for decades but had put their sonuvabitch, Somoza, into power and looked the other way when he ordered the execution of Sandino in the middle of the night. They funded the contras in Nicaragua, and in Guatemala they paid for the man-eaters that had butchered Honoré and Tequila. Since Trotsky hadn't slept much since his return from Guatemala, he was in no condition to speak in public. In fact, he felt like he did the day he returned from Vietnam.

For years his aunt had told him not to be Manichean in his thinking—that he shouldn't see things in terms of black and white, right or wrong, good and evil. The world was very complex, she insisted. But though he had tried, he could not. He could not get rid of the rage he felt when first betrayed years ago by his mother, his father, and then his country. His rage grew when he realized he and his friends had been duped in Vietnam and when he returned to California and discovered the history behind his brown face.

What could anyone say to a people who had everything, seen it all, done it all, and knew it all? Who ate and drank and snorted and fucked too much; who were not only the most powerful comedians of our times but who knew that history was all bullshit anyway and so understood that everything was staged; and who believed in nothing except their pocketbooks and their high opinions of themselves? What could he tell a people who the moment he opened his mouth would see him from the height of their power with sheer contempt as they had once when Che Guevara addressed them eloquently, though in translation, on an evening news report?

So he straightened and gazed into the depths of the camera and said something they wouldn't believe anyway, half-joke, half-truth, a cliché, a sound bite, Hollywood bullshit. "All I can say about my friend Honoré," he said, his voice trembling slightly but determined, "is that he died like a man."

The End

GLOSSARY OF SPANISH/ SPANGLISH TERMS

Spanish/SpanglishTranslation

acomplejado/s	neurotic/hung up
adelante	come in/come on
adentro	inside
aduana	customs
agua	water
agua de jamaica	hibiscus tea
aguas negras	sewage
águila	literally, eagle; slang for check it out, watch out
a la chingada	to hell
altiplano	high plateau/highlands
altos	top
amá/mamá	mom
a mover el bote	shake your booty/can/ass
ándale	let's go
apá/papá	dad
aquí	here
aquí están	here they are
aquí te curamos	we'll cure/fix/take care of you here (sexually)
arriba las mujeres	up with women
a sus órdenes	at your service/orders
auxilio	help, aid, assistance
aviéntate	throw yourself into it/go for it
ay, Dios mío	oh, my God
barbacoa	slow-cooked head, cheek, or tongue of beef or goat in a pit
bien chingón	badass
bienvenido/s	welcome (sing., pl.)

bienvenidos a la frontera	welcome to the border
borracho	drunkard
bote	booty/can/ass
bruja/o	witch (f./m.)
brujería	witchcraft
buenas tardes	good afternoon
bueno	hello (answering telephone)
cabeza	head
cabezón	pig-headed, stubborn guy
cabrón, cabrones (pl.)	bastard, asshole (m.)
cabrona	bitch
caca	poop, crap
calabaza	pumpkin, squash
calabozo	prison, jail
cállate	shut up, be quiet
camaradas	comrades, buddies
camión	bus
cantinuchas	dive bars
cantor	singer
capitán	captain
cara chueca	crooked face, paralysis of the face
carnalas	cousins, sisters (f.)
carne asada	mesquite-grilled meat—specifically, beef
carrizo	reed/s
casa	house
cementera	cement plant/business
charro cantor	singer of Mexican cowboy songs
chicharra	cicada
chicharrón	pork rind
chichi	tit
chilango	man from Mexico City
chinga tu madre	fuck off, go fuck your mother
chinga/chingao	oh, fuck
chingada madre	oh, fuck

chingazos	body blows, shots to the body
chingón	badass motherfucker
chingona	someone/something awesome (f.)
chingos	a lot, a bunch
chiquito	baby or kid
chisme	gossip
chotas	cops
'chuco	pachuco young guy, gang member
chula	cute, pretty
churro	joint
cine	film, movie theater
colonia	undeveloped, marginalized residential area
comadre	friend (f.), very good friend or god-mother to one's child
comandante	commander
comité	committee
¿cómo qué?	what do you mean?
compadre	friend (m.), very good friend or god-father to one's child
comprendes	you understand
con dinero y sin dinero	with money and without money
cordillera	mountain range
cosa mala nunca muerea	bad thing never dies
cosotas	big things
cubreviento	salt cedar tree
cuerno de chivo	goat's horn, AK-47
dale en la madre al güey	beat the shit out of that guy
dale gas	step on it, go ahead
danzante	dancer
de la chingada	bad, difficult, complicated, fucked up
déjenlo	let him be, leave him alone
desaguacatarte	"de-avocado you," castrate you
desde luego	of course
diablo	devil

diabólico	diabolical or devilish
diga	tell, speak (imperative)
diluvio	flood, downpour
Dios mío	my God
disculpe	sorry, excuse us
disfrute con una rubia	superior literally, enjoy a Superior Beer, a Mexican brand; implying, enjoy yourself with a blond girl since blondes are superior
échale	go for it
el cine mexicano	Mexican cinema
el convoy	the convoy
el gusto es mío	the pleasure is mine
el huracán me ha mandado todo a la chingada	the hurricane has sent me to hell
el placer es mío	the pleasure is mine
el pueblo unido jamás será vencido	the people united will never be defeated
el víbora	the viper/adder (m.)
embrujado	bewitched
¿en qué les puedo servir?	how can I help you?
en serio	seriously
éntrale	enter, go for it
entrevista	interview
es el diluvio	it's the deluge/flood
es un vato de atole	he's a cool dude
es una vieja bien buenota	she is a really hot chick
estás loco	you're crazy
estos cabrones	these bastards
estos hijos de su rechingada madre no valen madre	these motherfuckers aren't worth shit
federales	federal police
felicidades	congratulations
feminista	feminist

finca	ranch
frontera	border

gobernación	government security department; specifically, Secretariat of the Interior in Mexico
Guate	Guatemala City
guatemalteco	Guatemalan (m.)
güerita	little blonde, dear blonde, or blondie
guerrillera/o	guerrilla (f./m.), participant in guerrilla warfare
güey	dude, bro

hablar	speak, talk
hasta la victoria	until we achieve victory
hay te wacho	see you later, dude
hecho y derecho	full-fledged
hija	daughter
hijita	dear little daughter
hijo	son
hijo de tu rechingada madre	motherfucking asshole
hola	hello
huracán	hurricane

idiota	idiot
iglesia	church
Iglesia de los Descalzos	Church of the Descalced (literally, Barefoot)/Destitute
indios	Indians
indios patas rajadas	derogatory; literally, "Indian with a cut foot," implying Indians who still look Indian

jale	hassle, racket, job
jamaica	hibiscus
jefe	boss, chief

jotito/jotillos	little queer(s)/derogatory
joto	gay, fag
jóvenes	young men or young women
justicia a los asesinos	justice for the murderers
la causa	the cause
La Clinica del Barrio	The Neighborhood Clinic
la mano	hand, basalt pestle
la pinche rubia superior	damn superior blonde
la sultana del norte	the sultana (female ruler or power/sultan) of the north, nickname for Moneterrey, Nuevo León, Mexico
la zona	red-light district
las entrevistas en la iglesia	the interviews in the church
las partes nobles	private parts, family jewels
le doy mi palabra	I give you my word
lechuza	owl
loco/a	crazy (m./f.)
lógico	logical
luz de la calle	light of the street
machacado con huevo	shredded beef with egg
macho gacho	nasty/ugly macho
maestro	teacher, sir
malas noticias	bad news
malcriado	spoiled brat
mamacita	hot little momma
mamasota	big sexy momma
mamones	suckups/smartasses, cocky guys
mano	hand
manos arriba	hands up
maracas	breasts
masa	dough, cornmeal dough
matachines	dancers to indigenous ceremonial music

me fascina	I'm fascinated, it fascinates me
me la mamas	blow me
mendigo	beggar
menudazo	a big serving of menudo/sex
menudo	tripe stew
mi	my
mi casa es su casa	my house is your house
mi general	my general
mijito/a, mi'jo/a	my little and/or dear son/daughter
milanesa	a fried, breaded beef cutlet
mira	look
mírale las nalgotas	look at that big ass/butt
molcajete	basalt mortar
momentito	moment
monte	brush, scrubland
mordida	bribe
mosca	fly
mota	pot, marijuana
movida	mistress, a woman on the side
muchachos	boys
mucha vieja, poco hombre	a lot of woman, a little/insignificant/ less-than-manly guy
mucho gusto	pleased to meet you
mujeres	women
muy chingóna	real badass
nada	none
nalgas	buttocks
narcocorridos	songs about drug dealers
narcos	drug dealers (abbrev.)
narcotraficantes	drug traffickers
no a la discriminación	no more discrimination
noche de carnaval	carnival night
no chingues	don't bug me, don't fuck with me (sing., familiar)

no chinguen	don't bug me, don't fuck with me (pl.)
no mames	don't bug me, don't fuck with me (sing., familiar)
no'mbre	no way, man
nos mandan a la chingada	they're sending us to hell
oaxaqueños	Oaxacans
observatorio	observatory
órale	all right, come on
oscuridad de su casa	darkness of one's house
otra vez	again
otro	another
oyes	listen/hears
palapa	open-sided building with thatched roof
panocha	pussy
panza	belly, paunch
papacito	hot-looking man, big daddy
para todo mal, mescal	for all that ails you, mescal
partes nobles	private parts
pasen, por favor	please come inside/enter
pecho/s	chest, bosom; breasts
pechuga	breast (of fowl)
pechugonas	women with big breasts
pendejada	stupidity
pendejo/a	idiot, asshole, dumb ass (m./f.)
perdóname, papacito	pardon me, big daddy (an exceptionally attractive man)
perfecto	perfect
periférico	beltway, loop
pero sigo siendo el rey	but I'm still the king
pierna	leg
pinche mosca	damn fly
pinche puto culero	damn queer asshole
pinche tecato	damn heroin addict

pinche vieja	damn despicable woman
pinche huracán	damn hurricane
piscas en el norte	migrant farm labor up north
pito	penis
policía	police
politicos	politicians
por favor	please
primo	cousin
problemas	problems
profe	professor/teacher
pronto	soon/quickly
provecho	advantage, benefit/enjoy or bon appetit
público	public
pues	well
puro cabrón	complete bastard
puro pedo	complete bullshit
puro teatro	pure theater, lots of drama
puta	whore
putos	gays
que	what, that
qué buenota esta la gringa	that gringa is hot
qué chichotas	great tits/breasts
qué rey ni qué rey	king, no king, yeah, whatever
qué Satanás ni qué Satanás	devil, no devil, yeah, whatever
que viva la raza	long live my/the people (my people, in this instance, expression of Chicano ethnic pride)
¿qué?	what?
qué bruja ni qué bruja	witch, no witch, yeah, whatever
qué chinga	what a beating
qué chingados	what the fuck
qué envergadura	what magnitude, or what a long one
¿qué gustan tomar?	what would you like to drink?
qué hombre	what a man

qué horror	how awful/horrible (ironic)
¿qué loco, no?	crazy, no?
¿qué onda?	what's up?
¿qué pasó?	what's happening?
qué rico chorizo	what a delicious sausage
qué suerte	what luck
¿quién chingados?	who the fuck?
quinceañera	coming-of-age party for 15-year-old Mexican girls
rápido	quickly, fast
rápido, muchachos	hurry, boys/guys
raspa	snow cone
raza	race, people
regalo	gift, present
retén	checkpoint
rey	king
rincon	corner
ruca	slang for woman, old lady
sale	okay
saludos	greetings
Satanás	Satan, the devil
seguro que sí	of course
si no, nos mandan a la chingada	if not, they'll send us to hell
simón que sí	yeah, you got that right
somos amigos	we are friends
submarino	submarine; tequila with a Tecate, salt, and lime chaser
'ta bien buenote el cabrón	the bastard is well-endowed
taco de ojo	eye taco (treat for the eyes; eye candy)
tacos de huevos con machacado	dried, shredded beef and egg tacos

¿te gusto?	did you like me?/did you like it/him/her?
teatro	theater
tecatos	heroin addicts
tecolote	owl
telenovela	televised drama series/soap opera
teniente coronel	lieutenant colonel
testículo	testicle
tlacuache	opossum
todo	all, everything
todos los hombres son iguales	all men are the same
tokesito	little toke
toquecito	little hit
toro	bull
tortillera	lesbian
tranquilo	calm, tranquil
tu amigo está loquísimo	your friend is very crazy
un taco de ojo	a taco for the eye, an eyeful of skin
usted	you (formal)
vámonos	let's go
vato	dude
vato loco	crazy dude
vida loca	crazy life
viva la revolución	long live the revolution
vuelve a la vida	return/come back to life
vulcanizadora	tire repair shop
washatería	laundromat
ya	already
y abajo los hombres	and down with the men

ya basta con este gobierno	enough of/from this government/administration
ya estufas	that's it, I'm done
ya estuvo	that's it, I'm done
ya llegó el mero mero	the main man has arrived
ya mero	in just a little while
ya te chingamos	we screwed you good
ya voy	I'm coming
y el convoy	and the convoy
yo	I
yo sigo siendo el rey	I'm still the king
y tú	and you (sing., familiar)
y ustedes	and you (pl., formal)
zapatos de charol	patent leather shoes
zarape	serape
zona	redlight district

Included in *Merriam-Webster's Collegiate Dictionary*, 10th ed.

adiós	iguana
amigo	jacal
amor	loco
barrio	mañana
buenas noches	maquiladora
buenos días	mercado
caballero	mestiza/o
cabrito	metate
cacique	pensione
campesino	picante
cantina	piñata
charro	pronto
chorizo	pueblo
cilantro	ranchero
corona	salsa
dinero	señor
empanada	señora
gracias	sí
gringa	sombrero
gringo	taco
hasta la vista	tamale
hombre	torta
huarache	viva

ABOUT THE AUTHOR

A native of El Paso, **Carlos Nicolás Flores** is a winner of the Chicano/Latino Literary Prize and author of a young adult novel, *Our House on Hueco* (TTUP, 2006). As director of the Teatro Chicano de Laredo and a former director of the South Texas Writing Project, he has long been engaged in the promotion of new writers and writing about the Mexican-American experience. He teaches English at Laredo Community College in Laredo, Texas.